AF379644

The Memory Paradox

The Gift and the Curse of Human Memory

Series – Cut Copy Paste

T. E. Aravind

Being Indian, a Tamilian, and having interacted with people from diverse cultures, I firmly believe that this world is a beautiful chaos. Inspired by a love for storytelling, I began sharing short stories with friends and family, and with constant motivation from the lovely people around me, I started my dream project of this debut book series, "The Memory Paradox".

My writing delves into the mind's influence on perceptions, emotions, and behaviors, fueled by a fascination with new technologies and a deep interest in human psychology.

I am a bank professional with a passion for writing and embarked on a parallel journey as an aspiring author. Now my world revolves around finding the balance between numbers and words.

You can connect with via my personal website "AuthorAravindTE.com"

Printed in India

ISBN: 978-93-5776-896-2

First Printing, 2023

The Write Order
A division of Nasadiya Technologies Private Ltd.
Koramangala, Bengaluru
Karnataka-560029

THE WRITE ORDER PUBLICATIONS.

www.thewriteorder.com

Edited by Anagha Somanakoppa, Divya Balaii

Typeset by MAP Systems, Bengaluru

Book Cover designed by Sankhasubhro Nath

Publishing Consultant - Deeksha

Chapter 1

A strange sensation filled me; my heart began to race and thrill as if a missile was closing in on its target. Maaya's breath swirled in my ears, and I blacked out, despite my brain mumbling that she was inebriated and not in a perfect state of mind. I went into a trance-like state while my mind continued to debate... And suddenly, my mom jarred into my dream and woke me up.

I am not Lord Shiva, nor do I have a fiery third eye to incinerate those who disturb my peaceful moments. So I looked at her with half-opened eyes, still egging for that kiss.

"Hey, they have announced a lockdown again. Wake up! Go get the groceries for a week. Why are you sleeping until 8 in the morning? Would you be this irresponsible if you were married now? Oh gosh! You are still sleeping with your phone in your hand."

A typical Indian mother never misses connecting all their children's shortcomings to mobile phone addiction.

Apparently, 90s kids were doomed to remain virgin even in their dreams. What life is this?!

"Give me ten more minutes, ma," I muttered, going back to sleep.

I was hoping for my dream to continue and egging to complete the kiss at least in my dreams.

* * *

That night, it was around 12. I was watching a new YouTube channel – 'Committed Singles.' They generally upload many relatable videos that look like they're speaking of me and my life. Only a single guy like me would know the pleasure of settling down to watch these videos with a beer in hand.

Right then, my team leader, Maaya, messaged me.

Maaya is a bold, dusky, and beautiful woman. One look at her, and you would know she was a Tamil girl - well dressed, smiling face with a svelte body. She would tell anything directly to your face, and she never discussed any personal stuff at work. She perfectly fits the description of an authoritative Team Lead. So

I loved seeing her from afar but was hesitant to talk about anything other than work. I always felt that she never gives a damn about me.

'Hi, how are you?' The message read.

Why was she messaging me on the weekend? Was there something wrong at work? Won't they even let me watch videos on YouTube in peace?!

'Hi, I'm good. Tell me.'

'I just texted you casually. I am at a pub now. Since the last few days, you seem to be residing permanently behind my eyelids…'

'Oh wow!!! Which pub? I am also at my friend's house. There's a party here.'

I felt a bit embarrassed to admit that I was not partying like her, so I was just trying to act cool. But I was surprised by her reply.

'🙂'

I did not understand what that emoji meant, so I scrolled up again, only to realize why 90s kids get mocked repeatedly. I shamelessly replied with another message.

'Just kidding!! Thanks! 😊 Someone told me that my stars would send me some good luck, but I didn't realize that the star herself could send me a WhatsApp message!'

I was too surprised at her sudden message and wondered what was happening here. I had always assumed she was out of my league, but here she was, texting me something personal by herself. I did not know how to respond, so I focused on the other part of her statement.

'I want to tell you something!' The screen had read 'typing' for a long time for this message.

'Tell me.' I messaged again.

'I have a huge crush on you. I know I am older than you, but I can't resist this feeling.' Maaya sent a message.

I stared at the screen for a long while, feeling elated. My star had just made me feel like a superstar. Never had anyone in my life told me like this. Nor had I said such a thing to anyone. I wondered how to reply to that and flexed my fingers, not wanting to mess it up again.

'Is that so?! That's a surprise. But when a beautiful girl like you says this, it's something special!' I typed out the message in my excitement. But truth be told, I had no idea how to react.

'Shall we meet tomorrow?' Maaya asked.

'Definitely! I am ready even now.' I replied.

'Haha! Then let's meet now. Why don't you pick me up? I will join you in your friend's place,' Maaya said.

'Ayyo! It's a 'boys only' party.' I shamelessly lied again.

'Oh, okay! 😩'

'Why don't we go on a long drive? I can come and pick you up now?' I said.

'Oh, cool!! I have no mood to go back home. Text me when you reach here.'

'Done!' I sent a reply immediately.

* * *

I jumped up in happiness. I was thrilled as if MS Dhoni had again pulled up a nearly impossible victory with a last-ball sixer. There were thousands of questions running around in my mind as I drove there. I was also nervous about this unexpected date.

In 40 minutes, I was at the Pasha Pub. I texted Maaya.

'I'm here.'

She came out. Holy Shit! Was this the same Maaya I see in the office every day?! I stood slack-jawed at her. She looked like a different person in the black party wear. As she walked towards me, I ruffled and corrected my hair and wiped my face urgently. I muttered to myself, 'Don't drool, dude.'

I tried to think of a pick-up line using the moon, but before I could think of something, the moon entered my car, hugged me, and said, "Hi!"

"You look so beautiful. The actual moon is going to be jealous of you," I said.

"Thanks," she laughed. "Where are we going now?"

That was probably a very cliched pickup line! I needed more practice, I thought to myself.

"I don't have a destination in mind. I just wanted to drive around with you aimlessly," I confessed.

"That's an old movie pick-up line... But nice try," Maaya said with a cheeky smile.

"Oh, is that a movie dialogue? I do not watch Indian movies often," I said.

"Hmmm, so you only watch Hollywood movies?" Maaya asked.

"No... Every movie has the same story. There's nothing new, so I do not watch movies much," I said.

She laughed again.

"Don't overact, dude," I muttered to myself.

"Okay, where are we going?" she asked again.

"Let's go to Pondicherry," I suggested.

"Pondy? Now?!"

"Yeah, let's drive there. It will take 3 hours from here. We can have coffee together in the morning, refresh ourselves, and take a walk on the beach. Then we can decide what to do next," I said.

"Nice plan. You planned all this so quickly! Are you used to going on these trips often?" she teased.

"Haha! 'Information is wealth,' indeed," I laughed.

"Ah, right!" she smirked.

That laugh again. Seeing that, I felt so energized that I thought I could carry the car in my bare arms and run all the way to Pondy, even if it was short of fuel.

In that laugh, in that second, I fell for her. I knew she was special to me!!!

"Play some music," she said.

I had a romantic playlist ready for occasions like this. Dream settings, long drives, listening to romantic songs with a beautiful girl who confessed she has a crush on you.

"Everyone at the office says you're a boxer. Is that true?" I asked.

"Oh, God!" Maaya sounded mildly surprised. "Yes! I had kept this a secret for a long time, but we played a hand-wrestling game during our last off-site, and I won against the boys. Everyone was surprised, and our head, Raj, revealed this secret. Now the whole office knows, I guess," she confessed.

"It's a good thing he did! How did he know, though?" I asked.

"I had mentioned it in my CV. And that man remembered that nugget of information after all these years!" she shrugged.

"Wow! So I have an idea to make our first date more memorable," I suggested.

"What's the idea?" she asked, her eyes narrowed.

"You should arm wrestle with me. The winner gets to give the loser a task, which the loser has to do. Okay?" I asked.

"Oh, you poor dear! How eager you are to lose to me," she exclaimed teasingly.

"Let's see who wins. But the loser has to do whatever the winner says!" I insisted.

"Okay. But there should be no inappropriate moves, okay?" Maaya agreed, blushing.

"Hehe, this is our first date. So just vegetarian moves!" I grinned.

"Hello! You shouldn't even touch me. These are Covid times. We should maintain social distancing," Maaya said, gesturing funnily.

"That's unfair! Can't I even get a small, cute kiss?" I asked.

"A kiss! Ayyo da. No chance!" she said emphatically. Then she blushed as she added, "You wish!"

I fell in love all over again with her reddening, dimpled cheeks.

"Not even on my cheeks? If not on my lips?" I asked sadly.

"I'll give you a flying kiss at best. Just take it," she said.

"We should have side benefits for getting into a love marriage like we have internals before the final exams..."

"Marriage! We're just on our first date..." Maaya exclaimed, sounding surprised. "Us getting married is doubtful in itself. And you already want the side benefits. Look at you and your lofty ideas!" she scoffed.

"We shouldn't lament ceaselessly, saying that we're '90s kids. We should be like 2k kids. Otherwise, we'll end up marrying the bride or groom our families arrange for us," I joked.

"I don't ever want to get married that way. But no one would even propose to me. In our society, girls who like to party get judged, and even the boys who love partying have double standards when it comes to wanting those girls as their partners. Hypocrites!" she said.

"You're not like a normal girl. You're a bold woman," I smiled.

"I have more male friends than female friends. Guess why?"

"Why? I have no idea," I prompted.

"If a woman is bold like this, men easily label us as 'girl besties.' But you guys prefer girls who listen quietly and keep you happy," Maaya said.

"I'm not like that, okay?!" I said earnestly.

"I didn't mean you in particular," she backtracked.

"Hmmm... Don't worry. Just wait and see. We'll get along really well," I said confidently.

She laughed.

The 'Mannippaya' song played next. We drove along, silently listening to it.

I loved how the phrase "Will you forgive me?" had been composed into such a beautiful melody. My mind wandered, wondering how this song was about misunderstandings and asking for forgiveness, but it ended up becoming such a cult hit and an unforgettable romantic melody.

"Sorry! I messed up with my rant. Why am I telling you all this? Especially on our first date! I feel so ashamed..." she said suddenly.

"You're asking sorry when the 'Mannippaya' song is playing. So what will you do when the 'Omana Penne' song plays?" I asked cheekily, changing the topic. I didn't like seeing her embarrassed.

I paused to see Maaya's reaction. The 'Omana Penne' song was another cult classic, where the protagonists would accept their love and kiss each other! But she instead referred to that one scene I had forgotten, which was also part of the song...

"I'll probably slap you like the heroine of that movie does. Nothing else will happen. You really wish for too much. This is no train, and you are no Simbu," she rolled her eyes.

"But you look much more gorgeous than that heroine Trisha," I said fervently.

"Such seductive lies!" Maaya teased again.

"But your seductive eyes are more powerful than my seductive lies!" I turned to look at her and smiled.

She looked at me for a while and then said, "You really are a good man. I think your innocence and candid words have attracted me to you," she laughed, taking my hand in hers and placing it beside her. Then she took it to her cheek and leaned on it. Surprisingly, she kissed my hand!

"Enough?" she asked, holding my gaze.

I looked into her eyes. Those eyes held so many unspoken emotions – attraction, yearning, love...

I held her hand tightly with my left hand, even as I was steering with my right. We held hands throughout the drive.

Then the 'Omana Penne' song played, and we looked at each other.

I looked into her eyes again. They were brighter than the high-beam headlights of the vehicles coming towards us from the other direction. That was when I understood why so many movie scenes talked about the power of women's eyes.

"Why do mornings dawn your words and glances move my days and nights? If we separate or get together, half of my soul is yours. Your joy and suffering are mine. You became my beginning and end..."

I gave her a flying kiss, grinning happily. She came closer to me. I knew she was going to kiss me. There was a slight hesitation. When her warm breath fell on me, I could smell her and sensed a drop of sweat on my skin in an air-conditioned car at 2 AM. I could see the reason why people usually say that women are 'hot.'

I knew that she had been drinking. But I still did not have the heart to stop her. Instead, I tried to go along the service lane and park the car. It was as if my dream from that morning was happening in real life. She cupped my chin in her hands and came close to my face.

Suddenly, someone stopped their vehicle in front of my car. Two guys alighted. I could not discern who they were in the bright glare of their lights. But that was enough to break the magical moment. Maaya had already pulled back, looking surprised.

I groaned internally. Wondering how I had even hoped to get a real kiss when it would not even happen in my dreams, I parked the car and looked out to see who was outside.

They were my friends, Ilango and Sathyan. I got down from the car and asked, "Hey! How are you guys here?"

"Where are you going without us? We are coming along too," they declared.

"Hey, I'm going with her, dude. Don't interrupt like a rampant elephant in a crowded market," I said.

One of them looked into the car. Then they looked at each other.

"Don't worry, dude... Suja and Vidhya are with us. All of us can go to Pondy together. If we leave you alone now, you will mess this up too and remain single all your life. Only we know that you are still in your 1st stage of adolescence," Sathyan joked.

"Hell! She was just about to kiss me. But you, the biggest Casanova, just ruined it. Get lost, idiots." I muttered.

Before I could respond, Ilango and his girlfriend Suja got into my car and looked at me like they were asking, 'What are you still waiting for?' I turned around when I heard the sound of the engine from Sathyan's car.

Maaya did not like this at all. But she came along silently. I did not know what to do, either. I did not like my friends' behavior - it was completely unexpected and surprising. I wondered how and why they were acting like this, though.

"Hey! How do you guys know I was here?" I asked, trying to make sense of what was happening.

"We know everything. You take the next exit and go to Auroville," Ilango directed me.

"Auroville? Hey, we have different plans. Why don't we catch up for dinner later?" I asked.

"You sly dog! Don't think you can get rid of us. Suja's aunt is there. Let us just drop by to meet her, get the keys to the beach resort, and spend the weekend there. It's a private resort, dude," Ilango said.

"Your girlfriend's aunt is sending you to a private beach resort with her niece?! What a great family," I laughed.

"Hey... we are getting married next month, and she is fine with it. So you don't overreact like a boomer." Ilango said defensively.

Through all this banter, I looked at Maaya. She was silent throughout, and my friends were doing an equally great job of ignoring her. We eventually reached Auroville, and Suja's aunt Renu's house looked like a big healing center.

Renu welcomed us with lemon juice.

"Aunty, this is Maaya, my friend," I introduced Maaya to her.

She turned to look at Ilango and then back to me, saying, "Hi, Maaya. Please wait. Let me bring juice for you too."

She walked back inside, throwing a loaded glance at Ilango. I felt confused and awkward. Wanting to do something with my hands, I drank the juice.

I must have fainted soon after drinking that juice.

* * *

I was in a clinic-like setup when I woke up. I had probably fallen into an intense sleep abruptly and deeply and was now feeling exhausted. My first thought was, 'Oh god! What would Maaya have thought of me?!'

I had left her alone with them and fallen asleep. Will these fellows have taken care of her properly? I wondered.

Renu was talking to my friends outside the room. Maaya was not there. I felt nervous and upset. Of course, they were my friends. But I understood that I was responsible for the situation - after all, they did not know Maaya, and she did not know them, but I had brought her along to an unfamiliar place. I had to get Maaya safely back to her house. Was this really Aunt Renu's house? Why did I faint after drinking the juice? I wondered. Feeling suspicious, I went near the door and tried to listen to their conversation.

"On observing him since the last four weeks, and based on what he is talking... I think he is suffering from the beginning stages of erotomania. We should do some more tests to be certain about it," Renu was saying.

"What is erotomania?" Suja asked.

"It is a psychological disorder where someone - purely in their imagination - believes that another person loves them, is attracted to them, and wants to live with them. This illusory person can be a random individual they come across in their life or even a celebrity. Have we not seen this before... where some people target a big movie star, and spew lies about them, almost like they want their name to be ruined? This kind of madness is driven by misplaced desire. It is usually more common in women. But even men get it.

"So people could be afflicted by this condition, after wanting to get a name and fame in cinema and being thwarted in that attempt, or falling in love with a person but not having them reciprocate. It creates an emptiness in some people that they cannot deal with, so they create such perfect scenarios in their heads and believe them to be true. They believe that, finally, the object of their affection - or obsession, rather - has expressed their undying love and reciprocated the sentiment," Renu explained.

"Will the affected person understand if we explain?" Ilango asked, sounding worried.

"They will not understand even if we explain with proof. They do not have the emotional capability to handle this. They will get angry if we speak against their imagined scenarios or even indirectly talk about the person they have imagined being in love with. So we should go with their flow and handle this."

"What do we do next for him?" Ilango asked.

"We can start medication. We can then give him cognitive talk therapy and attempt to control it. But first, find out who that Maaya is. He keeps saying the same name every week. So, we must find out if that person really exists or if she is a figment of his imagination. Based on that, we can decide what to do next. But, more importantly, we should take his consent to treat him. We cannot give him medication without that," Renu said.

I was too tired to comprehend what she said. But I understood that my friends had brought me there for some reason. I also realized that my fainting was not by coincidence.

I went out to them and demanded, "Where's Maaya?"

"She left for her home with Vidhya," Suja said.

I felt speechless in shock and as if something was pressing me from inside.

"Just go inside and sleep. You'll be okay in a couple of hours," Renu said soothingly.

Was the Maaya who came in the stillness of my morning dream just an illusion? Her breath was a piece of music - it had emotions. I could feel it when she came near me. And that very minute, I felt a deep sense of life and completeness within me.

I went to sleep, believing that I would definitely meet Maaya again when I woke up. Somewhere, deep down, I realized that I could not even walk properly. I was way too exhausted to argue.

Was this a dream, my imagination, or love?

* * *

Chapter 2

I was not yet completely conscious, but I could hear someone entering the room where I lay on the bed. I noticed some movement out of the corner of my eyes. I half-opened my eyes and saw people milling around. Ilango, Suja, and Renu were now beside me.

Ilango gently took my hand in his and unclenched it. He was trying to unlock my phone using my fingerprint. When we are healthy and capable, we take measures to ensure our security and privacy. However, the same measures can become a disadvantage when we are vulnerable. It dawned on me that I could not even protest without giving myself away, so I remained silent with my eyes closed as they walked out with my phone.

"Check if someone named Maaya has really messaged him," Renu said authoritatively.

"Yes, there are a few messages… But he has not even stored her number in the contact list," Ilango replied.

"Hmm, check his photos and notes… We may get some clues from there," Renu suggested.

"His gallery is full of food photos… and selfies of him. What else can we expect from a single guy like him?" Ilango said cheekily, and the three of them laughed.

'How can one expect me to have a life after I spent my entire childhood and adulthood in the name of friendship with a dick like you?' I thought to myself angrily.

"Hey… Don't mock him now. That's for later," Suja laughed.

"Okay, you both finish getting refreshed and come; I have two more clients waiting for me. Let's catch up for dinner," Renu said.

Then Ilango asked, "What do we do with him?"

I assumed he was talking about me. "Drop him a message asking him to call you. Let's decide what to do next based on when he wakes up. I think it will take at least two more hours," Renu was ordering them. Suja and Ilango just agreed like obedient children.

So, I woke up earlier than expected! But I still felt very weak. I walked like a drunken monkey and somehow got into the attached bathroom to wash my face. I hoped it would clear the fog and the weird headache I had. I felt much better after drinking cold water.

With renewed energy, I walked out of the room into the silent hall. I looked around, but no one else was there. I had so many questions inside me. Why did these people bring me here? I could see and feel Maaya clearly, but why were they saying that Maaya was a figment of my imagination? How could she be my imagination if everything about her felt so real? Not just that… if these people were really trying to help me, why did I faint after drinking the juice? I did not have answers to any of these questions. My head spun, and I felt like I was wandering around like a headless chicken.

Confused, I checked my phone, which had been returned to me. I saw Ilango's text. 'Call me when you wake up.' I did not feel like calling him at all. Nothing felt right in the entire episode. I just wanted to see Maaya and ensure that she was alright. I could not stop thinking about her. I knew the name of the beach resort that Ilango had mentioned yesterday. He had already spoken about it before in some other context. So, I googled the location, deciding to go and check there.

Unbeknownst to any of them, I took my car and started from there. On my way to the resort, I noticed Maaya standing at a bus stop on the opposite lane. So I made a quick U-turn and went there.

"Hi Maaya," I said, stopping the car in front of her.

She glared at me.

"Hey, sorry. I had no idea about what happened yesterday. Please get in, Let's talk it out," I said.

"There's nothing to talk about. Just leave me alone," she exclaimed angrily.

"Come, please get inside… We'll go back to Chennai. Everything will be okay if we talk."

"No. I've booked a cab. I will go back alone," she turned to check her mobile to see whether her taxi was coming.

"Hey… Just get inside the car. We will clear this up. I need to talk to you in detail."

"If you are going to talk, then I am definitely not coming with you," Maaya warned me.

"Okay, come! I won't talk about anything… You get into the car. I will be relieved if I drop you home safely," I said.

Maaya reluctantly got into the car.

"I'm sorry! I don't know why my friends behaved like this. This won't happen again," I apologized.

"There's nothing left to happen. We are done!" she snapped.

"Why are you taking this hasty decision?! We can talk it over," I said placatingly.

"No… It won't work," she said quite firmly.

I tried to hold her hand apologetically. But she shook my hands off vehemently, saying, "Don't touch me!"

"Okay, okay… cool…" I said, casually trying to play the songs of the Vinnai Thaandi Varuvaya album again. But she stopped the player immediately and sat in frosty silence.

I tried to sing the 'Mannippaya' song myself… 'From a romantic date and long drive just last night to a slow drive with breakup songs now,' I lamented to myself.

I felt that this was not such a huge mistake. Despite my apologizing many times, why was she putting up such a scene and overreacting?

Out of frustration, I had spoken my thoughts out loud.

"Oh, you still blame me after all this and think I am overreacting? I'm leaving," she snapped and tried to open the door of the moving car.

"Hey! Don't behave like an idiot! This is the highway to Chennai, not to hell! Close the door," I yelled.

Right then, she received a text. She read it and looked at me. I asked her what it was about, but she did not reply and instead stared out of the windshield.

Neither of us spoke. After a while, Maaya said, "I feel sleepy. I will go to the back seat and sleep."

I nodded and stopped the car. She went to the back seat, texted someone for about five minutes, and then slept. I kept looking at her in the rear-view mirror while driving, listening to songs over my headphones. Mentally, I was thinking of the meme about expectation vs. reality regarding what happened last night. It looked like the Universe was telling me, 'Expect the unexpected.'

For the first time, a girl had confessed that she had a crush on me. But it did not even last for 24 hours, I felt like everything was crushed in my life.

I dropped her near the Anna Nagar Tower. She got down and walked away without bothering to say bye. I was upset. I had no idea about what had happened to her last night. I wanted to ask her what had happened, but she was in no mood to speak.

* * *

I felt like I had lost something huge, and I was feeling so heavy. I drove home thinking about everything that had happened. I didn't speak to my mom properly and went straight into my room. I shut the door and fell onto my bed. But sleep eluded me. My head was whirling. Unable to control myself, I texted Maaya within a few minutes.

"I had no idea what happened yesterday, and I am as confused as you are. But I can see that you are deeply affected. I want to know what happened to you last night. I tried to talk to you in person earlier, but you were not ready. So I am texting you. I want to see you. You will understand when you let me explain my side of the story. Everything has been deliberately framed on me, and I swear I am clueless." Yet, Maaya did not reply to that.

No matter how much I tried to think, I could not understand what Suja's aunt, Renu was saying. Maaya is real! She liked me, and I could feel it. I could not believe whatever they were saying about something called erotomania; nor could I accept their theory that Maaya was a figment of my imagination.

I wanted to sort out this problem. This was the only thing running through my mind. But I was feeling very restless. As I was thinking about all this, Ilango called me.

"Dude… Where are you?" He asked.

"I came back home. I was planning to call you myself," I said.

"What happened? You usually never call!" He asked.

"No… But I wanted to ask you about what happened last night," I said.

"Last night? What about it? It was as usual… Why are you asking?" He sounded very confused.

"What… Are you at home? Is your mom near you?" I asked, wondering why he was evasive.

"No, dude… I didn't understand what you were asking…" He said slowly as if trying to make sense of what I was saying.

"Hey! You were the one who ruined my date last night. And now you are asking me this?!" I demanded, my voice rising.

"What? When did I see you last night? Have you gone nuts? What are you blabbering?" Ilango asked.

"Bugger, your prank won't work with me anymore. What did you guys tell Maaya about me? Why did I faint? Tell me the truth!" I yelled.

"Dude! Wait… You're not making any sense. You're speaking like you've gone crazy. How will I know what happened to you? I have no idea about anything. I was at my office last night. I came home just early this morning. I called you now to ask if you'd be home today… I wanted to give my wedding invitation to your mother."

"Don't bluff, da! Are your parents nearby? Come away from that and talk!" I snarled.

"Now you are scaring me! What happened to you?" asked Ilango.

"Please stop your prank, dude. I am not in the mood for that," I pleaded.

"Really, I never met you last night. You sound very confused, and now you're confusing me too. I did not sleep a wink last night. I was at work. I will first get some sleep and come to your place this evening. We will talk in detail in person," Ilango said and cut the call.

As if all the confusion of last night was not enough, now I had this oddity to ponder about. I could not accept what he was saying. I thought he was pranking me. That was the most plausible explanation. He was just doing a damned good job of it.

I sighed in frustration. I had been happily whiling away my time with YouTube and munching on chips just a couple of days ago. But now I could not make head or tail of what was happening in my life.

* * *

Evening 07:30, At My House

Ilango came to my house on his Thunderbird bike. I was listening to songs, standing on my terrace. I looked at him from there and asked, "Hey! Where's your car? You don't usually come by bike!"

"No, dude... I have to go to many houses now to invite people. The bike works better than the car. Parking is easier," he said.

"Okay, come up!"

"Hey… This invitation is for your mother. Not for you… You come down!"

My mother had opened the door by then and was inviting Ilango inside. "Come in, son. How are you? It has been a long while since I saw you… You used to come here often while you were in college. Nowadays, you all have become busier," she smiled.

"Nothing like that, Aunty. Commuting to work takes most of my time. There's not much time for anything else," he said.

"How are your wedding preparations going on?" she asked.

"They're good. The wedding is just a month away. And only now did I get the time to give invitations."

My mother turned to me and said, "Learn from your friend; find a girl soon for yourself." Then she turned towards Ilango and said, "He is always sitting in front of his computer. And if I ask, he says things like robotics and machine learning and is always tied to his work. I think I should get him married to a robot."

"Yes! We will definitely create a humanoid robot like Amy Jackson in the 2.0 movie. It will be helpful for you, too," Ilango laughed.

"Hey, enough! Give her the invitation and come inside. I want to talk to you." I intervened.

I did not want to talk about anything else in front of my mother.

Ilango gave my mother the invitation and said, "Please do come to my wedding, Aunty."

My mother smiled and wished him while I moved aside. Then he followed me to my room.

"Hey, why are you so restless? You always play along with timely counters whenever we try to pull your legs! But what happened today? You sounded very crazy this afternoon too!" He asked.

"Tell me the truth! What happened yesterday? Or I will surely chew you out like a deranged man," I warned.

"That's exactly what I am asking, too. You tell me clearly… what is happening?" He insisted, looking very confused.

"Okay," I took a deep breath and started narrating yesterday's incidents. At some point, I was hoping to catch him laughing or explaining, but as I spoke, Ilango became increasingly confused. He then insisted vehemently, "Hey! I swear nothing like that happened at all! I did not even see you yesterday…"

He did not look like he was lying, either. I felt so confused. He relapsed into silence, apparently unsure what else to say.

Then I said, "Wait, I'll come," and went into the washroom.

I remembered what Renu had said in Pondy to them. Now with Ilango's staunch refusal, I was beginning to have serious doubts, too. If what Renu had said about erotomania was true, was Ilango lying? If what Ilango was saying was true, then who was Maaya? Who was I messaging? The trip in the car and the conversations on the way… what were they? Everything that happened felt so real to me. But everything around me was confusing. I went out and called my mother.

"When did I come home today?" I asked her.

"About two o'clock," she said.

I turned to Ilango and looked at him for a response, and he said, "Hey, trust me, dude!"

Now, I started to doubt Maaya too. How and why did she message me last night out of the blue? She called me to come out at night. All this was not just unusual but completely unbelievable. And everything that happened after that point now confused me to the core. I did not know which one to believe.

Was all this my imagination? If that was the case, where did I go last night? What the hell was happening to me?

* * *

Chapter 3

"Even after all of this had happened, I still found myself wondering whether Maaya would message me. I looked at my phone, which was lying on my bed, infuriatingly silent at the moment."

I turned to Ilango, who was still sitting there, looking confused. "Hey, give me another invitation card."

"For whom?" He asked.

"I want to invite Maaya too. I will bring her along for your wedding... I have to patch up with her," I said.

"Dude! Who is this Maaya? I'm so worried about you now," he said, now looking frightened.

"Why are you creating such a scene for just one extra invitation?" I demanded.

"Okay, whatever. You are not going to listen, anyway. I have no problem handing you an extra invitation. But I still think you are winding me up. I have to leave now. You get some rest, too. I will come tomorrow, and we can discuss all this in leisure. I have promised to come to many houses now to give out some invitations, so I can't do this today," Ilango said.

"Right. Tell me the truth at least tomorrow," I countered. He just shook his head and went out.

Once Ilango left, I went back upstairs and started listening to songs. That's when Maaya messaged me with just one word: 'Hi.'

I felt like my whole world had come back to normalcy. I replied immediately, 'Hi! Finally, you replied.'

'It's regarding work. That's why I texted. You need to come to the office tomorrow. Apparently, new projects are starting this week. So Raj asked us to come for some preliminary work and preparation. He is going to lead this project and asked me to inform you about this. Nothing else,' she replied.

'Okay. Who else is coming?'

'He said that it is only the three of us for now.'

I thought that this was the only good thing that Raj had done in all these days. He will anyway be there with us just for a while and then leave. So we both could be alone, even if we were just working. Even if I go to the office on Sunday, I could spend time with her. I replied 'Okay' and left it at that.

But the only thing running through my mind was to ask Maaya what had happened last night. My head felt like it would burst anytime.

* * *

The Next Day (Sunday Morning)

I went to the office by 11 AM. Raj had arrived in shorts and a T-shirt. Maaya was in a yellow dress – it was her usual attire.

"A beautiful yellow moon is here!" I said, winking at her.

In response, she just gave me a short smile. My heart fluttered. So her interest in me was real! Earlier, I would not have dared to make this comment to her. But now I had told her this, and she responded with a smile. But other than that moment, she behaved like a colleague on a usual workday and nothing more or nothing less.

What an accomplished actress! I wondered. How could she be like this? If anyone sees my face for 2 minutes, they can write my life history with every comma and dot in place. But she remained as an elusive mystery. What was going on in her mind?

Raj looked at me and asked, "What, Ilamaran? You look like you're immersed in some thoughts. Are you lamenting that we made you come here on the weekend?"

"No, Raj… I'm wondering where we should order biriyani for our lunch," I said.

"I like that you're focusing on the important things in life," Raj laughed.

"No, I was just joking," I laughed along with him.

"Right, we will speak about that in a while." Raj got to business.

Maaya laughed but asked, "Raj… Would we be able to complete this work in a couple of hours and leave?"

I felt she was asking that question to avoid being with me.

"Don't you both wish to know more about this project?" Raj asked, sounding surprised. Pointing at me, he exclaimed, "This bugger is asking about lunch as soon as he arrived. And now you are asking when you can go home… I am not seeing the usual energy in you both!"

I turned around to see whether I entered the NASA space center to get excited about some impending rocket launch, but no, this was just an IT company – the same office where I had been working for years now. So another rich foreign company decides to drain his money through IT projects, and you are expecting me to express enthusiasm for this, I wondered darkly.

Maaya immediately countered. "Not like that, Raj. I have some other work. I came to the office just for this project. You told me that this is with a new French company, and I have never been to Europe. So I will definitely not miss this."

'Oh! Look how smartly she expressed her interest in working on-site. Smart!' I muttered to myself.

"This is not just with a French company. Another Indian company will also be partnering in this. Besides, the Indian and French governments will also be sponsoring this important project," Raj informed us.

To me, it looked like Raj was already speaking in French!

"The government is working on brokering a similar partnership deal with 5 other companies. If this succeeds, you both may have to go to France for 2 years."

Suddenly, Raj looked divine to me. I was already in France and had started singing a romantic duet in front of the Eiffel Tower with Maaya.

"This is all top secret. You must sign a non-disclosure agreement, as we should not discuss this with anyone else." Raj's words brought me back to the present.

'My entire life is already full of mysteries. No one is even telling me the truth about myself. Who else am I going to talk to about this? Even if I did, no idiot is going to believe me,' I thought.

Maaya asked, "What, Raj? You've already given a lot of build-up to this project. What are we going to do? Spy on Pakistan?"

"Haha! Not yet! I'll tell you. But before that, you both have to sign this non-disclosure agreement. Even if we do not get this project, you both should not talk about this to anyone outside. That's all. Once you know the details, you can opt-out if you do not like the project idea or the working terms."

Maaya was deep in thought. So Raj looked at me for some response. Immediately, I said, "I need some time to think."

"Even I want to give you ample time. But as we speak, 5 other companies have been collecting data for this project for a month. We are already very late to the party. I have gotten this opportunity after a lot of effort. I've even spoken to central ministers to get this… If you trust me, you can agree to this," Raj said.

"Right… I'm okay with this. I'll join," Maaya agreed.

Raj turned to me.

"Raj, give me one hour. I have to think. If you had asked me the same thing last Friday, I would have agreed immediately. But certain things happened in the last 36 hours. So I have to think a bit…" I said.

"Hey! You're building this up like a weather report on a news channel… The last 36 hours, indeed!" Raj laughed.

I stared at him, not knowing what to say. I then looked at Maaya, but she was busy with her laptop as if she had nothing to do with this.

"Okay… how can I not give you even that one hour? You can take it. Let's meet after lunch," Raj said and left.

* * *

Maaya and I were now alone in the meeting room. Before I could even open my mouth, she said, "I have to make a call," and went out.

I called Ilango, but he did not pick up. I thought he must be busy flirting with his fiancée. So I called my other friend, Sathyan.

"Hey, what's up mental?" he asked in his usual way of greeting.

"WTF? What's with the 'mental' greeting?" I shouted.

"Yeah, dude! Ilango called and complained that you were torturing him with your imaginative stories, tall claims, and insane questions. What's gotten into you?" he responded.

"Dei! You were there too. You should know the truth. So why are you saying I am torturing him? They told me that Maaya left with your girlfriend, Vidhya..." I questioned, now feeling insane.

"Oh god! Leave me out of all this. Only Ilango can handle you patiently. I cannot do that," Sathyan interrupted.

"Oh... so you're going to spew the same lies as he did?" I demanded hotly.

"Okay... why did you call me then? Let's talk about that," he changed the subject.

"I want your opinion on something," I said, realizing that I had a purpose for calling him. The other questions could wait since he was also going to lie to me.

"Opinion? Okay, I'll talk about this only if it has nothing to do with your mental stories!"

"Dude! You won't be this cocky if you were in my state. I cannot explain anything now... It's all my fate," I said.

"Okay, leave that! What's the matter now?" he asked.

"There's this new project in my office. They are asking us to sign a non-disclosure agreement. I am a bit confused about it. What do you think?"

"You need such a project now. Distract yourself. It is a good thing for you. Take it up and do it properly," Sathyan advised.

* * *

Maaya came back inside. I was sitting on a chair, leaning back as I was talking to Sathyan. She came near me and leaned on the round table before me. I cut the call.

I looked at her. But before I could say anything, she asked, "Why are you thinking so much about this?"

"I am just confused. You know what happened, right?" I asked desperately, wanting her, at least, to confirm that I was not going insane.

"Don't confuse that and this. You come... we'll do this project together," she said reassuringly.

"You know I would love to do that. But I doubt if I am mentally ready to sign such agreements now."

Maaya looked at me for a long moment, as if deep in thought. Then she said abruptly, "I am a bit skeptical about your friends. I am afraid they are the reason for all your confusion. I don't know how to tell you this. You agree to this project now. We can speak about it more this evening," she said.

"Why are you saying this? They've been my friends for nearly a decade now," I said.

"This is exactly why I did not want to tell you. You trust them, it's natural. But now trust me and sign this agreement. We can discuss this later today," she said.

"Are you saying this as a team lead or…" I hesitated.

She grabbed my cheeks and gave them a good pinch. "Aww, you're my sweetie," she said, looking at me with a loving smile. But then she got serious, "I can't stay mad at you for long, babe. You sign this. Let us not miss our chance to go to France."

Whoa! When she looked at me with those eyes, I was like, 'damn!' I couldn't even talk. But I finally gathered my senses and asked, "You tell me one thing… I will decide based on that."

"What?"

"What happened after I fainted on Friday night?"

"I fainted too. They gave me the same juice, right? Then I was with Vidhya in her room. I asked about you the moment I woke up. But Vidhya told me, 'Wait, Ilango will be coming… you can ask him!' And I waited for a while. But I was afraid to be alone there. Though they were your friends, I did not know them at all. So I left without informing them."

"What? You fainted too?! Then why is Ilango swearing that he never even saw us on Friday night?" I asked, confused.

"What?! Did he say that?" Maaya looked shocked.

"Yeah… I asked Sathyan now. He was also saying the same thing. Not just that… Their aunt Renu is telling me that I have something called erotomania…"

Maaya looked contemplative for a moment before she answered. "I am with you here, and you need to trust this. Something doesn't smell good here, with whatever they were doing. They said the same thing to me as well. You were creating an imaginary relationship with a person called Maaya and roaming around with her. And if your imagination is true, then it is not erotomania but extra-sensory perception! You got this before I texted you the day before yesterday," Maaya said with a very excited tone.

I did not know how to react to that and was watching her unblinkingly.

"Do you know one thing? Three weeks ago, when you sang in our team event… That was when I fell for your voice. Look at our names… Maaya – Ilamaran… Like how they were named in the movie 'Kakha-Kakha'… but this time God's design is to pair a heroine named after Maaya and the hero, Ila, who was unfortunately named after the villain," she whispered.

When Maaya said this, her eyes danced expressively.

"Forget the villain's part. But will we get together in life?" I asked.

"Let's see… God would have decided that already. But how did you get to know about it? I mean, how did you hear about this thing?"

"I swear I don't know. I do not even remember such a thing happening," I confessed. After such conflicting words from friends, everything looked confusing to me.

"I like you. But when I think of all this, it makes me nervous. Don't mistake me," she said worriedly, biting her lips in tension.

"I am afraid of myself right now. There's nothing wrong with you feeling that way. I would understand if you no longer want to be with me for this reason…" I said that with a heavy heart. I had to be the bigger person, for she was really looking scared and my instinct was to protect her.

"I really like you… if you are ready to try that, shall we go and check with another psychiatrist?"

"Hmmm… so all of you have decided that I am mental!" I muttered.

"Darling! Don't worry. It's not like that. This could be due to depression as well. I had also troubled you a lot yesterday in the car. Sorry."

"No, no… I can understand." I said automatically. "I felt slightly calmer only after knowing you were safe."

I couldn't bring myself to look at her. To my shock, tears were welling in my eyes. Man, my life is a total mess, I thought. Everything looked messed up from every angle.

Maaya leaned in closer, looking concerned. "Hey, what's wrong? Why are you crying?"

"Nothing… I am very petrified. I don't even know if I should be with you. What if I am endangering you? My own friends are lying to me, and I have no idea why. What can I do?"

"Don't worry about anything. Let's wait and watch how this goes." She said, taking my hand in hers and squeezing it gently. "Everything will be okay."

I looked at her. No matter how difficult our life gets, we feel confident and happy when our loved ones say they will be with us.

I smiled at her. Maybe she was right. With her by my side, there was always a ray of hope. I wanted so badly to believe her.

She then ruffled my hair and said, "Your hair is so soft… how do you have such soft hair?"

I understood that she was doing this to change the topic. But when a gorgeous woman says such things, we do lose ourselves in the moment. I smiled at her. No, I drooled at her. She laughed at me too.

"Your touch on my hair got my heart pumping like crazy. I'm losing it! Are you Maaya or a damn magician?" I demanded, with a mix of awe and amazement.

"Your timing sucks, but your rhyming is good," she laughed.

This was the kind of reply I was bound to get if I spouted such random cinematic dialogues, I told myself.

"Let's finish work today and go to Marina Beach," she said abruptly.

"Wow… Let's go!" I agreed with enthusiasm.

"But before that, you must agree to this project."

"Hmm. Sure. How could I refuse when you insist?" I folded.

Then she got a call and went out to attend it. Though I had spoken to her that way and accepted when she insisted, I was still confused. This confusion increased after Maaya's sudden (apparent) change of mind.

On first seeing me this morning, she did not say anything to me. But she went out to attend some call, returned, and apologized by herself. And then she spoke lovingly to me. I could not help but doubt her intentions. I wondered if these doubts were justified or if I was overthinking everything. If I could doubt my friends who I had known for years, I could also easily doubt Maaya, who had come into my life fairly recently.

Everyone seemed to be lying, but they all were vehemently insisting that they were truthful. So much so that after everything was said and done, I was the one who felt wrong-footed everywhere. There were so many questions and doubts in my life, which had been fairly simple just a couple of days ago.

One thing was clear. I should not ask any of them to find an answer. I should go along with their plan and work it out myself. At this point, I was not able to trust anyone. Nor could I confront anyone without any proof.

* * *

Chapter 4

I hadn't even had my lunch before Maaya and Raj returned.

"Ilamara… What have you decided?" Raj asked me.

"Okay, Raj. I'll join this project. It's hard for me to refuse you," I said, winking at Maaya. She gave me a cute smile in return.

"That's great. So we will be here for the rest of the day," Raj said as he logged into his laptop to give us a printout.

The words 'Non-Disclosure Agreement' were prominently displayed at the top. Maaya and I read it once and signed it. Raj then scanned it and sent it to our head office.

"Raj… could you tell us more about the project now, or my head will burst?" Maaya asked.

I snidely thought that it had been 36 hours since my head burst. I did not share Maaya's curiosity as I did not prefer such intense projects. I had accepted this just for her sake. I wanted to breeze through work, keep it easy, and relax.

"Okay, I'll ask you a question," Raj began.

'Questions again? He answers a question with another question. Wah!' Although such thoughts were running amok in my mind, I smiled and said, "Yes, Raj."

"What do you think of India's healthcare system?"

"I think it is the most important industry in the post-COVID scenario. But we have to improve it a lot. For example, I read somewhere that we do not have enough facilities to cater to our population," Maaya said.

Raj turned and looked at me.

"I think we need to give more attention to our mental health issues as well," I said.

"That's exactly why I chose both of you for this project," Raj grinned. "Your thought process fits perfectly with the project's goals."

I had blurted out my mind's voice, but this man was elated with my response! 'He needs treatment first.' I told myself, but silently this time.

"Our healthcare system is weak. As Maaya said, the ratio between patients and hospitals is so skewed, and corruption is rampant while people suffer, unable to get proper treatment. So it's incredibly tough to even diagnose people who come for treatment. Our Indian government is going to experiment with something novel. They want to automate the basic diagnosing methods for common diseases. They have approached many healthcare and IT companies in this regard," Raj said.

"How can we do this, Raj?" I asked.

"They're saying we should use machine learning," Raj explained.

"Machine learning? How do we use that for this?" I asked again, as he was not providing me with any clarity.

"In a nutshell, we should create a machine learning algorithm and train our computers with the medical history of patients that exist with our doctors. So when we become ill, if we input our symptoms into the computers, they would compare those with the existing data and help us diagnose our problem…" Raj said.

Maaya and I looked at each other. Raj looked at our faces and realized that we had not understood.

"What exactly is machine learning? It involves using existing data to analyze patterns and predict outcomes. Essentially, it's using past data to make decisions about new data and can be used for a variety of tasks such as analyzing behavior."

"Yeah, we know that, Raj. But how are we planning to bring that concept into this project?" Maaya asked.

"We all have a device at home now to check our blood sugar levels, right? We could connect that to a smart device and automate all the blood tests. Nowadays, they are even exploring whether they could take x-rays with cameras. Everything is getting digitalized these days, and people could be consulting with their doctors from the comfort of their houses," Raj explained.

"And what are we going to do in this space?" I asked, trying to bring it on track. I needed to know what the scope of our work would be.

"For this project, we are going to focus on software development. There would be partnerships with companies in the hardware and healthcare sectors. And the Indian and French governments are also getting involved in this," Raj replied.

"The idea is great. But is this really feasible?" I asked.

"Every invention in today's technological world began with just the same doubts and uncertainties. And today, machines do more than half the jobs that humans have been doing for years. This is also one such concept, that's all."

"So, we can diagnose anyone without visiting a doctor at all?" I asked. It sounded impossible and slightly dangerous, like self-medication.

"Think of it this way… You're going to share everything online about yourself with the doctor. He is going to track your data live, and he may suddenly call you, saying, 'Ilamara, you're going to get a cardiac arrest in another 30 minutes… you have to come and get yourself admitted.' In other words, he'd get the timely alert and could warn you so you could get medical intervention on time. How many lives could be saved this way?!"

"Ayyo! What happens to people's privacy then?" I asked, seeing how intrusive this sounded even verbally.

"That's going to be your choice. In today's terms, privacy is just a difference between your details being shared with or without your knowledge and consent," Raj pointed out.

"I think Apple has already thought of this concept," I said.

"Yes! The big tech companies have already begun their research on this," Raj agreed.

"Then what are we going to do innovatively with this?" I asked. Something was not adding up. Why were governments getting involved in this project if it were not path-breaking or dicey about the law?

"Now we come to your second point… We are going to focus on mental health," Raj explained.

"How is that going to happen? Should we be able to predict if someone is going to go into depression and try to make them happy?" I asked rhetorically.

"Hahaha… Not like that. We have to analyze if there is a possibility of that happening and discuss how to take care of it."

'I am in that state where I need a few people to tell me how to take care of myself. Already some people are calling me mental. And what am I going to do for this, now?' I controlled my thoughts and said, "I don't get it at all."

"We should gauge someone's emotions ahead of time with the help of machine learning. For example, some people feel happy while listening to a particular song. So if they lose their mind or do something else that indicates sadness or emotional imbalance, we could notify their phones and prompt them to listen to the song. Then there's a chance that they would relax and become normal," Raj explained.

'Oops! If you hear my mind's voice, you will fire me the next minute. And here you are, asking me to identify everyone else's mind voice and cater to that,' I thought.

"Likewise, when you speak to your mother or your friends, you may feel happy. During those times when we see that people are sad, we could notify them to call or text their parents or friends. If we have the details about their friends, we could also see who is in the right frame of mind to handle that and send the text to the right person. All these are just ideas, and it is up to us to make this real," Raj said.

At this rate, we wouldn't know whether we are talking to a machine or with humans. They would even earn by giving therapy and treatments with devices.

"How would we know when they are going to lose their minds?" I asked.

"I don't know. First, we have to talk with healthcare companies about this. Then we would get a better idea," Raj suggested.

"The idea sounds good. But how are we going to collect the data for this? How are we going to train the computers?" I asked, voicing only a part of my concerns.

"I don't have the answer for this either, as of now. But this is a huge challenge. Again, we have to talk to the healthcare companies and get the details from their psychologists," Raj explained.

"Patient confidentiality and privacy are very important. How will the doctors or hospitals or mental health professionals share the data indiscriminately?" I pressed on.

"I'm not sure. We have to work out the methods for that..." Raj said.

While Raj and I were discussing intensely, Maaya was pretty much silent. Finally, Raj turned to Maaya and asked, "Why are you so silent? What's your opinion?"

"No... all this sounds a bit extreme, and I am wondering how this could be possible," Maaya said.

Usually, Maaya is quite sharp. People used to joke that even the quick-igniting camphor is slower than her. Thus was her reputation for catching onto concepts quickly.

"If we finish this project successfully, our company will become one of the top 10 in India," Raj said, sounding strangely hopeful.

"But why should we do this so secretly? We are doing a good thing, right?" I demanded.

"Our government is trying to dominate the global healthcare industry. Russia, China, and the USA are also doing such research as we speak. Besides, the general public and opposition parties would bring politics into such issues in our country. Once we complete everything, they may decide how to do it formally. These things are not an issue for a country like China, for instance, where there's an autocracy," Raj explained.

"Okay… Why France?"

"That seems to be some other deal, the details of which we are not completely aware. Our government has insisted that we must have a partnership with them. We cannot ask for reasons if we want them to give us permission." Raj explained.

Shaking herself out of her thoughts, Maaya said, "I don't want to sound too negative, but I don't think this would work out for all practical purposes. It's a huge project with diverse verticals."

"Yes! But that's the challenge here. This is why we have selected you guys," Raj agreed.

But before we could reply, Maaya's phone rang.

"Hmmm. Just a minute! I have to take this call," Maaya said and stepped out.

I wondered who she was talking to so often. I thought that I should at least earn some extra money to recharge her phone if we start to date regularly.

Raj looked at me and prompted, "What do you think?"

"I'm not sure, Raj. The concept sounds outstanding. But the challenge is in completing it within the timeframe that you have mentioned. We have a lot of work to do even in the preliminary stages. But it is just the three of us working here. We need more people to handle such a big project, or we are setting ourselves up for impossible deadlines," I said candidly.

"We don't have to do all the work by ourselves, Ilamaara! We'll just have to prove that this concept is feasible and get the government's approval. Then, once we land the project, we will bring more people on board. Then, you and Maaya could lead it," Raj said reasonably.

Maaya entered the room and said, "Raj! I need to speak to you alone for a moment."

"Ila! Can you stay outside for five minutes?" Raj requested.

* * *

I stepped out. Ilango had called me meanwhile, so I returned his call.

"Dude! Did you sleep well? How are you now?" He asked.

"Yeah, I'm okay!" I responded.

"Okay! I wanted to discuss something with you. I am a bit concerned about you. Can we go and see a doctor? Suja's aunt is also a psychiatrist, dude."

"Is she the one from Auroville?" I asked dully.

"How do you know it?" He demanded, sounding shocked.

"Weren't you the one who took me there? But now, if I ask you, you'll refuse and act innocent," I muttered.

"Dude! Even I have not seen Suja's aunt. But how would you know?" He asked, sounding really worried.

"That's great! Now you are the one who needs to consult this psychiatrist aunt."

"Dude… You're going to get it from me. If you are not interested, just say no. Don't make up stories like this."

"Leave it! No one here is going to believe what I say. I don't want to argue. So this was why you called?"

"Yeah, but no! Forget that… I'm arranging a bachelor's party."

"I'm not sure I'll be able to attend. Here they've called me for some new project, so I don't know if I'll have the time for this," I said.

"Try. It is not happening immediately. I have ten more days of work pending. Then we'll all go on a long drive somewhere… Even Sathyan is doing a project for some Russian company. He's roaming around with Russian chicks and refusing to share any details. Bugger! He's silently doing something, I don't know what," Ilango said.

"It'll only surprise me if he's not roaming around with girls. How does Vidhya feel about all this?" I asked.

"He's a playboy, and I am sure she has lost her case. Take care. We'll catch up later," Ilango said before ending the call. Then I absently scrolled through my mobile, waiting for the conversation inside to finish.

* * *

About half an hour had passed by then. Was this their 5 minutes? I looked towards the closed door casually, noticing that Raj and Maaya were still deep in conversation. I was grumpy, seeing that I could have gone out and had a good biriyani by now. I had not had lunch, unlike them, and my stomach was growling.

I then moved a bit and glanced through the glass windows of the room. Raj was calling someone, and he gestured at Maaya to step out.

Once she came out, I asked her, "What happened?"

She just shook her head and shrugged.

"You spoke all this while for nothing?" I demanded.

"I'll tell you, wait," Maaya said and went back inside, noting that Raj had completed the call.

In a short while, they came out together. Raj looked at me and said, "Maaya has given me a good idea. I've also spoken to the head office. We are starting a research team. It will be a hub, with members from the healthcare industry, hardware companies, and government representatives. I suggested that we all work together from one place for fifteen days, and everyone has agreed."

Maaya stood behind Raj and silently mouthed at me, 'You and I are going to be together.' She then formed a heart symbol with her fingers. I could not even react. She looked happy.

"Raj, this is great! I wondered how the three of us alone will do it, but this is a big team now."

"We have to thank Maaya for this. She was the one who gave this idea," Raj smiled.

Behind him, Maaya was gesturing silently as if she were hugging and kissing me. And I stood there, unable to react to any of that because I was facing Raj. She looked adorable. I did not know what she had in mind while doing this.

"I'll meet the project partners and decide what's next. It won't get us anywhere if we discuss this matter in the office. I'll take them out to have drinks and finish the deal. We'll meet tomorrow," Raj said and left.

* * *

Maaya laughed and came near me.

"I see a cute monster here. What are you up to?" I asked.

"Yeah, you take this monster on a date now! This evening… is for us alone," she said.

"How did you think of all this?" I asked.

"Easy-peasy!" She laughed. "I have a lot more to teach you this evening."

Ilango called me again, but Maaya took the phone from my hands and cut the call. Her face reddened in anger. Then she sighed deeply, saying, "Today, your time and your attention are for me alone… come, let's go to Marina Beach."

She switched off her phone, too. Then she grasped my hand tightly and led me out. There was no one in the parking area. So once I got into the car, I turned to her.

"What are you looking at?" she asked. It wasn't a question but an invitation for more, with the way her seductive eyes were focused on me.

I closed the distance between us. Her eyes roved around, searching for any onlookers. I kissed her eyes gently and her eyes shut automatically. Her warm breath mingled with mine, and at that moment, I knew that every breath she exhaled was my life-giving oxygen. I kissed her cheeks, and she kissed mine. Though my nerves fluttered with anticipation, all I could focus on was the softness of her lips and the connection we shared.

"Sir! We have to close the parking lot. Today's a Sunday. Parking is allowed only until 6 PM," the security interrupted us.

'You idiot! Couldn't you have come just ten minutes later? It's not funny to intrude on the privacy of poor 90s kids,' I muttered silently and started the car.

Maaya laughed and said, "I'm hungry… Let's go somewhere to eat, and then we can go to the beach."

I switched on my phone. Ilango had called me 24 times. Before I could check what he wanted, Maaya plucked the phone out of my hands and said, "When I'm with you, your phone should not be with you. This is our dating rule number one!"

That was a day when I felt elated after a long time. I forgot myself and all my problems for a while. I hadn't gained much clarity about whatever was bothering me, but these moments with Maaya were good and a dream come true.

But once I thought about everything else that had happened, I couldn't shake off the nagging doubts in my mind.

Why had Ilango called me so many times? What was his problem? Why did Maaya insist I shouldn't talk to him? She was accusing Ilango… But was he really to blame? I didn't know when I would get answers to these troubling questions!

Chapter 5

Raj called me the next day and said, "Ila, pack your bags for a 15-day trip to a resort. We will have brainstorming sessions over the next two days there and set up everything we need for the project. Then we can finally get started on our proof of concept."

"Okay, Raj. Send me the address," I said. But, in the meanwhile, I lamented that I had never wanted to go to a resort for work purposes, especially when Maaya was around.

But now I felt that I should take up this chance. I informed my mother and left. Once I reached the resort, I immediately felt like a fish out of water, as everyone was dressed in casual attire while I was in formal wear. The only saviors for me were the delicious hot coffee and breakfast.

Many new faces were also there. There was the hardware team from Mugilan Computers, representatives from Chola Biotech Limited, the French company Graft Pharma, and our company, Indra Software. This group included doctors, psychologists, and psychiatrists.

Alexander, a French government representative, and Keshav Patel, representing the Indian government, were also present.

I wondered what I was doing amidst all these people. I felt like I would forget what little programming I knew!

They thoroughly checked us before admitting us inside. First, they had everything set up and ready to go. Then, they took away our phones and gave us new ones for communication among ourselves. We were allowed to call our homes once daily. And social media sites were strictly off-limits.

I understood one thing clearly that day. In our country, we could achieve anything in one night if we really wanted to. Just last evening, we had discussed the project, but this morning, everything was ready. Usually, it would take at least two weeks to achieve such a feat. But here, we were hoping to complete the entire project conceptualization in two weeks. Where there was a will, there was a way, indeed.

Maaya was dressed in beautiful blue jeans and a black t-shirt. The guy from Graft Pharma was literally drooling over her. I wanted to confront him, but I kept my mouth shut. Maaya could surely hold her own.

The workshop started, and they discussed and debated numerous ideas. I was initially waiting for lunch, but in about half an hour, everyone, including myself, got immersed in the intriguing ideas being presented.

They explained how doctors could determine if someone was sick by listening to their blood flow. Then they delved into the workings of our nervous system and detailed how it triggered our emotions. They explained the logic behind certain recent technological advancements, such as using capsule cameras for internal body examination, and MRI technology to capture images from the brain based on an individual's thoughts at a specific moment.

Then it was Raj's turn to speak.

"It is human nature to make decisions for our future based on our past experiences. When we get new information, it changes the decisions we had made. Even our body alters itself according to the situation. If we do the same thing with computers, it is called machine learning. Now, based on what you're all saying, there's a good chance the computers could learn about this machine called humans and offer a lot of help. This attempt would be a giant step in taking artificial intelligence to the next level. We're proud that our company is participating in this journey," he said.

* * *

They had organized a team-building session that night after all the intense morning meetings. A bowling game was planned, and they put me with a bunch of older folks. And, to top it off, Maaya and that French guy were on the same team. Just my luck!

Maaya and I were in different lanes, but my eyes were always on her. The French guy – whose name I still didn't know – was all over her, high-fiving, hugging, and acting like he had just won the World Cup.

Maaya looked at me with a teasing smirk, and I was standing a little apart, trying not to knock the guy out.

An older woman, named Thyda, who was also a psychologist, noticed all this. She came to me and asked, "Are you feeling jealous?"

Shocked, I turned to her. Was I that obvious? Had I spoken my thoughts out loud? But I collected myself and looked at her. "Of course not! There's nothing like that!"

"You both make a wonderful couple. You have fifteen more days here… use them well," she smiled at me.

I laughed too, not knowing what to say. She raised her wine glass at me and said, "Cheers," before going to bowl her turn.

So when the bowling was over, they split the teams for the next game, Antakshari. But the catch was that we could only sing English songs. Great, just my luck again. The only English song I knew was 'Twinkle, Twinkle, Little Star', and I'd probably mess that up too. So, not wanting to make a fool of myself, I quickly changed the topic and suggested that we play hand wrestling instead.

Maaya gestured at me, raising her eyebrows, asking what I was doing. I winked at her and whispered in her ear, "Our challenge isn't over yet."

She laughed and tapped my shoulder.

I turned around and said, "First, we'll have a contest between the ladies, and then the gents."

I knew Maaya would win in the ladies' game. But I surprised myself by winning in the men's segment. The French guys were unbelievably weak. Winning had been easy!

Then Thyda said, "We need a champion, so let Maaya and Ilamaran go head-to-head now."

Everyone exclaimed happily at that. I winked at Maaya again, and this time she winked back at me. Both of us laughed.

Maaya came near me and asked, "Should you have gotten into this? If you wanted to lose so badly, you could have done it privately. Why should you lose to me in front of so many people?"

"Let's see… But one thing. Our bet still stands. No holds barred here," I said.

"I'll be the one winning anyway… So yeah, okay," she laughed, waggling her eyebrows.

"One more condition!"

"Yes?"

"While we're hand wrestling, you should look into my eyes. You shouldn't look anywhere else."

"You think you're some bright-eyed, alluring sex idol… as if I'll be enamored just by seeing you," she teased.

"Your overconfidence is not good for your health. We're going to be alone here at this resort! I already cannot control my mind," I said.

"Get lost, idiot! I'm going to the restroom," she said with a smile and winked at me while walking back.

"Would you want to win this game or win her over?! Think about it. But if you lose to a girl, everyone here would come to know… what are you going to do?" Thyda asked me.

"I'll win the game and win her over, too. Wait and see," I said, looking around to see if Maaya was coming back.

As she stepped out of the restroom, I noticed some change in her. Before I could think of what it was, Thyda explained in detail, "She has touched up her make-up. A bit of eyeliner and a splash of red lipstick."

I understood that Maaya was trying to seduce me. Thyda went to the other side and told Maaya, "It's quite easy for you to win now!"

Maaya blushed and looked at me. I wondered what the French woman was trying to do… she was talking for both sides!

Coming near me, Maaya smiled. She looked devastatingly beautiful. Boys like me would be seduced by just a bit of black eyeliner. What power did girls' eyes have?! That look from her disturbed something deep inside me. The eyes that overflowed with love, the seduction on her lips, and her beautiful, even teeth between those ruby-red lips that looked like a sudden flash of lightning on a reddened sky of dusk... all of this completely bamboozled me.

I could not take my eyes off her. Everything around her blurred, and only she stood in stark focus. She was also looking at me exclusively.

"Is it enough if I don't take my eyes off you?"

I did not reply but took a sip of the wine, trying to calm myself. She kept her arm on the table, indicating that she was ready for the arm-wrestling match. I lost even before I had begun, due to her body language and her unwavering gaze.

But still, I gulped down all the wine and kept my arm on the table. Everyone had gathered around us. All the guys supported me while the girls supported Maaya.

Someone there ordered tequila shots, saying, "The winner will buy the shots."

Everyone was a bit tipsy. I noticed Raj exiting the place urgently. He looked a bit upset. I thought he probably did not like whatever was happening here. But I could not ponder that much. I had a game to play.

We then started the game.

Maaya's hands were so soft. I, who was supposed to kiss her hand, was wrestling her instead. Initially, we played just for fun. But in about half a minute, we became a bit more serious. She kept looking into my eyes. Then suddenly, she winked at me. I responded automatically, and everyone around us cheered.

She started pushing my hand with surprising force. I was surprised to see such strength in those tender hands. Just as she was going to push my hand down, I proposed, saying, "I love you, Maaya!"

Surprised, she took her hand away. Everyone around us exclaimed, some in shock. I drained the next shot in one gulp and announced myself as the winner.

"This is cheating! I won't allow this," said Maaya.

I gently picked up another shot glass and knelt before Maaya, handing her the glass. Everyone laughed and cheered as Thyda said, "Come on, Maaya, accept!"

Maaya laughed as she took it from my hand and drank it before saying, "One more!"

Then Mark came out, saying, "Guys! It's karaoke time."

I thought he was trying to impress everyone with his singing. That's probably why he was saying this all the time. I found that boring because I could not sing. So I searched for Raj, wondering if he had come back and if he was really upset at all the fun and games here. He looked like he found all these distractions a problem, considering he was intent on completing the project soon.

But he was not around, so I realized that he had left for the day. I too left the place and went into the nearby bar. Maaya was staying back with others for the karaoke. Boy, she could sing, too! Absently, I ambled around to the bar. The guy from the healthcare company, David, was drinking alone. I hesitated, wondering if I should join him. But he beckoned me. "Come, join me for a drink."

It looked like he had been drinking for a while.

"It's quite boring. Look here, we have the bar to ourselves. They are not letting anyone else inside... I mean the general public in the resort," he said in Tamil.

"Do you know Tamil?" I asked, stunned.

He laughed and said, "I studied here in Auroville. I went to France only to work."

Oh my god! Auroville again. I could not take it anymore. Even hearing that name was triggering me.

Quite unaware, David continued, "My wife is Indian, too. She is a psychologist working in Pondicherry."

I wanted to ask her name, wondering if it was someone I knew, but then I decided that I did not want to know. We were there until 3 AM. Then I went back to my room. David stayed back, still heavy on the drinks.

* * *

I was late to work the next morning. I had a severe headache. But David had come to the meeting before me. He had a cup of green tea in his hand. Would that guy need to have a drink of some sort in his hands always? How could he come to work on time despite drinking the whole night? Was he even human, I muttered to myself. My eyes searched for Maaya, meanwhile. But she was not there. Had she not arrived yet? I did not know when she went to sleep last night, either.

Raj had come, looking well-rested. His wife, Kavya, was a lawyer. She was also in attendance that day and was speaking to the government's lawyer. I was seeing her for the first time. She was clad in a cotton saree and had cut her hair short. She looked like a stereotypical journalist straight out of a movie.

Maaya came behind and tapped me on my shoulder. "Hey, why are you looking at that aunty?"

"Dei! Is that not Raj's wife? She's a lawyer, right?" I asked.

"Yeah! She's a feminist and a Periyarist too. She has written a lot of books as well," Maaya said.

"Wow. Have you met her before?" I asked.

"Yeah, once. Raj took us out to dinner," Maaya said.

"Oh! Do you know her that well?" I asked.

"Not like that... Raj had called all team leads once..." Maaya began explaining.

I changed the topic and asked, "Why were you late?"

"You're the one who's late. I had a breakfast meeting at 08:30 AM," she said, settling down.

"Breakfast is for eating... not meeting. Silly people!" I said and sat in the only empty seat available.

No matter what I did, I always had one eye on Maaya. We were communicating a lot just with our eyes. The occasional smile. The blush. The stolen glances. And I was loving every minute of it.

I wanted to eat lunch with Maaya, but she had a lunch meeting, too. So the first day went by with just discussions. Though I was with them most of the time, I was invited only for specific meetings. So I would simply be meddling with my computer at that time.

That evening, they separated us into different groups.

One team was assigned to enter the data from the doctors into the system. They had to finish entering all the data in three days. Meanwhile, Maaya and I had to build algorithms for that data to analyze the behavioral patterns. Only based on this result would they tell us what the next step would be.

Once the actual work began, Maaya came near me and lamented, "At this rate, they won't complete the project even if it takes two more years. They are very slow. It will be great if we have live data for demo and practice. Now they have just given us old and obsolete data… how can we do a project with this? How do they expect us to get proper results with this?"

"Why should I be worried about that? They are giving me free food and accommodations that are allowing me to spend two weeks with you… what more do I need?" I answered casually.

"Sir is always in a romantic mood! Do you have any idea of actually working on what we came here for?"

"Weren't you the one who said it will take them two more years at this speed? That's good news for me… Why should we hurry now?" I laughed.

"Oh, hell! Don't forget that I am your team leader!" She exclaimed.

"Forget leading the team… Let us talk about how to lead our lives!" I quipped.

"You are unbelievable!! I have to go to a meeting. Will come back and take you to task…" Maaya muttered.

"You can take me anywhere. I will come willingly," I laughed, spreading my arms wide.

"Stop and get back to work," she admonished, rather ruining the stern effect with a smile.

"I am doing my work," I insisted, giving her a hearty smile.

She turned around, blushing and laughing.

* * *

We worked for 15–16 hours daily. The healthcare companies would come up with new requirements, and Maaya and I would make changes in the development based on that. They would then check it. They were trying to discover the early symptoms of depression and anxiety disorders. They believed that this would be the primary level and understandable for everyone.

We met for dinner again after three days. Only Maaya and I were there. And at first, we discussed only the office issues.

Then I slowly spoke, "Since we started this project, we barely have time to breathe. We are always working. We have no phones or the internet to get some respite from our stress, nor do we speak to any of our friends. We have to distract ourselves in some other way, at least. We don't need to speak of work even during these dinners. Let's talk about something else."

"Don't you know I love my job?" She asked.

"With all the stress surrounding us here, you'll definitely break up with your job. Then I'll have to take care of you," I said.

"I think you're the one who is more stressed about all this. What happened?" She asked gently.

"I don't prefer such intense projects. If not for you, I would not have joined this project. I came here because I thought I could spend more quality time with you. That was my only objective. Instead, we are constantly working and trying to meet impossible deadlines. While I was home, you'd kiss me at least in my dreams. But here, even my dreams are about giving status updates to the other teams. The only woman appearing in my dream is Thyda and not you," I complained.

Maaya, who had been drinking water, spat it out and snorted with laughter. "Continue," she managed, still laughing.

I stared at her. "I am not as committed to working as you are. I just want to take care of the people with me. So I have to go to work and earn money. That's all. All this intense work is not my cup of tea."

She held my hand as she said, "I understand… I won't talk about work hereafter. Let's use this time to understand each other."

We decided to go to a spa on the resort premises and inquired about massages. But they informed us that we were not permitted to have massages; and if at all we really wanted them, we had to come before 10 PM. Usually, it took us until midnight to even finish our work for the day, and we worked even on weekends. So that was a no-go, too.

The following day, Maaya and I were together starting from breakfast until dinner. It was not just the project that advanced; everything else developed too.

Despite us working until 11 the next night, the work remained incomplete. We had to give an update the next day to the government representatives. Raj was also working with us. But he could not sit with us beyond 2 AM. He became a bit grumpy and annoying. Work was progressing at a good pace, but he sounded unhappy. It was very unusual to see Raj behave like this. He was generally a very soft person. But ever since we started this project, I noticed that he was becoming a completely different man.

Maaya finally lost it and spoke boldly to him. "Raj! Nothing will work out if you are here any longer… You're only making us nervous, too! You can come at 8 AM for the demo with us. We can then give the government officers a demo together at 10 AM. You go sleep now."

I was looking at them, wondering who was the boss here. To my surprise, Raj also nodded and agreed, wishing us a good night before leaving.

"I've noticed that Raj has been acting differently since we came here. He's always so wired up and tense. He often goes back to his room and drops his work midway. I've never seen him behave like this in the office. He looks overwhelmed and probably sees this project as a life-or-death issue. I am finding it more difficult to manage him than the project." Maaya ranted out of frustration, confirming my thoughts.

I nodded in agreement.

She then added, "Come, let's go to our room and work."

We called room service and ordered vodka. Then we refreshed ourselves and started work again. 'Work with Vodka' really helped, and we finished both – the whole bottle and the work – by 6 AM. We ensured that everything was wrapped up perfectly and mailed Raj.

Maaya took a deep breath, looking relaxed after finishing the job. Then she came and hugged me as well. I was tired, but the happiness of completing the work made it all worth it. I hugged her back and kissed her on her forehead.

"Shall we go for a walk? We've been sitting inside for far too long. We cannot rest now, either," she suggested.

We both stepped out for a walk on the beach just as the sun was rising. The moon was still visible as well. And the orange blanket over the sea looked majestic and alluring. The waves sounded peaceful in the early morning. I could not help but think that if we had such an experience every day, we would not need yoga or meditation at all.

David was alone there, lying on the beach on his back, looking like he was doing yoga. I wondered how he could drink all night and come here to exercise in the morning! We were amazed. Did that guy ever get sleep? Or was he that crazy about fitness?

"How is this guy like this?" Maaya asked, echoing my thoughts.

When we got closer to him, we quickly realized that he wasn't doing any fancy yoga poses. Turned out that he had had too many drinks at the party last night and gotten completely wasted. He had ended up passing out on the beach like a champ, unable to make his way back. We woke his drunk ass up and walked him back to his room, laughing our heads off at the irony of thinking he was some kind of enlightened yogi while he was merely drunk.

Then we walked back to our rooms to get ready.

Outside my room, Maaya hugged me again and gave me a smoldering kiss. But realizing we were in a public place, she moved away and said, "Come by 8 AM, sharp."

Then she went to her room while I stood there, watching her go.

She went to her room and took her access card to open the door. She turned to me before stepping in and queried my hesitation with her eyes. I winked and gave her a flying kiss, while she gestured at me to come inside, leaving the door open.

I hesitantly went inside. She was standing by the door and pulled me in for a kiss. I closed the door behind me and kissed her in return. It lasted for a long while.

Since that day, we were both together. We had never even proposed to each other, but we had one hell of a honeymoon that week.

For us '90s kids, this was a major achievement. In those 8 days, we got to know each other fully. Some people even jokingly asked us, "Why should the company waste money on two separate rooms for you guys?"

We just laughed it off.

But I'd always say that those 8 days were the best days of my life.

* * *

Chapter 6

I had an early morning meeting at 7 AM; yeah, you read it right, it's at freaking 7 AM. With no choice, I got up, gave a good morning kiss to Maaya, and left. The discussion got over only by 11 AM. When I came out, there was some disturbance and everyone inquired about Maaya's whereabouts. I had no idea, so I went to our room to check. She was not there, either. We all got worried and searched all over the resort. We even checked the CCTV footage, but she was nowhere to be found. Her bags and dresses were still in the room. She would never have stepped out in her pajamas. I felt sick to my stomach with worry.

After searching for a while, Raj suggested giving a police complaint. But the government officers refused and said, "We'll take care of this." They then made some calls, but they either kept a poker face or didn't seem to have bothered much about a missing member. Only I was really nervous and worried. And I was furious on seeing them all being so callous about it. Maaya was missing, and they were not allowing me to even leave the premises or call anyone else to ask about her.

I did not have lunch, nor was I in any mood to work. So I went to the bar inside the resort and started drinking. I ordered a Kingfisher Strong and sat at a table there. Right then, a woman working at the bar came to me and handed me a small slip of paper. On it were the words, 'First kiss + Friends + Fainting'

I understood that this must be from Maaya and that she was talking about Auroville. When she first tried to kiss me, my friends stopped me. Then I had – we both had – fainted after sipping that juice in Auroville. So I guessed that she must be there.

I rushed out of the bar and went to the government guys. I lied through my teeth. "My mother is not well. I have to go home today. I'll come back tomorrow." First, they hesitated, but they eventually agreed. Then, they instructed me to use the mobile they had given me. I just nodded my head to express my agreement so they'll get off my case. I took my car and tried to go straight to Pondy. While I was on East Coast Road, Raj called me. I did not attend and quickly switched off my mobile. I wondered why Maaya had gone there without informing anyone, especially me. In the next three hours, I reached Pondy. But once I was in Auroville, I did not know what to do. I looked around aimlessly. They would only allow me inside if there was a solid reason.

But right then, a meditation class was happening, so I pretended to go for that. It was a big place. On one side were small cottages. On the other side stood gardens. A little way inside were the places where they taught meditation and yoga. There were a few shops and a business center. Behind all this stood a huge forest. There were a few French colony people there. Many foreigners also came there to learn meditation. I was searching around for Maaya. I did not remember which exactly was the psychiatrist Renu's house. But a short distance away, I saw someone who resembled her. Deciding to follow her, I ducked behind a wall and started following the woman, trying to keep out of her sight.

Right then, a red Mahindra Bolero came into the area. Inside were Sathyan, his girlfriend Vidhya, Ilango, and his fiancée Suja. Ilango was in a wheelchair and looked to be unconscious. They were urgently carrying him out of the car and taking him inside in a wheelchair that someone had brought. Unbeknownst to anyone, I went right behind them. Some way into the forest, there was a building that they entered. I followed. Beyond a point, it was a restricted area that required access cards to enter. So I waited there and tried to see what they were doing.

I was worried and shocked at seeing Ilango's state. Maaya had often told me not to trust my friends. But I could not remain impassive after having known Ilango for so long. When Ilango had called me so many times in the recent past, Maaya had not allowed me to attend, and I had let it go, too. But now I felt incredibly guilty. I could see, however, Sathyan was the one calling the shots now. It was all so confusing.

About twenty minutes later, everyone except Ilango came out. I wondered if I should go inside or follow these people. There was nothing I could do to help Ilango without knowing more. In a split second, I decided to follow them to find out what was happening. I could not shake off the feeling that Ilango had wanted to say something important when he had called me so many times. And now, after seeing him in a wheelchair, I felt like I had made a mistake in not attending his calls on time.

To add to my confusion and worries, Maaya was also missing. I was not sure if something was linking both of these events. If so, were Maaya and Ilango caught in the same web? Something was seriously odd here. What was going on around me?

I followed Sathyan and the others. They went into Renu's house, which was nearby. Once I saw that house, I was able to recollect how they had brought me there and how I had fainted after drinking the juice they had given me. I was not even sure what they had done with me. At least today, I would get the answer to that. Then I could turn my back on this dark confusion and continue leading my life in peace.

I was following close behind them and heard their voices floating over. Suja angrily yelled at Renu, but I could not catch her words. Sathyan was trying to control her. "I did not know all this would happen. This was a 50-million-dollar project. That's why you accepted this, right? Some of the world's best doctors are treating him right now... They have reassured us that they could cure this. So have some patience," Renu was yelling back at Suja.

With a chill running down my spine, I understood that Ilango's life was in danger. These people had done something to him in their mad desire for money, which had apparently now backfired.

Now I was even more confused about why they had brought me here that day when I was with Maaya. What could have been the purpose of getting me to this place? Were they trying to do something to me as they had done to Ilango? Who were these people? And where did Maaya fit in?

How did Maaya know about all this? Why had she called me here now? Most importantly, where was she? Was she facing some problems here? Had she been forced to come here but managed to leave me a hint in some way before she left the resort? So many such questions were running through my mind.

Ordering Vidhya to remain where she was, the others came out. Renu turned to Sathyan and said, "Take a proper backup of all the data here. We should leave this place by tonight." Vidhya was speaking to someone over the phone. I slowly entered the place, making sure my footsteps were silent. Maaya was asleep in a room inside. I snuck in, too. Some electrodes were stuck to her head and neck. A machine that looked horribly like the one giving electric shocks stood beside her bed. A VR headset was over her eyes. I went inside and woke Maaya up.

The scene setup matched the ones from the best Sci-fi dramas and was arranged in a secluded place near Pondicherry. 'Unbelievable' was my only expression. At first, Maaya did not get up. I overcame my fear and tried again. Eventually, she managed to stir. When her eyes opened, she blinked at me uncertainly. She looked exhausted and could not even speak properly. I tried to carry her outside.

Vidhya returned after finishing the call and looked at me in shock. "Where are you going?" In return, I demanded, "What's going on here? What happened to Maaya?" "I'll tell you. Just get her back to bed first. It is hard to escape from here. We have to switch off the machine that is connected to her first. I did not know how," she said.

I did not want to listen to her, and I wondered if she was in cahoots with the people outside. But something in her eyes told me that she was genuinely worried for Maaya. So thinking quickly, I went inside the room and switched off the mains. That looked like the simplest solution. I then turned to Vidhya and demanded an explanation. "They're trying to erase Maaya's memories. They are planning to turn her against you," Vidhya confessed.

"What? Deleting her memories? Is Maaya a computer? How is this even possible? Who is doing this? Are they gods? Why would they want to turn Maaya against me?" I asked, trying to get my head around her words. "I don't know. They were trying to do something similar with Ilango, and now he is fighting for his life," Vidhya said, looking near tears. "Shit! What happened to Ilango?" I asked, trying to hold myself steady. She was not lying. Ilango's life was in danger, and now probably Maaya's, too!

"I came here to save Maaya. I am the reason Maaya is in this state now. She is my younger sister," Vidhya cried. "Sister? Ayyo! You're confusing me. Please tell me clearly…" I asked. "Renu is Suja's maternal aunt. Sathyan and Suja are business partners. They are both working for a Russian company on some big project. The project's worth is 50 million dollars. Maaya and Renu are also working with them. And because Ilango is Suja's girlfriend, he also helped Suja," Vidhya tried to explain.

"What? Maaya is working with them?" I asked incredulously. "And Ilango too? What are you saying?" "Yeah! As far as I know, they did some kind of experiment with Ilango and you. I do not know the full details. I tried hard but I could not contact Maaya for the last 8 days. And I guess the testing they did with you did not go well. Thankfully, you were not affected much, it appears. What they did with Ilango backfired, though, and now he is in a coma. They are not allowing me outside and are keeping me under their watch. I have not understood what is going on, but I have gathered this much since I came here. Maaya knows everything. I repeatedly tried calling Maaya to let her know about Ilango but in vain. I was only left exhausted. I could not reach her at all," Vidhya repeated as if in a shocked daze.

I could explain one part of it, at least. Maaya had been in the resort with me, where they had taken away her phone, so she was out of contact for that time. "Are they doing some tests with me?

And is Maaya working with them? So the last 8 days I spent with her… was all that a drama? I never did feel like that even once… I was with her the whole time!" I said, shocked.

"I don't know that, either. But I understand there's something seriously wrong here. I am going to break up with Sathyan. He's doing something illegal and hooking up with the Russian girls. I am here only for Maaya. I tag along with them all the time, but I do not know or understand half of what they are doing. Now I don't know what is going to happen to Ilango either. They are also seriously trying to control Maaya like this, against her will… I think this is the last straw for me."

Even as we were talking, Sathyan came back inside. Hearing his footsteps outside the door, I hid behind the shelf there. Vidhya tried to bring her expressions back under control. Sathyan entered and I heard him speak to Vidhya, "It will take her four hours to wake up. I must go and see Ilamaran before that and collect the data from him. We have to start from here by tonight."

Vidhya remained silent. "If at all Maaya wakes up earlier, give her this juice and make her sleep again. She'll drink this only if you give her. Remind her that her 5-million-dollar deal still stands and that she should not betray us." He left abruptly.

I could not understand what was going on around me. They were talking in millions. One of my friends was speaking like a villain, and another was fighting for his life. I did not know which side Maaya was on now. With a start, I realized that I did not know which side she had been on since the beginning. Had she had a change of heart and fallen in love with me or had she been around me for the sake of this project?

Forget all that! How were these fiends deleting people's memories? That was some serious sci-fi-level shit! And not at all plausible, no matter how much I thought of it. It felt surreal. I felt like I had gotten the answer to a few of the questions that had been plaguing my mind, but now I had more questions than before.

* * *

Chapter 7

Once Sathyan left, I tried waking Maaya up again.

"Let her sleep. These people have sedated her," Vidhya said.

"No… These people could have done something even for her to sleep. I have to wake her up and know more," I said.

Vidhya and I woke Maaya up and took her to the bathroom, where we washed her face. Then we gave her some cold water. Vidhya squeezed a lemon into it and asked Maaya to drink it.

Maaya eventually recovered. She did not look shocked to see me but was confused. Eventually, she collected herself, looked at Vidhya, and asked, "Did Sathyan say anything about how much time is left for us to leave?"

"He said we have four more hours," Vidhya replied.

"Then we have only that much time to leave this place without them knowing," Maaya said.

"Leave that. First, tell me what's happening here. I cannot understand anything," I snapped.

Maaya sighed. "You will not be able to understand… This is a huge game. These people are doing the same project that our company wants to do. They have a different aim, though. We are trying to use machine learning to understand humans better. But they are using the same technology to try to alter human thoughts… and teach them certain patterns forcefully…"

"How is that possible?" I demanded, horrified. I was still trying to wrap my mind around the concept of my company's project and was debating the ethics involved in that, but here they were, presenting me with the horrific reality of the other side of the project.

"As far as I know, they're doing two things here… First, they took me on board to control and emotionally manipulate you. They wanted to create a lot of confusion in you and push you into depression. They wanted to monitor all your body movements and train the computers based on that data. I would get orders in real time when I was with you. 'Do this. Say this.' And so on. I would follow those to the T. Then those people you believed were your friends would call you and confuse you with different versions of the story. Your confusion is their data," Maaya explained.

I was shaken to the core. "But how would these people get my data?" I asked disbelievingly, unable to take in all this.

"They've inserted skin-colored chips in two places in your body," Maaya informed me.

"What? Inside me?! What are you saying, Maaya?" I demanded, shocked beyond words.

"Yes, in your body. And you cannot even feel them. That was why we brought you to Pondy that first time. They have fitted you with that chip, but it would be indistinguishable from your skin. And in about sixty days, it would dissolve naturally."

"Is all this possible?"

Maaya laughed sardonically, "There's a lot more."

I tried to wrap my head around the shocking revelation. I gently trailed a hand over my forearms, imagining chips fitted there. "How would they get the data from me, then? I mean, how is it shared with them?" I asked, confused.

"Do you remember they accessed your phone when you were here last time? That's for this, actually. First, they took your fingerprints and installed certain software on your phone. Then, every time you unlock your phone, it would take the data collected in the chip and transfer it to their database," she explained.

"Oh, so that's why you asked me to stop using that mobile in between when we were alone?"

"Yes."

"Why did you switch sides again? Did you change because you fell in love with me, as they show in the movies?" I mocked.

"Nothing of that sort. I joined these people because Vidhya told me about this. Besides, they told me they would give me 5 million dollars. And they promised to make me a partner if the project went well. So I agreed," she said coolly, with no regrets.

"That's fine… but why did you come with us halfway through?" I demanded.

"I spoke about the same deal with Raj. He also agreed to pay me the same amount if the deal went through. The same price, but lesser risks than this, so I decided to ditch these guys," she explained as if it was apparent.

"Does Raj know about this project?"

"Why should he know about this? I made a deal only to finish that project with him. I have never spoken with him about this other one."

"You're unbelievable!" I exclaimed, still unable to believe this was Maaya talking. I felt a dissonance when I remembered all the loving private moments we had shared and how she seemed to reciprocate my feelings. "What about whatever we shared?" I blurted.

"I like you very much. But my career is more important to me," Maaya said unfeelingly.

"It's fine to say that you 'like' me… But I am specifically asking about whatever happened in the last 8 days! Are you such an open type of person?" I asked, wondering if that intimacy did not mean as much to her as it did to me.

Maaya looked shocked. "What happened in the last eight days?"

"Hell! We were together for the last 8 days in the resort. And I mean… completely. So much so that everyone knew we were a couple! I believed they were the best days of my life…" I said.

"What? I don't remember any of this!" Maaya said.

Vidhya supplied dully, "They are erasing your memories."

"Oh! My memories too?" She asked, turning to see the bed she was on. Then she thought a bit and said, "The last thing I remembered was being in the car parking area…"

I looked at her intently, not knowing what to say. Had she really forgotten all the beautiful moments completely? Was that even possible? Had she been with me only for some ulterior motive? Was that Maaya real, or this one? How did we progress to such deep love in such a short time? Was all that planned ahead of time?

Questions swirled in my mind as I kept looking at the woman I thought was my life's love. I felt crushed as if all my trust had shattered.

After two minutes of awkward silence, I asked, "Now, what happened to Ilango?"

Maaya seemed to collect her thoughts as she replied, "Suja used his existing migraine problem and told him she is giving him shock treatments for a quick recovery. She's using that and erasing his memories at a specific time and replacing them with some other memories using VR technology. So basically, they are overwriting his memories with artificially created incidents. Then they will make him talk to you and confuse you, too. This was their plan."

"So he has no clue about any of this?"

"No, they are using him to test the procedures' success rate. They are using him as a guinea pig to see how they can erase memories… Suja clearly knew that Ilango would not do anything against you. So they wouldn't ask him directly to do anything like that. But they can confuse you only by using someone you trust, who they had to bring under their control… That person is Ilango. But he was just your friend. So his hold was limited when it came to you. Unfortunately, that was not enough for their plans. So they wanted someone to control you more intimately. That was me."

"How many more people are involved in this?"

"Thousands of people. Not just in India, either. Sathyan said they are doing such things in 12 countries across the world. They just have the data from India here. They are collecting data from other countries and cultures to ensure the accuracy of their algorithm. The more the merrier!"

"Isn't it illegal to erase people's memories? It feels so wrong to artificially manipulate human experiences," I said, trying to wrap my head around the concept.

"Don't they operate on people to remove their malignant tumors? Likewise, they can remove people's bad memories and replace them with good, happy memories. That is all. When we talk about someone, we recollect their face in our minds. These people scan our memories and try to identify the person based on that face. They see how we associate certain people with certain emotions…

With this, they can analyze who we think of when we are happy or when we are sad, and so on. This will give them an idea of how we see people. This is useful when they want to change our emotions… For example, if you are sad and they want to make you happy, they can modify your sad memories by associating them with happy people's faces. They are also wondering how to treat people based on this."

"Oh, God! Is all this actually possible?"

"Yes. But legally, it is complicated to get approval. Just look at how secretively they are, in our company, while doing the procedures and asking us to sign non-disclosure agreements."

"Okay, how did you come here from the resort?" I asked the question that had been bugging me for a while.

She thought for a while and said, "I don't remember anything. I heard about the resort only from you. I do not remember any of it."

"My head is reeling just thinking of all this. The Russian company's involvement is scary, seeing what they do here! And all my friends are also involved in this in some capacity… you know the truth, too… Only I have been an idiot!" I exclaimed.

"Consider Ilango and me in that list of idiots who fell for love," Vidhya muttered, looking angry and pained.

"Hey! I came to this project because you told me about it first," Maaya protested.

"You did not tell me these details. When Sathyan mentioned it to me, I thought it was some ordinary project. I knew you were talented enough, and the pay was good, too. I never knew what the project was about! But you did… I did not know you and Sathyan were such greedy people who would do anything for money," Vidhya snapped.

"You would not have accepted if I had shared all the details with you. Will they just give me 5 million dollars for doing something usual, legal, and normal?" Maaya demanded.

"And even Sathyan being with those Russian girls looks okay according to you, right?" Vidhya demanded.

"I swear I did not know that. If I had known, I would have warned you for sure…" Maaya said earnestly.

"I honestly don't care anymore. I have nothing to do with him hereafter," Vidhya snapped.

"Okay, I will call Raj now. If we tell him the truth, he can speak to the government officers there and decide on the next step," I said, taking my phone out.

Maaya immediately plucked my phone out of my hand.

"Hey! Why are you always plucking my phone away from my hands? When are you going to stop this?"

"What can I do? You are such a straightforward and naive guy. I am not like that. I want to do business," Maaya shrugged. Then, as if she had thought something over, she turned to Vidhya and said, "You stay here. If Sathyan comes over, distract him by saying that I am in the bathroom or something like that."

Then Maaya turned to me again and said, "You come with me."

Maaya kept giving me orders as we went into the basement. There was a massive server room, and a few people were working on the servers. Maaya used her biometric identities – her fingerprint and iris print – in the appropriate devices and was granted access.

The huge metal doors opened to a big room inside, which seemed to be some area that only she could access. I wondered what she was doing in this place that looked straight out of a sci-fi movie setup.

She logged into a computer and said, "We can access all the data here. You have to find some way to copy all this. Later we can sort through the data and see how to use that. I will go back to the room and pretend to be sleeping. We will get caught if someone comes in. We still have three hours left." She then turned to leave, but turned around again to ask, "What excuse did you give to come here?"

"I told them that my mother was ill. But I guess they found out that I was not at home like I said I would be. They kept calling me. So I switched off the mobile. So, no one knows that I am here…"

"Super… Just don't call your mother from here. If you do, they'll track you. We can take care of everything after three hours. We have to leave India today. What country do you have a visa for?" She asked.

"Hey! I won't leave my mother and go anywhere. I will be here only. I have not done anything wrong here, to consider leaving."

"Okay… You just copy the data. I will think of what to do next," Maaya said and left.

I did not know when I would stop listening to her without uttering a word of protest.

I started accessing the data. They only had the data pertaining to India stored in that location, as Maaya had said. But they collected it in 23 different languages.

* * *

Once Maaya went up, she addressed Vidhya, "We have to leave India today, or they'll arrest us. Ilamaran does not understand all this and is still speaking some age-old useless mother sentiment. Let us collect the data from him and leave. First, we will go to Mumbai and then plan our journey after that. You book flight tickets for three places – Mumbai, Delhi, and Goa."

"Why for all these places together?" Vidhya demanded.

"So they won't know where we are going. Also, book a big SUV for long-distance driving," Maaya instructed.

"You should take some time to think. Are you not curious to know about the 8 days that Ilamaran keeps talking about with such conviction? Even after knowing what you have done to him, he is still working to help you. But you still want to use him for your personal gain. Don't you ever regret doing such things to Ilamaran? Imagine how much he must have loved you to come here in search of you when you went missing. His friends had backstabbed him. And the woman he thought was his love also ditched him, not to mention having ulterior motives. Will you never think about what will happen to him after you leave India? Won't Ilamaran feel betrayed, like how I am feeling now after Sathyan betrayed me? I will book tickets like you said, but you have to pause and think. Would you be happy if you lost him and earned all this money?" Vidhya asked and turned to make a call without waiting for Maaya's reply.

Maaya did not say anything in return and just went to bed.

* * *

Chapter 8

Three hours later

I finished the work and went upstairs. But I was in for a shock. In the main hall of the place, a few men were moving about with purpose. There was a general ruckus, and I had walked right into it.

Raj and the government representative were there, along with three policemen. They had arrested Sathyan on the basis of suspicion when he went to the resort to collect data about me. And on further inquiries, they had known about this clandestine project in Pondy.

They roused Maaya, who had been sleeping then thanks to the exhaustion and the medication. She looked surprised to see them and was shocked to learn that they had arrested Raj, too. Even I was shocked and frightened to hear about that. I stood back and observed them from afar. What in the hell was happening?

Keshav Ram Patel looked at Maaya and asked, "How are you, ma?"

"Why has Raj been arrested?" Maaya asked, looking disoriented.

"He's the main reason behind everything that happened here. He wanted to get a project patented using your company, Indira Software. In parallel, he planned to build another software – even a huge setup – for nefarious purposes. They just used the name Indira Software to get government clearances for certain procedures and to avoid apprehensions about the whole process. Sathyan's company is helping them obtain the data illegally and also helping with other fraudulent activities under his company's name. Their plan is to eventually merge these two companies. Raj had honey-trapped Sathyan and made him agree to this!"

"What! What nonsense is this?! Sathyan… what else have you done?" Vidhya yelled.

Keshav looked at Vidhya and continued speaking.

"The only mistake Raj made was giving full responsibility to Sathyan. This meant an overlapping of common people. So you,

Maaya, and Ilamaran got involved in both projects. That is how we found out that such a thing was going on."

I was growing increasingly shocked upon hearing all this. I could not believe it at all. Raj was my mentor. I have always held him in great respect. And Sathyan was my friend. I was terribly upset that Maaya and Sathyan had betrayed me. And to now hear that Raj was also a part of it was impossible to bear. I could not control myself any longer.

I rushed inside in anger. "Raj, I never expected you would do such a thing. You are my role model… Why did you do this, Raj?" I demanded.

Raj looked back at me with his head held high, almost defiantly. "I made no mistake here. These people are still secretive and hesitant about technology that should have existed fifteen years ago. But the world is evolving so fast. I am trying to bring in the technology today that would only be possible for general use 20 years into the future. You will not understand this."

"So, are you fine with framing someone as mentally unstable and pushing them to depression so you could serve your purpose? Just think… does this sound right to you?" I demanded, feeling a strange urge to yell at his face.

"Ilamaara! This is exactly the problem. Why would you call anyone dealing with mental health issues mentally unstable or a retarded person? Why not treat mental health issues like you'd treat a fever or cough? Give it the right medical intervention as you'd do for any other physical illness."

I immediately remembered Sathyan calling me mental. So their ideals and outlook were not the same! I wondered what had brought them together then.

"They took even our ancient heritage of yoga and made politics out of it to divide us on some pretext. This is such a country. No government or healthcare industry bigwigs have ever taken mental health issues seriously. That is why I took things into my hands. So what's wrong with this?" Raj demanded.

"What you are saying sounds right. But you could have done all this safely and legally," I countered.

"What can I do? If I had to go the legal route, we would spend the next 50 years just talking about it, with no actions."

I felt angry. "Now Ilango is fighting for his life. What are you going to say for that?" Did he not see how his actions had such consequences?

"Imagine if a girl got raped and she got into depression because of that incident. Immediately, everyone will try to express their rage and condolences and give rousing speeches on social media. No one can or will do anything else. But imagine… if we could erase that memory from the girl's mind and replace it with some happier memory, we could solve her problem. Sometimes, the memories inside us are like cancer cells, So there is nothing wrong in removing them," Raj said.

This looked like a long-standing sour topic that had been festering inside him. He was speaking with such passion and hatred and frustration – all of which were vying for space on his face.

"Likewise, we call the rapists and murderers psychos. But each one of them will have stories or incidents behind their actions… some trigger in their past… that is urging them to become such detested criminals. We call for them to be hanged to death and express our rage when such incidents happen. But we never pause to think of why they are happening. Instead of talking left and right on social media and punishing the wrongdoers, we could remove the bad memories from their brains and replace them with good ones so they have a new chance at life. Think of that! When we are attempting such a good thing, we have to accept a few sad side effects!"

It looked good when he put it that way, but I could not accept it wholeheartedly.

"What you said sounds good. But this also has the power to turn normal people into deranged maniacs. With just one small incident and some confusing, irrelevant information that was planted, even I started believing I was mentally disturbed," I said angrily.

"That cannot be helped. Don't we have a black market for kidney transplants now? Did that mean they have stopped doing kidney transplants at all? Or could we discount all the lives that are saved thanks to this miraculous technology? So we should find a way to counter all the negative effects of this new technology, that's all! But we should not be rethinking and doubting the need for this technology altogether," Raj argued.

"You are trying to artificially alter and manipulate human experiences. How is this correct? It sounds morally wrong as if you are taking away some parts of people's lives and replacing them with fake memories that they will think are their lived experiences. You are actually taking away a part of what makes them a person. It is one thing to use machine learning to understand people. But how is it ethical to completely change their thoughts and memories?"

"It's very simple. Even for physical ailments, surgery is often the last resort. We will not perform surgeries for issues that could be cured with medicines or therapy. Likewise, we could do this memory modification only when it is absolutely necessary. Or we could just give some other therapy based on the data we get.

Let me tell you, in another ten or twenty years, there is a chance that mental health issues will be much bigger than cancer. They will be more common. Every single person now is suffering from some form of mental health issue thanks to all the stress and the hustle of everyday life. Our lives now are different from what they were 30 years ago! If we do not take preventive measures now, we will suffer greatly.

What could we do? If we have to do all this legally, we will take at least 2–3 decades, by which time the technological world will have grown leaps and bounds and this very concept may become obsolete!" Raj said.

I did not know what to say. Raj continued.

"That was why we had to collect and work on data this way. Why? All the government officials are here, right? Ask them to make all this legal now. They cannot. What's more… They will not even take it to the Prime Minister for a discussion or do anything proactive about it."

Keshav Patel intervened. "Raj, your arguments are solid and thought-provoking. But you have to speak all about this in the courts. Let us believe that something good will come out of it. From our side, we will surely speak to the PM... But it is not easy to implement such a policy in a country like India. You will not understand the political intricacies and roadblocks we may need to face.

As I was ruminating, the place buzzed with activity.

Raj, Sathyan, and Suja were arrested. They were the owners of the companies involved in this. But because Maaya and Renu were just working under contracts, they were not arrested. They were let off with a warning to appear when summoned. It was ascertained that their roles in this nefarious scheme were not that big.

But the officers were saying that Renu could lose her practicing license. It would serve her right, for she was one of the people who should have understood mental health issues best, thanks to her profession, but she had been callous and played with people's lives instead. She knew the risks best but still had been money-minded and greedy enough to ruin people's mental and physical health.

I stood unmoving as the officers took my friends away. The shock was still hard to process.

Maaya came to me and said, "Sorry, I should not have done this. In my blind desire for my career, I did not respect human emotions. My career is important to me. But on seeing what Vidhya told earlier and with whatever happened here now... I realized that I had made a grave mistake. I feel ashamed of myself," she said.

I did not know what to tell her. But Vidhya pulled her into a hug after seeing her cry.

"Now I really want to know what happened in the last 8 days. There is no better punishment we can have than forgetting the good things that happened in our lives. I want to know how I saw you, and how I fell in love with you. Can you please tell me what happened? Or we could try to do something based on the data these people had taken. I want to see you the same way you see me... With love and trust... That is how I can completely understand your emotions and feelings," Maaya said.

"There's no need for that. Let's stop everything here," I said immediately.

Her face fell in shock. But she recovered quickly and said, "Oh! But that's right. You deserve a girl who prioritizes you. Not like me… I cannot explain everything I did, because most of it was for my career and money. But I understand that you don't have to love me the same after knowing all this. I… I wish you luck… you'll surely get a better girl," she turned to leave.

But I held her back by her hand and said, "I love you. I will always love you, no matter what. We don't need to think of our past now. We need to be together for life. And we must love each other anew every single day. If you had liked me in the last 8 days, you will definitely find that feeling again. Let us start over. I believe you will love me again like you already did, and I will also love the experience of falling in love with you all over again, this time with none of the confusion that marred our relationship. Then our love will become even more beautiful."

I took her hand in mine and dragged her close. She hugged me gently, reaching up to kiss my cheeks. The power of that kiss was as if she was feeling everything that I had felt in the last eight days over just eight minutes.

Then she looked at me as I said, "My friends are not coming, now."

We both laughed. I ran my finger over her smiling lips. "The promised walk in Pondicherry beach is still pending. The waves are apparently angry that you have not visited, and are refusing to grace the beach!"

She looked intently at me, blushing as she said, "You were my date, but now you are my fate."

✳ ✳ ✳

Chapter 9

The news that a software company based in India had tied up with Russian companies to build a technology that deleted people's memories had become the most sensational news across the country. At first, it was just the local print and visual media, but pretty soon, national news channels were covering the same on a larger scale. So much that all of us had lost what little modicum of privacy we had.

The authorities had only arrested Raj, Sathyan, and Suja. But even Maaya and I felt the brunt of the media glare. The involvement of Russian companies and the concepts of data security and data privacy all made national headlines and were the subjects of debate programs across languages. The entire became a huge controversy.

On one side, people were saying that this was an apparent show of the government's dictatorship and that the government was funding this technology to infuse their ideology by erasing people's memories. On the other side, people were debating security and privacy issues. They had brought up everything including people's biometric data that the government held and the other such 'breaches' into people's privacy, and they linked those with this new revelation. Overall, none of them seemed to have grasped the real issue, but everyone had an opinion on it. As a result, conspiracy theories abounded, and social media exploded, too. The videos of armchair experts prophesying doom and the memes with our caricatures also became viral.

We had become quasi-celebrities, much to our displeasure. Based on our agreement to keep us away from consequences, the government officials had given us strict orders to not talk to anyone about anything, including friends and family. The media frenzy made this look like a logical demand, but that also had negative effects on us. Maaya and I had escaped the legal repercussions, but we could never land work anywhere else. As long as the case was still in court, no one was ready to trust us with any job. We applied to many companies and tried asking all our contacts, but nothing helped. In between all this, the media people were also hounding us. They had almost set up a camp outside our houses.

It was incredibly difficult for me to even see Maaya in person. I was constantly griping in my mind, 'Hey do you know how difficult it is for the 90s kids to have a girlfriend? I finally found one because someone decided to do some ambitious IT project! I would never have had one if not for this project. But you guys cannot accept even this! Why are you roaming with cameras around our places and following us wherever we go? Even inside the privacy of our rooms, we feel like we were stuck inside the Bigg Boss house with cameras all over us!'

* * *

While I was ruminating on the sad and sorry state that we found ourselves in, Maaya got a call from a US number.

"We're calling from Dhiraj Systems. We are a US-based company. We are aware of your recent project and all the legal problems associated with it. We are also doing a similar project but on legal terms and would like to offer a job on a contractual basis for now. After seeing your performance, we can look for a permanent position in our company."

The representative came straight to the point.

"Thank you very much. Could you tell me what kind of project you are talking about?" Maaya requested.

"As I said, it's similar to your recent controversial project. But this time, we will follow all the laws and get the government's approval. We will take care of all that. You just need to do the programming. We will take care of the rest," they said.

"Okay, When do we start? Can we discuss the salary packages?" Maaya asked.

"You can start immediately. We will give you 100,000 dollars once you complete the project. But we have a few conditions. First, you have to sign an agreement," they said.

'Agreement again?' Maaya's thoughts ran in all directions. Out loud, she asked, "What conditions?"

"You should hand over all the rights to this technology to us. You are not our permanent employees, but this technology would belong to us. We will pay you for that. And you should not work for anyone else during this contract period."

"Okay, these are reasonable expectations. I will have to speak to Ilamaran too. Let me discuss it with him and get back to you," Maaya said.

"We will speak with him too. And you could discuss and let us know," they said.

Once the call ended, Maaya googled the company. Dhiraj Systems was a surprisingly well-founded company. They were doing a lot of research in neuroscience and were using that to develop new technology. They have also published many research papers. A former employee of Google had started the company.

Maaya was excited. She wanted to do this project mainly because an Indian woman had founded the company. Her name was Dhivya. But she was apparently born and brought up in the US. We dug up some information on her. Her words and accent sounded American, though. It was not a big company – they just had a few hundred employees, but they had churned out some impressive work so far. In an interview, the founder Dhivya also mentioned that they wanted to start a branch in Chennai. Maaya immediately wished to complete this project successfully and eventually take over their Indian operations.

In the same happy mood, she called me! With her words and enthusiasm, I understood what she was calling about.

"What is it, my dear wifey? Do you want to go to America?" I asked

"Yes, partner. You're okay with it, right? Or are you going to say something about this, too?" She asked.

"I am still thinking about it, wifey!" I replied, a smile in my voice.

"Hey! Why are you calling me your wifey? It does not even sound good. No one does this nowadays," she said and blushed.

"How else would I call my wife?"

"Call me your partner. We are not just life partners. We are business partners too."

"Hold on, partner; let us not rush into this. I am still scarred by everything that happened. Do we need to do a similar project and risk it again? The media is still behind us. I am unsure how such a project could be legally feasible. Do we need to get into all this right now?" I said.

"I know you will say something like this. Thanks for proving me right yet again!" she laughed and continued. "But listen! At this point, we don't have any other options. We will only get a chance to move forward if we start something like this. We cannot do anything by just sitting at home…" she chastised me.

"You're right. But for some reason, I still think we need to help Raj… We should try to get him out of jail." I said.

"Excuse me! Did you misplace your brain in the resort? Are you trying to be a superhero? Talk about something that could happen!" She retorted.

"Why do you say this is not possible?" I demanded, confused.

"Are you even following what's been happening around us? Have you seen the news that has not yet died down? The debates and theories in the media? The entire spectrum of analogies and narratives – including politics, national security, data privacy, and terrorism – are being discussed by every common man these days. Even the sound of these words sends a shiver down my spine. And you want to be a hero in all this?" She almost yelled at me.

"Hey! It's not like that, sweetheart! We have known Raj for a long time now… We have seen his leadership and know how passionate he is about his work. Have you ever had a reason to doubt him so far? I think he is a straightforward guy with some misguided motive this time. I don't think he is generally corrupt. No one could have acted that well for so long. But despite thinking for these many days, I cannot find out the one valid reason that he could have done something like this without a reason or a purpose," I said.

"Shall I tell you the obvious reason that you won't even think about? It's money, man… money! Everyone needs money. Why did your friend Sathyan dare to desert my sister? He wants to go to Russia and earn money there. So he felt he would be better off with those Russian girls. They are his fast ticket to big money. That's the only reason. If we both have to settle in life, we need money too. Otherwise, no one will respect us," Maaya said, her voice rising in anger.

"What you say might be right. And I may be the naive one here. But if I have to commit myself fully to this work, I have to know the truth. I strongly feel that there is some other reason for Raj doing all that. So I think we should not sell this concept or our talents to anyone else until we know the truth," I said.

"What, now? Are you suggesting we go to the prison and meet him?" She asked almost sarcastically.

"Do we have any other option?" I countered.

"Okay, so you come and pick me up at 10," she said in a resigned voice and cut the call.

* * *

I had not expected her to agree so quickly. Maybe she wanted answers, too. Or she was just appeasing me? Or, somehow, she was just sure that nothing could move forward unless this was cleared. Whatever it is, she had agreed. And I did not want her to back out, either. So I diligently took my bike and went to pick her up.

When she came out, she asked, "Hey, mister! Where's your car? Why are you coming in a two-wheeler nowadays?"

"It's very tedious to drive a car in this traffic. So we will use it only for a long drive. Otherwise, a motorbike is the best," I said.

"Mr. Romeo! Don't I know why you prefer bikes nowadays? If you unnecessarily use those brakes, we'll surely break up before marriage, I swear…"

I laughed and muttered, "Why are you putting up such a scene after everything that happened in the resort?"

"What did you say?" She asked, looking simultaneously nervous and shy.

"Nothing… We should not break up for one misapplied brake. Indian roads teach us that we should cross many ups and downs together. When that happens, we will feel much closer, and our intimacy will increase. And this happens only when we go on a motorbike," I said,

"Look at that! Full-time Romeo thinks of life and marriage all the time. I think I have to be careful with you from here onwards," she laughed.

We were on our way, and the journey was quite enjoyable. Once we reached, I removed my helmet and corrected my hair by looking at the bike's mirror.

Maaya had gotten down and was looking at me. I turned to her and grinned, "What are you staring at? Is your beau looking great?"

"As if," she laughed teasingly. "Come, let's go in."

* * *

We finished some processes there and went inside. The jailer told us to go to room number 777. Once we went in, Raj came out. The place was a designated meeting point for visitors. I had expected Raj to have thinned and grown a beard during his stint at the jail as they showed in the movies, but he looked clean-shaven and perfectly groomed like he was ready for an office meeting.

Immediately I quipped, "Raj? You are looking smart!"

"Look who has come to give me a surprise visit!!" he smiled sardonically.

I wondered if he was angry that we had not come sooner to visit him.

"Actually, Raj… It was a bit overwhelming. Whatever happened – and is happening right now – is too much to process for us. It took so long to sort it out in my head, and I am still trying to understand what is happening. Besides, we are also basically under house arrest," I explained.

"What? You've been arrested?" Raj asked, shocked.

"Yeah, the media are hounding us. Even now, about ten people are waiting outside the jail. They will start to torture us the moment we step out," Maaya said.

"Hmmm… we will be their prey until the next big news comes. Okay, tell me! What do you want? You must be here for a reason," He came to the point.

Immediately, I chipped in. "Raj. We are not able to land jobs anywhere. Now, an American company is asking us to do a similar project. That is why I wanted to talk to you first."

"I am not in the right mindset or position to give you advice," Raj said.

"We have not come here just for advice. We want to know why you did this. We still cannot get our heads around why you did something like this. We want to know the truth."

Raj looked startled for a moment, probably at our insistence and the fact that we had sought him out despite the apparent betrayal. But he recovered quickly.

"Money, guys! Money is the sole reason. What else?! They told me they'll give me millions, and I am not a fool to refuse such an opportunity," he shrugged and laughed out loud.

But his laughter sounded off-key and he could not even look at our faces while talking. It was evident that he was feeling ashamed and guilty.

Maaya and I looked at each other. I could see that she had her doubts, too.

Eventually, Maaya managed, "Raj! Don't try to spin your yarn even now, and try to fool us too. You're definitely hiding something. You're not the person who goes behind money, I know you well."

I looked at her with some sort of shock. Had she not said the same thing this morning, about money being everyone's motive? Now she had flipped 180 degrees in front of Raj. I had always known that she was smart, but I was surprised to see her do this with such a straight poker face. I tried to hold her gaze, but she avoided me and continued talking.

"When you spoke about this project in our office, you had high ideals and passion. I have not seen such energy in you before for any project that our company has done. There is no way all this was just for money," she insisted.

"I feel like laughing at you both for your naivete. Money is everything, kiddos. Go. This is the age to earn more. Don't be sentimental idiots and second guess my intent or try to sniff out some other motive. There's no meaning in anything. None," Raj said bitterly.

"Raj... we did not think of you as just our boss. We see you as our mentor. If that were not the case, we would not have come so far to talk to you amidst all the risks and knowing how many tongues would wag and create a big issue out of this now. We could have sold the program to that American company, earned money, and simply walked away into a better life. But I feel that is not how we thought of each other. Raj, please tell us what happened. Only then we would know if we can do something. We beg you, please!" I said.

"Stop making me emotional! I did not want to talk about it at all. Every effort I took has been wasted, and I am in jail. My professional life has been ruined, but that is nothing compared to my personal pain. So how can I even begin to explain? And even if I did, will it matter?"

Maaya and I waited in silence. I felt a lump in my throat after seeing Raj's pain. But eventually, after letting the silence reign for some time, Maaya and I both spoke together, surprising even ourselves.

"Please, Raj!"

Raj looked up in surprise. "Okay, I will tell you the truth. But this is too personal, and the story should not go out. Only my wife and sister know about this. Now I am telling you because I feel guilty for dragging you both into this project."

We both felt relieved and sat back in our seats, prepared to hear the truth at last.

"Don't tell us it is a love story, Raj," I muttered to lighten up the mood.

Maaya looked at me and countered, "Should it always be a love story? Won't something else have happened in his life? Why are you always thinking of that?"

Raj blushed a bit, laughing. Maaya and I could not control our laughter.

"We cannot trust these 80s kids. They have super love stories compared to us 90s kids. We are the poor ones," I said.

Raj laughed. "This is not some great love story. But this was something that turned my life upside down… and I am yet to come out of it. I don't think I ever will," his voice had turned heavy.

"Raj?! Come back from your dreamland, we are waiting to listen to your story with imaginative popcorn in hand," Maaya joked.

* * *

Chapter 10

Hereafter, Raj is narrating his story.

It was the final year of my college. The summer vacation had ended, and it was my first day back to college. I felt quite happy on seeing my friends and regular bus mates.

Back then, the people we meet on the bus, the shopkeepers with their petty shops near the bus stand, and even the old peddler grandma who hawks things on the bus… all these people would have some impact on our life. It is not unusual for the bus conductor who sees us every day to wait for us without blowing the whistle when he sees us running late so that the bus could stop for a little longer. And when we, in turn, see him in the local saloon, we'd feel a familiarity with him.

That day, I was late. And my usual bus had left by then. I took a lift from someone nearby and rushed to the next bus stop to somehow get on the same bus. Engineering college girls would usually sit in the back seat of the bus, and we'd always give our books to them, and travel by standing on the steps.

Back then, I had long hair. When it was ruffled by the air, I'd show off by adjusting it. We always ogle at those engineering girls but seldom talk to them. They would alight four stops ahead of ours. So we'd get back our books by then, and the bus will also be less crowded by then.

And this was how I saw her for the first time. She was a new entry to that backseat girl's group.

She was a beautiful Tamil girl who had come in a green & yellow salwar. A small black bag was in her hands, and she had a thin silver chain around her neck, a black bindi on her forehead, and a slim streak of sandal paste above it… She had such a beautiful face that would make you lose yourself at first glance. She did not even see my face properly. She just gave me back the books I had handed to her and got down.

'Ah, not surprising. The moment they realize we are looking at them, they would start pretending that they did not even notice us,' I thought. But out loud, I said, 'Thanks!"

Ilamaran, who had been listening to this, interrupted, "Girls are still like that, Raj."

Maaya immediately countered with, "If not for me, no one will see you. So stop!" She then turned to me and asked, "Raj, was this love at first sight?"

"Wait, I'll tell you! Have some patience," I smiled and continued.

"She would come at 7:30 AM for an 8 AM bus and sit in the same place all the time. I would wake up only at 7:30 for the same bus. I always gave my books only to her, and we shared a glance at each other every single morning. She was a studious girl. I had seen her carrying books written by Periyar and Osho and had also seen her reading them. So many boys would keep their distance from her. But I liked her since the first time I saw her. And even today, I still have no clue why I was so attracted to her."

"Aha! Ahem, okay," Maaya and Ilamaran teased me.

"I had not spoken even a word to her until college was over. I had a fledgling, one-sided love track with one of my neighbors' girls at that time. So I never felt like approaching this girl any further than sharing a look every morning. She was more like a crush at this point."

"Raj, this is too much. We are all roaming around without even one girl for our love stories... But you were having two – one in college and one at home!" Ilamaran exclaimed.

"Wait, da... listen fully, don't lament! One year had passed quickly, and my college life was over. On the other end, my one-sided love track had hit a dead end, and I became a depressed single guy again. I was working as a school teacher then. Though I did not like teaching, I thought of working at that school until I got a better job. I was spending my free time roaming around with my friends. Sometimes, I would stay the night in their rooms. We would drink all night. I had no work or personal goals then and nothing to look forward to in my life. I wasted about six months of my life like this.

And one day, my friend Varun took me along to enroll me in a computer course. The place had a 24-hour lab. He just wanted to keep me busy and occupied. Everything else was a side benefit. The class was between 06:30 PM and 08:30 PM. So I'd head straight to the computer center after my day job. After the class, I would only have time to go home and sleep. This was my friend's intention – he wanted me to do something constructive and have less time for any other distractions.

* * *

We went to the computer center for the first day. It was some time before we could complete the registration process and get inside. My first class was Java Programming. When I went in, the first person I saw was that girl from the bus."

"I am not surprised," Maaya said and giggled.

"This is not a movie to have a twist. Just stop talking and listen," Ilamaran said.

I continued.

"We both smiled at each other, recognizing our faces easily. I felt like I had met my long-time friend. She was in a grey and black salwar that day. Her dressing sense was still intact. She looked the same, too. But I had put on some weight. Once the class was over, she approached me by herself and spoke to me.

"Hi, how are you? I don't see you on the bus these days?"

"Unfortunately, my college life is over. If I had to come, then I should do it only to see you girls," I joked, smiling.

"What a nice, pretty smile! By the way, my name is Subha," she said and extended her hand.

A girl had called my smile pretty! I blushed and shook her hand, saying, "Raj."

Her hand was too soft, and I could feel a different vibe when our hands touched.

"I know," she said.

"How?" I asked, surprised.

"You'd give me your books, right? I have seen your name written on the first page," she explained.

"Oh, look at that! But I've not made an effort to know much about you, I guess," I said.

I noticed my friend Varun approaching. He gave me a sour look as he walked towards me. Subha was gently twirling the chain around her neck while speaking to me. I had never seen her talking much to anyone.

Varun finally neared me and asked, "Dude! Where have you gone?"

"To London… You were the one who was gone from class, and now you are asking me that. Dumbo!" I said casually. Then I turned and pointed to the girl. "She's Subha," I introduced them to each other. "Subha, this is Varun."

"Hi, I've seen you on the bus, too," Subha greeted him.

"Yeah, it's been a while since I saw you," Varun nodded in response.

"Okay, I should get going… will see you guys tomorrow," Subha said and left.

* * *

We left from there, too. Once we came out, the first words from Varun's mouth were, "Wherever you go, you will find a girl to flirt with. Your stars are made this way dude. But I am not going to pay for your drinks during the aftermath. Your relationship sagas and your break-ups seem never-ending. Focus on getting your life together," he said.

"Why would you always assume it is romantic love if girls and boys talk?" I asked back.

"That's not true for me, dude. But that's definitely how it is with you. You've been having a series of love affairs & break-ups since you were in the third grade. I am tired of helping you out with all that. If I had tried to fall in love with someone myself, without focusing on helping you, maybe I would have gotten something for myself," he said.

"Don't tell me you did not try at all. Accept the fact that you didn't get a girl to love. So you started pretending as if you were the one not interested in all that. I am like a movie hero, dude. You are like the hero's sidekick. Sad reality!" I laughed.

"It's all my fate. If I had saved up everything that I had spent for your break up and the drinks after that, I could have spent it on my marriage," he muttered.

"You have the money now, but still no girls," I teased.

Talking thus, we reached home.

* * *

The friendship that began that day between Subha and me blossomed like a beautiful lotus. We worked together in the lab during the weekends. We had fun roaming around the city in our free time. Another girl joined us, and Varun was already attending the classes. The four of us stayed together most of the time. Our time passed with fun chats, games, roadside pani puri, snacks at the famous Gangotree Snacks shop, bowling, movies, and so on. We would never talk about anything personal. Just general things and the merciless teasing we did with each other.

Varun did not want to get attached to anyone. So he never discussed anything personal with anyone. And, of course, he never allowed others to speak about personal stuff either.

He often said, 'The connection that comes with us being together now and whatever we share now will be the only true connection. We can take it as is. The friendship that is formed based on our past or our backgrounds will never last long!'

Though I liked what he said, I am an emotional guy who gets attached to people easily.

In the time we spent together, Subha and I had a lot in common. Including our likes – AR Rahman, Rahul Dravid, computers, food... She spoke a lot about politics. I started following the news so I could discuss that with her. I had never seen girls talking politics before, so I loved her a lot for that.

She was knowledgeable and had a down-to-earth and practical approach to life. I always felt she was unique. And beyond all this, she would always say that she wanted to do something big. So in no time, I started getting enamored by her and whatever she said.

If we like someone, we will also start loving everything they do. And on the flip side, when we start liking the things someone did, we start liking them too. I liked Subha in both ways – as a person and for the things she did.

Six months passed thus. Though we roamed around as a group of four, Subha used to speak to me more.

Varun got a job in another company. So he changed his classes to some other center near his office. Unfortunately, the other girl had also stopped coming to the classes for some reason. So now it's only the two of us."

"Do we expect the romantic Ilaiyaraja BGM hereafter, Raj?" Maaya asked.

"Did they not say they were AR Rahman fans? So it would be ARR playing the BGM," Ilamaran pointed out.

"Correct. No one can beat the 90s' AR Rahman," I agreed.

They laughed. "Continue, Raj," Maaya prompted.

* * *

"We usually went to eat something after class. But that day, she asked if we could go to a temple. So we went to a nearby Ayyappan temple. She did not pray there. Instead, she just looked around the temple and read the inscriptions on the walls.

I asked, "Why? Won't you worship God?"

"No, I don't believe in God," she shrugged.

"Why did you come to the temple, then?" I asked.

"We'll get good vibes here. We both are coming out together for the first time. So I thought we should go to a temple," she said.

I looked around and spotted a pillar. We both went and sat beside it. She gave all the prasadam to me.

"I cannot take all this home," she explained.

"Won't you even apply this sandal paste?" I asked.

"I will, but I did not inform my parents about this, so I prefer not to!" She said hesitantly.

"Here, take it," I said, extending my hand. "If they ask, tell them you got it from a friend in class."

She took the sandal paste from my hand and kept it neatly on her forehead. "Looking good?" She asked with a shy smile.

She was in a black salwar that day. And when she applied the mild yellow paste on her forehead, in that color combo, I was bowled over. Wordlessly, I looked at her intently. She shook her hand in front of my eyes and gestured, 'What happened?'

But she was smiling when she asked that, and that smile seemed to convey a thousand truths to me.

"You look so beautiful, like an angel," I said immediately.

"Ayyo da!" She exclaimed. "This is a temple, and you are lying so callously here?"

"No, no! If I were not speaking the truth, Lord Iyappan would punish me," I said.

"He is a poor God, still unmarried. Did he teach you that pickup line? This is such a sham. Come, let's go… Or you'll kill me with your over-the-top words," she said, still smiling.

We walked out casually.

"Let's walk for a while and then catch an auto home?" she asked.

I nodded, and we started walking. After a while, she asked abruptly, "Tell me your break-up story."

I stood and stared at her for a moment. I had not seen her face while walking, so I took a moment to orient myself. So far, we had never discussed anything that personal.

"Why are you asking this suddenly?" I asked.

"I just wondered. Why? Shouldn't I ask? Won't you share it with me? Is that such a secret?" she demanded.

I did not want to discuss anything personal yet, but I did not have the heart to say that out loud, either, as it would hurt her. So I managed, "Nothing like that. It's not such a big story. Just a one-sided love story, right? Why should we speak about that?"

"Okay, leave that. You are not keen to share this with me as you don't consider me your close friend yet," she said.

"No, it's not like that… It's just a closed chapter in my life, and there is nothing much to share," I tried to explain.

"Just say that you won't share! Why are you beating around the bush? I won't ask you about this hereafter," she said. "Get an auto. Let's leave."

"No… Let's talk about this in leisure one day," I said.

"Whatever!" She said abruptly and held her hand out to hail an auto.

* * *

We boarded an auto. On noticing her, suddenly, the auto driver said, "Good evening, Miss! How are you?"

"Hello, Anna! I'm good. How are you?" Subha asked in return. But her smile was strained.

"I'm good, Miss. How is sir?"

Subha did not directly respond to that, but neatly diverted the question. "When did you come to Chennai?"

"It's been a while... about six months... How is your sister, madam? She would have grown up by now, right?"

"Yes, brother! She's doing her 1st year in college now. So how is everyone at home?" Subha countered.

"We're getting on, ma. My son is more interested in cricket instead of his studies... he does not listen to anyone," the driver lamented.

Subha pointed to me and said, "Anna, he is a cricket player too. He has passed college with flying colors even without attending classes. And today, he's a school teacher. So likewise, your son will also grow up to become successful... don't worry."

"Am I your only example for this?" I demanded.

"It is true, right? Only from you should one learn how to skip classes and still pass," Subha laughed.

"Hey!" I objected. Then I looked at the driver via the rear-view mirror and said, "Anna, don't listen to this girl. Find a good cricket coach... your son will shine in that."

"We need a lot of money for all that, brother... an auto-driver's son should not have such lofty dreams," the driver said.

"Here... like how he became a teacher without ever attending a class, he would teach your son to excel in cricket without ever playing cricket himself!" Subha said.

"Won't you give me a break? Why are you butting in when two elders are talking? Go and sit in a corner," I said.

Before I could complete my sentence, the auto driver intervened, "Oh, God! Brother, madam was so talkative even in her childhood. You'd know whose granddaughter she is! The talent is in her blood, sir... What, madam? Am I not right?"

"It is in her blood? And whose granddaughter is she?" I asked, turning to Subha, "Hey, why have you not told me about all this?"

"You did not ask, so I did not say," she shrugged, laughing.

"Oh! So madam is a VIP?! I should be careful hereafter," I joked.

"Anna, look at him! This is why I never tell anyone about all that. Now look, even he is talking like this. You have outed me," she lamented to the auto driver.

She looked cute even while doing that. The auto driver did not allow me to enjoy that scene, though. He said, "Brother... she is really a great girl..."

Subha laughed and gestured at me with a wink as if asking me to listen to him. I laughed and turned to the auto driver.

"Okay, I will get down now. I can walk home from here. I think only people from high society places should pay the fare, not a commoner like me…" I said.

"Which law is that?" Subha asked.

"It is called Raj's law," I laughed. "Okay! I will leave now. We'll see tomorrow," I said, smiling at her.

She looked at me and said a wordless goodbye with her eyes. I laughed and walked away. While I was walking, a lot of questions arose in my mind. Some strange happiness filled me, but along with it was some irrational fear. Subha's gestures and appearance… the way she spoke to me today… The girl who had never talked about her personal life taking time to ask about mine today with some rights… and especially, her anger… Everything looked new to me.

* * *

Chapter 11

(Raj continues)

The next day, once class got over, Subha came to me and asked, "Shall we change our class timings to 5 PM?"

"Why should we change? Our current timings are good, right?" I asked.

"Just like that… shall we change?" She asked again.

"Yeah, we could. But that would mean I have to come here straight from school," I said.

"You won't lose your crown by coming here directly. Creating such a scene is not good for your health," she said.

"Who, me? Alright, I get that!" I hit back.

"Ah… We can change, right? You're okay with it?" She prompted again.

"Why should we change? You tell that first," I demanded.

"Because you are a madman and you go mad after 8 PM, that's why." She replied.

"Yeah, I am the madman. But you are very clear! Yeah, right!" I laughed.

She blushed and said, "What about me? I am Ms. Perfect!"

And without waiting for my answer, she went straight to the admin room.

I thought she was kidding, but she really went there to change our class timings. They asked her the reason for this change.

"It is getting quite late in the evening to go home. That's why," she explained.

They then looked at me and asked me for a reason, but I could not respond immediately as I had had no time to process it, and she made a decision for me. She was doing things her way. I wondered what I could say here.

Subha looked at me as she said cheekily, "I am changing, right? So he wants to change as well."

The admin gave me a look and said, "Oh, is that so?"

Only I could discern the reason behind her look. 'When is this no-good guy going to come up in life?' her gaze seemed to ask.

Subha winked at me, laughing. Her eyes danced with a question, asking me teasingly if I knew what the admin must be thinking.

The admin said, "Your classes will start next Monday… you can take a break till then or use the lab."

Subha immediately said, "We'll take a break."

And needless to say, she had answered for me too…

I did not give any other reaction. I sat there like a side artist in a movie scene as they both decided and finalized the changed timings. The admin looked at me and laughed, saying, "Have fun!"

I decided not to react to that, either. It was not like I had a lot of say in this, anyway.

When we came out of the center, I turned to Subha and asked, "What happened there? You gave them all the answers, even mine. You look like my school principal now."

"If I were the principal, you'd not have a job by now, dear. And I will also resign and roam around the place with you!"

"Ayyo… I cannot tolerate even two hours of roaming with you. If I were to do it the whole day…" I exclaimed.

She laughed, saying, "Ahh, that's rude, you must be lucky to have me as a.." she paused noticeably and then said, "friend."

"Okay then, what's the plan now? You'd have surely thought of something… Let us do that, then," I said, ignoring the pause and her comment.

We went to the park nearby. A lot of people frequented the park for walking and jogging. Some skating classes were also being conducted for kids in a corner of the same park. And in another corner, karate classes were going on. These were the usual sights there.

The busy park had many green trees and shrubs too. A lot of old people sat around, talking. And there was also a small pond with a few steps on its banks. This was the hotspot for lovers who wanted privacy and to avoid public nuisance.

We started walking around the pond. It was peaceful there. After a few minutes, Subha said, "Okay, tell me."

"Tell you what?" I asked.

"That thing you keep saying you will say some other time… that time has come now, so tell me."

"Oh, that… You look really beautiful when you apply this sandal paste on your forehead. And if you wear a saree, you'd look even more amazing," I deflected.

"I know that I am always surplus beauty, dear. But that's not what I was asking."

"Look… You should compliment me back if I compliment you. When such a handsome guy like me with an amazing personality is near you, you are still talking about yourself?" I asked.

"You're actually fishing for compliments… Don't you feel ashamed?" She asked.

"Being shameless is my birthright. You don't know that," I joked.

She rolled her eyes and then looked at my eyes, I was looking at her with a smile and expecting a sarcastic response, but she surprised me with a compliment.

"You aren't that great! But since you are begging me for a compliment, I will give you one. You will also look good with that sandal paste on your forehead. When your hair is ruffled, you look stylish whenever you adjust it. I love your bushy hair."

She then reached out and ruffled my hair, and looked at me unblinkingly while I adjusted it.

"Continue," I prompted.

"That's it. There's nothing more to say," Subha said. "Stop drooling. Wipe your face," she laughed.

I went and sat on a bench nearby, and she joined me. She then took my hand in hers and placed her hand in mine, checking it out. "Ayyo! Look at how small my hands are. Your hands are so rough," she said, holding my hands tight. "But they are so special to me. I cannot begin to tell you how well I know them… Every line, every blister, every callous… I feel so close to you when I do this. When I am with you and hold your hands like this, I feel so safe and secure," she explained.

Her soft fingers were gently clasping my big ones, and the fingers of her other hand were running over the back of my hand. She had expressed it well! But though I felt like I knew every inch of her soft, dainty hands, too, I kept quiet. I felt like I wanted to talk to her and gently caress her hand. But I resisted for some reason and didn't know why. She was apparently not waiting for my answer. She just continued.

"These six months were the most favorite days of my life. You have become so special to me. Our house does not have this gaiety and laughter at all. My parents are always focused on education and earning. Only my father and mother would make all the decisions. They would never consult us even if their decisions affected us. We won't know what they are doing and are expected to just obey. Sometimes, I have doubted if I am their daughter. I am myself only when I am with you. I always spend my time alone, otherwise. I once read in a book by Osho that love and affection are born when we are alone. I was born into loneliness, and I grew up as a lonely girl. I did not have anyone for myself. Now, when I am talking to you, I understand how a world without loneliness would look. This is nice, too…" she said.

"Didn't you have friends in your school and college?" I asked, surprised.

"I was not allowed to have friends. Only now, I have fought to get the privilege to roam around with you guys. And after a point, they could not do anything against it."

"What tyranny is this!" I was still trying to wrap my head around this revelation.

"It is like that only! I got used to it," Subha shrugged.

I did not know what to say to that. Nor did I want to press her for more information. She already looked melancholic behind her casual mask. I did not want her to think more about whatever was making her sad. So I changed tracks and instead spoke reassuringly.

"Okay, leave that. Things will get better hereafter. I am there for you, don't worry!" I consoled her.

Until then, she had been holding my hand and looking elsewhere as she spoke. But when I said, 'I am there for you,' she turned to look at me. Her eyes shone with happiness. But she did not say anything in response. After a long moment of looking into my eyes, she turned away.

I was overcome by emotions too. I did not know how best to tell her everything I felt. But even our silence together was comfortable. After a while, I said, "Okay, come, let's leave. They'll be waiting for you at home."

"Amma has gone to Madurai to be with my grandmother. She looked quite harried when she left…. Did not even tell me the reason, of course."

"Oh!"

"Let's go. Anyway, Amma would call home and ask about what I was doing the whole day. If she gets some unnecessary doubt about me, then we both will lose these precious moments, too," she said.

* * *

Chapter 12

"My mother called me from Madurai. Apparently, my aunt is unwell. She has to go to Delhi to take care of her. She just told me that she'll be staying there for six months. She did not even bother to tell me what else was going on!"

This is what Subha told me one day. I quelled my surprised reaction at that.

We used to go for long walks regularly, almost every day. We would walk about 7 kilometers a day. We would talk endlessly about everything under the sun. And most of the time, we wouldn't even remember what we spoke about. We cared more about being together and spending time with each other. We had a lot of commonalities in our areas of interest and kept talking about them. Even if I did not like some topics, I loved to hear her talk about them. Her eyes, hands, and sometimes her entire body danced with emotion, and I felt like I could sit and listen to her talk passionately all day long.

Initially, we walked about a foot apart from each other. But soon, we started walking with our arms twined together. We did not need to sit in front of each other and see our faces to talk. Instead, hand-holding was where most of our communication happened. Like how the mythical Duryodhana's life force was in his thigh, my life force was in her hands. Words are not enough to describe the language that our hands spoke and the feelings we exchanged with the mere touch of our fingertips. People say that we could usually gauge someone's thoughts based on their eyes and expressions. But I felt that I could do the same by holding Subha's hands.

It was so potent that even if we were in a coma, we could speak with just our hands and fingers. Her hands were so soft while mine were rough due to playing cricket since childhood. She would gently caress my hands while saying, "I will soften them up."

But my heart was softened and melted on hearing those words.

Many weeks and months passed this way. We had not officially proposed anything between us until then. I had drastically reduced talking to my other friends, and I had also forgotten about cricket, which I used to be so passionate about.

Not wanting to leave Subha alone in Chennai for so long, her mother called her to Delhi. It was her summer vacation in college. So she would be there for at least a month. We had not expected that. She took a break from classes, and so did I. We could not make calls between us at this time. Only the occasional email was allowed. She promised to try chatting through IM when possible. Her mother had booked tickets to Delhi before telling her, so she did not even have enough time or warning. They had to leave in two days.

We decided to meet once before she left for Delhi. So she asked me to come to her friend Lavanya's house. There was a huge overhead tank on the terrace, and we stood under its shadow. I was sitting on the steps, waiting for Subha. Lavanya was keeping me company.

* * *

Subha was teary-eyed as she came. She sat near me and took my hand in hers. She kept it on her thigh and held it tight with her other hand. She then leaned her head on it. When her tears fell on my hands, tears pricked my eyes too.

I composed myself and said, "What happened to you now? Just one month… It will fly by in a blink."

She rolled her eyes up to see me and said, "What have you done to me? I have never missed anyone like this. It has been more than a month since I spoke to my mother properly. I did not spend even a second worrying about it. But I am breaking down completely when I think that I cannot see you for a month. I do not know if this is good or bad. They are saying they will take my aunt abroad for treatment if she does not get better. If that happens, they will not leave me alone here. I don't know what they'll do. What if they take me along?"

"Nothing like that will happen. Just go. You will feel refreshed too. You'll get a chance to meet new people. It will be a good change for you," I said.

"Oh, are you saying you need a change?" She demanded, looking annoyed.

"I am going to be here only. Everything needs a break. That's when we get clarity about what's happening around us. Go and see some Delhi boys, maybe even hang out with a few of them. You will get some guy, and you can get settled in Delhi. If I ever come to Delhi, you can be my guide," I said jokingly.

"Are you crazy? Ah, anything else I can do other than being a personal guide to you, my lord? Here I am, lamenting that I'll miss you… and you are trying to chase me off permanently," she said.

"Why are you getting emotional now? We can chat on Yahoo! every day. Email me often. Wherever you go, get me a gift from there," I said.

"Robots like you don't deserve a gift from me. At least for a namesake, you could have asked me not to go. Or do lip service and say things like 'I will miss you!' Robot… Robot Raj… What do I do with a person who has a robot-like heart?" She said, faking her disappointment.

"Hmm! I will miss you too! Terribly… There, I've said that. Enough?" I laughed.

She laughed along with me, muttering again as she held my gaze. "What am I going to do with you?"

Then she sat up straight and said, "Just because I am not around, don't you dare start drinking again every weekend."

I was just wondering what to say to that when thank heavens for great timing, Lavanya came up. She heard what Subha was saying and interjected with, "This is what my mother would tell my father too. Why are you telling him this?"

I laughed and said, "Your friend is quite emotional now."

"Ah! There was this girl who once asked us all to be practical!" Lavanya laughed. "Wonder where this is heading!"

Subha immediately countered with, "Why did you come here now? Don't you have some other work?"

"Look at you! Hello! This is my house… you are the one romancing here, and you are asking me this question! My mom is back home! I cannot let you two be alone here," Lavanya replied.

Then we decided to leave.

Subha hugged me and said, "I am going to miss you terribly."

Lavanya looked at that and said, "How much longer are you both going to pretend that there is nothing between the two of you? Or worse, pretending that to yourselves?" Then she added, "You both look good together!"

Subha quickly said, "Hey, idiot. Don't assume just anything… Why? Should friendship not have any emotions? If my family had been a bit open-minded, I would have taken him home. But they're not, so that's not possible. That's why I had to choose your house. It is nothing like what you are assuming."

"You go to Delhi now. You'll get better clarity once you are apart. I won't say anything more now," Lavanya replied.

We did not speak much after that and left for home in an auto. She leaned on my shoulder silently. With her fingers, she traced the words, 'Miss you. You are special,' on my hands and laughed at me with tear-filled eyes.

I wiped her tears away and gently kissed her forehead. I got down at the corner of her street and said, "Mail me soon after you reach. We can talk whenever possible. You're going to forget me once you see those Delhi boys," I laughed.

She was just saying "hmm" to everything I said. She looked a bit overwhelmed with her emotions and could not put that into words any further. I left immediately, not wanting to show her my emotions.

* * *

From the next morning, I was checking my emails frequently. I would try to chat with her in the evenings. But there was no reply. I was growing increasingly anxious with every message and mail that went unanswered. Seeing my listlessness, my family started asking me what was up. My elder sister knew everything. She liked Subha, too, and had promised to meet her after the family returned from Delhi. She did not believe me when I insisted that this was just friendship.

Subha did not mail me even once after reaching Delhi. Only I was sending many emails a day. I started missing her a lot. So many unwelcome thoughts would cross my mind then. If she did not love me as I had assumed she did, would this break bring about any change in her? Will she leave me? But her eyes and hands had told me a different story! Was that all not what I thought it was? Such thoughts would run through my head and confuse me, giving me a dull ache in my chest.

I could not be myself at all. I was flummoxed. Every day, I would walk alone, tracing the same route we had taken from the class. Though I felt melancholic and missed her, I would laugh alone, recollecting many of our old conversations. Sometimes, I would suddenly realize the hidden meaning in her layered words and then wonder why I had been such a daft idiot.

I kept buying small gifts for her every day, collecting them so I could give her when she returned. I had not given her any gift so far. Even on her birthday, she took us to dinner. This was the habit between us friends - we never needed to share gifts. But now, I was buying random things I saw and thought she would like.

She was the one who had brought our relationship to this level. And I decided to take it to the next level. I finally decided to propose to her once she returned.

* * *

Chapter 13

Thirty days had gone by, and the mere prospect of seeing Subha again had me feeling ecstatic like the sun breaking through the clouds after a long spell of rain. Despite the no-contact month, I was sure she would return on the said date. I decided to wait for her. I could also feel the nervous energy dominating every cell in my body.

The day before she was due to return, I kept waking up throughout the night and checking the time. Everyone at home started to show their disapproval of my behavior. Finally, she sent me one mail before leaving Delhi after all my emails and messages.

'I am sending you this email because you told me to email you from Delhi. I read all your emails. It was so much fun reading them. When I confessed that I'd miss you, you were putting up such a scene, talking random things about me meeting Delhi boys, settling down here, and being your tour guide. But a virtual tour of your emotionally professed emails made up for that. We will meet at our usual place tomorrow. I have a surprise for you.'

I felt elated on reading that mail. Every word boosted my energy. My sister was joking about how nothing could rein in my enthusiasm that day. I bought a saree and a ring for Subha and waited in our usual place. One of my friends had a beachside restaurant. They usually were closed for business on Wednesdays. So I asked him to keep the place open for us. I planned to propose to her, and he had decorated the entire place.

While I was happy that I was going to see Subha, I was also equally nervous about what I had been planning. Will there be any change in her? Why had she not mailed me for those many days? Was she occupied and busy with life? Was she moving on? After all, she had repeatedly insisted, even to Lavanya, that we were just friends! I could clearly see that I no longer thought of us that way.

But was she firm in that opinion? Did she mean for it to be that way always? But she did sound her usual self in the mail. She had also mentioned a surprise... What could it be? Many such questions were running through my mind. I was very confused. I had heard that being in love makes butterflies flutter in your stomach, but there appeared to be an anaconda rolling in my stomach.

I felt like I was lost alone in a thick forest. Sometimes, I was speaking aloud to myself. But despite my apprehensions, my desire to meet her came to the fore and I went to the usual spot eagerly, on time. Subha came in an auto. She was dressed in jeans and a red and black checked shirt with the sleeves folded halfway up her forearm. It was the first time I had seen her wearing a shoe or jeans. Only her chain was the same old. Everything else had changed.

She looked beautiful even in this attire, but I started overthinking and worrying about this little change. The little courage I had also faltered into pieces, and I wondered whether I should wait for a few days before I made a move. As if all this was not enough, another girl in similar attire accompanied her. I wondered who she was, intruding on our time like a villain from a soap opera.

At this point, I knew all my plans were a wasted effort. There was no way I could go ahead with it in front of a third person. Many monkeys had taken refuge in my head by then. Maybe Subha was not the same girl I thought she would be. She did look like she had changed during the break. I saw her get down just thirty feet away, and it took her about thirty seconds for her to walk towards me, but almost thirty thousand thoughts ran through my mind.

She came near me. "How are you, sir? It looks like you've put on some weight?" she teased, looking me up and down. Seeing that expression on her face reassured me that everything remained the same. I felt a bit calmer. "What is this? You went there like south-Indian actress Revathi and came back like a Rani Mukherjee?" I asked. "Just so! I wanted to surprise you a bit," she smiled knowingly.

"Oh, so is this the surprise? I thought it was something else," I muttered, my hopes crashing. Subha smiled at my face. Then she turned and introduced her cousin Keerthi to me. "She has come here for her holidays. My mother asked me to take her along because she'll get bored at home otherwise," Subha explained.

'All mothers were like this! They give the right advice at the wrong time.' I thought to myself. "How was Delhi? How is your aunt now?" I asked. "She's better now. She's able to manage her daily activities. Only I was restless there, wondering when I would come back here…" Her gaze fell on the bags in my hand, and she asked, "What's this?"

"Nothing… Just my dress," I lied. "So… you and your friends…" she started to scold but stopped abruptly. Her eyes went to her cousin, and then she turned and stared at me. Finally, she managed, "Come, let's go eat." Her cousin had noted all this and laughed, but she did not ask any questions.

Subha held my hand while walking and that touch answered many questions. After that, I felt much more confident and my heartbeat started pacing to normalcy. More than the words we spoke we expressed many things with our hands that we could not say out loud.

She sat beside me in the restaurant and kept holding my hands. We were skirting around general topics. Her cousin's eyes were on our clasped hands while we were busily talking. Suddenly, Keerthi asked, "Shall I ask you guys something?" "Yes?" I responded.

She looked at Subha and asked, "Are you two just friends? Or am I intruding on something else here? Is this why you tried to leave without telling me where you were going?" Subha took her hand away from mine and said, "Hey, trust me… There's nothing between us."

"The vibes here do not look like that at all… But don't worry… I won't tell anyone!" she said. "Ayyo… there really is nothing like that," Subha insisted again. "Okay, okay. I believe you," Keerthi laughed. We both laughed, too. Then I changed topics and asked, "How was Delhi for you?"

"Your girl ruined it! She had a severe fever. So we did not even go out anywhere. Just stayed home. And we all had to go to the hospital for her too," Keerthi informed me. "Ayyo, what happened?" I asked, trying to check the temperature on Subha's forehead. "Hello! Hello… This is too much! Her fever reduced a week ago," Keerthi said and laughed again.

"You never told me she was okay now," I managed stupidly, cringing at how bad that sounded. "Now that she's seen you, everything will become alright for her. I did not know she had left her medicine back in Chennai," Keerthi smiled. Subha and I looked at one another, laughing. Subha blushed but did not say more.

"My dinner is done. Let me go for a short walk. I do not want to be the cursed witch separating you guys," Keerthi said and walked out before we could object. I turned to Subha and asked, "How are you?" "I missed you a lot. I have never been like this before. They had to admit me in the hospital for fever and administer drips… it was such a mess," Subha confessed.

"I don't know if I should be happy or sad about this," I smiled. "What did you do?" Subha asked. "I was happily roaming around," I said cheekily. She laughed and said, "Yeah, right! I read all your emails…" I laughed too, not even bothering to challenge her. We spoke for a long time. She never took her hand away from mine.

Though I had regained my confidence about us, I could not propose to her that day since her cousin had accompanied her. My plans were ruined! I surely had to tell her tomorrow. So I had to plan something else…. Or I would have to wait until next Wednesday…

I did not know what to do after they both left. I was not in the mood to return home. So I went to the computer center. I was going there after a month. I browsed the net for a while and sent myself an email. If ever my memory worsened and I forgot these golden moments, I wanted to read all these emails and remind myself of this again. So I told myself that I should not forget these until the end of my days.

Then something occurred to me. The whole proposal idea sounded so cinematic. I understood that the happiness one would get in subtle confessions would not come with what one does blatantly. But I still wanted to express my love to her, capture her reaction, and fix it in my eyes, safe inside my eyelids…

I had kept the gifts safe at home secretly. I could not sleep that night. I took off from my work the next day as well.

* * *

I roamed around the city throughout the morning and came to the center at precisely 5 PM. She was also there punctually. I was happy that she had come alone that day.

But as soon as she saw me, she said, "Hey, I have to leave immediately. Amma has said we should all go to a movie with Keerthi. I somehow managed to get some time to see you." She looked so nervous. When she said this, I wondered again if I should propose. Then I was afraid that I might not get another chance if I missed this moment.

No matter in which part of the world she lives, I would be financially settled in life when it is time to marry, and I will go and get her. But I felt that I would miss Subha if I missed this moment. I had no idea from where that thought invaded my mind, but now it looked more important that I convey my feelings than think of how and where I do that.

Immediately, I said, "Hey! I have to tell you something. You should come somewhere with me." "Whatever it is, you can say here. I have to leave in twenty minutes," she said. "Okay, get on the bike. I will somehow drop you home in forty minutes," I promised.

Though she looked flustered, she could not refuse. In twenty minutes, I took her to the bus stand where we had first met. The lucky bus we usually went in was standing there. And fortunately, her usual seat was empty too. So we went and sat in those seats.

She understood what I was trying to do. But played along without asking questions. She kept looking at my face. I held her hand and looked into her eyes. Tears clung to her lashes. For a while, I wordlessly stared at her.

Then, squeezing her hand, my gaze unwavering from her eyes, I said, "I waited for thirty – no, thirty-one – days for this moment. I felt like I was on fire." Before I could say the next word, she took her hand and kept it on my chest as if she could feel my rapidly beating heart. After a five-second pause, she whispered, "Yes."

Her eyes were teary, and there was a shy blush on her face. A soft laugh danced on her lips. I felt overwhelmed by all this and felt tears sting my eyes too. I kept looking at her unblinkingly.

At that moment, I felt how a staunch theist would feel when God appeared in front of them. She recovered first and took the bag from my hands, looking into it.

"Hey, look at that! You've got me a saree. You've outdone yourself... I did not expect such thoughtful things from you," she said. "I will come as your official girlfriend tomorrow, wearing this saree. We will go to the Iyappan temple, and you put this ring on my finger there. After that, wherever I go in this wide world, I am yours. I will live only for you," she said.

I had come there wanting to talk a lot. But as usual, she did not let me speak at all. She said whatever I wanted to say and then casually suggested that it was time to leave. Eventually, she confessed, "I wanted to talk about this to you myself. But you brought it up yourself! I am very happy."

"You wanted to say this, too? Where's my gift then?" I demanded. "I am yours, unique and exclusive... What better gift is there?" she laughed.

Because it was already late, we could not spend a lot of time together. "Tomorrow, we should go to a place where we can sit and talk in peace. Find a nice place!" She instructed as she was leaving. "I am waiting to see you in a saree!" I said.

"I will come adorned with your favorite sandal paste," she said, winking at me. That 20th of July was the most unforgettable day of my life.

* * *

Chapter 14

I dropped Subha off near her house, but before I could go much farther, traffic police stopped me and checked my documents. They sent me off once they saw everything was in order. But I was surprised. I had never seen traffic police at that spot before. It looked odd. But my mind was not in it. I did not think much of it.

From there, I went on a long drive. I was riding around aimlessly without a destination in mind. I had my dinner alone and relived the happy events of that evening without anyone's disturbance. I had never experienced a happier moment.

The following day, I told my sister everything. She was also delighted and suggested that I bring Subha home that evening.

"Mom is going to attend a wedding. I am also going to a temple and will return only by 8 PM. So you both can be alone until then. Then Subha can have dinner with us before leaving," she suggested. I also thought that was a good idea.

As usual, I was there at the stop at 5 PM. We had not even taken a photo together so far. But that day, she would be coming in a saree. I did not want to miss this chance, so I borrowed a camera from my friend and brought it along.

Time passed. It was 6 'o' clock and then 7, 8… But Subha never came. I went to the center and mailed her. I was getting increasingly worried. Finally, when it crossed 8 PM, I decided that she wouldn't be coming that late. So I took my motorbike and went to her street corner.

The lights were off at her house, which was odd. I kept roaming around the street for a few minutes. Finally, I realized that there was no one at her home. I panicked and started going crazy, unable to process what to do next.

I came back home and confessed everything to my sister.

"Go and see tomorrow! Where could they have gone? She probably could not communicate with you in time due to a family emergency… She'll be back soon, don't worry!" She consoled me.

But I could not stay put because deep in my gut, I felt something was terribly wrong. I went to her place again that night, and there was no change in her house.

The next day, I took my sister along to their house. We asked the security guard there. He told us that the family had gone out of the station for an emergency. I felt devastated, something telling me inside that I was not going to see her again, but desperately hoped that she would return someday. I wondered if her aunt or grandmother who had been ill had probably worsened in condition. Subha could have gone there urgently for a visit. Like a madman, I was waiting for some news from her.

After that day, I went to their house many times a day. I sent countless emails. I even called her landline number for an answer, but nothing worked. No one could answer my questions. There was no one who I knew and could approach for answers. Even the so-called friends she had knew very little about her and were of no help.

The day I had proposed to her was the day when I had last seen her, too. And I have been searching for her until today… But I don't know where or how she is. There's just a small voice in my head telling me that she is alive and well and that one day I would get to see her.

* * *

The Story Flows From Ilamaran's Narration Hereafter.

"What do you mean, gone? Where?" Maaya asked, surprised at the abrupt end to Raj's story.

"I don't know. I did not get any other information after that. We asked everyone… but there was no news about her…" Raj said, his voice heavy.

"What is this, Raj? Is it so difficult to find someone in this day and age of social media?" I asked, confused.

"I have tried all that. She's nowhere to be found," he said.

"What horror is this!" I exclaimed. This story sounded so odd.

"They had come to Chennai only two years before I met her. I did not even know where she was originally from. The people in her street knew the family existed, but they had mostly kept it private and did not speak to anyone. Even the people in the shops nearby said that the family did not speak to them much. Even her parents' name is missing from her college registration. The admission was done under some 'guardian's' name. No such person was living there when we went to the address mentioned under the guardian's name. The people in that address had been living there for twenty years. That address was real, but the name was fake, obviously.

"It was a similar story in the computer center as well. They had gotten a college admission based on the recommendation of a minister. As I said, the only friend I knew of her was that girl Lavanya, who also claimed to know nothing more than what I know! She repeatedly insisted that she had only known Subha at college and that Subha had always been a very private person. They had just hung out together."

"Raj, can I ask something?" I interrupted.

"Yes, Ilamara?"

"What is the relationship between this and our project?" I asked.

"You must have heard about PTSD, but you may not know how deep the pain is when one is affected by this. No matter how many days have gone by, I could not take the loss of Subha normally. If it was a break-up or even a sudden accident or death, I could have handled it with time. But this is different. There has been no proper closure. The last word she had spoken to me was that she would wait for me, wherever she was. But 18 years have flown by. I could not even gather one bit of information about her so far. I cannot forget her at all. I can never stop wondering what happened after that fateful day.

"I spent a few years in depression too. I could not gauge what I would do when I got swarmed by memories of her. Even now, I feel like I am talking to her at night. And at times, I would feel as if something wrong was happening to her and I was being selfish without saving her. On occasions, I have driven my motorbike in the middle of the night to the computer center. I would not even remember going there, but I would be lying at the entrance of that building.

"A lot of people started calling me mad. Even today, I hear the words that they had thrown at me. But they could never understand my pain unless they experienced it themselves. Only I know how futile it is to try to make others understand."

Raj broke down completely, sobbing softly, his hand pressed over his chest.

"Losing Subha led me to this level. Even today, I can feel her presence with me. It is not a mere memory. It is a part of who I am. The moment she kept her hand over my chest… Even after these many years, I—"

Before he could complete the sentence, Raj fainted.

Maaya and I shouted in shock. One of the constables there rushed forward to rouse Raj.

"Raj, are you okay?" Maaya asked.

"Don't worry… This happens to him often," the constable assured us and called the prison doctor.

Maaya and I looked at each other, unsure what to say.

Eventually, Raj recovered a bit by himself and said, "This is why I wanted a solution for this… Our mind is like a monkey. If it wants a thing desperately, it will not bother about ethics or anything else. When I first spoke of this concept, everyone laughed at me. But only one person said that this was possible and we could try. And it is with his help that we have come so far now…"

He continued, "If you could make it happen, at least not all our efforts would go wasted. So please take this up and do the project. Crores and crores of people like me exist, hiding their pain and suffering every day."

"Raj! Very sorry… I swear we did not know you had so much pain inside you. Even I had thought bad of you when I first heard of your involvement in this," Maaya apologized.

"Raj! This project has not gone anywhere. You must first come out of prison. Then we can think about how to do this," I said.

"Don't wait for me. It will take time for me to be released. There are many legal issues. You take this up. Just ensure that you also have intellectual property rights to the product. And don't do this for a namesake. If possible, negotiate a deal that says you would be using this technology on me first. Talk to my wife, Kavya. She's a lawyer. She could help you with drafting the contract. All the best," Raj said breathlessly.

* * *

I still could not wholeheartedly accept this project. If I could find Subha, we could sort this out. That was the more straightforward, logical solution. How could one woman – and her entire family – disappear so suddenly? How could this be possible? There must be something else that Raj had not tried. How long could it be before we found a missing person in this digital age?

But it looked like people wanted to do a lot of other things instead. Maaya looked excited.

I looked at her and asked, "What?"

"A lot is going to happen," Maaya said, looking as if her whirring mind had found many solutions. "First, we are going to start a company. You are my partner in that. We have a huge purpose. We are not doing this just for money anymore. You will be happy to work on this now. I can work with Kavya. I have heard a lot about her. And now I have a chance to work with her. What else do I need?"

I did not tell her what was on my mind. I wanted to wait and see how this panned out. We exited the prison complex. Before we could think of taking our bike from there and going somewhere to eat, the media people surrounded us. We escaped them somehow and drove for a while. Then I called my mother and said, "I'll be coming home for lunch. Maaya is also coming along."

Maaya was hesitant at first about meeting my mom. But eventually, she agreed. When we reached home, Mom was busy cooking. She was preparing something special for Maaya. I introduced Maaya as my team lead and Maaya gave stared at me incredulously for that.

Before I could talk further, Mom addressed Maaya. "Come inside, dear…" Then she turned to me and exclaimed. "What is this? I thought you would introduce her as your girlfriend, but you are saying this!"

Maaya laughed and said, "Hello, Aunty!"

My mother brought water for us and spoke to Maaya. "How are your parents? Where are you from?"

I had never asked all this before. But that was my mom's first question.

"My father is working in Singapore. My mother is in Madurai. My sister and I are here," Maaya replied.

"Why are all of you in different places? Your mother could come here and stay with you, right?" My mother asked.

"My parents are divorced. My mother remarried. So my sister and I are here alone," Maaya said, her voice pensive.

I was shocked to hear this! My mother's expression changed. Maaya looked at me. I managed to intervene and said, "Amma, I am hungry… shall we eat?"

My mother did not speak much while we were eating. She was talking to someone on the phone in between. Maaya looked slightly flummoxed at her reaction. Even I was wondering what was going on.

When we left after eating, Mom handed Maaya the traditional kumkum and said, "Your mother is very brave. This is how women should be. Only we should take care of our lives. We cannot expect others to make our decisions."

I was quite surprised to hear that. I had never seen my mother talk like that. I realized that something else was running through my mom's mind, and I decided to ask her about it later.

* * *

Chapter 15

Once we came out, we called Kavya and spoke to her. She asked us to come and see her on Sunday evening. Maaya and I wondered what to do. Earlier, we had agreed to the American company Dhiraj Systems that we would respond by the next day, but now we had to ask for three more days of additional time. A lot of other things were also running through my mind. I was confused about whether I should talk about that to Maaya.

At that moment, I got a call from Ilango's father, "Can you come home?" He asked on the phone.

"How is Ilango?" I asked.

He was silent for a few seconds and then said, "Come home and let's talk."

Amidst all the other major issues, I had not even visited Ilango. I still could not get over how he had called me many times before he slipped into a coma. I had not attended any of them because Maaya had taken my phone away and then I had been in the resort, working. I often regretted that I could have saved him if I had taken the calls. This was guilt-tripping me, and hence I avoided visiting him. I was also not sure what I could do to help him.

I dropped Maaya at her house and went to Ilango's house.

But Ilango was still at the hospital. He had regained consciousness, but they had apparently diagnosed him with a brain tumor. I also learned that the doctors had said the surgery would cost about ten lakhs.

"We have already spent forty lakhs. Now we do not have any money in hand. I am going to file a case against your company. You have to help me. Ilango had told me they had cheated you, too… so you must also file a case with us. We can ask for compensation up to 2 crores. We can use that for Ilango's treatment. Then you both can start a business together to secure your future. What do you say?" Ilango's father demanded.

It sounded like a well-rehearsed, nicely-thought-out plan. I did not know what to say. I did not want to file a case against the company when things already looked so black for Raj. But I also did not have the heart to let Ilango suffer. Nor could I say anything about the new offer for a similar project I was planning to do with Maaya. I was sure that the entire concept was a sore topic for them.

Besides, based on what Ilango's father was saying, it looked like he was angry with Maaya too. Ilango had probably told his father about Maaya's involvement. There was also a chance that Ilango himself knew more about everything that had happened, and Maaya's involvement in this, which could have been on a larger scale than I was assuming. I first had to know what it was. Only then could I decide about other things properly.

"I have to meet Ilango and talk with him," I said to Ilango's father.

His face flushed with anger. Obviously, he did not like that I was asking him something for clarification and not answering his question. But I did not have any other option. He went into a room, got dressed, and came out.

"Come, let's go," he said.

"Are we going to Pondy now?" I asked.

"Are you even my son's friend? You don't even know where he has been admitted or how he is now," he said angrily.

"Sorry, uncle. It's my mistake. I should have visited him earlier."

But he did not reply. Instead, he stalked off to his car and started it. I got in beside him, too, and he drove to the hospital.

I saw Ilango there, lying on a hospital bed. His face was dull, and he had lost a lot of weight. If things had not taken this drastic turn, he'd have been married by now and on his honeymoon. But he was at the hospital thanks to his fiancée. I felt sad just thinking about it all.

Ilango started crying a few minutes after seeing me. I had never seen him cry before that. Feeling shocked, I consoled him and asked, "How are you?"

He did not say much. But I detailed everything that happened and asked him about what had happened to him and what else he knew.

"I don't remember anything of those days, nor do I know how they managed all this. But I could recall one thing clearly… Suja used to speak to someone when she thought I was sleeping. But sometimes, I was only half asleep. It definitely did not sound like she was talking to Sathyan. She mostly spoke in English, so chances are it could be a person who does not know Tamil. I did not listen intently because I trusted her so much. I genuinely believed she will tell me if it was important for me to know. Little did I know how much she was working to ruin me."

When Ilango said that, his melancholy was evident. He choked on his words but recovered and continued, "It is not just Raj who masterminded this. A lot of people are behind this."

"Must be those Russian guys. Sathyan was roaming with them often," I said.

"Maybe. But it is good to know who else is involved. Don't get me wrong... it could even be Maaya," he said hesitantly.

I could not answer that. I kept quiet because he had, after all, been cheated on by his fiancée. So it was not wrong of him to speak like this.

"Don't mistake me," he muttered again.

I just shook my head, trying to reassure him. My mind, however, was running at the speed of light. I had gotten some answers, but the puzzle in my head remained unresolved. I asked Ilango about the case his father had been discussing with me earlier.

"He's very stubborn with this," Ilango said, shrugging.

I told Ilango about meeting Raj in prison and his story. I also spoke about the offer from an American company for a similar project. "If there is only this way to cover the costs of your treatment, I will do this. But this guy has been suffering for 18 years... We should think about him, too," I said.

Ilango did not reply. Obviously, he was not satisfied with whatever I was saying, nor was he interested to hear about Raj. But I realized that both sides had their justification, and neither was wrong. Now I just wanted to help everyone involved without troubling anyone else further. All these problems have to be solved. But the deeper I delved, the worse the confusion became.

I turned to Ilango and asked, "What do you think of Sathyan?"

Ilango was immediately furious. "What? Do you think he also has a sob story like your Raj? Yeah... go and ask Suja, too... maybe she will also tell you such a story and justify her betrayal. And you can go and help everyone. People can be fooled only once... I cannot fathom how you can be such an idiot and be with the very girl who wanted to make money out of your ruin!"

Rage flared up inside me, too. But I kept quiet because he was speaking in anger, and I did not want to escalate the issue. His father came inside and handed me the papers with the case details.

"You can decide who is important to you: him or your other friends. If you think he is important, sign this paper and give it to me. Or we will fight alone. Ilango will also understand that he has no friends. He is still trusting you. I did not even want to call you," the man said and stalked out of the room.

I turned to Ilango. "Dude, there's so much more to this tangled web than I realized. But I would never let you down. Out of everyone involved in this, I know Raj and Maaya to an extent. And I feel there is a semblance of truth in their words. I will first arrange for some money for your surgery. Then we can see how we can take this case forward. I am sure you will get your justice. I will come and see you tomorrow," I said and left.

* * *

The moment I stepped out, Ilango's father went inside. I took an auto back home, thinking about the many things overwhelming me. I recollected everything Raj had said. I could clearly see that only finding Subha would be a solution to Raj's problem. But Maaya would never accept that. So I have to manage her too. And now I also had to work to help Ilango.

Since childhood, Ilango had always dreamed of starting a company. He had been fooled by Suja and Sathyan. If we think big and expand our scope of work beyond just working for Dhiraj Systems, Ilango could join us as well. Maaya would agree, as she always wants to work on things that would lead us to do bigger things.

I also wanted to meet Sathyan, Suja, and Renu and hear their side of the story. I would not have to believe that, but at the minimum, I wanted to know why they had done all this and who else was involved.

And when I saw my bank branch on my way, I got an idea. I could take out all my savings and help Ilango with his treatment. Then I could figure out how to manage the other things.

First of all, I had to earn Ilango's trust. Then there's a chance that he would trust Maaya, too. He would agree with the idea of starting this company. It would take a lot of time if we had to file a case and get justice and compensation via that route. I felt that he need not wait for so long.

I went to the bank and withdrew money, went straight to the hospital, handed that money to Ilango's father, and said, "First, use this to begin the treatment. Even if we file a case now, it will take time to get money from them. We don't have to wait that long."

I looked at Ilango and said, "This is something we can't fight in court alone. If we work together, we can do a lot of good. You get well and come. Then we will do some things together and get our answers."

I then continued. "Thanks to Maaya, I now want to do something good in life and secure my future instead of wasting my time. Beyond the question of her goodness or sincerity, she is a fighter. Right now, I have also gotten the urge to fight. After seeing you like this, this fight got a lot more meaning. You must first get cured, dude, then we will do something big together."

And I left without waiting for his reply.

* * *

While I was with Ilango, Maaya had gone to meet Vidhya. Wanting some alone time to forget everything that had happened, Vidhya had taken her car and gone somewhere without telling anyone. No one knew where she had gone. She had returned only recently and informed Maaya about it, so Maaya went there immediately. We got to know that Vidhya had gone into depression too. It was understandable. She had been affected by Sathyan as much as – if not more than – Ilango had been affected by Suja.

Maaya eventually returned home and said, "We must do something for Vidhya."

I agreed and then explained Ilango's state to her.

"Whatever you have done is right. Unfortunately, the situation is worse than what we anticipated. We got together through all this, but others have suffered serious consequences. If you think of it, every problem we are facing now is because of something else that happened 18 years ago..." she mused.

We decided to meet Sathyan and Suja in prison before meeting Kavya at her house on Sunday.

Suja apologized for her part in the entire fiasco and said she had made a mistake. She confessed that she had done this due to her aunt, Renu, who had drawn her in with promises of money and a good life in the future for her and Ilango.

"Renu promised me that nothing would happen. But I should not have ruined Ilango's life like this," she cried. "I just want Ilango to get well soon and be back safe. I am ready to spend my whole life in jail in penance."

And in an opposite tangent, Sathyan was not repenting even one bit. He claimed that what he had done was right, and such a technology must exist, though it won't be understood in today's world. When we told him that the way he had approached this was wrong, he responded that only those who did not understand the ramifications were in a position to make decisions.

"When that is the case, people like us will approach this in the way we know. This is not a heinous crime. Once I come out, I will do it again," he said.

What was worse is that he didn't even feel bad about Ilango's or Vidhya's state and the long-term effects on them.

"You do not have the foresight and vision. You are still thinking emotionally. So it is extremely easy to fool you," he sneered.

I felt that he had not done it just for the money. While it was one of his motives, there was a bigger picture. The entire process had given him a high. He wanted to stand apart from others, tower over them, and prove to someone that he was brilliant… He looked like he'd do anything for that. So I did not tell him anything else. I felt that this was also a psychological disorder.

"Why is he talking like such a fool? Did he not even spare a thought for Vidhya? He did not even ask how his friend of so many years was doing!" Maaya kept lamenting.

"There's no use talking about him anymore. Leave it. Let's focus on what should happen next," I said.

Maaya and I were standing on my house's terrace, talking.

I then began slowly, "Our job is not just to do the project. I want to find Subha. That is the only medicine for Raj. The concept of deleting memories is a complete waste. It is not right to want to change people's memories and perspectives of their life experiences. There is always more to it. This is not something that only we both could do. We need more trustworthy people. I want Vidhya to take care of the admin work, and we could have Ilango as another trustworthy person on the team. He will add value to the development side, and he has managerial experience, too."

"Why are you tormenting and confusing yourself so much? Would Raj not have found out about Subha if he could? Now if we bring two more people into this, there would be more expenses. And we will have to give them a share of the profit. But neither of them has the money to invest in this now. Do we need all these complications now? You are thinking very emotionally," Maaya chided me.

Though Maaya had meant it as an explanation, I remembered what Sathyan had said. Why was everyone saying the same thing?

"You are branding the care I have for others as me being emotional. And based on that, you're calling me wrong... Is it wrong to show care and affection to a fellow human being?" I demanded.

"That's not wrong... But we should take care of our life, too. We should not complicate a business with emotions and relationships," Maaya countered.

I laughed and said, "I am not seeing this as just a business. Were you, not the one who said there was a huge vision behind this? We have to focus on that, too. How can we do this wholeheartedly if we do not have empathy and care for the people affected?

"You have a lot of time to do social service in your older age. But now we have to earn money and also secure our future. If we can help others while doing this for ourselves, I am ready to do it along with you. But you are approaching this the other way around... Your main aim is way off," Maaya huffed.

"This is just like four friends getting together to start a company. Our work with Dhiraj Systems will give us the money needed for our lifestyle. And if we do something better than this, we can grow even more," I said.

"How can you do this, though? Are you going to manage all this by this Sunday? Talk realistically," Maaya replied.

"Maaya... if you really want something, you won't accept no as an answer. Think of yourself! Do you remember how you fought tooth and nail to succeed? I know how much work you will put in for something when you really want to do that. I am sure you will find an idea to sort this out. This time, can you please do it for my sake?" I beseeched.

Maaya did not know what to answer. Eventually, she agreed.

"As you said, the reason for everything that has happened here is the incident that happened eighteen years ago. So our project's name is Mission Subha."

Maaya looked at me intently. She probably did have an objection to this. But it looked like she wanted to stop arguing just for the time being and tackle it later. Then she laughed, saying, "Then we should name this company Mibha Systems."

So Mission-Subha became Mibha.

***

Chapter 16

Maaya had already emailed Dhiraj Systems, asking for more time to make a decision. They insisted on receiving our answers by next Wednesday. They had also sent a mail stating, 'Many others are approaching us daily for this project. We chose to contact you due to your relevant experience. However, your decision-making is taking longer than expected. We require your answers by 9 AM EST on Wednesday.'

Maaya agreed and scheduled the meeting. It was 9 AM IST that Sunday. Whatever we intended to do, we had just over 84 hours to accomplish it. Within this time frame, we needed to talk to Kavya, come up with another project idea, and prepare a presentation. The American company had offered us a mere USD 100,000. Hence, all our tasks had to be completed within this budget. Moreover, the company stipulated that we should work exclusively with them and not take on other projects.

I was uncertain how we could achieve any of these tasks within the given 84 hours. If this were in the past, I might have spent 60 of those hours glued to my phone. But now, I didn't even have time to take calls if someone rang me.

The following day, I picked up Maaya, and we went to Kavya's house in Anna Nagar. The house was spacious and impressive, complete with a car parking garage holding four cars. There was a staircase beyond the main gate leading to their living quarters upstairs, while the area downstairs was dedicated to Kavya's office. Surprisingly, Raj had been running a separate office called 'Subham Technologies' on the side, with a few employees. He had never mentioned this venture to us throughout our years of knowing him. The offices named 'Kavya Enterprises' were situated on the right-hand side. Inside, we noticed a few more people working. Additionally, there were two separate rooms, one of which belonged to Kavya. The other room remained mostly hidden from our view.

Kavya greeted us warmly, appearing just as well-groomed as she had been at the resort. Her demeanor was composed and pleasant, quite contrary to what one might expect from a woman whose husband was in prison. I had anticipated needing to console and reassure her, but her strength was evident, surprising me positively.

"I'm delighted to meet you. I've been an ardent reader of your books and blogs. Unfortunately, we couldn't discuss this thoroughly during our previous encounter," Maaya mentioned to her.

"It's good to know that, Maaya. Raj has told me a lot about you. Based on what I've heard, it seems we share many commonalities," Kavya smiled.

As we conversed, coffee was brought to us. During our interaction, Kavya laughed, "Ilamaran, if our meeting extends until noon, we should order biryani for lunch."

Maaya jokingly added, "Then he'll definitely stay for lunch."

Although their comedic timing was off, I joined in the laughter. "After all, food comes first," I remarked light-heartedly.

Kavya chuckled, saying, "Absolutely! Nothing surpasses the importance of food."

She proceeded to call someone in her office, instructing them to inform the cook upstairs to prepare biryani and to prepare side dishes to accompany drinks. Kavya then turned to us and revealed, "I met Raj yesterday. He briefed me on all the details. Sorting out the contract shouldn't be an issue. But before we proceed, there's something I need to clarify with you."

"Please, go ahead," Maaya encouraged.

"I want to know if you're pursuing this work for your personal gain and future or if it's primarily for Raj," Kavya questioned.

Maaya and I exchanged glances before responding.

"Of course, we want to help him. If it were solely for our future, we wouldn't have reached out to Raj. But I won't deny that our involvement could also benefit us," Maaya answered honestly.

Kavya studied us intently before continuing, "How can I be certain that you won't abandon this endeavor halfway through and opt for better opportunities if challenges arise again? This might require a fight. Presently, you don't have other commitments, so taking this on seems logical. However, if you secure another job elsewhere soon, what guarantees you won't abandon this project midway?"

"We're looking at this as an opportunity to start a venture. Successfully completing a project of this magnitude could bolster our reputation in the industry, potentially leading to more projects. We won't need to seek external employment afterward," Maaya explained.

"Raj had lost all hope during his imprisonment. Yet, you've rekindled his hope. He mustn't lose faith again. A man shouldn't be plagued by a series of losses throughout his life," Kavya emphasized, her voice sharp.

I interjected immediately, "This is why we're also focused on finding Subha."

Although Maaya attempted to intervene, I blurted out, "It's true... you don't understand Ilamaran... he's quite emotional. If finding Subha were that simple, Raj would have located her long ago. Yet, he insists on pursuing this seemingly futile quest."

While I didn't appreciate her response, I sensed that Maaya was saying this to spare Kavya's feelings.

"But still, we will try from our end for our satisfaction. So please share the detective's details," I said.

Before Kavya could react, Maaya changed tracks. "You can believe us. We will not go anywhere else or seek another job leaving this in between. Maybe you could add this as a clause in the contract!"

"No, that's not necessary. Raj trusts you completely. I just wanted to make sure of your plans. I will prepare the contract and come and meet you in a couple of days at your place," Kavya said.

Immediately, I said, "We don't want the contract that they suggested. We should draft a new contract and discuss it with them based on that... Will you be able to help us?"

"New contract? What do you want me to do?" Kavya asked, frowning.

"We want two things mentioned in the contract. One is that we should be able to do projects with other companies too, and not just be limited to working with their company alone. Besides, we have some new ideas. We will also do our projects, and there should not be any restrictions for that, either. We may even hire people from outside. Not just that... They should do nothing illegal in this project or indulge in anything without consent. We will also retain our intellectual property rights and have a say in the end product." I kept on adding points without taking a breath in between.

Kavya did not say anything and kept looking at me intently.

Maaya said, "These conditions don't look like you're coming from a start-up. They sound like someone who is on par with Ambani would say!"

Kavya laughed. "Do you have any other project ideas that would bring you credibility? It won't be enough if you just claim to be a start-up and ask for all this."

"We have nothing so far. But Maaya will find out something by Wednesday," I shrugged.

Maaya looked at me and said, "You're talking like the CEO before we have even started the company. I don't know what else I will have to bear!"

"Only now are you seeing my other face," I winked at her.

Kavya agreed, "You're thinking the right way. When starting a business, you should not limit yourself to just one company or just employ the same people you know. But no one will support you if you do not have the right ideas. Besides, you don't have many other options now. So, think about it a bit before proceeding."

"I understand that. Whatever I told you now were my options. This contract opens a door for us, but that does not mean we have to close all the other doors to land this. I have a lot of belief in Maaya's abilities. She will find an idea soon," I said.

"Okay, I will prepare a contract that gives us our best options. We can try talking with them," Kavya suggested.

While we were talking, her cook informed us that lunch was ready. We went upstairs to Raj's house.

During lunch, Maaya looked at Kavya and asked, "Shall I ask you something? It is a bit personal… But I'm curious if you won't mind."

"I can guess what you want to ask. But first, you ask. Let me see if my guess is right."

I thought she would either ask something about feminism, Periyar, or the dress, so I was focusing on the succulent leg-piece in the biryani.

"Raj is still thinking of his ex-lover. How are you supporting this so staunchly? Are you and Raj really a couple?"

When I heard Maaya's question, I felt a swooping sensation of shock as if the chicken whose leg piece I was eating had suddenly come to life in my hands and was flapping its wings angrily at my face.

Apparently, even Kavya had not expected this question. She raised an eyebrow at Maaya.

'Do we need this detail now? Can we not enjoy this superb biryani and just go home… Why is Maaya asking this now? How will Kavya answer this?' I wondered. That was when I realized that our women were ready to talk about all topics. They had absolutely no filter when it came to their curiosity.

Kavya eventually said, "Wow, Maaya! You asked this so directly! I thought you would ask something else along these lines, but I did not expect you to ask this question so directly."

"Ayyo! Forgive me if I have asked something wrong. You don't have to answer this," Maaya apologized.

'Going ahead and asking what is on her mind and then backtracking by saying something like this. Such a nice trick,' I thought to myself.

"Nothing like that. But it is a big story. Do you want to hear it?" Kavya asked.

'A story again? Looks like my life will end just by listening to the stories of everyone's past. The first thing we must do is find something that will delete everyone's memories beyond the past ten years. People were going to flashback mode just because they could!' I thought.

"I am always ready; please say," Maaya encouraged.

"Let's start from the time Subha disappeared without a trace. Not knowing what happened to Subha and being unable to see her, Raj went into depression. He would start crying randomly at night. He has even attempted suicide twice. Only his sister was with him at that time. As long as she was around, she took care of him. For six months, Raj did not even go to work. At this time, his family did not think he was psychologically affected and needed medical intervention. They just kept him home and took good care of him. That's it. After some time, his sister got married and moved out of the house. They even kept Raj's issues a little secret during her marriage because they were stigmatized and could have ruined his sister's chances of getting married by mere association.

"I knew the story and started getting involved in the search for Subha. We hired a private detective and searched for her. But nothing happened. We only got to know what we knew already. Everything in their house was under the guardian's name. A judge had shifted to the place they had been living in, and it was not even their own house. So Raj and I decided to go to Delhi to search for Subha's family. We were able to go there only a year after everything had happened. We could not find anything, though. Her cousin — that girl, Keerthi — we did not even get any information about her either. There was not even a trace of such a woman having existed there," Kavya said heavily.

"How could this be possible, Kavya?" Maaya asked.

"Yeah, it is frankly astonishing. I feel there is some huge mystery behind this," Kavya agreed.

"Tell us more," I prompted, my lunch almost forgotten. I needed all the details I could get.

"When we were returning from Delhi, I proposed to Raj. At that age, I had this unshakeable faith and belief that I could cure him with my love. But he did not accept it as expected." Kavya said.

"Look at that! Did you think you could change such a stubborn man with love, Kavya?" Maaya asked.

"It was my silly age," Kavya laughed. "Raj is a gentleman. He would always be careful that my name should not be dragged into the problem. He felt that my reputation would be ruined. My mother had more belief in him than in me."

'He has first impressed the aunty, apparently… Such an aunty-hero,' I thought to myself.

"As usual, the families got us married, saying that everything would be okay post-marriage. But until today, he has not changed. I am not able to make him forget Subha. If that happens through this project, I will be happy," Kavya said.

Wordlessly, Maaya hugged Kavya. "This is such a magnanimous thing. I did not expect you to have such a side. Feminists usually try to be on par with men. But you have given a guy a life and social status and have been taking care of him so far."

"No… you shouldn't understand this like that. I do love Raj very much. You should not term my love for him as some kind of sacrifice. I also have a selfish need for this. We should not confuse feminism and love," Kavya clarified.

Maaya nodded her head mutely.

"Was there no change after the marriage, Kavya?" I asked.

"There was some change. He started going to work regularly. He became responsible so that he could take care of me. But he would always regret moving on in his life as if he had betrayed Subha by doing that!" Kavya sighed.

Her eyes teared up even as she was saying this. Her words choked in her throat. It felt painful to even hear about. I did not know if I should feel sorry for Raj or Kavya now. My resolve strengthened. I had to get to the bottom of this.

"Did you not try to take him abroad and live there?" Maaya asked.

"I have tried asking that. But it will become a huge issue if I even suggest it. Once, he even sent me a divorce notice because I suggested he should stop searching for Subha and start living his life," Kavya shook her head.

"What! What horror is this?" I asked.

"That's how it is, Ilamaran… this disease…" Kavya said, her voice quietening and going heavier.

"You're great, Kavya. You have grown in your career and have taken care of him for so long. Really, this is an amazing feat!" I said fervently.

Kavya smiled in response. "Thanks, Ilamaran. I believe this too shall pass."

* * *

Chapter 17

Kavya promised to meet us again on Tuesday. We were both confused when we left there. I definitely was. And I guess Maaya was, too.

I wanted to find Subha, for Raj's sake. But now, after hearing what Kavya had said, I wondered what would happen to their lives if Subha returned. I was afraid I would ruin their marital life.

Maaya was not speaking much to me, either. She was also deep in thought. I dropped her home and returned to my house.

"I will meet you tomorrow morning. We have to get prepared for Wednesday," she said.

"Bring your laptop while you are coming," I said.

* * *

Once I reached home. I cleaned the guest room on our terrace and brought in the computer table from my room. I also set up a table fan that we already had. Then I went to a shop and got a whiteboard, marker, and a new mobile phone. I got a separate mobile for office purposes. I also put up a board outside our office that said 'Mibha Systems.'

I converted the additional bedroom in our house into a guest room. I was hoping that Maaya would stay there. It was midnight before I had finished doing all this.

I could not sleep that night. All the problems loomed in my mind. I could not discern what was right and what was wrong. I did not want to do any wrong to anyone under the guise of doing some good. It was 4 AM when I drifted off to sleep.

Maaya came home at 6 AM.

"Hey! You're here so early. What happened?" I asked.

"No… I could not sleep at all last night. I got an idea as you had asked. So I did some work regarding that. I wanted to tell you immediately. So I left as soon as it was dawn," Maaya confessed.

"Is there no limit to your sense of duty? Okay, wait, let me join you," I said and stepped inside my room to get ready.

When I came out, my Mom had already taken Maaya to the terrace. They were looking around the room I had organized and discussing something enthusiastically. When I eventually went upstairs, my mother teased, "This is the first time I have seen your work! You have become so responsible after Maaya came into your life!"

"What are you two doing here? This is an office room! We have to work here. You have to leave, ma," I said and tried to send my mother downstairs.

"Wait, da… Don't start already. Let me do a quick pooja before you start," my mom chided me and went to the pooja room of our house.

Maaya turned to me and asked, "What is this, sir? Is this our office? You have set it up well, though. This looks like that unfinished house from the movie Alaipayuthey. If we eventually become a big company, this will be a great memory," she said and took a photo of the room.

"If this were like the 'Alaipayuthey' movie, we need to put a bed here. But we don't have the room/space for that," I said, frowning.

Maaya laughed, "Yeah, right! Then no work would get done. But this room will be enough for only the two of us. So what do we do once Ilango and Vidhya join us?"

"We will add another room outside when required. But, for now, we will start here. Then we can expand. Once we add other rooms, we can convert this to a bedroom. Okay?" I smiled.

"Stay away. Don't get any ideas!" Maaya nudged me aside and switched on the computer. In the meantime, my mom had brought a photo of Lord Ganesha, some incense sticks, and lamps and set them up. She also performed a small pooja.

"You start your work hereafter. I will go and prepare food for you both," she said and went downstairs.

Maaya began telling me about her idea.

* * *

"We are going to do this like a social media site. This is mainly for people who will need psychological help or intervention. So there will be three types of people who can get involved in this.

"The first is those who currently have psychological issues or those who have recently come out of them. They could share details about their problems or how they came out of them. The second kind would be the volunteers who will just listen to the people's rantings and maybe give some general advice to help them. The third kind would be psychiatrists. They will give clinical support online. Using this platform, we can bring the patients and the doctors together. People will pay for this service and we could get a commission out of this."

Maaya continued. "There's no need for anyone to give their details. We can even set up encryption for security and privacy purposes and give them a pseudo-name. They can call each other via the app itself securely. We can advertise this with the USP that no one needs to provide their true identity to anyone.

"If our people can keep their identities private, their true selves will be revealed. Also, many people still do not believe in psychologists. They are talking just to vent about their issues. So if we give them such an option, they may be able to share what ails them. Couples can come and talk without each other knowing, and children can talk without fear of their parents knowing. Everyone has something private and secrets that taunt them for life… and they need a medium to talk, rant and get some consultation. So we must capture that market," Maaya said.

I listened to all this patiently and said, "The idea sounds good. But does all this not exist already?"

"It might exist – either together or in individual bits, in some form. But none of those ideas has become popular. If we can find out why they aren't successful, then we can develop a better product than what exists today – maybe bring them all together in a better, fluid manner. Or provide some additional features. Most of them simply look like they were made to help people rant. There are no options to consult psychologists and psychiatrists. Also… our objective is to collect data for our project, and we can tell Kavya about this and add this to our terms and conditions. No one is going to read them anyway," Maaya smirked.

"Okay, but can't we do this a bit ethically?" I asked.

"We just need to do it legally. We can take care of everything else once we grow bigger," Maaya shrugged.

I did not know what more to say. I did not have any other ideas either. So I said, "Okay, let us do this. You keep this ready for the meeting on Wednesday. Let us see what they say."

"I'll work from here itself. I'll go home in the evening." Maaya said.

"I want to tell you something. Don't get angry," I began.

"What?" She asked, an eyebrow raised.

"You can stay here at my house if you want… I have prepared the guest room already. My mother will anyway be home. So there won't be any problems."

Maaya did not reply for a while and was deep in thought. Then she said, "No… I will be with Vidhya. I cannot leave her alone now. She still has not come out of the Sathyan episode."

"She can come, too! Anyway, she is going to work here. The room is big… you both can share," I suggested.

"No, that's not necessary. We don't know what everyone would say! All this is an unnecessary issue… Did you ask your mother first?" She demanded.

"My mother won't have any problems with this. I know. Why should you care about what outsiders are saying? We have to do what we think is right. Once we begin this project, we have to work day and night. We have to work even on American time. If we work and live together, it will be beneficial for all of us. You don't have to waste time traveling back and forth, right?" I tried to convince her.

"What you're saying is technically correct... But this does not sound right to me. Anyway, I will speak to Vidhya and let you know."

"Okay. I'm going out now." I said.

"Where?"

"Will come back and tell you," I said and started to leave.

"I have to tell you one thing now... don't mistake me..." Maaya began.

I laughed. I knew what she was going to say. Anyway, I nodded, "Say."

"Trust is the most important factor in such partnerships. I need to know what you are doing, and you need to know what I am doing. I am your partner here in every way possible. You have to ensure that such things won't become huge issues in work and our lives. So think on that and act," Maaya said, frowning.

"I know and I understand. Why do you have to say such a big dialogue? I am going in search of that detective. I want to talk to Raj and seek his advice on how to arrange for funding. He might have friends who would invest in startups... Any VC contacts would help. I wanted to ask him if he could arrange something!"

"Don't finalize investments without discussing them with me first..."

"Okay, madam," I laughed. "Shall I leave now?"

"Get lost! You're not gonna listen anyway! I will do something about this next week, or else you won't behave," Maaya muttered.

I laughed and came out. I had to do things on my own. I hated informing others before doing something. So far, Maaya had been my team lead, so nothing could escape her notice at work. But now, it was not like that. She was not used to not being the lead. So I have to manage this expectation as well.

I stepped out, got ready, and called Maaya to eat. While we were eating, my mother asked Maaya to stay at our place. She added that since my father was not at home, there were no other men either, and Maaya could stay here freely.

Maaya's eyes were teary. Then, she smiled and said, "It has been ages since we went to our house. Months since we ate home-cooked food. Now when you said this, I felt so touched."

My mother wiped her eyes and said, "What's in this? This is your house, too. If you marry him, you are like my daughter. I already see you as a part of our family."

Maaya looked at me. I did not know what to say and stared passively at them both. I was extremely surprised at how my mother had been approaching the whole issue since the beginning. I had never spoken anything about this with my mother, but she had somehow found out.

"Amma! Why are you talking about marriage now? When did I tell you anything like that?" I demanded.

"Should I wait for you to say all this to me? Won't I know just by seeing your face? I noticed you looking at your phone and smiling like an idiot. Only yesterday, I knew that you know to make a bed and get a room ready to stay. I have never seen you do any household chores so excitedly," my mother laughed.

I could not control my laughter. Maaya wiped the tears from her eyes and laughed softly.

"Should I not have to take care of the girl who is coming to my family?" My mother asked in a tender voice.

"Ayyo, Amma! You are rushing things. She still has to talk to her family. We also have to understand each other better," I said.

"Get into the marriage only after you understand each other well. Until then, you can live together! I will also be there while you live-in together, that's all. Only then can I understand my daughter-in-law, and she can understand me too," she laughed.

"No one would have heard of such a live-in relationship," I muttered, hiding my shock and grin.

All of us burst out laughing!

* * *

Chapter 18

I left immediately after breakfast. My Mom and Maaya were busy talking and were getting on like a house on fire. I smiled and left, feeling happy about what was happening at the dining table.

First, I went to the detective's place after getting the address from Kavya. I had tried calling them before, but there was no response. So I decided to visit directly and check them out.

There was a board proclaiming 'Detective Charles' at the given location, and I went in via the open door. There was just a table and a chair in the room, other than the walls. A man clad in a shirt and dhoti, sporting a military cut, was sitting inside the room, reading newspapers. The room and that man brought into my mind images of a south Indian temple kitchen owned by a military cook.

He looked me up and down when I entered, wordlessly took all the papers there, and went inside. I was surprised by his abrupt action but decided to wait it out, wondering if he had gone inside for some other errand. He came back after five minutes and looked me up and down again. His look clearly expressed, 'why are you still standing here?'

Slowly, he asked, "Was it you who called yesterday?"

He had not answered my calls but had guessed it correctly. Maybe no one else would call him, I thought.

"Yes," I confirmed.

"Will you come directly if I don't attend the call? I did not take your call because I don't want to talk to you. You can leave," he said.

"Sir, I have come on important work. I need some answers, and I believe only you can give them to me. When can I come again?" I asked insistently.

"No. I have stopped detective practice. You can leave," he repeated.

"Your board outside is still bright, and so are you. So you are just bluffing," I insisted.

"I don't have to explain anything to you," he said, stepping out to take the board off. He put it in his table drawer and shut the drawer with some vehemence as if daring me to question further.

"It's okay if you don't talk now. Just call me when you are ready. I want to discuss with you… regarding one of your former clients Raj. I need some clarifications about the missing woman, Subha," I said, not wanting to back off.

"One minute! Who is Subha? That Delhi girl?" He asked, frowning.

"Yeah, but I believe she was originally from Chennai," I said.

"What do you want to know about her?" he demanded.

"You were the one who had searched for her when Raj hired you. So how is it that, in this day and age, no details could be found about a person?" I asked.

"Think whatever you want. But I did not get much info about them. And you won't get it even if you search hereafter," he said, bristling in anger.

"Why are you saying this?"

"I have been on this job for ten years. Some cases will drift without any closure even when there are a lot of leads, and that's expected. But only in this case did I not get even one bit of information other than what was publicly available and what Raj told me. I roamed around Chennai and Delhi like a dog for six months. I could not find out even a small detail. For such a thing to happen, there are only three chances… "The first is that Raj is hiding something. Secondly, whatever details the girl had given or shown him should be false and a concocted story. It could have been a planned attempt where the girl's family had decided that no one should know anything about them… If that is not the case either… then this should be some psychological disorder that your friend has where he could even be making up a story and imagining such a character. There is no other way this could pan out," he said firmly.

Could Raj really have some problem similar to erotomania? They had tricked me, too, with this issue earlier. I wondered if they had not known about this so far. I kept that information aside and said, "There's no chance of Raj hiding things intentionally. But why would Subha give him the wrong information? When we hear their story, we cannot even think of her betraying him that way… Why would anyone do that?" I asked.

"We won't discount anything like this. We will always go by the facts," he claimed.

"You need proof of its existence too!" I countered.

"Yes. That's why I am surmising that it could be like this. The details they've given are not right, even in her school and college. Something else huge is behind this. She has studied with the backing of a politician. Subha is a star student, so there was no need to force her way into a college with a politician's recommendation. She could have gotten in on merit. So the help from the minister would have been required only to hide the details," he mused.

"Why are you talking like this? Who could this Subha be to necessitate all this?"

"I don't know! She could even be a terrorist. Or maybe a Naxalite. Or part of a suicide squad. She could have packed and left one night suddenly to go back to her group. Such people will not want the attention turned on them… There could be any number of such reasons," he sighed.

My heart jumped to my throat. "What is this, sir? You are saying such tall tales! Are all these claims based on things you found out or are you just guessing? Could such things even happen?" I asked.

"I don't have enough information to refute anything concretely. Likewise… I do not have factual information to confirm anything, either."

"Okay, even if what you say is true, will the whole family be like this?"

"How do you know they are all from one family? If there was a family set-up, why would they require a guardian to vouch for them? Won't the girl have used her parents' names in her college? No one even knows what job her parents were doing," he said.

"Are you saying they could be sleeper cells?"

"Why not? Anything could have happened," he shrugged.

"If they were people with such motives, could she have loved Raj so deeply that he is now scarred permanently?"

"She is a young girl, she could have crossed paths with her love over Raj. But once others get to know this, they could have moved places to avoid any further attention."

"Raj told me that she used to read books by Osho and Periyar. He also mentioned that she wanted to make a big name in business and had big ambitions. And now you are saying this?"

"Why? Should big CEOs not be terrorists?" He countered.

I had no answer. I remembered what Raj had told me about Subha's relationship with her mother and father. Even he did not know her family, and the whole story about the impossibly authoritarian upbringing put up so many flags in my mind.

"I want to help Raj. Is there a way for that?" I eventually asked.

"There are a thousand ways to help him... but what you are thinking of now is impossible. If you want to do something good for him, forget this Subha route," he shrugged.

"If you cannot do it, does that mean no one else could do it, either?" I demanded.

"Brother! You can try. But I was once with the military. I have seen many such things. I am telling you... this is an unnecessary headache for you."

"Okay, I'll leave now. Let me think of what to do further... But I cannot keep quiet about this," I declared.

"I will tell you one way to save your friend, maybe..." he volunteered eventually.

"What?"

"Approach another detective... Ask him to prepare documents claiming that Subha is dead. If Raj believes this, there is a chance that he can get cured of this mental disorder... since there will be some closure to Subha's story. I had already suggested this to his wife. And only now do I realize that she has not done it so far," he said.

"Why don't you do this yourself?" I asked suspiciously.

"I won't condone lies on the job. It goes against my ethics. But there are many others who will do such things. You can try with them."

"Okay, I will talk to Kavya about this again," I said and left.

I understood one thing after talking to that guy. He was not just guessing blindly. He had a lot of information, based on which he was talking all this. So I decided to hire another detective for this purpose. After hearing all this, I was not in the mood to speak to Raj. So I returned home.

* * *

When I reached home, I noticed a new car standing in front of the gate. I went in, wondering whose car it was. Ilango was inside. I was a bit shocked and wondered how he could have returned so soon after his surgery.

I did not know if he had told anything to my mother. I had a shrewd doubt that he could have done something due to his distrust of Maaya.

"Dude! What are you doing here? Is your health okay now?" I asked, rushing inside.

"I am good. I wanted to talk to you… That's why I came here," he said.

"Tell me the truth! Is your tumor cured? Are you fit to drive a vehicle again already?" I demanded, voicing my concerns rapidly.

He stared at me weirdly and looked around as if wondering what to say.

"What, da?! Answer me!" I prompted.

"There's nothing wrong with me! It has been more than a month since I was cured. My father and I were on a fact-finding mission as we were unsure whether you were also involved with everything that happened. That's it. I wanted to confess the truth, apologize to you, and return your money," he replied.

I felt furious. "What? You played me as well? What are you saying?" I yelled.

"Yes. My father wanted to file a case against you, too. But I did not doubt you… So I refused. He did not believe that and wanted to confirm the truth. That is why he did this. Once you gave me the money and left, he followed you and checked what you were doing. We realized you were really trying to solve the problem. That's why I came here… to apologize and return your money," he narrated.

"I don't even have the heart to rage against you now. But I would have been happier if you had asked me about this directly. You need not have done all this," I snapped.

"Sorry, dude. I did not know whom to believe or trust. I just saw Maaya upstairs. Vidhya is here too. They told me about your idea. I am very happy for you. Don't mistake me," he said, looking contrite.

"Okay, leave that. We were all in a bad phase and doing things against our nature. No one is doing all this on purpose. Did Maaya tell you everything?" I asked, feeling a strange relief.

"No! You could tell him all the details yourself," Maaya said, walking inside. Vidhya followed right behind her.

"Hi, Vidhya! How are you? Is our palace upstairs good?" I asked.

She laughed, saying, "It is great. But I don't have a table!"

"We'll arrange for it soon," I said and turned to Ilango. "Dude, I want to ask you something!"

"Yes?" he asked.

"Do you want to work with us? We could all do this together. Maaya and I will find it hard to manage everything just by ourselves. We need trustworthy people. So who else could it be if not you?"

He thought a bit and said, "Okay. I had also wanted to do something like this for a long time."

"Great! Then it's all set. I have arranged for a mason to build a room upstairs. Let us build just one huge room. Maybe we can set it up so four or five more people could work comfortably," I said.

"We can take care of all that after Wednesday… First, let us land this project. They have to agree to our conditions. Only then we should think about these things," Maaya interrupted.

"Yeah, we'll do that," I agreed.

"I'll leave now… I will come tomorrow morning to start working with you. Let us see what's next," Ilango said.

"Okay. Take care! Call me before coming tomorrow," I said and sent him off.

* * *

Chapter 19

Once Ilango left, the three of us went to the office upstairs to see the slides that Maaya had prepared and worked on how to present them.

Maaya had done a good job on the presentation. She had put herself as our lead in that. I felt bad that she did not put our names as partners, but I did not bring this up as an issue. She used to be my team lead and wanted to maintain that in our new set up too. Besides, I did go to her for project ideas, so I understood why she was trying to position herself as the lead.

In the meantime, I was focusing on other work like starting a banking account in the company's name, building the room upstairs, and other such admin work. We were working until midnight.

While Maaya was still fine-tuning the slides, I wrote the project details on the whiteboard. Then suddenly, I felt that a 3rd party review of our idea would be good, so I called Ilango and asked, "Can you come home now?"

Maaya turned to me immediately and asked, "Why are you calling him here now?"

"Nah… Let's share our plan and get his views on this! Ideas only get bigger when they are shared," I said.

Maaya did not reply but turned around.

She and I had many differences even while discussing the slides. But we both kept quiet to avoid any friction in our relationship. But ironically, it did not even look like we were in a relationship nowadays.

We were alone in a room. My mother was downstairs. It was past midnight, but I had just called Ilango to come here. I did not know if this was the reason for Maaya's anger or if it was something else.

Ilango arrived in thirty minutes. We explained everything to him. He listened patiently and said, "The idea is great. But I am not sure if it will be a commercial success. How are you planning to commercialize it?"

Maaya and I had not thought about the commercial aspects of this project.

"The success of this venture depends on how many people we will be able to reach. Without that, we cannot ask anyone to invest in our idea," he pointed out.

Neither of us had an answer for that.

"Then you should talk about this only superficially. Don't give them too many details. Just mention that you are still working on it. Insist that you will approach investors only hereafter and can therefore not work with them exclusively. But you can say that they could pay us the contract money upon completion of the project." he suggested.

Ilango's clarity and approach were good. Neither Maaya nor I had that acumen. He was a valuable addition to the team. I could see that, and I was sure Maaya could, too.

* * *

Kavya came to our office the next day.

She had already emailed us the contract details. There were two contracts. One was between Dhiraj Systems and us. The second was between Kavya and us as partners in Mibha Systems. And in the partnership, the name 'Sukumar' was mentioned. We did not know who he was. Kavya had added someone's name without even discussing it with us first, and Ilango's and Vidhya's names were missing. So we thought we would talk about it to her in person.

Kavya looked around our office setup and wished, "Nice! Let this company become huge, like the next Google or Apple."

"We don't even have the money to buy an apple, forget about building a company like Apple!" I said.

"That's why I added this Sukumar as a partner. He is living in the United States. He works in the health industry as well… he is my schoolmate. I have spoken with him. He knows many investors in the healthcare industry there. He'll be of great help to us, not just in investing in this project but also in getting the relevant approvals from the health industry. We need not restrict ourselves to coding. We can also offer help in obtaining approvals and providing relevant contacts etc. But he will not do this for nothing. We have to give him a share. I think you will be okay with this proposal," Kavya said.

Maaya and I looked at each other, gauging what the other was thinking. Neither of us was interested in this idea. But I did not know how to say that to Kavya without hurting her. I also wondered why she was basically forcing this on us.

Maaya eventually managed, "Kavya! We don't have a problem with you becoming our partner. But we are hesitant to add someone we don't even know as our partner!"

"Neither Raj nor I can be partners in this. It will garner unnecessary attention and probably ruin your chances!" Kavya said.

"I understand that… but it does not feel right to add an unknown person as a partner," Maaya refused.

"I can vouch for him. You trust me, right?" Kavya countered.

"Ayyo! How can we not trust you with this? Why are you talking like this?" Maaya hesitated.

Maaya respected Kavya a lot. So she could not push much further now. I was hesitant, too. But I understood Maaya's situation and spoke out.

"Kavya! Don't mistake me for saying this. But I don't even know you that well. I know you only as Raj's wife. Is that enough?"

I was so hesitant to ask this, but Kavya replied calmly. "I have already spoken to Raj about this. He suggested this was a good idea and said I should talk to you. It was my mistake to prepare the contract without asking you. I did this because we had limited time. This is my mistake! I will remove this name and prepare another contract. You can think and let me know.

"For you guys, this is just a job. Even if you fail in this, you can go to another job. You also have the age for it. But this is my life. I want to live happily with Raj at least for a few years now, putting all this behind us. I have put my full faith in both of you. I feel all kinds of emotions on that Subha, including anger, jealousy, pity… I'm not able to categorize them at all.

"He was with her only for eighteen months, and she became an indelible part of his psyche. But I cannot make him forget that even after being with him for fifteen years. When it comes to Raj, I am also just an ordinary woman… who wants to feel loved."

She was sobbing softly as she said this. Maaya and I felt very bad about seeing her break down. Maaya immediately reached out to console her. "Ayyo! Kavya, why are you saying this? We are there for you. No matter what happens, we will do this. We just wanted to work with the people we knew and trusted. That is why we were hesitating about this. So don't mistake us."

"If you want to conduct business, it is not enough to just work with the people you know. You have to make new acquaintances. More importantly, there should be no fear. You should have to make decisions bravely. These are the signs of good leadership. You will learn, though, with time… I believe in that. Think of this and let me know of your favourable decision," Kavya said and left.

As soon as she was out the door, I turned to Maaya and said, "No… this is unnecessary!"

"Did you not hear what she said? Look at how bad she is feeling… How could you refuse her?" Maaya asked.

"We have to! As she says, working with new guys and refusing to rope in unknown people are business decisions, I agree. But saying no is also part of the leadership qualities she just mentioned. We can't keep everyone on board," I said.

"That's right. But I feel so sorry for Kavya," Maaya muttered.

"Were you not the one who said we cannot earn money if we keep feeling sorry for everyone around us? And now you are saying this?" I demanded.

"Are you throwing my own words at me? I was firm with all that. But you were the one who involved her in the first place. And now you are saying that we should not listen to her," Maaya pointed out.

"I am not saying we don't need her. I am okay with it if Kavya wants to become our partner. But she is asking us to allow someone else inside who we don't know," I said.

"I cannot refuse her directly to her face," Maaya said.

"You already did…" I smirked.

Maaya stared at me. "I hurried to do that because I was worried you would say yes unthinkingly, as you are the emotional one. But after seeing her cry, I felt terrible," Maaya hesitated.

"You're thinking very emotionally!" I said.

"You are telling me this! It's my fate that I have to listen to all this from you now. Let this be between you and Kavya. You answer her. I am not doing this," Maaya said.

Meanwhile, my mother brought us lunch. "What are you two fighting about?" She asked, coming inside.

"Ayyo, aunty! We would have come down. Why are you taking the trouble to bring this up here?" Maaya asked.

"Not an issue. What's there in doing this for you guys? I asked if you two were fighting," she looked at both of us from the corner of her eyes while she kept the plates on the table.

"There's no fight, mom. We were discussing work issues," I said.

"Take care! Make sure your work doesn't affect your friendship. You can earn money any day, remember that." she said and went downstairs. Maaya and I looked at each other.

Maaya eventually said, "Shall we go on a trip once we sign this contract? We have not had time to relax at all. Only if we are relaxed can we make the right decisions… We will have to face so many issues hereafter."

"Shall we go to Pondy?" I asked.

"Won't you leave that damn Pondy alone? I wonder what's there in that place," she laughed.

* * *

That evening, workmen had come to unload the building materials for constructing the room. "We can build the room in four days, sir," the contractor told me. I felt that I had so many responsibilities with all these new developments. I feared that I might get into trouble if I was not careful in handling issues that came my way. As a result, I felt 1000 times heavier, with the stress weighing down on my shoulder.

Maaya and I were discussing until 9 PM about the contract and our project. Ilango joined us in the evening. We were doing mock presentations by asking Ilango to role-play as the decision-maker from Dhiraj Systems.

* * *

There was an unused barren plot in front of our house. Ilango was sitting there. There was some hole underneath his feet. Wondering why he was even there, I approached him. He reached into the hole with his hand, took a white snake, and threw it at me.

I am deathly scared of snakes! Once the snake turned its eyes on me, I started running. It chased me relentlessly. Ilango brought along a motorbike and said, "Climb aboard, dude."

I got into the vehicle in the back seat. But the snake loomed over Ilango's shoulders from the front and tried to bite me. Now that snake was black. Its yellow eyes looked aggressive. I jumped down from the bike. The snake also jumped onto the backseat and then slid down from there. It was about four feet long. It was now white again, with black dots all over it. Its colour kept changing. I panted as I ran. At one stage, I could not run further, so I rushed into a house that stood alone. There was a middle-aged woman inside, clad in a classy cotton saree. I went in and tried to close the door behind me to stop the snake from following me. But the snake had already entered her house.

"Wait, brother! Why should you fear this snake?" the woman asked softly. Then with just a broom in her hand, she went to chase it away as if it were a mere cockroach. I wanted to shout and warn that it was dangerous and had been following me, but I could not speak. And when I found my voice, the snake disappeared. So did that woman.

Shaken out of my sleep, I sat on my bed in shock at this bad dream. Though I was awake, I vividly remembered the snake chasing me. Why did I dream that Ilango was throwing a snake at me? Who was that woman? Why did that snake disappear on seeing her? In the darkness of that night, wherever I turned, I felt like I could see the snake. I went and switched on the light, drank some water, and came back to bed. But the dream was still on my mind. I did not understand why I had had the nightmare. I drifted off to sleep uneasily.

The next day, I was at the airport. There, I met Dr. Joseph, a famous psychiatrist. He approached me as if we were dear friends. I was speaking to him about my dream. And he was saying, "This is the fear inside you... you think that you have many enemies, and, they may get you into trouble. That's why you are getting such a dream. Some incidents that happened recently would have affected you deeply. So you may have gotten this dream because of that, too."

My mother gave us coffee in our office room, scolding me for wasting time with unnecessary searches instead, which was no better than me wasting time with YouTube videos...

Losing sleep again, I woke up. I was speaking about the previous dream in this dream. And while I was speaking with a doctor in an airport, my mother was giving me coffee in my office room.

Airport & office room... both in the same dream... within moments of each other. The places and the people kept changing. And halfway through the discussion, the psychiatrist had disappeared! I felt like I had watched some thriller series. I had completely lost sleep by then.

It was past 3 AM. The next night, at 9 PM, we had the presentation. We had to answer Kavya within then, too. I put all the worries aside for the moment, though, and started watching YouTube videos. This was always my stress buster.

There was some inexplicable happiness in watching such slapstick videos, even when we were in an awe-inspiring tourist spot like Niagara Falls. 'People waste thousands on holidays when they could simply see such videos! Those idiots!' I thought, watching the videos even as the sun made his subtle entry through my room window.

* * *

Chapter 20

Maaya and I logged into the meeting at exactly 9 PM. Ilango, Vidhya, and Kavya were also with us. Two people – Karen and Rick – were representing the other side.

We had already mailed the contract that we were proposing to Dhiraj Systems.

"We saw your mail. But it was sent at the last minute, so we had very little time to read it. So if you can explain it now, we can speak further," Karen said.

Maaya showed them the presentation we had prepared and explained our idea. Then we also gave them an overview of the project we were planning.

Rick waited until we had explained fully and said, "This is very childish. A thousand apps like this are already available in the market and are unsuccessful, too. Besides, this is completely useless and irrelevant to our project. I had assumed you were really good with the latest trends in technology. But what you just 'explained' is a rookie idea, and even college kids do better here in America.

"We do like your efforts. It is good that you are trying to do something you think is big. But you do not have enough exposure yet. You should think of something else. These concepts and technologies have been available in the States for the last five years. In the world of technology, five years is a long time. Companies are dabbling in metaverse and cryptocurrency these days. You have to update yourself and try again. Meanwhile, you could just sign our contract and start work," said Karen.

Feeling embarrassed at being dismissed like this, I wondered what to say.

Maaya recovered first and said, "Why would we give you the full project details now? This is just an idea, and this will be improvised as we spend more time on it. We only wanted to say that we cannot work exclusively for you. But we will be able to complete your project on time. You could pay us after we have completed the work. If you don't like our work, you don't need to pay us. But don't insinuate that we don't know the latest technological advancements. If you are going to insult us, we don't want to work on this project. We do not wish to work where we are not respected. We are not here seeking charity from you."

I was sweating bullets when I heard this. Maaya had just steamrolled over their words. Kavya was sitting there, immobile in shock. She also looked a bit hurt at how Maaya was probably blowing this whole thing away despite Kavya reiterating how important this project was. Kavya had clearly told her that she was banking only on this project to cure Raj, but Maaya had dealt with this quite strictly. Vidhya and Ilango were watching Karen and Rick's reactions intently. But the Americans did not react much. Rick wrote something on a piece of paper and handed it to someone off-camera.

A voice sounded from that direction whence he had handed the paper.

"When it is ready, you could share your idea with us formally. We can have a non-disclosure agreement, and we will not be using that anywhere else. If your idea is good, we will invest in it completely. If we do that, you should do the current project we have discussed for free. But if we do not invest in that, for some reason, we will pay you the hundred thousand dollars for this project as specified. And until this decision is finalized, you should not work with anyone else."

We did not even know who was speaking there, but we guessed that it must be Karen and Rick's boss.

Maaya turned and looked at Kavya, who said, "Ask them to update the contract and send it. Tell them that we will respond after reading the details and fine print."

"Sorry! But who else is there? We need transparency and loyalty," Rick interrupted. His tone implied that he was not interested in us getting this project.

"Our lawyer. We have not seen the person who just spoke and proposed the new terms, either. Transparency and loyalty are two-way streets. In principle, we are fine with the revised terms suggested, but please send us the updated contract. We will review and confirm," Maaya said.

Kavya came into the frame and said, "Please send us your non-disclosure agreement and your terms and conditions."

It was clear that Kavya had used this as a chance to show her presence there. She probably was not happy with her being side-lined in the discussion. I was bearing all this for the sake of Raj. I noticed her shocked expression when Maaya told she did not want to proceed with the contract, so Kavya wanted to make her presence more solid.

"You have to tell us before tomorrow. Or we will hire people locally," Karen said.

"We'll definitely give you our answer," Maaya said and logged out.

Ilango immediately shook Maaya's hand. "You spoke quite confidently. Whether or not we do this project... you should not let these people talk this way!"

Kavya looked at Maaya and said, "For a minute there, I was scared. But you spoke well. If you had capitulated to those demands today, the whole project would have gone that way. Very good!"

While everyone was appreciating Maaya, I was staring listlessly, feeling confused.

Maaya turned and asked me, "What happened to you?"

"Do you have another idea?" I asked.

"No. We need to work that out. Once that jerk spoke like that, I was furious. That's why I blustered," she laughed.

The others laughed too.

"Oh hell! Now we are in soup," I said. "But who was that lady?"

"No idea! Do you remember we saw the name 'Dhivya' on their website? The founder and ex-Googler? I think it must have been her," Maaya said.

"What habit is this, speaking without showing her face?" I asked.

"Leave that... we have only one more day to work out the project scope. We have to confuse them by claiming something humongous. Then we can work out the logic behind it," Ilango said.

"Do you have any ideas?" Maaya asked.

"No, but let us brainstorm. They spoke about metaverse and crypto. If we think along those lines, maybe there's a chance they will accept our new project," Ilango said.

"We don't need to hurry! Let us take some time and do this properly. Any more half-baked ideas will hamper our reputation and credibility. So take time and do it right. I have some work and will be back in a couple of hours," I said.

"Where are you going at this hour?" Maaya demanded.

"I have some work," I repeated vaguely.

"Your girlfriend is here! What work do you have outside at this hour?" Ilango asked.

I looked at Kavya. Not knowing what to say in front of her, I countered, "Should I do everything only after telling you? I will finish the work and tell you. You guys do your job," I said and left.

Vidhya, who had been silent for so long, looked at Maaya and asked, "Wouldn't he have told you if he could? Why are you forcing him?" Then she turned to Kavya and said, "Kavya! I'll order food. Please have dinner with us."

"No… That won't be necessary. I won't eat this late at night," Kavya responded and left.

Ilango later video-called me that Maaya's face had fallen when I started my car and left.

'Don't hide anything from her, dude. It might become a problem later on,' he advised.

'There's nothing to hide in this. I will come back and explain in detail,' I replied.

* * *

Dhiraj Systems sent us a contract within two hours of that call. Maaya forwarded that to Kavya and also sent her a message asking her to review it.

When I was outside, Ilango video-called me. Kavya was also on the call. Maaya, Vidhya, and Ilango were still speaking from the office.

"I have read the contract. This looks okay to me. They have put only whatever they told over the call. But I wonder whether this will lead to a long-term problem," Kavya began.

"What?" I asked.

"They may make you something of a subsidiary company of theirs. I doubt if they will let you operate with autonomy," Kavya said slowly.

"How are you saying this?" Maaya asked.

"According to their proposal, if they invest in your company, you will have to work only for them. You can work for others or be on your own only if they don't invest in your idea. This kind of puts the decision in their hands and does not allow you any room to manoeuvre or change anything later," Kavya explained.

"Maybe they would delay the investment decision until the current project is completed and then decide against investing. In the end, they will get what they want, and we will be the fools here," Ilango said.

"This project will take at least one year. Can they drag it until then?" Maaya asked.

"We are just two, three people here… We will not add anyone else to work with us without further investments. If they keep us busy in this project and do not give us time to work on that other project, they could easily achieve what they want," I voiced my doubts.

"That's why we need someone like Sukumar… he'll give us the money. It is always better for us to have someone in America. Think of that," Kavya said.

Maaya nodded, but I still did not like that idea.

"This looks like a good idea too," Ilango agreed.

"Could he be just an investor? We can give him shares, but we will be the decision-makers, and he should not interact with the clients or whatever," I said.

"You're saying no to the most significant benefit of having Sukumar on board. I will tell you another thing. The moment I left your house, I called Sukumar and enquired about this Rick. Apparently, Rick is very strict and firm in his ways. Besides, Sukumar has learned from some other people working in the company that Rick is not interested in giving you this project. He said only Dhivya was pushing to onboard you guys for this project.

"He got these details by hiring a private detective. Dhivya is a brave woman who speaks directly to people's faces. She only trusts people's talent and skills and would never get emotionally attached to anyone. If you work, you get the money. That's it. She is famous for never getting work and personal life mixed up.

"Many companies that had gotten into such contracts got nothing due to non-performance. Some don't even exist today. If you work well, you will be around. Or else you will be fired immediately. I will ask Sukumar to look for other companies there. You can use his help to come up big. I guarantee you," Kavya said.

"I agree," Maaya said.

"It is better to have good support, and I don't see any downside here," Ilango agreed.

Maaya looked at Vidhya, who said, "If all of you guys are okay with this, I am okay too. I don't even know what I am going to do here. So I have no opinion either way."

"Then the majority is okay with this," Kavya noted.

It appeared that they didn't need my concurrence, and I did not like how Kavya pushed us to get Sukumar onboarded.

"Kavya! Can I ask you something here? What we will be losing here would be just the other projects. But our original project is in our hands only. If we do that, we will get a minimum of 100,000 dollars. So… Why are you so interested in the other projects? Your husband is not affected anyhow by this," I said.

"What are you saying, Ilamara? Do you think I have a hidden agenda with this?" She sounded upset.

"No, I am not saying that. But I feel that you are pushing us into this decision, which I don't understand why," I responded.

"Your wish. I will send my assistant if you need someone to draft a contract afresh. Raj had asked me to be with you and take care of things. That's why I came in person. Raj believes you. You just do what you have to do for him. I will not get directly involved in this hereafter. Why would I put myself in this position unnecessarily," Kavya said abruptly.

Maaya intervened. "Let us speak in person tomorrow. We are all exhausted now. This is going wrong."

"Kavya, this is not about you. I trust you completely. But if someone who invests money comes inside, everything changes. That's why I am hesitating," I said.

"It's your wish, Ilamaran. There's nothing left for me to say," Kavya said with finality.

I understood that she did not want to speak further.

"Kavya… Let us speak tomorrow… We will come to your house," Maaya spoke placatingly.

Even I felt that was the best way. Kavya exited the call.

"Dude, when are you coming home? No idea is working out here. Come soon," Ilango said.

"Where are you now?" Maaya asked.

"Will come home and say! I will be back in an hour," I said.

"What's with this build-up? Why can't you just say what you are up to?" Ilango demanded.

"Coming! Won't take much time," I said and cut the call.

Ilango messaged me saying that Maaya had noticed that I was in Anna Nagar and she saw the famous Iyappan Temple in the background. She was lamenting what I was doing there at that hour.

'Keep this in mind… you have to sort it when you are back home,' Ilango had added.

* * *

I returned home only at 3 AM. That was also when Ilango left for his house. Vidhya and Maaya had decided to stay at my place. As my mother had already slept, none of us talked much. We just retired to our rooms.

Maaya messaged me, 'Where did you go at this hour?'

'I went to meet someone. I will tell you the details in person. Cannot message the whole thing,' I replied.

'What are you doing that you cannot share with any of us?' She demanded.

'Everyone else was around us then… That's why I could not say anything. But now it's quite late at night. I will definitely tell you tomorrow,' I replied.

She did not even answer that text. I understood that she was furious with me

* * *

Chapter 21

While I was working on the computer in the room on my terrace, there was a sudden earthquake. I fell into a hole that appeared to be a deep borewell with only enough space for one person. And there was a laptop on my lap. No one else was there. The place was pitch dark.

Suddenly, I got a message on my laptop. 'Thank you for coming into this world in a hole. Press either the green or red button.' Not understanding anything, I pressed the green one. And immediately, I was shifted to a beach, where Maaya was waiting for me.

"Come, Ilamara. You won't listen to me if I say we should go on holiday. That's why I brought you here like this," she said, her voice echoing.

She looked resplendent in a light blue-colored dress. I went near her, but suddenly she screamed. When I turned, a huge tsunami-like wave was rushing at us. I turned around to run and escape from it and tried to hold Maaya's hand safely, but then I realized Maaya had disappeared.

Raj was stuck in the wave, screaming, "Ilamara! Save me!!"

While I was wondering what to do, I started riding a whale underwater. There was a laptop again, but this time it just had two buttons — green and orange, and there were no words. Before I could press the orange button, my hand slipped into the water and pressed green.

Suddenly, the whale broke the surface and started flying through the air. I could not understand what was happening. Amidst all this, I was searching for Raj. Suddenly, I felt the hot sun on me. I was now flying on the back of a large eagle.

The eagle dropped me on top of a big mountain full of red snakes. They were in clumps as if they had a collective mission and were going to some political rally. Then suddenly, a white snake came out. Its eyes lit up, and it stuck a tongue out at me. I felt that the snake was reacting in the same way I would have if I saw the well-cooked biriyani at a Muslim wedding — almost as if gazing at a particularly succulent piece of food. Then it started chasing me.

I started running again. I ran for a long time and jumped from that mountain. I fell into a house through the roof. A middle-aged woman was inside.

"Is a snake chasing you again today?" She asked.

She looked beautiful, with a small streak of sandal paste on her forehead. She was wearing a blue colored saree. I had never seen her before. Raj's photo was hanging in her house. She had garlanded it. Raj's photo had been smeared with sandal paste, too. The date of death was mentioned as today. Ayyo! I was feeling sad that I was not able to save Raj... I lamented that I alone had escaped.

While I was crying thus, I realized that it was indeed a dream, but I could not come out of it. I felt motionless, and at that minute, I felt as if the snake was climbing over me again. I yelled in paralyzing fear. Maaya and my mother had heard my screams and rushed into the room to see what was going on.

And until they came in, I couldn't even get up. My mother shook me.

"What horrible dream did you have today?! This has become a habit for you. Earlier, you used to blabber in your dreams that some girls were kissing you. But now it looks like a snake is kissing you," she asked, looking worried.

Maaya laughed and said, "What are you saying, aunty? Would he really claim that girls are kissing him in his dreams?"

"Ayyo! He has always been like this, ma. If we sleep in the same room as him, we can easily figure out what is running in his mind. This is my tip to you. Now he is worried about some work issues. Did he not spin yarns to me that day that you both were not in a relationship? But I knew long ago that he was running behind you."

Then my mother turned to me and said, "Dei! Go wash your face and come. You can drink some buttermilk and go to sleep."

Once my mother had left, Maaya mouthed at me, "Are you okay?" I nodded.

She laughed softly and said, "Take care!" Then she gave me a flying kiss and left.

It was true that I get such dreams. In fact, just before all this had begun, I had dreamed of kissing Maaya as well. I considered those normal, but I never had such random, disjointed, senseless, and insanely frightening dreams. Mountains, oceans, beaches, snakes, whales, and eagles... All made a debut appearance in my dream today.

It was already 5 AM. I didn't think I could sleep again today.

My mother brought me some buttermilk.

"I don't want buttermilk. Give me coffee instead," I said and went straight to the bath.

"Where are you going so early in the day? I want to know what you are doing. I'm a bit scared to see your actions nowadays. I am hiding my fears in the face of that girl who is with us now," my mother demanded.

"I will tell you, ma! You know me, right? My mind is like this. It won't let me sleep until I have some answers. But there is nothing to worry about." I consoled her.

I left on my two-wheeler. Maaya came out of the room and saw me leaving, but I pretended I had not noticed her.

I had booked a flight ticket to Madurai. Raj had mentioned that Subha's grandmother was there. So I went to detective Charles's house again last night and asked him if he had inquired about Subha in Madurai.

"What should I inquire about in Madurai?" He asked.

"Subha's grandmother is there. Raj had told me that Subha's mother had gone there because her grandmother was ill! So Subha could have gone there, right? That's what I am asking," I said.

"I don't know anything about this. He did not tell me that she had such a side," Charles said, looking flustered.

"Raj had also told me that some auto driver told him that her grandfather was a big shot."

"Auto driver? I don't know about him either," Charles huffed.

Then I called Kavya and asked her about this. She answered, "Yeah! But we don't know where in Madurai she was. So we just did not mention it."

"How can we ignore such an important fact so casually? Isn't it a common trope even in Tamil cinemas to send girls to their grandparents' house when the parents do not accept their love affair?" I asked.

Immediately, she countered, "Ilamara... Is all this necessary now? Did you ever pause to think about my state if Subha comes back? I was supporting him unflinchingly so far. But now, with the option that his memories can be deleted, I had raised my hopes of having a normal life with him finally. But if, by chance, we find out Subha now, what happens to me? This is an unnecessary problem, right? Please don't do this, Ilamara… I am begging you…"

I was a bit shocked to hear this from her and felt pity for her when her voice choked when she said this. No woman deserves this! Her husband was mentally disturbed, unable to forget his ex. But she loved him so much that she could not leave him. She was ready to go to any extent to cure him. Now there was a chance that she could have him only for herself. So her heart was yearning for that, too. But for the world, she is a bold feminist. She has written many books and is an inspiration to young women like Maaya. I did not know how one woman could have so many different facets.

I consoled Kavya. "Don't worry, Kavya. Everything will end well for your good heart. I will not just think of Raj. You are important to me, too. So I won't create any issues for you," I said and cut the call.

Then I called Charles and informed him about this.

"Bro, let's go to Madurai tomorrow and see what we can find there," he suggested.

If I had informed Maaya about this, she would have said that all this was unnecessary. Kavya should not know I am going, either. But the only way to cure Raj was to bring Subha in person. Only those with no other option should resort to this memory-deletion process. Thinking thus, I reached the airport.

There, one more person had accompanied Charles. The detective introduced him to me. He was Joseph, a famous psychiatrist, who said he was going to Madurai for a meeting. I immediately sweated bullets.

"What happened, Ilamara?" Charles asked.

I looked at Joseph and asked, "Have we met before?"

"Not as far as I know… Besides, it has only been six months since I came to India," he said.

I blinked, not knowing what to say. I felt deeply uncomfortable.

"Ilamara! What happened to you? You look like you're going to have a heart attack," Charles said.

I then explained how I had met him before in my dreams before meeting him today for real.

Joseph immediately said, "What I had told you in your dreams is factually correct too. These are supernatural dreams. To be specific, we also call them precognitive dreams. This is like a warning we get before something happens for real, like how you met me today," he said.

My head spun. I could not follow what he was saying. I felt that I should talk about the other dream as well, but there was a boarding announcement before that. So we hurried onboard.

Joseph was in business class. Charles, too, was traveling business class, making use of his military subsidy. I was alone traveling economy class.

I did not know how the journey from Chennai to Madurai went. I kept thinking about the dreams and how they happened for real. Once we alighted in Madurai, I got Joseph's contact details and said, "I will definitely come and meet you, sir."

Maaya had called about ten times and dropped about twenty text messages. She was a little worried when her messages were not even getting delivered. My mom had called me a few times, and Ilango sent me a text, 'Dei! Where did you go?'

I replied to everyone with the same message.

'There's nothing to worry about. I was in a meeting this morning. I will come home and talk to you.'

Maaya called me and said, "Where are you now? Who are you meeting at 6 in the morning? Keeping all of us in the dark and doing things your way is wrong."

"Just adjust for today… I will tell you in detail once I am back home," I said.

Charles intervened. "Brother! Call from home? They won't leave us alone. Come… I know a high court judge here. Let's go and meet him first. We will try inquiring with him first."

From the house's security guard, we got to know that the judge's name was Chandrasekhar. But there were no further details.

So we went to a nearby police station and inquired there. It was hard to gather details about an event that happened 18 years back. Except for the name 'Subha,' we had no other concrete information to inquire further.

Where exactly could I search in Madurai? I didn't even know that grandmother's name.

"You go back home. There's no use of you being here. I will wait a couple of days to see the judge and check if there is any other way through this." Charles told me.

I wanted to stay back with him. But remembering Maaya's tone, I decided against it. For this, I could have remained at home and need not have come all this way to return empty-handed. Such was my life's setting! What could I do?

I agreed with what he said and left. But while I was going by bus, I saw a death anniversary banner at the end of a street. The deceased's name was Subha. This immediately caught my attention, and I read the details. It was mentioned as the 18th death anniversary. The date of death was 22nd July. Raj had told me that 20th July was the date he proposed, exactly 18 years ago. Immediately, I stopped the bus, got down, and went to the address mentioned in the poster.

I called Charles to inform him about this. He came to that address soon enough and asked me to send that photo of Subha in the banner to someone and ask them to confirm with Raj if this is the same person.

There was one 82-year-old grandma in the house who gave us some information. That grandma's son was Ganapathi, who worked in Delhi. Her daughter-in-law was Gayatri. Ganapathi and Gayatri had two daughters. They were named Subha and Preethi. They were all killed in a car accident – they fell from the mountain while traveling to Ooty, and were mutilated so badly that no one could even recover their bodies.

That grandmother looked senile. She could not even speak properly. There was a young woman, her caretaker, who informed us casually that she was an orphan. Apparently, a government officer brought that caretaker to this house when she was 20 to take care of the grandma. She did not have any other information about that government official, for he had also died shortly after that. Since then, the woman had been staying at that grandmother's place, taking care of her. She was not even married yet.

It was that young woman who had organized the posters for Subha's death anniversary, and she also usually gave alms to a hundred homeless people in the nearby temple on this occasion. The family looked like they had once been well-off and now lived off that glory.

It was only then I noticed that – there were three more people's photos on the poster.

* * *

Chapter 22

No one in that village had seen Subha. They all claimed to know that Subha existed only based on the grandma's stories. So I sent the photo to Maaya and asked her to confirm with Raj.

"Where are you? Tell me the truth," Maaya demanded.

Having no other choice, I told her everything and said, "Go and check with Raj now, please… Kavya need not know about this right now."

"We need to confirm the partnership agreement with Kavya and sign our contract today and look what you are up to!" Maaya demanded.

"If this is Subha, then there's no need for our project… Nor is there any urgency to sign the contract. We can do it slowly," I replied. I was sure Maaya would consider this a lame excuse.

"Seriously?! I can't believe you! You just do whatever you want without even thinking about how it affects other people," Maaya exclaimed in frustration.

"Me, not thinking about others? Woah! I am in Madurai now because I care about others. If we find Subha, then Kavya will no longer ask us to include Sukumar in our contract. There's a good chance that Raj could get better. If he comes out, we can run this company with Raj. Let's face it, we don't have enough experience to handle it all by ourselves," I explained.

"You will believe anyone and everyone else in the world. But you won't trust me enough to tell me all this beforehand. You will even go to Madurai without the basic courtesy of informing me!" She yelled.

"This is not about trust, but we just have different priorities. You somehow want to close that deal and start work, while I am more focused on finding a way to get Raj better," I said.

"You're giving excuses. You just don't think about me any longer because now you have me with you. You think of everything else and want to do so many things at once, in between forgetting the dreams I have for myself and us. When was the last time you even talked to me sweetly? Instead, You always look so serious and never wanted to spend time with me. Then, to make it worse, you invite Ilango for a work discussion when we are alone. And now that we're together, you don't seem to care about spending time with me. You keep saying about what happened in that resort, so you obviously don't need me anymore," she said, pouring out her hurt.

"Hey, listen, it's not what you think. My mind's just been so caught up in all these problems lately, and it's been hard to shake off all that. I'm sorry, babe! I promise to change my behavior and make it up to you. Once all of this is over, I'm sure I'll be back to my usual self," I assured her.

"Look, no matter what's going on in the world, I should be your top priority. But you are saying you will come back to me only after finishing all your work. Of course, work is important. But we also need to make time for each other. I have left everything behind and am now living with you at your house, but I feel like we are drifting away," Maaya's voice broke with emotion.

I got her message loud and clear. Deep down, even I did not like this version of myself lately. I used to be carefree and happy-go-lucky, but even my smiles and laughter have become rare. I had to come out of this soon.

I spoke softly to Maaya, who had fallen silent after her outburst. "I promise everything will be okay soon. But we have to do this now. Don't tell anyone about this. Please go to Raj and ask him about the photo."

"Your wish," she said and cut the call.

I understood that I should speak with Maaya in person. If we had this conversation over the phone, this could escalate. I understood that she was immeasurably furious and rightfully so.

Charles and I went to a shop nearby and had bun parottas. We then got some flavored milk from the Aavin milk booth nearby. I bought some palkova for my mom, as it was her favorite.

* * *

About two hours later, Maaya called me. She sounded tensed and was crying.

"Hey, what happened?" I jumped up from my seat in shock.

"Deiiii! The person in the photo was Subha! Raj saw it and got very emotional. He fainted. He is in the hospital ICU right now because he might've had a heart attack – his second one. So we are all at the hospital. You come here immediately," Maaya stuttered.

I turned to Charles, who asked, "What happened?"

I told him everything, and he bracingly said, "Everything will be okay… Don't worry… You start for Chennai immediately. I will remain here and collect some more details. We can talk about the rest when we meet in Chennai."

* * *

I left immediately, bound for Chennai. I went straight to the hospital from the airport. It was 6 PM by then. I asked Ilango, who was standing there, about Maaya's whereabouts.

"She has gone home… We have to sign and send the contract… Ilango informed me.

I turned to Kavya, and before I could even ask my question, she cut me off with a curt reply.

"Sukumar's name is no longer there."

"Ayyo. Not that. You don't lose heart! Raj will recover soon," I said.

"You don't talk! I told you beforehand that all this was unnecessary. You did not listen to anyone and brought this mess on us. Why? Couldn't you have just sent me the photo? I would have taken that to Raj and asked him carefully, watching and carefully analyzing his responses. But no, you went behind my back and involved Maaya just because I asked you not to do this last night. If something happens to Raj, the onus is on you, and I will never forgive you for that. Even now I hold you responsible for this mess," she seethed.

All I had wanted was to do the right thing, but it had backfired badly and things had gotten worse for everyone. I didn't know what to say, so I just walked out.

Ilango requested Vidhya to be with Kavya for the moment and followed me outside. "Dude, let it go… You didn't do anything wrong here. You did this keeping Raj's best interest at heart. Maybe this is a good thing. If he gets better, as the Subha puzzle is solved, then everything else may get sorted too. Don't worry, go home and talk to Maaya. She is really mad at you," he said.

Not having the mood to go anywhere, especially home, I stayed there. That was when the government officer, Keshav Ram Patel, arrived.

"Ilamaran! What are you doing here?" he asked.

"Sir! Good evening. Raj has been admitted here after a heart attack… He's still in police custody so we could not see him. That's why we're waiting outside," I replied.

"Come with me," he said and took us inside.

Ilango and I went into the room with him. We explained everything that had happened – starting with Raj's health condition, mental health issues, and why he got involved in a project like that.

He expressed his apologies. "How could no one know how an entire family had disappeared?" He asked.

"No… We found out just now," I said.

When we told him about detective Charles, he said, "I know him very well. I will speak to him."

"Is there a chance of Raj coming out of jail?" I asked.

"Give me a letter about his health condition. I will see what I can do," Keshav Ram Patel said.

"Sir... even those who have committed serious crimes are roaming around happily without any fear. He did not make any huge mistakes. It would be great if you could help," Ilango said.

Patel looked at Ilango and asked sharply, "Was it a small thing when you were in a coma?"

Ilango did not speak for a minute. Then he cleared his throat and said, "No, sir... But when we hear his story, we cannot help but feel sorry for him"

"Hmm... That's your magnanimity. But we have to see beyond his motives and focus on what the law says. I will do as much as I can. You should get going," Patel said.

* * *

I left for home, alone. There, Maaya was lying on my mother's lap, crying.

"What happened?" I asked.

"What kind of habit is this? Going to Madurai without informing anyone? No matter what you do, don't you think you should keep people informed?" my mother yelled at me.

"Let's not worry about it! Raj will be fine. Everything will work out... We have no control over anything now. Things are slipping out of our hands," I said without directly responding to my mom's statement.

"Did you hear what he said, Amma? Despite everything he has done, see how he is talking," Maaya grumbled to my mother.

"Maaya! Our problem is solved. We have found out what happened to Subha. So we may no longer need this project. Let's see what we can do next, once Raj is discharged from the hospital." I said.

"How do you know Raj has been cured? You are talking based on what Charles said. Is he a doctor or what? He is talking as if he knows everything," Maaya said.

"We have to believe that Raj will be okay. Likewise, we'll have to believe we'll get another job," I said.

"The contract has been signed. We did not include Sukumar, since you had concerns about that. You and I will get a 30% share each, while Ilango and Vidhya get a 20% share each. Our investments will also follow the same percentage," she informed me in a matter-of-fact tone.

"How did you decide all this without informing me?" I demanded.

"When you leave town without even informing everyone, we cannot wait for you to return when we involve – and are answerable to –other parties. You knew we had to decide today, but you did what you wanted anyway. You did not even answer my call… The world won't wait for anyone, so we made the decision ourselves," Maaya snapped at me.

"Wow! That's nice.; keep at it," I said sarcastically and then added, "I am not in the mood to talk about it now, we will talk later."

"Nothing will be set right without proper discussion. This applies to our work as well as our life. Get this into your head for your good. I have nothing left to say to you," Maaya said and went into her room.

I left as well, feeling upset at how everything had gone.

Per the contract, we were expected to work starting the 1st of August. Our office on the terrace was ready. Ilango and Vidhya were also working with us, of course. We set up a bar there and also added a dining table. We had hopes of working throughout the clock.

Raj had been in the ICU for a week and was then shifted to the general ward. But he was still not completely well. Occasionally, he would faint. But he had slowly started accepting that Subha was dead. He needed some medical treatment and therapy for his mental stability. But Kavya hopefully said that he would be okay.

* * *

Kavya came to our office and expressed her happiness seeing our office setup.

She approached me and said, "Ilamaran. I am very sorry! I should not have spoken to you like that. If we had thought of that Madurai angle before, this would have ended long back. You did the right thing. Don't mistake me."

"Ayyo, Kavya! Why are you apologizing? I am happy that you understood my intentions. All this should end well. That was the only thing on my mind. Otherwise, I did not intentionally want to do anything by myself," I said and turned to look at Maaya.

She ignored me. "How is Raj now, Kavya?" She asked.

"He's a bit tired... He will take a few more weeks to get alright. But now he's not yelling at night as frequently as before. I hope that Subha's death will not lead to any other problems. I am afraid only of that. I have requested to put him under house arrest. I am not sure what they're going to do," Kavya expressed her worries.

"Oh, will they allow all that?" I asked.

"No idea... they have set the hearing for the 5th of August. Let's see," Kavya said.

"Everything will end well, Kavya. You don't worry," Maaya consoled her.

"I will never forget the help you both did," Kavya said fervently.

"Why are you thanking us already? There's a lot more to do," I said and narrated everything that Keshav Ram Patel told me. I then added, "He's asked us to give a letter regarding the same."

"He spoke with me. This August 5th hearing is about that only. If they don't agree to it, he suggested we ask for house arrest," Kavya explained.

"Oh, wow! I guess it's time for Raj to come out, then," I exclaimed.

"Our Mibha Systems has completed the delivery before the official inauguration," Maaya said.

"I don't get it... What delivery?" Kavya asked, sounding confused.

Maaya and I laughed. "Don't you know how we named it Mibha Systems?" Maaya asked.

"What is the reason?" Kavya asked.

"MIssion SuBHA became MiBha Systems," I explained.

"But now we are going to start the company only after Mission Subha is actually over," Maaya said.

My mother laminated Subha's photo and brought it, asking us to keep it in the office.

"Why, ma?" I asked.

"In a way, her death is the reason for all of you to have come together… why, even for you to get together with Maaya… When something happens randomly, we may not be able to correlate the reason why it is happening. Everyone will die one day, everyone will face hardships in life based on their karma. Everything in life that happens has a reason. But when can connect all these happened to bring all of us together for a purpose, then we should keep that person in our memory and thank them. Let her soul rest in peace," she said.

None of us had any words to say to that. We listened to her silently, wondering about the profoundness of her statement.

"Everyone should have lunch at our house today. I have already started cooking… Kavya… I am talking to you, too. Please stay back for lunch," my mother insisted.

"Aunty, I'll come and help you too," Ilango said and went down.

* * *

Chapter 23

"Shall we all go on a trip? I feel very stressed. We should start work next week, and we don't know how hectic it will be thereafter… Shall we go somewhere before we get into all of it?" Maaya asked.

"Hey! Yes… We will go to a hill station. Even I feel it would be better to go somewhere," Vidhya agreed.

"Shall we go to Kolli Malai? It is an eight-hour drive from here. If we all take turns driving, we can go by car," Ilango suggested.

"I have to ask my mother… I can't leave her alone here. Now my mother knows about Maaya too, so I don't know how she will react to going on an overnight outing with her," I said.

My mother came upstairs and said, "Dei! You go with them. I will stay at your aunt's place. Your cousin is getting married and the groom's family is coming to see her. I will stay there for a few days and help them out."

"Aunty! He was trying to use you as the reason to avoid the trip, but you spoiled his plan," Ilango laughed.

"Yeah! he doesn't want to miss kissing girls in his dreams. That's why he wants to stay back here," Maaya teased.

"Don't remind me of the dreams! These days, I only have nightmares… and you have stopped visiting me at all in my dreams these days," I said.

"Yeah, da… I am standing in front of you here, and you don't notice me. How will you notice me in your dreams then?" Maaya hit back.

"I think he's saying that you are coming as an anaconda in his dreams…" Vidhya said snidely.

"Cha! Why are you calling Maaya an anaconda? She is gold! This fellow doesn't listen! He's seeing random videos on the internet and dreaming about them… how many times I have told him not to!" My mother said.

"Oh, right! When did you switch to her side?" I asked.

"Amma is always on my side!" Maaya said and rushed to hug my mother.

"I had to see all this! My awful fate," I said, scowling. But I was internally happy to see them bonding.

"Yeah… according to you, this beautiful bond is awful… but those who come in your dreams are your angels…" Maaya said.

"You know… Nowadays, beyond the whales and eagles and tsunamis, my dreams are full of a big white-coloured snake. And it is laughing at me and chasing me," I said.

"What is this, da? You seem to be sleeping in the zoo and dreaming about animals." Ilango laughed.

"Why are so many animals coming in a monkey's dream?" my mother joked.

"Amma! You too! I have lost sleep. I am scared to switch off the lights while sleeping. I always feel as if that white snake is coming at me," I said.

"Nothing like that… I will have to ward off the evil eye that has fallen on you. Then everything will be okay. For the last few months, you all had too much attention from the media and others. All this could have been because of that," my mother said.

"Yeah, that reminds me… where are the media people now?" Maaya asked.

"Some caste group has filed a case against an actor because their caste was insulted in his latest movie. The media's attention has been turned his way. So we have escaped!" I said.

"It's good that we have a lot of loose nuts creating issues for a publicity stunt... that is helping us," Maaya observed.

"At this rate, we will not even cross Chennai before 1st August if you guys keep talking shitty stuff." Vidhya mocked us.

"Dude! You drop your mother at your aunt's place and come to my house. We can then go and pick them both up and leave," Ilango suggested.

"Dei, wait! Should we not book resorts and all? You're talking as if your grandfather has a place there..." I asked.

"Yes, actually. It is not my grandfather, but my uncle who has got a resort in Kolli Malai. I can book our rooms while we are on our way. You get going," Ilango said.

"Go tomorrow morning... avoid night travel when you travel with girls." My Mom said.

"No, aunty! If we leave now, we can reach Pondicherry by 11 PM. We can stay the night there and start by 5 AM from there... We will reach Kolli Malai by lunchtime," Ilango explained.

"Ilango... were you working in IT or were you a travel agent? You are talking as if you have this schedule by heart!" Vidhya commented.

"Exactly! We would have taken at least a week to plan this otherwise," Maaya agreed.

"Suja and I had travelled to every nook and corner in the past six years," Ilango said, his voice lowering in pain. We noticed his face falling when he spoke of her.

"Were you in the relationship for six years?" Vidhya asked, stunned.

"Since we were studying in our eighth standard, actually... When I say the last six years, I mean... that's when we went on many trips together..." Ilango said.

His eyes teared up even as he said that. Wiping them away, he turned to me and said, "Why speak of all that now? You get ready to leave."

Then he turned to the others and said, "Let's go."

Vidhya was looking at Ilango intently, her face inscrutable, but Maaya dragged her away by her arm.

* * *

Once everyone had gone, I turned to my mother and asked, "Why did you lie now?"

"Oh, that's nice… You have grown up enough to find that I am lying!" She laughed.

"Tell me, ma," I insisted.

"If not at this age, when will you go on trips? I will be with you always and that doesn't mean you can't go anywhere with your friends," she said.

"Where will you go now? Are you planning to stay home alone?" I demanded.

"What's going to happen to me? I will ask your aunt to come here for company… you don't worry," she assured me.

"Had that man been here, all this would have been unnecessary! I am furious when I think that he has run off, heaven knows where," I said angrily. Even thinking about my father upset me.

"Why are you blaming him, da? I did not know how to live my life as Maaya's mother did. I always hesitated and worried about this useless society, wondering what everyone around us would say. Your father, however, did not worry about all that and is living life the way he wants. It is my mistake! Why blame him?"

I did not know what to say. For a long minute, I kept staring at her, looking at her afresh.

"Why are you looking at me like that? We alone are responsible for the decisions we take," she said.

"If everyone thinks and behaves like you… there'll be no problems in life," I said fervently.

"Dei! Tell me something about your business. So I can also talk about it to others and show off proudly," she changed the topic.

"Look at that! Let's do that when I am back. Who else am I going to tell all this to if not you? I will explain everything in detail," I smiled.

"Okay… you get ready to leave," she said and went inside.

* * *

I went to my room, got ready, and went to Ilango's house. Maaya and Vidhya had gone to their house to pack their bags. So we picked them up on our way and started to Kolli Malai.

With a lot of fun banters and pulling each other's legs during the drive, for the first time, we forgot all the work issues. There's nothing quite like the ecstasy of grooving to great music with your pals while on a road trip.

After a while, Maaya sighed.

"How carefree we were! And look at how we are now! So much has happened in one year. Everything looks like a dream," she said.

While she was talking about dreams, I put both my legs up on the seat.

"What, da? Do you feel like a snake is about to bite you? Your legs went up on the seat automatically," Ilango asked.

I laughed, trying to circumvent it.

"Okay… tell us about your dreams… let's hear the whole story now," Maaya asked.

Before I could start, Ilango interrupted, "Can we eat first? I am hungry."

We all agreed and went to dinner. We took a break in Tindivanam Junction. It was a busy place. Many buses had stopped there for dinner. While we were eating, I saw Keshav Ram Patel's secretary Muruganandham there. He had not noticed us, though.

I approached him and said, "Hello, sir! How are you? Are you able to recognize me?" I asked.

He looked at me uncertainly and said, "No… I don't recognize you."

He knew me very well, I was sure. He had just seen me at the hospital with Raj a while ago. I did not understand why he was pretending otherwise. Then, I noticed who was sitting opposite him. It was none other than our detective Charles.

"Charles! How are you here?" I asked.

"I have come to visit my relatives here," he said casually.

"Do you both know each other?" I asked.

"No… no! He had come here to eat, and we both got talking."

"Oh, okay!" I said and turned to Muruganandham. "Sir, I was with that Raj in the project. Keshav Ram Patel knows me very well. That's why I thought you'd know me too," I said.

"Ayyo! Yeah, I remember seeing you in his office… Sorry… many people come there every day… that's why I could not recollect you immediately," he said.

"That's correct, too! Okay, please go ahead. Charles… let me know once you are in Chennai. We'll meet," I said.

"I'll definitely let you know… It could take a week more," Charles said.

The whole thing with Muruganandham and Charles gave me negative vibes, and I felt something was wrong.

* * *

We booked hotel rooms in Pondy. Ilango and I stayed in one room while Maaya and Vidhya took the other.

"Dude! I have booked three rooms in Kolli Malai. I know you were not expecting me here, but adjust for tonight," he said and laughed.

"Oh, forget that! Now listen to this," I said and related everything that happened in Tindivanam.

"What's looking wrong in this?" He asked.

"No, da! I have seen Charles many times and spoken to him at length too. He is a brave man. He always looks a person in the eye and speaks boldly. So whatever he says would mostly be believable. But today, he was hesitating a lot as he spoke. He never once looked me in the eye," I said.

"He was probably drunk or something, da!"

"No… He does not have that habit. When he came to Madurai with me, I asked him to join me for a drink. He took me to drink juice instead," I explained.

Ilango laughed and said, "So you took a milk drinker to task and tempted him with beer."

"Dude… he did not look right today. Something is wrong!" I insisted.

"What are you saying, da? I am not following anything," Ilango looked confused.

"I think he knows a lot more about Subha. He is not sharing everything with us. I want to go to Madurai again and inquire around. Once Charles got to know that she had died, he immediately asked me to leave. He promised to call me once he was back. But he never did. And I had also forgotten to call him amidst all the issues around Raj. But now I feel I should have done that because something is majorly wrong." I explained.

"Okay. You meet him in person once you are back in Chennai. I will come along with you. Let us first go to Madurai and see the people there, too. We can do our own inquiry about Subha. Then you can meet Charles and ask him about this. You'll come to know if he is telling the truth or not," Ilango suggested.

Even I felt that was the right thing to do.

* * *

Chapter 24

We started from Pondy the next morning around 6 AM. Once Maaya got into the car, she began, "Do you know everything about Kolli Malai? Are we still going there after knowing all this?"

"Knowing what?" I asked.

"Did you see any videos about the mysterious happenings there?" Ilango asked her.

"Yeah! Do you know about them already?" Vidhya asked.

"I have seen the videos, too… but when I went there, there was nothing out of the ordinary," Ilango said.

"I don't know much about the place. But my mother has told me about Siddhas living there," I said.

"We could have gone to Ooty to relax, right? Why should we go to a place like this?" Vidhya asked.

"Those are usual tourist destinations. But it will be a special experience to drive on the hairpin bends in out-of-the-way places like Kolli Malai. If we only go to some place and take pictures, we could remain in Chennai for that. We have to visit new places to get new experiences," Ilango said.

"You let go of the IT field and start a travel agency… you will do much better. You should probably ask Dhivya to invest in your venture," Vidhya laughed.

"Do you know one thing? I have always wanted to drive like this and spend time with nature. But, instead, I am doing random things like working in IT, working on projects to delete people's memories, keeping chips in their bodies, but also stuffing my face with chips and snacks…" Ilango trailed off, ruminating.

"Dude, that's so true. This is so boring! Your words are gold," I said.

"Hello! He's saying we should travel and gain new experiences. He's not advocating that we should sit at home eating chips and watching random YouTube videos!" Maaya intervened.

"Silly fellows! What you guys get with traveling is what I get while watching these videos and living my life to the fullest," I said.

Having such fun discussions, with food and songs to fill our souls, we came to the foothills of Kolli Malai. We had to take seventy hairpin bends from there. Ilango asked us all to wear our seatbelts.

The ambiance there was ethereal. It was full of natural beauty. Bikers and hikers were everywhere, and families were having a blast on their vacation. You could hear the roar of the engines and the buzz of people having a good time. On the other side, people had also come to visit the eight-handed local deity, Ettukai Amman. Though there was not much traffic, we were going slowly. After crossing 30 hairpin bends, we took a break. I took over the driving.

During the break, a boy came and spoke to us.

"Brother… if you have alcohol with you, please leave it here with me. Or the Ettukai Amman will punish you! I will be here only. You can get the bottles on your way back," he said.

"You'll be there, of course, but how about the drinks? Will they be there?" Ilango asked jokingly.

"Brother! The Ettukai Amman will punish you up there if you take alcohol. I am saying for your good," the boy insisted.

"You are a smart kid. But did you see this girl behind us? She drank everything last night. I asked her to leave some for you. But she didn't," Ilango said.

He had meant Maaya, but Vidhya slapped him lightly on the shoulders and said, "I'm going to kick you one of these days."

"He's talking about me. Why are you getting into this?" Maaya teased.

I turned and looked at Vidhya in surprise.

"He's talking in general! Why do you think he means you?" Vidhya asked.

When she fumbled like this, Maaya and I laughed.

"You go, dear! As a sister, won't I do at least this for you?" Maaya asked.

"Hey! You're going overboard!" Vidhya complained, blushing.

But as if he had not noticed all this, Ilango was speaking to the boy. Eventually, we left that place, drove uphill, and finally reached the resort.

* * *

Ilango called his uncle, who asked us to go inside the resort and tell them his name. He assured us that the room would be ready. He also told us he'd send a number that we should contact for any further help.

While Ilango was talking to the resort people, I was casually looking around. The area was quite peaceful and serene. I was admiring the foliage and the general ambiance.

Suddenly, I noticed Joseph, whom I had met at the airport, standing in a tea shop on the opposite side of the road. He appeared not to have noticed me. I was surprised to keep seeing these people at odd places. I stepped out of the car to talk with him. On seeing me, he reacted with a startled expression, like Charles and Muruganandham, and pretended to remember me only after a while.

"How are you here, sir? Are you on holiday?" I asked.

"No, actually... I have come here for some research," he said.

"What research are you going to do here?" I asked.

With a small smile, he said, "There are many local legends about deities possessing people and predicting the future. I want to talk to the locals and learn more about all this."

I laughed along and said, "Then you'll surely have a lot of work to do here."

"Yeah, they claim that even the ancient Siddhas still live here. Unfortunately, there are also a lot of cheaters who claim to lead people to these Siddhas. So take care, or they'll fleece you too," he said.

"Definitely, sir! Even if the Siddhas come in person, we won't believe them!" I said.

"Are you going to stay at this hotel?" he asked.

"Yes, sir… we'd be staying here only," I replied.

"How many days?"

"Two days!"

He thought a bit and said, "Okay, we will see then. I'll be here, too. Let's meet."

I was still confused about what had happened in Tindivanam. And now his reaction looked odd, too. He did not look entirely pleased to meet me and looked further uncomfortable when I told him about staying in that resort. But he had composed his face quicker than the other two had done.

I took my leave and went back to the resort. Ilango had arranged for everything by then. We were tired from the drive, so we went directly to our rooms. Ilango had said that we could rest for an hour and go for lunch.

* * *

While the room was not big, it was clean. Maaya and I were in the same room reminded me of our good times in the resort in Chennai. Those were the best times of my life. Maaya was looking at herself in a 6-foot mirror in the corner of the room, appreciating her beauty.

"Darling, this is not a time for self-love, I am here!" I demanded playfully, trying to lie down on the bed.

"You'll call Ilango when we are alone anyway," she said tartly, reminding me of the recent past.

"Really! Which idiot does such silly things? By the way, who's this Ilango? I don't know anyone by that name," I muttered. I walked up behind her, wrapped my arms around her, and pulled her close. As I rested my chin on her shoulder, our cheeks touched, and I gazed at her through the mirror, whispering, "As long as I'm here, no one's getting close to you, not even yourself."

"You're not going to look at me anyway… You are so busy nowadays! I am not even in your line of sight," she pouted adorably.

I pressed my lips gently against her cheek and murmured, "When you are inside my eyes, deep inside me, why won't I see you outside?"

As she locked her eyes with mine in the mirror, she reached up and tenderly caressed my cheeks. "I always thought I had very dark skin But standing next to you, I look much lighter and am glowing, too," she whispered back with a smile that lit up the room.

"You're here to bring light to my life. This is an indication of that," I said.

She turned to face me and traced her finger over my lips. "What's gotten into you, making you spout so many dialogues? Did you go for extra tutoring of these sweet nothings just for this trip?" she teased, with a glint of mischief in her eyes.

I laughed. "As they say, you just have to enjoy what's being said… not delve into the meaning or the source. Enough talking," I swept her up in my arms and playfully tossed her onto the bed. All of a sudden, we heard a commotion outside. It sounded like people running around frantically. We rushed to the window to see what was going on and noticed many people banging on Ilango's room door. As we stepped out to check, Ilango burst out of his room. Behind him was the same snake that had come in my dreams – the long, slimy white snake, hissing and very much alive.

The sight of the snake sent everyone into a frenzy, and they began darting around nervously. Maaya and I joined the panicked crowd, running as fast as we could. The snake then turned its focus on me and chased me relentlessly, just like in my dreams. I freaked out and bolted out of the resort, but the snake was hot on my heels. Fortunately, some people started shouting and whacking it with sticks, making it slither into a nearby ditch.

I could not understand anything. I was in complete panic. Whatever had happened in my dreams was real now – only the situation and place were different.

Maaya came running to me and asked, "Are you okay?"

"Should I tell you the truth… or…" I trailed off, still shaking.

Unable to explain how badly my heart was palpitating, how its noise was deafening my ears, how the fear struck my heart, and how shocked I was at seeing something in my dreams happening in real life, I fainted right there.

Ilango reacted quickly, buying water from a shop nearby and sprinkling it on my face to wake me. When I sat up slowly, he said, "Dude! It came into my room via the window and fell on the bed. I was stunned and immobile. But the moment it saw you, it started following you as if it had missed its long-lost friend and it wanted to hug you?"

"Dump your stupid jokes elsewhere," Vidhya scolded him.

Then one of the car drivers standing outside the resort rushed in and said, "It is normal for snakes to come here, but I have not heard of one finding its way into rooms via the window. I also have never seen such a white snake in my life!"

I looked at him, wondering how he was talking about the snake as if it were a frequent visitor from overseas who had come there without a visa. Everyone except us moved on and everything appeared normal in a surprisingly short time.

"What, da? You look so terrified!" Ilango asked.

"Get into the car. We're leaving," I said.

"Dei… we've just arrived… Everything will be okay if we stay here for some time," Ilango said, trying to talk sense into me.

"Dude, I will not be able to sleep the whole night. I can't get over the feeling of the snake coming in real life. This will haunt me in my dreams. I cannot be here. Let us go to Pondy. Or Ooty. I will not stay here," I said firmly.

"Dei! It is a six-hour drive from here, minimum, to any place. So we will just have time to sleep there and go back home. You come inside and stay with me… I will take care of you," he said.

"I'll leave. You guys stay back, relax, and come," I said.

"Hey! Wait… we'll go have lunch first. Then go to the Agaya Ganga waterfalls. If you feel the same even after that, we will return to Chennai or Pondy." Ilango said.

And as we were speaking, someone approached us. He was wearing saffron clothes and a necklace made of large rudraksha beads. His forehead had holy ash on it, and his uncut brown hair seemed like it had been growing for ages. He looked so intense and scary that it wouldn't have been a shock if the snake from earlier had been hiding in his locks.

He said, "Brother… you must leave this place at once. Amman did not like you coming here. If you remain here, your life will be in danger."

None of us ever believed such claims. We have always looked at voodoo and dark magic as lies and fabrications.

"I have heard a lot of such stories. So let us stay back here and see what happens," Ilango said.

I could not speak much. I was not in the mindset to give my opinion. Ilango then called his uncle and said, "The person whose number you gave is not picking up my call. There are a lot of problems here, now."

I did not know what his uncle spoke, but I could gather the general idea from Ilango's response. The uncle apparently claimed that he had left on some urgent work and such happenings were not new here. He had also said that this was the first time he was hearing about a snake coming inside a room.

"I am not in town… Or I would have come to meet you," the uncle said. "The boys at the hotel are too young. I cannot do anything with them at the helm."

"What would be the general response of the people who have had these experiences in the past?" Ilango demanded.

"Most people leave. A few brave people stayed back, and only a few left with their life intact… Some people are claiming that this is the work of the Ettukkai Amman. But I think this is just an excuse people use to take revenge. There are no proper answers for this mystery," Ilango's uncle stated categorically.

Ilango was looking at me as he spoke over the phone. When he noticed I was looking back at him, he turned around as if he was speaking about some normal topic. While all this was happening, we were standing near the resort's gates. We never went back inside.

I wanted to call Joseph and ask him where he was and if I could seek his help regarding my confusion. It was one thing to have a dream based on my subconscious warning me. But it was something entirely different for the dream to come true and involve such fantastical elements. But my mobile was in my room. My laptop was in the car, though. So I took the contacts from that and gave Joseph's number to Ilango, saying, "Call this number for me."

Ilango called the number and disconnected immediately. He looked at me and demanded, "How did you get this number?"

"This is the psychiatrist's Joseph's number. I met him at the airport earlier and saw him this morning in the tea shop over there." I explained.

"Dei! My uncle gave me the same number and said this person would extend all the help here with the resort. But he claimed this man had also gone out on some urgent errand now," Ilango said.

"What?! This guy claimed to be going to some big meeting or conference in Madurai. And he also said he was here to do some kind of research! But now you are saying he is working here, with your uncle?" I asked incredulously.

"How do you know the psychiatrist?" Maaya demanded.

"Charles introduced us at the Chennai airport. While I went to Madurai to meet Subha, this guy claimed to be going for a meeting there."

Ilango and I looked at one another, remembering whatever we had discussed last night. I thought for a while and said, "Let us go to Madurai."

"Dude! After coming all the way, we should not leave without seeing Aagaya Ganga." Ilango said.

"Okay. Let us finish lunch, go to these waterfalls, and then go straight to Madurai," Maaya said.

"Fine. Then I'll book our hotel rooms in Madurai," Ilango said.

"Our house is there… we can stay at our place," Vidhya suggested.

Maaya stared hard at Vidhya as if she was not happy with the suggestion. But she did not say anything. I did not go back to the room at all. The others went inside and packed our bags. While we were about to leave, the snake came there again. I was safe inside the car, but still, I screamed upon seeing that. The woman from the tea shop poured some boiling water in the snake's direction, and it immediately slithered back into the ditch.

The four of us looked at each other. Though everyone was afraid, they tried not to show it. I remained silent.

We had driven for about three kilometers over a small road. There, the mendicant who had seen us in front of the resort came. He had the same snake with him. It was a deserted area, and no one else was around. He looked horrific with that snake looped around his neck.

While we were staring, wondering what was happening, he cleaved the snake in half with a machete and threw the pieces on both sides of the road. He was doing this intentionally, we could see. We were all shocked, and our hearts came to our throats. Vidhya threw up. While that man moved aside a bit, Maaya floored the accelerator.

We stopped the vehicle after we had covered some distance. Still speechless in shock, we looked at one another. Ilango looked at Vidhya, muttering, "What the hell is this?"

Vidhya had vomited all over him in the car.

"Did you not feel nauseous? How could you not feel like you had to vomit after seeing that?" Vidhya asked all of us after apologizing profusely for soiling Ilango's shirt.

We eventually crossed all the hairpin bends and reached the foothills. We decided to eat at a restaurant there. The image of Kolli Malai and whatever happened in those mysterious curves of the place had completely shaken us. We all threw up eventually. But finally, we thankfully stepped out of the car and got on solid ground. Then we just drank water to calm our roiling stomachs, feeling the calming breeze in the air soothe us a bit.

Ilango changed his outfit.

"I wanted to bathe in the waterfalls, yes… but you need not have done this," he looked at Vidhya.

"You look even better in this dress," Vidhya complimented him glibly.

"Oh! So this is why you vomited?" Maaya asked.

"She is your Agaya Ganga, dude," I chipped in.

Maaya winked at me and asked, "We should start this project next."

"Shall we change the name to ViGo Systems now?" I asked.

"Vigo? Oh! Vidhya-Ilango! Look at that… you already have a hashtag," Maaya laughed.

"Stop it, guys! After all this, you guys are still looking for new content at my cost. Come, let's go eat," Ilango cut our conversation short.

We laughed a bit and relaxed. There, the boy we had seen earlier rushed to us.

"Brother! Did I not tell you that you should not take drinks up the hill? Look at what happened now…" He said.

I thought he was talking based on us coming down almost immediately. Ilango, however, spoke with the guy. The boy heard our story and said, "You are very lucky. The Ettukai Amman did not aim for your life."

He ran away before we could speak further.

There was a hotel nearby and a car service center. We left the car there for a wash and went to eat.

Whatever the boy had said was running in the back of our minds. Was there something more to his warnings? Or was it all a ploy to prevent certain people from going there? Or was it just an attempt to take away tourists' drinks and such objects?

How did that boy come to us just as we returned from the hill, and how had he spoken as if he knew exactly what had happened? Had word traveled that fast from the resort? If so, who had told him? And who the hell was that mendicant who intentionally tried to scare us?

Even amidst all this, how was my dream coming true? What was the mystery behind a man who claimed to be a psychiatrist, who was definitely in cahoots with a local private detective, but who was working as a helper at a resort? Which part of it was true?

* * *

Chapter 25

After a long and tiring five-hour drive, we finally arrived at Maaya's house in Madurai. It was already midnight, and Maaya's mother was out of town, attending a wedding in Kodikarai. Luckily, Vidhya had a spare key and called her mother to let her know that we were there, and her mother promised to return the next day after the wedding.

We were tired and fell asleep remarkably quickly. Since we had started from Chennai the day before, we had travelled about 660 kilometres. Except for Ilango, no one had even changed dresses. We woke up the next afternoon at 2 PM. Maaya asked me not to talk about our relationship with her mother.

Her mother came at about 4 PM. We had just ordered lunch and were eating it. Maaya's mother looked so strict, like the matronly women who are featured in Maniratnam's movies in the roles of mothers and sisters. We were in Madurai, the heart of the Tamil land, but even her Tamil sounded like English to me.

Noticing that we were all tired, she offered us coffee and went inside. "I'll cook tonight so you can have home food," she declared.

"It has been so long since I saw you! Why don't you come here more often?" she asked her daughters.

"Why don't you come and see us instead?" Maaya retorted.

Vidhya stared at Maaya as if chastising her for that comment. I could see that the relationship between Maaya and her mother was a bit sour. Vidhya probably adjusted better, for she was mostly a diplomatic person. Maaya, however, was always feisty.

Immediately, I waved a hand towards Ilango and said, "We are leaving now. You guys catch up. We will finish some work and be back."

* * *

I figured this would give the daughters some alone time with their mother. And we could also finish our work here as we had discussed. Ilango and I left and reached Subha's grandmother's place. We wanted to ask for more details about that woman and the family. But there was no one in the house.

When we asked around, we learned that the people who had been in the house had left town rather abruptly. The neighbours claimed that the family had not informed anyone about where they were going, nor had they given any other details.

"What happened to all the land that they said they had here?" I asked.

"No idea! Everything remains as such. But they have left," one guy said.

"You came here last week, right?" Another guy asked, squinting at me suspiciously.

"Yes," I said.

"They were gone the next day. The man who came with you stayed here after you left. He kept calling people and was on the phone for a long time, standing around here. When we woke up and noticed it the next morning, the house was locked. Who are you to them? Who was that guy who came with you?" The guy kept asking questions.

"I left my ring here when I came last week. I told them that I would come and get it later. That's why I came now," I tried to evade their questions.

"Give us your number. If they come, I will inform you immediately," the man offered.

"No, thanks… I will call them myself," I said and left the area.

Then Ilango and I went to the place where I had seen the obituary banner just days ago. But there was no sign of it anywhere. The place was bereft.

We asked the people standing around the area.

"Don't know, brother… Usually, the posters remain until some other posters take their place. But this time alone, they have removed the earlier one without another coming to take its place…" One man said, pointing to another banner nearby. "Look at that! It is very old banner, but it is still there."

I showed him Subha's picture and asked, "Do you know about this woman?"

"I don't know anything… You can go ask in the shop where they printed the banner, though," the guy shrugged, pointing me in the general direction.

We went to the banner shop nearby. Only a small boy was manning the establishment.

"Hey… Do you have anyone else in the shop?" I asked.

"You can tell me what you want. Why are you bothered if anyone else is here or not?" the boy replied cheekily.

"Ah! Look at the attitude, man," Ilango said, showing him the picture of the banner and coming straight to the point. "Who gave the order to print this banner?"

"It was that lady from that house," the boy answered.

"Do you know about the people in this picture?" I asked.

"They are that old lady's son and granddaughters. I know only that. It's been a while since they kicked the bucket," the boy answered.

"What? Kicked the bucket? What is he saying?" Ilango demanded.

"I mean… they died," the boy explained.

"Look at how he is talking!" Ilango said, turning to me, visibly surprised at the callousness with which the boy was talking about death.

"All of us are going to die one day… why do we need to fuss about it?" The boy said, being cheeky again.

"Right! Now he's spouting philosophy!" we said and left the place.

I turned to Ilango once we came out and said, "Something's fishy about Subha's death. Why did they take her granny away like a thief in the night? And Charles's actions are all mysterious, too. I know I had to come back after I got the call about Raj, but Charles just looked to be glad of the excuse for me to leave this place soon. He asked me to return home immediately when we confirmed Subha's death. What's he hiding? Who was he involved with? And why has it been all so hush-hush since then? Now I am starting to doubt whether Subha's death was an accident, even."

"I get what you're saying, but I'm scared shitless about these people! They're actually abducting folks now. We may be risking our necks here. For the sake of Raj, you wanted to find out what happened to Subha… That's where this started. And now we know she's dead. Kavya already said that Raj is going to be alright as he is recovering slowly. We don't have the power or resources to investigate the hows and whys of these things anymore. It's time to focus on the work and move on from this mess. I don't know where the hell this is going to lead." Ilango voiced his worries.

I did not have any reply to that. But I did not have the heart to leave it be, either. But deep down, I simply could not accept that an entire family would just get up and leave their place one day – for some reason not leaving behind their belongings – and then be involved in a brutal accident that would kill all of them.

But conceding that there was nothing more to be learnt from our enquiries here, Ilango and I went back to Maaya's house. Maaya and Vidhya were ready to leave. They both looked upset; Maaya looked angrier.

Maaya walked out and said. "Let us leave… I won't be in this place a minute longer."

Vidhya also brought our bags to the car and loaded them in the trunk. They both got into the car and got settled. Neither Ilango nor I knew what to do. I opted to drive and took the car via the judge's house that Charles had taken me to. The gate was locked now as well.

"Where are you going, da?" Ilango asked.

"No, da… I think I came via the wrong route," I managed, not wanting him to start dissuading me again.

About a kilometre from there stood a police station. Charles and Joseph were there in front of it, discussing something agitatedly. Along with them was the woman who had been the caretaker for Subha's grandmother. I immediately parked the vehicle in a corner and looked intently at the police station.

"Why did you stop the vehicle now?" Ilango demanded.

I told them what I had seen at the police station. It was only then that Maaya and Vidhya spoke their first words since getting into the car. Ilango explained whatever had happened that day. Maaya did not respond much, but she listened intently. All our eyes were focused on the police station.

In half an hour, many people came out. The grandma, the caretaker, Charles, and Joseph got onto a Scorpio and left. A police van followed them. In two minutes, an old man came out, too. He looked like a lawyer, dressed in a court gown. I wondered if he could be the judge that Charles was referring to that day. That vehicle was also marked as a government vehicle. The police station looked like the hub of activity.

We all felt that there was something wrong with the whole affair.

"Why are such important men coming for this grandma? There's some mystery surrounding Subha's death!" I said.

"Dude! You are getting involved in this unnecessarily… I'm not denying that there is some huge mystery here. I am just saying that our doing this is unnecessary. This is not good for us. Just let this go," Ilango insisted again.

I followed the police vehicle, but they escaped traffic with the help of their sirens. I could not tail them after a point. I drove out of the city, thinking wordlessly. Maaya and Vidhya were looking out of the window. Ilango was checking his mobile.

We had planned a vacation to relax. But when I thought of the trip, it had been anything but relaxing. Seeing Charles in Tindivanam, everything that happened in Kolli Malai, and Maaya's fight with her mother… I felt that it would have been better if we had stayed home.

It was an eight-hour drive to Chennai, and I knew this silence would not work for long.

I looked at Maaya in the rear-view mirror and said, "You look beautiful even when you are not speaking."

"It will be good if she does not speak at all," Vidhya agreed.

"I won't talk hereafter, and you can continue enjoying my silence," Maaya said, still angry.

"I have not completed my dialogue yet… I meant to say, 'you will look gorgeous when you speak,'" I said.

Despite herself, she smiled. Slowly we started to converse, and the mood lightened for all of us.

"You tell me about your dream. I asked you yesterday! But you have not answered until now," Maaya said.

I told them about the snake chasing me, how Ilango was involved in the dream, how the middle-aged woman hit the snake with a broomstick, and how I spoke to Joseph about all this in the second dream, and his explanation… everything.

"Wait a minute! So have you met Joseph even before going to Madurai?" Ilango asked.

"I met him in person only after seeing him in my dreams," I replied, still confused about how that could have happened.

"How is this possible, da?" He asked.

"Dei! Forget that. Come to the snake. In my dreams, it was you who threw the snake at me from a bush. In real life, it came from your room and started chasing me. Also, it was the middle-aged woman who drove it away in my dreams. And now the snake went only after the woman in the tea shop threw boiling water on it. In my dreams, it was just one woman throwing a broom at it, though. Even if certain finer details change… whatever came in my dreams happened in my life, too," I said.

"Are you saying this for real? So that is why you reacted so badly today?" Maaya asked, looking stunned.

"I was frightened out of my wits," I admitted.

"Okay! But why did you shout the other night?" She asked.

I told her about the dream that had come that night… the quicksand, sea, Maaya, tsunami, Raj, eagle, mountain, snake, and the multicoloured strobe lights…

"Dude! If this happens, I will accept that you have some special power," Ilango commented.

"It has happened, actually… in a roundabout way," Vidhya said.

"What are you saying, Vidhya?" I demanded, looking at her via the rear-view mirror.

Maaya and Ilango also turned to her.

"Let me put it this way – when you were taking Maaya to the beach, we met you midway and got you involved in that project without your knowledge or consent. It was actually meant to help Raj indirectly… but it didn't work out, and he went to jail. Now you're trying to build your business and climb to the top like ascending a mountain, but the higher you go, the more problems come your way… like snakes in the game of snakes and ladders. And these snakes are actually related to the Subha problem. They're like a constant threat, always chasing you, even if you leave them be." Vidhya said.

The way she expressed the connections made sense. We were all looking at her in various degrees of surprise.

"So what does the quicksand represent?" Maaya demanded.

"I don't know… Maybe it was an indication that by loving you, he fell into quicksand," Vidhya shrugged, grinning.

And we all burst out laughing.

"If that were the case, he could never escape. Once he's fallen, that's it for life," Maaya said, smiling.

* * *

Chapter 26

"I have a project idea based on all the dreams… If you all are ready to hear it now, we can talk. Or we can discuss this tomorrow in the office," I said.

"We still have five more hours… you say, we will listen! We don't have any other important work to do," Ilango encouraged.

"While talking with the guys from Dhiraj Systems, they spoke about two things mainly. Virtual Reality and Crypto," I began.

"Correct! So, what are you suggesting? Should we mine crypto, now?" Maaya asked.

"Listen! In my dream, I was in a fantasy world, holding a laptop while stuck in quicksand. Suddenly, I was magically transported to a beach, and the whole experience felt so real that I could feel the heat from the fire and the sounds from the beach waves. I even saw a smiling snake, which will never happen in real. It made me realize the potential of Virtual Reality to create positive experiences for people. We could help others have similar experiences with VR."

"One minute!" Ilango stopped me. "If you are going to talk about Virtual Reality like in the games, stop right there. There are thousands of such games already – and most of them are RPGs based on fantasy worlds."

"Listen fully, you idiot!" I said and continued. "We could create a digital world like this. We are going to do something like a metaverse. Now, aren't they buying NFT art with crypto-currency? So we could do something like that…"

"One minute, wait just a minute!" Vidhya interrupted. 'I am going in one track steadily. If you stop me in between, I will forget,' I thought crossly.

"First, tell me what these things like Crypto and NFT mean. My head is spinning. You guys are rushing ahead," Vidhya said.

"Haha… Now look, he will pretend as if he knew it already," Ilango said.

"Dei… if we do it after knowing everything about it, we're going to be just another company. But if we innovate and learn as we go, we are leaders. Ask Maaya, she'll term this correctly," I responded, smiling.

"You tell your idea clearly, first. I will tell you the terminologies later if the idea is good," Maaya said. "Just talk about whatever's in your mind, so we get clarity."

"I am your boyfriend, Maaya," I pointed out. That was always on my mind, after all.

"Shabba! You're joking like a boomer. Just tell me your idea," Maaya said.

"Haha! Cryptocurrency is like digital currency. You cannot touch it or feel it. You cannot keep it in your wallet. It does not have a permanent or fixed value. Like, the share market, the value of the digital currency would change based on the market conditions. We could buy other products with this and we could send this to anyone in this world, irrespective of geographic borders. Governments all over the world are still working out the right level of governance and policies for this, but they have not been very successful. They may try to garner some control over the transactions soon enough, but that's a debate for another day.

"NFT is quite simple. Say you are drawing something now. A picture. Using a process called Mint, you can make it your 'property' in one sense of the world. You can think of it like getting a patent for something. They will give you a number like a token, and you have to keep it safe without sharing it with anyone… say, like a password. Then you can sell it to anyone. Or even gift it to others. You can also track the transfer of ownership from one to another and claim royalties from these transactions. We can do this for anything, technically, from art to music etc…" I said.

"Okay, I think I get it to some extent! You continue. I will ask my doubts later," Maaya said.

"Now, where was I?" I asked, trying to get back on track.

"You were talking about some metaverse…" Maaya prompted.

"Okay! So think of these like real estate NFTs or digital real estate. You are going to create your own world with your own rules. It's like a virtual Disneyland where people can come and play games and activities and pay you using cryptocurrencies. We can create an army with people in our world and go to other virtual worlds and start wars. We can create our virtual world with all the elements we want in it – beaches, rivers, waterfalls; you name it! We can even digitally market our world and attract more visitors. And imagine the possibilities – we can sing and dance to our favourite songs from movies like Bahubali and even create a virtual passport for our world!

We've all wanted to visit the worlds in the movies but we could not. So this could even open up a new dimension to make money for the movie industry… They could create recreations of their elaborate sets and characters and let users have the experience of actually being there. And the best part is, we can create anything we want with our imaginations! Even the places we never got to go to!" Ilango exclaimed.

"Exactly… on one side, we can have battles and wars. But on the other side, we can have romantic and beautiful scenarios. We can go wherever we want, do whatever we want, and become lawmakers and gain more popularity, too. As in, the more interesting your world is, the more popular it is going to become. And the more people who visit your world, the more powerful and sought-after you'd become," I said.

"All that is great, but how are we going to get data through this venture?" Maaya asked.

"We have to work out those options. But I can see that if we do such a thing, there would be no dearth of data. People will want to belong to this, and they will happily share their data with random strangers in real time. We all know how people are more comfortable behind anonymity. We can also ask for some of their data directly, saying we will be curating their experiences to match their sensibilities. Then we can also observe their behavioural patterns and analyse some more… We can work this out as we go. Maybe do it like a reality TV show?" I asked.

"I don't get you?" Maaya prompted. Vidhya and Ilango just raised their eyebrows.

"If instead of a VR glass, we have a lens. We can organize a show like Bigg Boss in the world we have created. And we can ask for the common public to be there for a hundred days in our universe and do the tasks we set for them. We could fix an admittance fee for the people who come to visit us. We can create a contract and draft terms and conditions. If they have to leave in between, they have to pay us. And if they remain for the hundred days as we specified, we can pay them from all the money we get with the marketing and advertising revenue, and the interest shown by others. And if we manage to translate the language accordingly, anyone from any corner of the world can participate without language barriers…" I kept building on the idea, my excitement creating new paths in my mind.

"Did you think of all this based only on your dreams?" Ilango asked.

"Yes, da. Virtual dating, virtual relationship, even virtual sex options…" I said, the idea blooming.

"What? Virtual sex?" Maaya asked, sputtering on the water she had been drinking.

"As if the problems we have with social media and online sites are not enough, you are creating new issues," Vidhya said.

"Problems are everywhere! If we don't do all this, someone else somewhere is going to do it. Why? Someone may even have already started all this somewhere. We could be talking about it here as if it is all new and something that only we have thought of," I pointed out.

"That's correct, da… The idea is good. But all this is not the work we could accomplish from your house's terrace. This would be the job that big companies with huge resources would do… First of all, we would already need the infrastructure in place for development and testing. Not to mention the user base where we can market the product and call for participation by offering early-bird rewards. All this is possible only for bigwigs – for instance, the companies like Apple and Samsung. Think like a start-up," Ilango said.

"Remember how that fellow, Rick, spoke to us as if we were clueless schoolkids? And now we can go up to him and boldly say, 'Our idea is big. Can you work on this? Do you have enough infrastructure and user base to tackle this?'" I countered.

"You were quiet that day, but now you are creating such a scene?" Maaya asked.

"It appears as if my dreams are happening in reality. So I thought maybe my dreams were an indication to do something like this till Vidhya gave us a different perspective." I said.

"No, no! It could be like you said, too. All these are things we think for ourselves. If everything you said is possible, there is no harm in trying," Vidhya chimed in. "Also, no idea is too big."

"It is possible, Vidhya! But we need a lot of capital for this. And space. As I said, we cannot do it from his house's terrace," Ilango said.

"Correct! Besides, it is easier for social media companies with a large user base to try this rather than us," Maaya said. "Even if we do build a top-class product, we will have to spend a lot on popularising it whereas those social media companies can just run trials with their existing user base."

"Guys… we don't have to do this ourselves. That's not my thought at all. I just think we should patent this concept first. Then if some big company is interested in this, we can sell our idea to them for some good money. Maybe if Dhiraj Systems would want to invest, this can happen automatically. We have to peg this idea to Dhivya directly. We should not go via Karen or Rick, because they won't take it to her properly. If possible, we could go to America and talk," I said.

"You're hell-bent on going to America!" Ilango commented.

"Not only me! All of us have to go. We go, we see, we conquer!" I said.

"Instead of calling us all to America to do the project, won't they rather hire someone locally and get their work done? Now I am thinking about something else, too," Maaya said.

"What?" We all asked and looked at Maaya.

"Firstly, they may want to ensure we are not working for anyone else by promising us this money. Chances are that when we are doing this here, they could also be hiring someone locally there to work on the idea. Or they could be trying to get this work done by hiring us for cheap. So based on these two assumptions, they won't be calling us to America," she said.

"Why are you saying this suddenly, Maaya?" I asked.

"No… I was thinking of what happened the other day. Why should they come down from their high pedestal and do this for us? Even after I spoke that way, Dhivya still spoke back normally… And she has the reputation for being a no-nonsense woman… See what Kavya said? But the Dhivya we saw acted almost as if she would do anything to get us on board this. She even encouraged us to broaden our ideas and implement them on a larger scale. I am wary of that action from that seemingly bold woman. Because, beyond anything, she's also a shrewd businessperson. Hence I got the doubt," Maaya explained.

"Why? We're Indians, and she's an Indian too. Could it not be because of that?" I asked.

"We are our first enemies. There's no chance this is the reason," Maaya said firmly.

"If given the money, for the right price, they will do anything," Vidhya noted.

"There's a big chance for what you're saying to be true," Ilango agreed.

"Then this is even more of a reason for us to go to America. We should pitch a newer idea that they can market and which could become a roaring success. A businesswoman would see the potential in this idea. We have to do something huge. Or we could get stuck here," I said.

"Did I not tell you? He has planned to go to America. So he's dragging every topic to that conclusion," Ilango laughed.

We all agreed and laughed out loud.

***

Chapter 27

"We discussed my idea in detail during the entire journey and finally reached home. So many ideas had come up from all of us, and most looked like a wish list. We had to bring it all together and plan on the feasibility and how to build such a wonderful product. But merely even talking about it made us feel like we had done something significant.

August 1st was an unforgettable day in our life. The day we started our company. Ilango's father, my mother, and Kavya had come for the small ceremony. My mother had gotten Subha's picture and a few more pictures of gods.

"There's a surprise waiting for you all," Kavya said.

Right as she was talking, a car came to a stop at our house entrance. Keshav Ram Patel had brought Raj on parole. None of us had expected this pleasant surprise.

Raj came inside and said, "I am delighted, guys! You should all get immeasurable success in life."

"It's nice to see such offices in terraces in our country. Companies in the US that were started in garages have become global leaders.

I hope your company reaches greater heights, too. Whatever you do, do it honestly, within legal bounds. Once you become a big company, people could thwart your growth by bringing up stories from your early days… If you remain honest and do your work diligently, you don't have to worry about anything," Keshav Ram Patel said.

Raj looked at Ilango and said, "Very sorry! I did not expect these things would take this bad a turn. I am living proof of how not to run a company. You must do all this legally. Everything will turn out well."

After a while, we all took photos. We had ordered lunch for everyone at our place. Once we were done eating, Keshav Ram Patel took Raj back. Kavya looked happy.

Ilango's father presented us all with books written by Abdul Kalam.

The day was filled with positive happenings. At about 9 PM, Karen had set up a meeting. All four of us were named in the company contract, so she insisted that we had to be present at the meeting.

Only Karen came to the meeting from the other end. After the welcome notes, she gave us the details of the project.

"A few people are already working on this project here. We can collect the data from our end. We will send you only the scenarios based on that. You can work on them in your time. We can speak every Monday to catch up on the progress. We can also have calls in between if necessary. Or we can communicate through emails," Karen said.

"It would be great if you could give us more details about your project. So please do send us the relevant documents if you have any," Maaya requested.

"I will speak with Dhivya about this and let you know," Karen said.

"Okay. It would be easier to work if we knew all the details. In our earlier project, we worked directly with a psychologist. I am not sure how effective it would be if we communicate only via email," Maaya said.

I interjected immediately. "It would be great if we could come to America and meet in person once."

"That's your decision! It would not be a part of our contract. At best, we could give you an invitation letter for visa processing. Don't expect anything else," Karen said firmly.

"We could decide on this after working for about two to three weeks," Maaya said.

"And one important thing… Until you present your new idea to us and we accept it, you should not take up any other project. So keep that in mind," Karen reminded us with an almost smug smirk on her face.

Flaring up with irritation, Maaya replied quickly. "We signed the contract only after reading it thoroughly.."

"Okay," Karen nodded and ended the call.

Ilango turned to me. "Hey, idiot! Will you ask on day one about going to America?"

"I just asked casually. Is that wrong?" I asked.

"You should not ask all this directly, dude. First, we should delay the work. And when they ask for the reason, we have to say that every time we ask a doubt, it takes us 24 hours to get a reply, so we are taking more time to complete the work. If we do this, they will call us there by themselves to reduce turnaround time. But now that you asked it directly, we would be actually expected to pay our way to the US," Ilango explained.

"Had he known all this, he would have become a team lead long back," Maaya muttered.

Feeling nettled, I turned to Vidhya and asked, "Why are you quiet? You could add to this list of complaints!"

She shrugged and pointed to Maaya. "Don't get caught in her web. Escape while you can and run far away."

"You keep quiet! Lest he takes your words and actually runs away!" Maaya replied, grinning despite herself.

While we were talking thus, a mail arrived with about 20 scenarios, asking us to develop code as applicable. They had mentioned that this work had a week's deadline and had to be completed within that.

Maaya looked at me and said, "Check if these are things we had done for the earlier project or if we should do them afresh?!"

In that mail, they asked us to share out codes with them. But Maaya responded, 'The codes we write are our intellectual property. We cannot share that.'

'Data privacy rules in the US mean we cannot send American data outside the US. So you will have to send us your code,' Karen replied.

'This was not specified in the contract, so we will not share our code.' Maaya insisted.

'You people are creating issues with every little thing. You are laying so many rules since day one. I think you are speaking as if our companies are on par with each other! As far as we are concerned, you are working for us, not with us. That's all!' Karen had replied.

"Don't reply to this. Let us talk to Kavya first, reassess the contract and then talk to them," Ilango said.

So we decided to sleep over it and reply the next day.

* * *

This issue stretched for the next three weeks and we delivered nothing. Rick had scheduled a contract review meeting. We had called Kavya for this meeting from our side.

Maaya was nervous.

"We have not invested much in this project so far. So whatever it is, we can face it. If we all get together and try, we can do something better. So don't get tensed over this," Ilango said, trying to cool Maaya down.

Ilango and Vidhya had gone to Kavya's house to take care of the work regarding formally registering the company. Maaya and I were alone.

I looked at Maaya and questioned, "What happened to you?"

"What do you mean by 'what happened'?" Maaya responded, frowning.

"Nah… Not too long ago, I knew a girl who had simultaneously brokered deals with Raj and Sathya for millions of dollars without breaking a sweat. But that girl is getting tensed and worked up for a mere hundred-thousand-dollar contract?"

Maaya smiled and said, "I don't know da! Your entry into my life… Getting to know about what Kavya had done – and is doing – for Raj… your mom treating me like her own daughter… all this has made an impact on me. Now I want to marry you and lead a happy family life. But I'm scared about what will happen if we lose our jobs. I need financial security and stability in our life. I want to be holding a job firmly and build our future together. I want to settle down with you and be a family."

"We can settle down and have a family when we are their age. I want to see my old Maaya. Only that Maaya could bring this company up. Only that Maaya is hot… only that Maaya turns me on…" I said.

She laughed, still deep in thought.

"See… we meet and interact with a lot of people in life. And we will change based on that. This is reality. But you have to work with courage and vigour. And I will be with you throughout," I said reassuringly.

She held my hand in hers, squeezing it tightly. I went closer to her but looked around.

"What are you looking for?" She asked.

"I am seeing if the snake is here. When I come closer to you, something or the other interrupts me – be it the snake or my friends…" I replied.

"I guess my dear Romeo had some grand plans that day in Kolli Malai!" Maaya laughed.

"I don't get it! What are you saying?" I asked, smiling as innocently as I could manage.

"Don't you remember? I handled your bags and brought them back from the room that day. I noticed everything you had in the bag. You only look innocent, but you are such a naughty boy," she said.

"I missed it that day, but won't make the same mistake today!" I said, leaning forward to kiss her.

"SNAKE!" she screamed, trying to run. I held her hand and pulled her onto my lap as she laughed and squealed. I tickled her, laughing too.

"I have become quite weak, Ilamara," she said, gazing at me fondly.

"Whenever I look at you up close, my heart starts racing. I lose my words, my train of thought... You have this magical power that even God would be tempted to come down to earth to be with you and be enchanted by your romantic gaze. He would be powerless in front of your beauty. He may even start Krishna avatar 2.0 and choose you over Radha as his girlfriend."

"Even then, I will reject him and be with you only. I don't believe in God," she said, her eyes twinkling shyly.

"Look at that! I am the guy who won over God!" I said, pressing a kiss to her cheeks. "Do you know how many types of kisses are there?"

As her lips brushed against my skin, she whispered in a seductive tone. "No... What are they?"

"I will teach you. We will have practical classes for you today," I said.

I pressed my lips gently against her closed eyelids and whispered, "This is what they call Angel's kiss, my love. You are my angel!"

She replied with a kiss on my closed eyes and said, "You're an angel too."

"The word Angel could mean either a man or a woman," I responded, then I moved in closer, brushing my lips against her cheeks and leaving a light trail behind with my fingers. "This is what they call an Eskimo kiss," I said, enjoying the sensation of her warmth on my lips.

Touching her cheeks, she climbed astride my lap. I pulled her in, our lips meeting in a sweet, lingering kiss. "That's a peck," I whispered because it seemed too short for my taste.

Then I gently parted her lips with mine, and our tongues met in a passionate dance. "This is a lizard kiss!"

"Damn! Lizard!" She exclaimed, slapping my head playfully.

I whispered, "Just a single kiss on your lips," before placing a soft kiss on her lower lip. But our passion quickly ignited, and we lost ourselves in a deep, sensual French kiss. As we came up for air, I trailed kisses down her neck, savouring the taste and feel of her skin against my lips. "This is called a neck kiss," I murmured, my voice thick with desire.

She pushed me onto the bed and said, "I don't need to know the names of kisses. I just need you."

She then trailed a path of fiery kisses all over me, and we lost ourselves with every passing moment.

"What is this, then?" she asked, planting a kiss on my cheeks.

"I will teach you. We will have practical classes for you today," I said.

When I woke up the next morning, she was curled up on my chest.

She woke up and tried to rise from the bed, but I pulled her back, saying, "I forgot to mention one important type of kiss yesterday!"

"What are you doing early in the morning without even allowing me to brush my teeth?" She demanded.

"We can do this only in the mornings. This is called a raw kiss. We have to kiss without brushing our teeth," I said, grinning goofily.

"Chee! Get lost! How can we kiss without brushing our teeth? Idiot!" She exclaimed, getting up.

"Hey, wait! It would be a sin not to do it!" I said, pulling her closer.

I went near her and kissed her softly.

She pulled back with a laugh. "You're such a dirty boy, da! Look at the names you give… Raw kiss, it seems! Idiot," she blushed and ran out of the room."

* * *

Chapter 28

Raj's hearing did not happen on the 5th of August. They said it was postponed due to his health. But at the same time, the Russian President was visiting India. So we thought they had paused the proceedings to ensure that such a scandal did not leak to the public at that time or create unnecessary media hype. But Kavya said that Keshav Ram Patel had promised to do whatever he could to ensure that things got resolved quickly.

In those three weeks, I had tried to call Charles and Joseph at least 50 times each. Neither of them responded. I went in person to check on Charles's house, but he was not there. No one back home knew I was calling them or following up with visits.

Maaya and Ilango moved on from that issue already, saying, "Raj is getting better. We now have to focus on this project."

But I could not just let it go that easily. I had this dream where I was chatting with Subha and she thanked me. I was convinced that there was some mystery behind her death, and with every passing day, I only felt more certain that I was right.

The truth was that the others did not even want to talk about it anymore. That was the major difference between them and me. The people behind the mystery did not even let the 80-year-old granny living in a remote village be at peace, and spirited her away discreetly. My head was still reeling on this, and I can't get over it.

Maaya and Ilango were focussing on resolving the multiple project issues at the office. The American team was putting us under undue pressure. The contract review meeting was coming up. But we had not delivered anything so far. They never even allowed us to meet Dhivya in the last three weeks.

They clearly believed that we were not that important for Dhivya to interact with us directly. Maybe whatever Dhivya told us that day was to keep us in her control. They also seemed to be playing the 'Good Cop, Bad Cop' game with us. Rick acted tough so Dhivya could swoop in and appear sympathetic like she was backing us. They had played us together as a team and ensured we signed the contract that specified that we should share our idea with them first, and not work with anyone else.

Trusting them, we even refused to onboard the guy whom Kavya had suggested. Kavya herself was a bit sour about this, and she had indirectly taken a jab at us a few times already. I feel Kavya was still sticking with us only because she is grateful for us, as we are the main reason behind Raj's recovery in a way.

Amidst all these problems, there was barely time to discuss our new project idea. It looked like everyone had gotten stuck with one issue or the other. Only Vidhya had not gotten deeply involved in any of these issues, keeping a clear head and giving us the right advice at the right time.

"I'm running a fever! I'm going to the clinic and will come to the office later. I'm not sure if I can take the call tonight," Maaya had messaged me.

"What happened? Why are you suddenly having a fever?" I asked.

"Don't know. Maybe I got a fever with all the kisses you rained on me yesterday," She texted back.

"Look at that! So I can cure it by increasing the heat tonight." I said.

"Rick will anyway increase the heat and pressure tonight. So no thanks!" She replied.

"That Rick has Dhivya, if not Karen. But only I am there for you." I said, at once teasing and earnest.

"Is that so? Will you always be there for me?" She asked, all pretense forgotten.

"What other job do I have? I have to tell you one more thing…" I said.

"Did you have a new dream yesterday? What color was the snake this time?" She teased.

I called her.

"Dream, yes… But there was no snake in this. It was you who came into my dreams. We were having a beach wedding… Your mother, Raj, Kavya, Dhivya, Rick, Karen, Ilango, Vidhya, and my mother are gracing the occasion. But what's weird is David and Thyda from our old project were present too," I said.

"Yeah, right! Oh, so sir needs a beach wedding?" she asked.

"Yes! That too on a beach in America! Based on the others who were a part of the dream – all foreigners – that is what I think," I said.

"It would be great to have such a memorable wedding," Maaya agreed.

"As far as I'm concerned, it feels like we are already married. Everything else is just some ceremony to appease others, da," I said.

Before she could reply to that, there was a sound. "The doctor's calling me!" Maaya informed me and cut the call.

* * *

I often imagine myself riding in two boats simultaneously, with one leg in each. Sometimes, I dream about being out in the ocean and someone trying to drag me back while I try to jump out of either boat. I would shout and scream, but no sound would come out, and no one could hear me speak.

I wasn't sure if the pictures in my head were just from my stress, or if they meant something else was going on around me. But I didn't dwell on them and just kept going ahead with my daily tasks.

* * *

We all got ready at 08:30 PM for the 09:00 PM meeting. Maaya said she could not actively speak on the call and asked Ilango and me to handle the meeting in her stead. But she was a silent participant in the call. Kavya said she'll join from her house.

Rick and Karen joined the meeting at exactly 09:00 PM.

"Everyone knows why we're all here for the meeting. So let's hear what you've got to say," Rick said.

Karen turned to one side and looked at someone out of frame. I knew it was Dhivya. I thought they were playing the same trick again.

Immediately, I said. "We have already clarified our stand in previous meetings. You organized this meeting, so you go ahead and start.

"Ilamaran! We want to cancel your contract and fire you. You have not delivered anything so far," Rick said.

"Feel free to do that! We came prepared for that. Like Maaya said that day, we deserve some respect. If you are looking for a 'yes man' and someone to work as your slaves, then we're not the right people for the job," I said.

"Okay, done! There's nothing left to talk about. We'll send the termination letter. We will end this here," Rick said, indicating that he would cut the call.

Dhivya immediately said, "Wait a minute!"

She came into the frame and said, "Ilamaran! Can't you speak properly with decorum? You can grow in your career only if you can understand where to make compromises. You don't even have another job right now. If you cannot work on this, you have to start looking for work. We are giving you a huge opportunity. You should use it and be grateful for this chance to grow big."

"Oh! Today is a day for 'bad cop – bad cop' tactics, is it? I asked,

"What?" Dhivya asked, sounding surprised and annoyed.

"We have nothing to lose here. If we lose this work, I could simply make a living as a car driver… or we could all start a travel agency and run it together," I said, looking at Ilango and Vidhya.

Vidhya immediately understood that I was echoing her words about Ilango and laughed softly.

I continued speaking to the US team. "But you have a lot to lose here. You want to control us by throwing money our way, so the data and info we've collected don't go anywhere else. If we hand everything over to you, you'll probably just fire us later anyway. You should rather do that now. We're not expecting anyone's charity here. Don't try to enslave people in the name of the business!" I was pretty worked up.

My voice had risen beyond the acceptable limits for office culture and had taken a weirdly personal turn. Even I could sense that. Consequently, the reply was as I had expected.

"What is this, Ilamaran? You first have to learn how to talk to people. Are you under the impression that you are some movie hero here who can get away with speaking such dialogues? Rick was right. I should never have brought you into this. I take responsibility for this mistake. We can cancel this contract," Dhivya said.

"Dhivya! One minute… I have an idea now. You can listen to this and make your decision," Maaya interrupted.

"What's left to talk about beyond this? First, you people should learn how to talk professionally. We can work after that," Dhivya said.

"Instead of canceling the contract, we can alter it a bit… We'll come to the US. We won't get into any other project until this gets over. We are already onto another idea that is easily a million-dollar project. You'll surely like it. We will pitch it to you shortly. But this is not something we can do with the facilities and infrastructure in India. We can give you the details in person when we come to America. If you like that idea, we can work out a partnership. For now, we can alter our contracts a bit. The real issue is that you have restrictions in sharing data outside the US… And from our end, we want to protect our rights over our lines of code and don't want to share them as is. So it will be much easier if we all come to the US and work together. It's a win-win for all of us," Maaya explained.

"This looks reasonable. We'll discuss it here and let you know. But I have a condition, I will say it right away. Ilamaran should not be involved in this project anymore," Dhivya said firmly.

"Very sorry, Dhivya! We will not work on this project without Ilamaran. It was he who built half the programs that we have now. He has paid a huge price for that," Maaya said.

"We will not budge on this issue. Anyway, we will discuss it and let you know. Let us have a call same time tomorrow," Dhivya said firmly and cut the call.

Maaya gave me a headlong stare, and then wordlessly got up and walked away.

"Dude, learn how to speak in a work meeting! Don't you have any sense? You're behaving like an idiot," Ilango said and followed her outside.

"Just leave them… Whatever you said was right. But your words and tone could have been better. Did you think you were a mass actor? I am seeing an underdog speaking punch dialogues only today," Vidhya laughed, handing me a cold beer from the fridge.

I laughed along as I took the beer and started drinking.

* * *

Chapter 29

Maaya had gone to bed to rest since her fever hadn't subsided. Ilango had stepped out for a smoke break and had just returned. Seeing Vidhya and me drinking beers, he grabbed one for himself and came over to join us.

"What, hero? Did you get sloshed before the meeting? You were blabbering so much that we couldn't even rein you in. Without giving us time to recover, without letting us speak in between, without even looking at us once… you kept steamrolling the conversation."

"I know you guys would stop me. That's why I didn't even turn in your direction… Dude! Look… It is not like only they can play good cop-bad cop with us… Can we not do that? Now I am the bad guy, and you all are the good guys. You also have gotten a way to go to America now. I am sure they will be okay with it," I said.

"Dei! It was you who always wanted to go to America! Now they are saying you can't come…" Ilango pointed out.

"If you guys go, then I will surely follow you later. Maybe it will take a few weeks. Let them first respond. We can decide based on that," I said.

While we were talking like this, my mother came upstairs. We quickly tried to hide the beer and frantically searched for a non-existent hidey-hole.

"You don't have to hide it from me. I knew a long time ago that you guys have stored these here," she said.

She then looked at me and said, "Don't be like your father. Maaya is downstairs, feeling ill. Go and be with her. Even if you don't do much, just being with her will help her heal faster. She told me she'll need to take tablets every two hours. So you go and help her with that and take care of her."

"Go, dude! Do at least that work properly," Ilango said, pushing me out of the room.

"I am going!" I said, feeling nettled. I took my beer bottle in hand.

"Leave that here and go," my mother said.

"It'll lose its cooling, ma! I will take it downstairs," I said, dodging her outstretched hand.

"Look at his audacity?! I thought I should not lay down strict rules because you guys are adults, and now he is saying this to my face," she said, calling Vidhya and Ilango downstairs to eat.

Vidhya and Ilango laughed and followed her downstairs.

"He's been crazy throughout the day, aunty. I mean, I know he is crazy, but I never knew he was such an idiot," Ilango said.

"I know he is an idiot, and he often surpasses my expectations in that," my mother laughed and agreed.

I went downstairs to check on Maaya and felt her forehead. She was still running a high temperature. She looked beautiful even when sleeping. I finished my beer while watching her sleep but realized that being with Maaya was more intoxicating than the beer.

When you're into a girl, you think she's beautiful no matter how she looks. Maaya is special because she is strong, brave, and bold. She wasn't afraid to show her love for me, and she managed to keep our relationship balanced by giving me space to do my thing while also keeping us close.

Vidhya came in after a while, saying, "I'll take over now. You go to sleep."

* * *

Karen had mailed us the next morning. She'd written:

'We're fine with altering the agreement. Likewise, Dhivya's decision on Ilamaran is also final. Let us know your decision.'

Everyone looked at me. Maaya turned to me and said, "You've completely ruined every last chance we could have had to go there as a team!"

I ignored that comment.

"How's your fever?" I inquired, touching her forehead. I had woken up late and was still in my night pants, holding a coffee cup in my hand.

"I can sense your care with your actions," she snapped. I understood that she was still angry.

"Wait! Kavya has said she'll be coming. We can check the contract and then decide," I said.

"Kavya has just mailed us. She said she won't be coming today. She has some urgent work," Vidhya informed me.

"You all should go to America first. And once there, you can sing my praises and allow room for me to come there. I am sure I will be coming as well, somehow," I said, winking at Maaya. "What do you say, Maaya?"

"What is this about?" Ilango asked.

"He's passing off his wishes as his dreams nowadays! Ignore him," Maaya muttered.

Ilango, though, turned to me with a puzzled look. I could see that he did not understand anything.

Vidhya immediately interjected, "Did you dream that you were going to America?"

"Not just going there, Vidhya… I dreamed that Maaya and I were getting married on a beach there," I told her.

Ilango laughed out loud. "What, dude?! We're all going there for a project… But you're planning something else entirely!"

"Everything will go well, dude. You mail them in response stating that the three of you will be traveling to the US, but I will be supporting from Chennai. Insist that I cannot be sent out of the project and that I will work remotely. Let's see what they do for that," I said.

"Or, you could swallow your ego this once and apologize, so we could all go!" Maaya said.

"No… I cannot apologize and turn tail today after speaking so passionately yesterday. Maybe the way I approached it was wrong. But you all know that what I said was right. You guys go there now. Maybe if, after that, you feel that our assumptions were wrong, I will apologize," I said.

"You were the one eager to go to America… But now you are talking like this?" Vidhya asked.

"I will definitely come. The right time for that will come soon. We'll see when it does," I reassured them casually.

"Do you really believe your dreams, da?" Ilango asked.

"I don't know, dude! But this has given me new hope. It has helped me with my decision-making. I feel that I can take care of the other things later. So whatever has to happen will happen," I shrugged nonchalantly.

Maaya kept looking at me silently. But I felt that she was liking my newfound version of confidence. Eventually coming to a decision, she sent an email as we had discussed.

In reply, they sent us an invitation letter, having accepted what we had said. I just realized that, on the whole, Dhivya was furious with me. I could not blame her, given how I had spoken belligerently yesterday. But I could see how I had touched a raw nerve. I had hit on something close to the truth, and she could surely not deny that. Overall, I said to myself, some people just did not like being challenged. Dhivya surely seemed like such a person.

We were informed that the visa process could take ten days. The company had booked tickets to the US for the 5th of September. They had also asked us to develop a few scenarios in between and bring them there. Everything had seemingly become normal again.

* * *

Kavya called us that night.

"Raj's custody has been suddenly shifted to Delhi. Keshav Ram Patel has also been transferred to Assam," she informed us.

"Why? What happened?" I asked, shocked.

"Someone had complained that Keshav was getting personally involved with helping us. Especially about Raj getting a chance to come out of the hospital to visit your office's opening ceremony," Kavya said, sounding listless.

"So they'd transferred him for this?" I asked, still trying to work my head around it.

"I guess so. Raj was also in the photos that we took during the opening ceremony, right? I believe those have come out. So I guess you're also being monitored even now."

I immediately wondered if this would create any issues with the US visa processing. For the first time since all this had begun, I was getting a bit concerned, probably even worried.

"What is your plan now?" I eventually asked Kavya.

"I'm also going to Delhi tomorrow. I have to get a feel of things once I go there and see what could be done further. I tried to get at least a visitation to see Raj for the whole day today. But they refused. I then went to Keshav to seek his help, only to realize that he had already left for Assam yesterday," Kavya explained.

She sounded extremely nervous and was breathing heavily as if she had been speaking while sprinting.

"Shall I also come to Delhi? Anyway, I am in a dummy position in this project as of now," I said and explained everything else that had happened.

"This is also good in a way. You remain in Chennai. I could use someone's help from here. I will feel happier if you are here," she said.

"We're always there, Kavya. Please let me know what help you need, anytime," I said.

"Thanks, Ilamaran. Please ask Maaya to call me tomorrow. I have some special news for her," she said.

"What is that?"

"I will tell that only to her!"

"What's with all the secrecy? Okay, I'll let her know," I said and cut the call.

* * *

Maaya, Ilango, and Vidhya had gotten their calls for the visa interview. I was worried Maaya's earlier project would be in focus, and they'd question her about it. But it never came up. So they asked the usual questions, assured her that she'd get her answer in four days, and sent her on her way.

"I want to go to Madurai and see Amma," Maaya said.

"Thank heavens! Your anger is gone?" I asked.

"A lot of anger is still raging inside. But ever since we were young, our mother always wanted us to go to America. While bringing us up, more than asking us to learn cooking to impress our future in-laws, she always said we should study and get good grades and good jobs and go to the US... and always be independent. So I want to see her in person and inform her about us going to America. That's all," she said.

"Shall I ask you something?"

"You're going to ask me what happened that day, right?" Maaya asked.

I laughed in agreement.

"It was a huge thing for you to have given me the space for so long without bringing this up! I don't know how to broach this subject with you… and I tried not to talk about it at all…" Maaya said.

"I refrained from asking you for this very reason. But I just felt you'd tell me now. So I am asking you!"

"How did you read my mind, da?"

"I should understand what you need without you having to ask for it. I don't know how to speak romantically like others, but the love and respect I have for you are immense. I will not bind you down emotionally. You have to be yourself, and I should be a part of your life, that's all. We should not confuse our interdependency with our need for freedom and personal space. If this remains a healthy relationship, that's enough for us, Maaya," I said.

While I was talking, she looked at me with amazement. And while she did that, she was extraordinarily beautiful! Especially her eyes that would widen and become huge like gulab jamun, tearing up slightly. Even the tears born out of happiness are beautiful!

"You occasionally floor me with your words… I never know how to reply when you do that!" she said.

"Tell me about your mother. What happened?" I asked.

"She wants to divorce again. And her reason sounds stupid, too. She claims she wants to become an ascetic and is planning to get her diksha this November. So she says she's going to divorce her current husband," Maaya said.

"Her husband? Shouldn't you call him your father?" I asked, frowning.

"My father is in Singapore… No… I… I'm not even sure if he is alive now. I don't know if he even remembers me," she said, choking back some emotions.

"So about your mother… Why are you angry about this? Is it not her wish?"

"How could that be her wish alone? Then why did she give birth to us? She did not spend enough time with us, and did not bother about our marriage and our future… but she got married twice and now wants to become an ascetic. How is this fair?" She demanded.

"Is it not her life? What right do you have to become angry at that?" I persisted.

"If not me, who else has the right to be angry?" She snapped. My questions had angered her.

"No one has the right to comment on another person's life decisions. Before you start blaming your mother for wanting to become an ascetic, think about why she might feel that way. You don't even talk to her much, so you don't know what's actually going on in her life or why she's considering this path. I will tell you from my limited experience that people become monks either because they are drawn by spiritual truths or because they want to escape the endless circle of family life. Now you need to figure out which of these reasons applies to your mother. If it's the first reason, then there's nothing much you can do about it. But if it is the second one, you know what to do!" I said firmly.

Maaya did not reply but remained deep in thought for a while.

"Just find out what state of mind she is in… or better bring her to Chennai. Maybe if her situations and surroundings change, things could get better. It would be great if you and Vidhya were with her for a while. Think of that!" I said.

"How could Vidhya and I be with her now? We have to leave for the US in a week!" She pointed out.

"Ayyo! Yes! I had forgotten that… Okay, leave it to me. I will be here, anyway. We can take care of her. Firstly, for now, you go and talk to her. Find out what the problem is. Then we can think of what to do. Importantly, lend a patient ear and listen to her. You don't have to answer back for everything," I said.

Maaya looked at me. "I will feel calmer if you come with me. I feel guilty now after hearing everything you said. I feel that I have not taken care of her properly either," Maaya said.

"Yeah, we could go together. What other work do I have here?" I agreed.

While we were talking about this, Kavya called me. That was when I remembered that she had asked Maaya to call.

"Ilamaran! You should go meet detective Charles immediately and bring him to Delhi," she said.

"What happened?" I asked.

"No… Here they're trying to press more charges on Raj. There's no other proof of his claims on Subha. We're all related parties. But if Charles comes and talks about what he has seen, it could help Raj. He's also an ex-military man, and it would look credible coming from him. I am calling Charles weekly, but he's not picking up my calls at all."

"Okay, I'll see him," I said.

"Maaya did not call me at all. So you please ask her to call me without forgetting," she insisted again.

"I forgot to inform her, actually. Maaya is with me now. You can talk to her right now," I said and gave the phone to Maaya.

"Maaya! You have to help me with this. Mrs. Revathi Periyasamy has come to Chennai. I told her that I would meet her on 1st September. But I have to be in Delhi now for an emergency. So I cannot meet her in person. She knows some details about Raj. She has also said that she'll speak about this project at the UN. She has offered to take it to the Human Rights Commission and get their permission. I have already told her whatever I know about this so far. But she wanted to talk about this in detail. I will join a call from here, but you have to go in person and explain to her," Kavya requested.

"Are you talking about the Padmashri Revathi Periyasamy?" Maaya asked.

"Yes, the very same. She's in the UN now as an Indian diplomat. There's a lot of increased attention on mental health now, so she has claimed she will speak about this there. You have to meet her in Chennai," Kavya said.

"I'll definitely do this, Kavya. I'm going to Madurai today. I will come back on the 29th and prepare for this," Maaya said.

"Thanks, Maaya! I'll speak to you later. Ask Ilamaran to call me if he gets to know something about Charles," she said and cut the call.

"Why is she sounding so nervous?" Maaya asked me.

I told her what Kavya said to me about Raj, "So now we have to find this Charles," I said.

"Did you meet him any time after seeing him in Madurai?" Maaya asked.

"No… I could not even contact him at all… Now, I will try again. If not, we can get video recordings from that granny's neighbors and send them to the authorities. At best, they would get some doubts about everything," I said.

"You're floundering only at office meetings. But you are not that bad at all these things." Maaya laughed.

"Imagine where I should be in life and how my talents are put to use instead! I am wasting away here and doing mundane work," I said and heaved a deep sigh.

"Enough, enough! Go and do some work. We have to leave tonight. Stop boasting!" Maaya laughed.

* * *

Chapter 30

I tried calling Charles again, and unsurprisingly, he did not pick up my call. The saga continued. Then I went to his place and checked. No one was at his house. There was a cycle shop nearby. So I asked the boy working there.

"Are you asking about the military man, sir? I have not seen him for days now. Last I saw, someone picked him up in a car from there. He never returned after that. Here, look… the cycle that he gave for repairs… He has not even come to take it back yet," he said.

"What dress was he wearing when he went out last?" I asked.

"He was wearing a kurta. As if he were going to some wedding!" the boy said.

Based on what he said, I understood that the last time Charles had left the house was when he had come with me to Madurai.

Next, I went to Keshav Ram Patel's office. But there was a Malayali called Balakrishnan Iyer there. He also had a new assistant, to whom I asked about Muruganandham. He told me that Muruganandham had passed away, but that he could not divulge any more details.

When I asked around, I learned that he had been murdered in a place called Kuroor near Tindivanam, and that police had not yet found who the culprits were. He had no family left behind. So no one was there to follow up with the police. I realized that no one else knew any more details.

On hearing all this, I feared that I was getting drawn deeper into this muck and would get caught in something big. A lot of things had been happening around Charles recently. But now I did not know if he was trying to help me or if he was a villain himself, trying to obscure the details from me and dissuading me from searching for Subha.

Without knowing an answer to this confusion, I took Maaya and Vidhya to Madurai. While driving, we kept discussing whatever had happened. We wondered if we could get some clue somewhere. Everything seemed related, but we were not able to connect the dots. I could not help but feel that I was missing something crucial.

When I first met Charles, he had warned me, 'Stay out of this! This is not an ordinary thing as you assume… There's no way that we could not get any details at all… They could even be terrorists…'

I told Maaya about this and added, "At that time, I thought he was just being dramatic. But his demeanor changed when I told him about the situation in Madurai, and we discovered the grandmother's involvement. And now, with news of Muruganandham's murder, things are starting to feel a bit more unsettling."

"You never told us all this!" Maaya exclaimed, looking scared. "You still went ahead with this, knowing he had warned you like this?"

"Yeah, as I said, I did not take it seriously. But now, seeing everything that is happening, I wonder if all this was possible, too!"

We eventually reached Madurai and went to Maaya's mother's house. I went straight to bed and fell asleep. Maaya and Vidhya were speaking with their mother.

The next morning, I went to the old grandmother's house. Like before, there was no one there. I asked for some details from the neighbors and recorded some videos, and sent them to Kavya. I went to the banner shop, recorded some statements from the workers there, and sent those to Kavya, too. After that, I went to the police station and the judge's house there. Now, there was nothing much happening there.

I called Kavya and gave her all the details, including what I had seen in Madurai.

"Why did you not tell me all this before?" She asked. "I'm not just Raj's wife. I am his lawyer, too. These are important details," she chastised me.

"Sorry, Kavya! I did not pay much heed to that fellow, thinking that Raj was anyway cured!" I apologized.

"Okay, leave that. Hereafter, whatever details you get, you have to let me know. Now I will see if I can use this detail to do something," she said.

It was 1 PM when I came back to Maaya's house. Everything was smooth there. Their mother was cooking. and I exchanged a silent glance with Maaya to check if everything was alright. She responded with a reassuring look. Apparently, Maaya told her mother about us and her mom began to ask me about my family. At the end of it, I felt as if I had just gone through four job interviews at once.

* * *

The following week went by with the speed of a bullet. We returned to Chennai, and our days were spent collecting the visa documents, shopping for the trip, and doing all the jobs that Karen had assigned to us. Raj's hearing was deferred again. Kavya was still in Delhi. She asked me to try reaching Charles, but I did not know what else to do to get him. He did not even have a family. He was a loner, as far as I knew.

My mother was a bit sad that I was not going to America. I reassured her, "I will go. This is just a temporary setback."

I wanted to spend time with Maaya alone and take her out, but we had no time for romance.

On September 4th, I went to her house. She was busy packing. I expected her to say that she'd miss me. But instead, she said, "Dei! I will have to keep you busy at home every day with work to do. Or you'll go in search of Charles or Joseph or Peter or Ponting!"

"Ponting is a cricket player, da! Why are you connecting him with Subha's death?" I asked.

"You will do that if you could. But instead, focus on researching the project we had planned. I will also try to talk to Dhivya, meanwhile. You have to try to come there at the earliest," Maaya said.

I laughed.

"Why are you laughing? As my mother says, we could live there permanently," Maaya said.

"Ayyo! No way! I love Chennai and want to live here. I want to be with my mom!" I said.

"Why? Won't your mom live there in America with us?" Maaya asked.

"I won't live there. We won't even get proper biryani," I objected.

"Dei! What's this? You're talking like those men in our office who try to call sour grapes when they do not get a chance to go to on-site opportunities? This is such a loser's statement to make. And now you are talking thus!" she scolded me.

"Let whatever happen. Did everything go according to plan today and even so far? Weren't we surprised by how things have been constantly shifting and changing? Then why all this? We will go where life takes us. Whatever comes, whatever happens, we will take it in our stride." I said.

"You're just saying something to manage the disappointment," she said.

"Truly da! Believe me, my dear," I said.

"Dei! For the last six months, I've never been without speaking to you or seeing you. But now I don't know when I'm going to see you next," Maaya said, getting emotional.

"We'll see each other soon and speak on the phone every day…" I reassured her.

"You and I have not spoken much… You're such an aromantic person. But while at the office, when I walk here and there, your eyes will follow me. I will always enjoy that. Now I am going to miss that too…"

"Me too… You'll use your big round eyes to wink at me. And now, who will ruffle my hair playfully?"

"Usually, when you go to Madurai and all, I will miss you. The memories will come in waves and wash over me, but they'll also recede when you return soon enough. But now, I feel like the waves will drown me… for when I don't know when I will see you next!" she said.

"Pah! Look at that… so romantic! I have never heard you speak like this. Wonderful!" I exclaimed.

She looked up at me. "I never thought I would miss anyone like this. I thought I could manage. But I cannot," she confessed.

I kissed her head and said, "This is one type of kiss, too. I did not have the time to show it that day!" I said.

"You won't have time for all this, really!" She said, kissing me back.

We were talking in the room, for we did not have the heart to come outside. We forcibly pulled ourselves outside eventually. And from there, we went to the airport. Maaya had to check in at 11 PM. Her flight was at 3 AM.

It would be midnight there, local time, when they reached the US. It was a nearly 22-hour journey. They had to go to Doha first and then from there to San Francisco. We spoke until she had a signal on her phone.

This small separation made us talk about the things we had never even discussed while we were talking in the same room. I had never seen Maaya become so emotional. Even while we were in the resort, she had boldly spoken that her career was important.

I always liked that. But now, today, she was crying and saying that she would miss me.

Though this transition of hers was natural, the Maaya I liked was that daring go-getter version. I just hoped that love had not softened her up completely and she will get over her emotions and get back to that uber-confident woman.

* * *

Chapter 31

Revathy Periyasamy had canceled her plans. We were not sure about the reason. But apparently, she had promised to meet Kavya in Delhi and talk to her. Kavya had told Maaya about that, who then informed me.

Before Maaya, Ilango, and Vidhya could land in the US, Dhivya called me directly. I was surprised.

"Ilamaran! It is good that you haven't made it to America yet. You have to go to Delhi immediately. A neurosurgeon from Israel is in town. You have to rope him in for an interview for your company. Then hire him under the name of your firm, and I will invite you both to travel to the US and work on this project," she said.

I was confused by her sudden change of mind. "Will you tell me the why and how of all this?" I asked.

"We tried to hire him for our company directly from the US. But he did not get a visa. He is quite essential for this project to proceed. He has done a few projects like this in Israel. There they also have very advanced technology. So I want him to be on board for this project."

"If he did not get a visa via your company, how will he get it now with us?" I asked.

"They won't give him a work visa, of course. But we can arrange for him to come for a meeting here. Once he lands here, we can think of what to do further," she said.

"I hope there will be no problems for us with this?" I asked.

"Whatever happens, I will take care. You just do this for my sake," she demanded.

"Yes, Dhivya. Since you approached me and put the disagreement behind you, I will do this for you. But what will we get out of this? I want a 20 percent commission on his salary. Not just that. When I come to America, I need your time to speak with you. I want to meet you in person, alone, and share our ideas," I said.

"We could do all this… no issues," Dhivya said casually.

I frowned, surprised. She had transitioned from a firm businesswoman to someone who capitulated to my random demands… What was happening? Her urgency scared me immensely. Dhivya usually was unflappable. But now she seemed positively tensed as if this neuroscientist was the crux of it all. Who was this man? What was the need to bring him there so urgently? I wondered. If I were to conduct an 'interview,' shouldn't he be coming here rather than me going there? Was he that big a guy?

On the other hand, though, I could get a chance to see Raj and Kavya, who were now in Delhi.

Eventually, I told Dhivya, "You send us the invitation. I will take care of the things to do here."

"No… no… Once you have given him the appointment order, call me. Don't email me. Just call. I will send you the invitation," she said.

This worsened my doubts. I thought I should discuss this with Maaya and Ilango after they land in the US and then take the next step. But before I could complete the thought, Dhivya said, "Let this remain between us for now. No one else needs to know."

"Why all this secrecy? What's the need for that?" I asked.

"There's no secrecy. We have a lot of office politics here. I have not spoken about this to my partners in detail yet. They do not have the vision or foresight to appreciate the importance of this move. This project needs Yadin Sharat. So I am forced to do certain things to get that result," she said.

"Hope this won't lead us to any other issues?" I repeated.

"Nothing like that will happen. As long as I am on board, your company will be involved in this," she reassured me.

When Dhivya said this, I remembered what Sukumar had told Kavya: that we were on this project due to her.

"Okay, Dhivya. You send me all the details, and I will do this. I will just have to talk to our lawyer about this. Since he is not an Indian either, I need to check on the possible issues, if any, with the recruitment process." I said firmly.

"Okay," she agreed.

In a short while, Dhivya sent Yadin's contact details to me from her private mobile number. I called Kavya immediately.

"You have to do this carefully. Thankfully, you did not refuse her directly. You go ahead and set up an interview. Ask Maaya and Ilango to inquire more about this man in the US. If this is just due to office politics, then there won't be any issues for you guys. It is beneficial for us if you remain on good terms with Dhivya. Not to mention the added commission. But I just hope there are no other issues. I will try to get more details on the Israeli man," she said.

Dhivya had sent the contact details with the name 'Yadin Sharat.' I called and spoke to him. The man sounded affable and also seemed to have been expecting my call.

"I'm staying at the Leela Palace in Delhi. You can come and meet me here," he said.

I messaged these details to Maaya and Ilango and asked them to keep it a secret. They had not yet reached. The same day, I took a 3 PM flight to Delhi.

I met Kavya there, who said they had not yet given her permission to meet Raj. She was managing everything all by herself in Delhi. She then gave me some information.

"I asked about the Israeli guy. He's a famous neuroscientist. But he cannot work full-time in America. They may call him there now citing that this is a business meeting, for two weeks at best. I think if he stays beyond this, there will be some issues. He has been banned from working in Russia and Europe. He is not just a neurosurgeon but also knows technology. He's also earned a doctorate in the field of Artificial Intelligence. So though it is risky to involve him, he could be a great asset to your project. So I can understand why Dhivya wants him on board. As for your company… There are limited chances for any legal issues arising in India. Besides, our government is on good terms with Israel's government. So there should be no issues here," Kavya said.

"Dhivya has asked us to do this knowing quite well that there will be no issues in India… She's planned it well," I observed.

"Dhivya is quite sharp," Kavya agreed.

"How did you collect so many details in a short span of time?" I asked with awe.

"There's no one that these lawyers in the Supreme Court would not know about," Kavya said, laughing.

* * *

I met Yadin Sharat the next day.

He was clad in a black suit, with spectacles and a French beard dominating his face. He was bald except for a patch of hair on the back of his head. There was no commonality between his expensive suit and the cheap pen he carried in his pocket.

When he saw me, he asked about our project as if he were interviewing me. I answered him patiently, keeping in mind his credentials. His questions were engaging too. Eventually, he said, "Dhivya has chosen you well."

I did not understand what he meant by that and probably expressed my confusion with my eyes and frown.

He laughed. "You'll understand everything with time."

Yadin was warm in person. His words, actions, and how he spoke were all quite friendly and almost loving. He looked like a thorough gentleman, and I could see his intelligence and compassion when we discussed the project. Now Dhivya's demand made more sense. No one would believe that this wonderful man had been banned from practicing. But he was, and now it was in my hands to bring him to the US. So I took a look at his face one more time and then decided to take that chance.

I got his email ID and said, "I will send your appointment letter soon."

He laughed again and said, "Okay, we're going to go to America together. We can talk in detail then."

I was the one who was supposedly hiring him for my company, but it turned out that he was the one telling me where I would be going and with whom. The weirdness of this situation made me laugh.

* * *

I started from Delhi and reached Chennai. Immediately, I sat down to prepare an appointment letter for him and sent it to him.

Maaya called me.

"Hi, wifey," I chirped.

"Wife? Oh, damn!" Ilango commented.

"Dei! Why are you speaking from Maaya's phone?" I demanded.

"Here we're all holed up in the same apartment. We just woke up," he explained.

"You're such an intrusive bear," I grumbled.

"Dei! We're leaving for the office now. You can talk your sweet nothings later," Ilango cut in.

"Why didn't any of you even message me after landing? Is everything alright there?" I asked.

"We're facing internet connectivity issues here. We're yet to get a local SIM card. We saw your message. That doesn't sound right. We will check it out here. You don't do anything until then," he said.

"No, da. I spoke to Kavya. She had checked using her sources and confirmed that he was a good person and we could hire him. I met him in person, too. He looks like a good guy. So I gave him an appointment letter," I said.

"Why should you have to do this so urgently? Can't you wait until we ask around here?" Ilango demanded.

"No, actually, Dhivya asked me to do this soon so she could apply for an American visa for both of us. So I did it," I said.

"Did we not decide that we should not have outsiders with us? So why did you rush into this?" Maaya demanded.

"That was for the partnership, right? Yadin is not like that. He will just be an employee. Besides, it will be Dhivya who will pay his salary. Not us. We would also get a 20 percent commission in that," I said.

"You are not the kind of person who capitulates to such demands… What's going on?" Maaya demanded, obviously having listened to the full tale.

"No, Maaya. I thought this was a chance for me to come to the US. If this could happen even after I had spoken like that against Dhivya, I should not miss this chance… My dream will happen, too! So I did not think much," I said.

"Dei… you're setting a lot of store on your dreams," Ilango commented.

"This is not about believing or otherwise. When such a thing happens, we should learn to accept it as is and use it to our advantage. It would have been wrong if I had gone and apologized and begged to be included in the team so that I could get to live my dream. This is just an easy way for me to come there with my head held high… They are the ones wanting me there. I just get to do what I wanted to do anyway," I said.

"We've heard a lot about your dreams. You've also given him an appointment order. There's no use talking further. We don't want to be late on our first day here. You just come here soon," Maaya said and cut the call.

I messaged Dhivya on her private number, informing her about the same.

Immediately, she replied, 'Great! I will send the invitation. You can go and apply for the visa.'

In an hour, she sent me the invitation. But it had a different project name, and even the location was different.

When I checked with Dhivya about this, she said, 'This is an offsite location and we are planning for a workshop there. It is happening in a place near San Diego. We will all come there from San Francisco. And you will land there, too.'

The invitation mentioned a company called 'Medat Solutions' from San Diego – a medical data solutions company. They were famous for working on projects based on clinical research and artificial intelligence and data. They were partnered with many pharmaceutical companies.

They were a big company too. I was a bit afraid. There were a lot of things I could not figure out. Dhivya asked me to come in this circuitous route, but she gave the others straightforward visa routes. She had also manipulated me so that Yadin Sharat would come with me, that too without Karen and Rick knowing about it. I did not know if these actions were to be trusted or doubted. Was all this good or bad? I did not understand what she meant by office politics. I was unsure if she was using our fledgling company to meet her requirements or if she was helping us grow.

In between all this, I also applied for a passport for Amma and got her a tourist visa to the US. All this was based on my blind faith that I will definitely go to the US and take my mother along for sightseeing. Of late, nothing that had happened in my life had been under my control. I was going with the flow of life. That's all.

Right or wrong, whatever it was, I was prepared to accept it.

* * *

Chapter 32

We had been given a separate space at the office. Karen was their only contact point, and she would be working with them always. Dhivya was working on the 56th floor of the building. And their office was on the 18th floor. So their chances of meeting her looked very thin.

Maaya and Ilango had not even seen Rick yet. A week passed, but no matter how much they had asked, Karen did not give them any proper answer at all – they were just asked to work on the project alone and not to bother about anything else.

Karen looked to be about 28 years old. She was a sharp person who spoke her mind and did that directly to people's faces. But her tone and approach did not hint at any disrespect or hidden intentions; she was always straightforward and matter-of-fact. She would clock in at 8 AM every morning and work until 9 PM. She would even be working during lunch and occasionally have her dinner at the office sometimes. She was such a workaholic.

She was also one of the very few people who had direct access to Dhivya and could speak to her in person. She was not only working on the project but also on the administrative side of the office.

Maaya was amazed at her multitasking abilities and repeatedly spoke about that with awe to me. While in India, we always thought Americans liked to party and mostly clocked off work on time and spent the rest of their day clubbing or partying. But Karen was not the only one who pulled off 12-hour work days. Many others were also as committed to their work there at the office.

Maaya, Vidhya, and Ilango did not find time to go out at all. They were slogging at the office. Karen had insisted that they should come even on the weekends to work. Vidhya was not a technical person, so Karen asked her not to come to the office. Vidhya worked from their apartment.

"You should not have brought her here at all," Karen had commented once.

"We never even thought about it from this angle!" Maaya said to me after that.

The constant complaints from Maaya and Ilango whenever we spoke over were always about their workload and their completely shattered expectations of life in America.

The apartment that the company had allocated for them was amongst private residences. Karen lived next door to them. Even the top honchos of the company, including the partners, lived in the same apartment complex. Dhivya lived just around the street, in the first house by the corner.

There was also a Buddhist medical center and a Buddhist temple nearby. Only those from the medical center visited the temple. It did not look like anyone from outside visited. Just beside the temple was an empty lot. And next to that was a two-story building.

Beyond all this was a service apartment, which was also managed by Dhiraj Systems.

The entire area was posh and boasted elite residents. So it was surprising to find Karen there.

Maaya tried asking Karen for some more details about Dhivya, Rick, and the others involved in the project. But Karen did not share information. She was firm on speaking only about office issues. Maaya did not know how to find a breakthrough. Ilango also informed me that he got only one-word replies when he talked to Karen. They did not even get a chance to speak to anyone else there for any aspect of the project as Karen had always provided them with what she thought they would need and also acted as their contact point for the rest of the company & team.

Maaya, who had high hopes of meeting Dhivya once she landed in the US, felt quite resentful that Dhivya had not even spoken to them since they had gone there.

The three of them felt quite stressed and spent their days lamenting once they returned home from work. After going to America, even Ilango, who was always optimistic about life, was only whining and complaining.

One day Maaya was ranting to my mother about all this.

My mother said, "Why don't you try our age-old Indian technique?"

"What is that?" Maaya asked, amazed.

"Celebrate Vinayagar Chathurthi! Do a pooja, cook all the good food as per our traditions, go to their house and share it with them. You can then use that chance to connect better with Karen and her family… and even meet some others with that chance. Is this not a successful technique we have been using for ages?"

"For that to work, I should know how to cook!" Maaya laughed.

"That's not a big deal. I will cook here and ask Ilamaran to record a video and send it to you. You can cook based on that… It will come out well," my mother suggested.

Maaya relayed this news to Vidhya, who said, "Surely there will be someone in America whom our mother knows. We could seek their help, too."

For the next few days, they searched for the right people and got ready to celebrate Vinayagar Chathurthi. Vidhya put her heart and soul into the work and prepared everything for the festival. She put beautiful rangoli and decorated the apartment grandly, trying to celebrate the festival on a large scale and ignite the curiosity of the American neighbors.

It looked like everything had happened for a reason. Vidhya going there but not being able to contribute much to the office work also turned out in our favor – she could spend her time working on such things instead. As she was the most diplomatic and approachable of the group, she could easily forge connections, too.

The festival fell on a Saturday. So the three of them went to Karen's house at 11 AM. Karen was of Chinese ethnicity. So

Vidhya made Indian kozhukattai sweets like Chinese momos. She had even bought a gift of a Vinayagar statue in traditional Chinese garb. Thank heavens for Vinayagar's versatility!

They had expected Karen's family to be Chinese, too. But the person who opened the door was a white man who towered over them at nearly 7 feet tall. Confused and at a loss for words, Maaya eventually found her tongue and said, "Hello… we want to meet Karen."

"Karen is sleeping. May I know who you are?" the man asked in Tamil, apparently having already noted them speaking amongst themselves in Tamil.

On hearing him speak fluent Tamil, they were shocked and amazed.

"Hello!" The guy said, waving his hand in front of their stunned faces, still waiting for a reply.

"We were a bit confused to hear you speak in Tamil. Sorry about that. We are celebrating a festival at home today. Back in India, we have the habit of visiting friends and family and sharing sweets with them. But here, we don't know anyone other than Karen. That's why we wanted to meet her and give her sweets," Vidhya explained, holding up the attractively packed boxes with delicious-looking momos and gifts.

The man welcomed them in and invited them to sit on the couch. Maaya and Vidhya had assumed that since he wasn't of Chinese descent, then his wife would likely be Chinese. But why was the Hindu prayer hymn Suprabhatham running mellifluously in the background? They could not make head or tail of it, and their confusion was evident on their faces! Finally, an Indian woman came out of the kitchen.

Seeing her age, Maaya and Vidhya decided that this must be Karen's mother.

"Are you the girls from India working with Karen right now?" the woman asked with an affable smile.

"Yes! Are you Karen's mother?" Maaya asked.

"Of course! What's the doubt in that? Please wait. Let me bring you some coffee," the woman said and went back in.

Maaya and Vidhya looked at each other. They wondered if Karen was a child from either the white man or the Indian woman's earlier marriage and thought that to be the likeliest option now.

Then a young boy came inside. He also looked to be south Asian. Based on that, the women thought that they had assumed right. Karen's mother addressed the boy, saying, "Go inside and wake your sister."

She then handed the coffee to the visitors.

In return, Vidhya handed her the sweets she had brought. Karen had come down to the hall by that time. Initially, she looked displeased to see them there. But eventually, she warmed up and started talking.

But there was a huge issue that they now realized. Assuming that Karen did not know Tamil, Maaya and Ilango had spoken a lot about her and the project in Tamil at the office. It turned out that Karen knew Tamil very well, and had been largely ignoring their comments.

Her house also looked weird. Karen was Chinese. Her father, Steve Barmer, was a white American. Her mother, Kundhavai, was Indian. Her brother Aayan looked like an Indian too – but he could be South Asian. It did not sit right. The entire set-up looked like an international version of the Tamil movie Bharatha Vilas, which portrayed a story of communal harmony amidst people from various states and cultures of India. This was just on a continental level.

Vidhya and Maaya were wondering how to broach the subject of this odd family. Eventually, Maaya attempted, "How are all of you living under one roof? This looks like such a love story?!"

Karen, however, nipped it in the bud. "Today is a festive day. Let us speak about this some other day."

Eventually, Ilango and Steve Barmer went outside for a smoke break.

There, Steve looked at Ilango and asked, "What? Are you confused?"

"Not confused… just curious," Ilango had conceded.

"About our family?" Steve asked.

"Yeah!"

"I'll tell you. But once you hear the story, don't bring it up in front of anyone inside. All of us are trying hard to forget our past and move on. We should be able to do it and not recollect the horrors that made our life into what it is now. That's my deepest desire," he said and continued with the story.

"In one way or another, we all have lost our lives – or whatever was the reason for our lives due to acts of human depravity. I was a general in the army. My wife and child died in the 9/11 attacks. Kundavai is a rape survivor. Karen and Aayan's birth parents lost their lives in a psycho shooting that happened here.

"Ayyo! I am very sorry to hear that, Mr. Barmer. How did you all come together?" Ilango asked.

"That's destiny. We all are affected by PTSD. When we remember such incidents, it triggers intense reactions from us. We were treated in a Buddhist medical center where we all met. They took us to the mountains and woods as part of the treatment, so we could spend time with nature and learn to meditate. There, we had seven other people with us. But they all had families of their own. Only the four of us were loners. And then, we all started talking and spending time together, getting to know each other. I invited everyone to come and live with me. A monk in that center suggested that we could all heal better if we were together and sent them to live with me..." Barmer said.

"Oh! Are you all healed now?" Ilango asked.

"Not yet... We are not able to forget those memories. But we are helping each other along. We are relying on your project to succeed. This is why Karen is working with Dhivya."

"Is there no other way for this?" Ilango asked.

"They have so many names for these in medical terms. But the wounds we have are not healing at all. Tell me, how can we forget such horrific incidents? The years I spent living with my wife and my love for her... It had been only six months since my child was born. They were my world. After getting married, I did not want to take risks with being deployed again and instead requested a transfer to admin-level jobs in the military. But at last, I lost the reason for my existence… and now only I am alive. Citing this, they found me unfit even to do my job. So now I am living on the state's pension. I am telling you all this now because you should not ask Karen about this later and upset her…" Barmer said.

"I can understand. I just don't know what to say," Ilango said, feeling freshly horrified.

"Tell me this! Can your project make us forget all this? Those were horrifying times in our life. We are all suffering deeply, unable to overcome the aftereffects. Can you change all that?"

"We're mere software developers. But our medical team believes this is possible. In an earlier experiment, some of Maaya's memories were deleted. So I think this is doable," Ilango said.

While they were talking, Maaya and Vidhya came out, saying, "Shall we leave?"

Once they had walked out of the apartment complex, Maaya asked Vidhya and Ilango to return home. "I'm going to meet Dhivya. All of us need not go. I will go alone and try to talk to her," she said.

But her attempts were futile, for Dhivya spoke to her only via the phone in the security booth.

"Sorry… I am currently not in a position to meet you. Please don't mistake me," she said.

"I'll hand over the sweets to the security so that he can give them to you," Maaya said and returned home, feeling defeated.

Maaya later told me that she had seen a name board proclaiming 'Congressman Peter Taylor' in front of the house. When we googled who that was, we learned he was a former politician representing the Democratic Party in the 80s. That's how we knew that Dhivya's father was an American.

The more I learned about all this from Maaya, the more I realized that it was not enough for us to do the project work. We had to do such things to get what we wanted.

I wondered if this was the difference between working for someone else's company and managing our own business.

* * *

Chapter 33

Dhivya had sent everyone the invitation for the workshop on Monday morning. It was only then that Karen got to know about it. People from Medat Solutions, Dhiraj Systems, Biomed Pharma, and our company were on the list of participants – a grand total of 18 people.

As per the workshop agenda, the leads were Dhivya and Yadin Sharat. The place was 'San Gabriel Wilderness.'

The most important thing we noted in the invitation was that Rick's name was missing from the list of invitees. When Maya and Ilango asked about this to Karen, she said, "They both had a huge argument regarding the issue with your company's contract. Eventually, Dhivya said, 'This is my company, so it's my decision.' So Rick immediately said, 'Then please take my name off this project.' Dhivya did so immediately."

We were surprised to hear this. This gave us a lot of confidence in Dhivya. But we also wondered why Dhivya would go to such great lengths to keep us on board. When we wondered this out loud, Karen answered with, "This is America… People will keep you around if they want some work done. They will cast you away if you are not needed. Today it was Rick. Tomorrow it might be you or me.

"Besides, Dhivya is a terror. No one can speak to her daringly. Her word is the law. She would never form an emotional connection with anyone. That is the main reason why investors like her very much. She will always look at what is good for the company and take relevant action. We have very few people like you who would insist that they will not be working if one team member is missing – as you did for Ilamaran."

"What expectations does she have from us that she wants us on board?" Maya asked.

"Only Dhivya would know that. I think only two people have the full details of this project. One is Dhivya, and the other is Yadin Sharat. She put in great effort to bring him here. He did not get a work visa to work here. He has spoken about a lot of controversial topics regarding neuroscience and human privacy, apparently. He has consequently been banned from working in many countries. But Dhivya has done something out of the box to bring him here…"

"Now he is an employee of our company. Please don't tell anyone about this," Maya told her.

"What? How is this possible?" Karen asked, frowning.

Maya told her all the details. Karen heard them with wonder and said, "I love Dhivya."

"I thought you'll be upset… But you're saying this instead?!" Maya asked.

"Dhivya does not like anyone saying that something is impossible. She would somehow do it and win. Earlier, she had given Rick the job of bringing Yadin Sharat here. He could not do it. He had told Dhivya, 'We should not try to do this anymore and risk it.' But she had been stubborn and persisted and eventually got him here." Karen explained.

"Karen… We thought you'd be angry that Dhivya spoke to us directly regarding this issue instead of communicating via you. But you love and admire her for doing this," Ilango said, surprised.

"This is not the first time such a thing happened, nor will it be the last. Suppose you go and tell her that 'You cannot do this. This is impossible,' she will tell you, 'Is that so? Okay!' and leave it at that. Then she won't bother with you at all. But she will find some other way to get the job done. She's a devil. But we cannot help admiring her acumen and talents. We will always be working with her, but she could still spring in a surprise at every turn and take us to another level," Karen said, her face shining in admiration.

"Will she not have a personal connection with anyone?" Maaya asked, wondering how such a person could exist.

Karen laughed. "She probably does not even know what you guys already know about my family. And I have been with her for years."

"Could any person be like this? I am amazed to hear this," Maaya said.

"This is how she is able to achieve on a grander scale than all of us. She could have been in a much better position financially if she had been in one of the big corporates. But she has chosen this path. She is trying to achieve something huge with this company," Karen said.

"Maybe she also needs such a technology?" Ilango asked.

"No… She may want to work for the United Nations. She also has the potential to make it big in politics. I have heard that she is already attending a lot of political rallies. Her father is also a politician."

"Who knows what's written in our fates? Maybe it is destined that Dhivya should achieve greater heights than what she is currently pursuing," Ilango said.

"We should take a selfie with her soon. It would be helpful in the future," Maaya said, smiling.

"If you can pull that off, I will take you to dinner that day. Dhivya will never allow room for such things," Karen said.

Maaya laughed along, saying, "I think she has planned something big. I went to her house, but she refused to meet me and sent me back," Maya said.

"You cannot talk to her in person, even in the office. That's why she has her space on a separate floor," Karen said.

The three of them had gotten quite close to Karen's family. Vidhya was the main reason for it. She had brought that closeness by talking to Karen's mother daily.

* * *

Yadin Sharat and I traveled from Delhi to San Diego. He was flying business class while I flew economy. I had thought I would get to talk to him during the journey. But he did not even bother with any conversations.

Maaya and I could not speak properly as she spent most of her time at the office. I was hoping that being with her would give me some time with her.

When I reached San Diego, a limo was waiting for us. We went in that together. But even then, Yadin did not speak to me much. "Sorry! I must finish reading this book," he said, pointing to a book in his hand.

I did not know if he had said that to avoid talking to me or if he did want to read the book.

Once I reached the resort, I understood that Maaya and the others had not yet arrived. They flew to Los Angeles and drove to San Gabriel from there.

I went for breakfast the next morning and saw Yadin and Dhivya deep in conversation there. I sat alone at a table. But shortly, Maaya came and gently tapped me from behind, asking, "What, sir? Finally, you are here! Did America welcome you with open arms?"

Ilango and Vidhya also joined us with their plates in hand. Karen had brought Vidhya along to help with some of the admin work – and probably also to include her in the project and not leave her alone back home.

The first day of the workshop was mostly about yoga and meditation. Then they organized some team-bonding games. Finally, after 6 PM, Yadin and Dhivya addressed the gathering.

Dhivya spoke first.

"Many companies worldwide have ventured into similar projects like what we are doing here. Some countries have also banned such projects. But in such sensitive projects, the biggest question that looms is – how legally or ethically are we approaching this entire idea? How socially responsible are we when we execute this project? And let me assure you, we will take every measure to ensure everything is within the limits specified by American law and true to the people of America.

"For the last two months, I have been speaking to Mr. Yadin Sharat. He's a genius neuroscientist. He has also gotten a doctorate in the field of Artificial Intelligence. Many neuroscientists are present at this gathering. There are also people adept at emerging technologies. In addition to that, we have legal experts on our team.

"We are all going to work together and win on this. We have already done a lot of work in this regard. Hereafter, we need to start clinical testing. And we can chart out our next plans only based on the results of those trials. Medat Solutions would be helping us with clinical research. And tomorrow, Yadin Sharat will tell us what the next step in this will be," Dhivya said.

It was weirdly funny because she had used our company to bring Yadin to America, but now he was portrayed as the most important person. It looked like they had brought us on board so they would have a way to get Yadin to the US – seeing as he was otherwise restricted.

Dhivya, however, was throwing her heart and soul into the work. We became energized by merely seeing her work. While she was with Yadin, she was different – far removed from the detached woman on a pedestal that she was when she spoke with us. They both had mutual respect and admiration for each other's capabilities.

A lot of people were staying with us. As usual, we had signed an NDA, and we were all lodged in a separate location.

Maaya said this was the first time they had heard Dhivya speak in person. Maya expressed her irritation. "Why is she doing so much? Kavya has also achieved so many things. Is she not getting along with us jovially? But it is an arduous task to get a hold of Dhivya for a meeting, even!" She griped.

"I have asked her for some time to discuss our project with her. She has to allocate time for that, surely. We can speak with her then," I said.

"Looking at what Karen is saying, I think Dhivya will easily say 'no' to this," Maya said.

I could not reply to that. What she said made sense.

We went to the dinner area. Again, Yadin and Dhivya were sitting alone, talking to each other. Weirdly, Dhivya was wearing an earbud in only one ear. Yadin was holding her hand. When we settled down to dinner there, they left immediately.

Karen came along for dinner only when we were almost finished with it. That's when Maaya realized that we had come without inviting her along.

"Ayyo! Sorry, Karen. We were distracted while talking to him and just walked down to dinner," Maya apologized.

"No problem! I will go get myself some dinner," Karen said, shrugging casually.

Maya went along to give her company. I returned to my room, saying I had to get some sleep. Vidhya and Ilango set out for a walk. It had been a long day, and we were finally beginning to see a clearer picture.

***

Chapter 34

The next morning, the workshop started at 9 AM. Maaya looked beautiful in a black suit, the first time I had seen her wearing one. I was clad in a blazer and hadn't bothered with a tie. I winked at Maaya, and she winked back at me with a smile.

Our happy times in the Chennai resort were running all over my mind with the little look and that wink. I sighed - those good old days...

Dhivya was, again, wearing her earbud only in one ear. She directly asked Yadin Sharat to address the gathering.

Yadin began speaking.

"It is something we use every day. But we won't even think much about it. At best, we would speak of it when we think of exams and tests. Otherwise, we realize its importance only when we lose it, or lose something because of it. I am talking about our brain… our memories and the power of retaining and recollecting them.

"Our memory is of three types. First is genetic memory – this is what we get via generations of our ancestors. Say your eyes are like your grandfather's, or some other feature resembles someone else in your family, and so on. We'd call a few children prodigies. They would be really skilled or talented from a very young age. No one would know how they got that talent. This could all be called genetic memory. We are not going to discuss this kind of memory in this workshop as the theories around it are still being debated in the scientific communities and no direct proof to support them scientifically.

"The next is declarative memory. In this kind, we would only remember the things that happened - facts, events, and experiences. We could recollect in vivid detail the events that happened and explain them with the same attention to detail. The place where it happened, whatever we saw during that time… everything could be recollected and detailed. And when we do this, we rethink the places we had seen and how they looked. The experience we had will come to us again, and we could feel it just as vividly – inclusive of the emotions we felt at that moment. This kind of recollection could be so potent that the resultant happiness or sadness could even affect our current state of mind.

"The next is the non-declarative memory. This is related to motor skills or emotions. For example, when we are riding a bicycle, we won't know which of our many muscles and tissues we are moving to balance ourselves on it and ride it. Even if we face a strong opposing headwind, we will automatically change our position to maintain the balance. We won't be consciously aware of which muscle we are using to achieve this, though. But no matter how many such things happen, our body would automatically react as if it is used to doing such things daily. When we smell the fragrance of the earthy rain, when our mother cooks some favorite dishes at home, everyone at home feels happy for the whole day. But no one can explain how all this is happening or how it even started. Some places and things trigger particular emotions in us, and we associate the events as such.

"The part of the brain where the declarative memories land is called the hippocampus. The place where the non-declarative memories land is called the amygdala.

"When we are stressed, our brain will react differently. In a normal, stress-free state, the hippocampus works better. This means we're more aware of the details like where, how, and when things happened and can remember and recall information more easily. We will be able to observe and retain more information. And we would be able to retrieve these memories better when needed. But when we are stressed, its function reduces drastically. So when we are in shock or under pressure, we don't store the details properly, and the amygdala takes over. We would only be able to store or retrieve the emotions we had at that place or time.

"This is why those affected by PTSD react emotionally in certain places or after certain triggering events. I have just described the basic distinction between the various kinds of memories. You all have also been working on this project for some time now. So you'd have some idea about all this," he said.

I felt like I had attended some kind of boring science lecture. While I looked around, wondering what I was going to do with all these lectures, Maaya and Ilango were taking notes like studious first benchers. They were writing down with such intensity that it looked like they may ask for additional sheets! I, however, was listening to everything like a story, enjoying the tea and biscuits there like a last-bench student.

Yadin continued talking.

"Nowadays, it has become a practice to give therapy for typical mental health issues. In the future, we can use smart devices to discover the symptoms, collect the data, and identify the underlying problem. And using machine learning, their heartbeats and the sound of their blood flow, we can set it right by about ninety per cent. It also does not have a lot of risks associated with it. The programmers from Mibha Systems, who are with us now, have already worked on a prototype of this concept. The biggest challenge in this would be data privacy.

"Secondly, we are trying to edit memories here. We are trying to retain only the declarative memories and remove the non-declarative memories. Many people across the world are researching topics related to this. They have already successfully tested this on rats. The process involves resurrecting the memories, so it is in edit mode when they are at the forefront of the mind. That is when they could be changed.

"During that time, with the help of a few tablets and medicinal procedures, we can delete the emotional memories and retain only the events. By doing this, we are not changing the core of anything. We are just changing your reactions to the bad memories - and the associated fear, stress, and tension. After giving tablets, we will use the high-beam laser to control your mind and perform hypnotic therapy to edit the emotions associated with the event.

"We need volunteers for this. We need to do clinical testing on humans. In some places, researchers have tried using strong-minded people. But we have to do the testing across a wider gamut. Only then we can be confident of our results and the efficacy of this method.

"In the first option, we used technology. And in the second, we used medical methods. But this third way is a mix of both. We are going to use VR – Virtual Reality – to achieve this. With this amazing technology, we will not just delete older memories but also replace them with newer ones. We have to confuse declarative and non-declarative memories. That is, we have to stir their memories, and when they are in edit mode, we change the memory of their experiences. Using this, we can absolve their fears and shock. This is something like surgery to transplant memory.

"Currently, there are no other methods to cure PTSD, which means this could be path-breaking. This memory editing or altering concept can lead us to handle and fix extremism. And in a world that thrives on polarization, we can even bring people together because the core reason for most problems is hatred and divisiveness due to caste, creed, religion, race, language, gender, etc. These stir us up emotionally and make us react with that force. Suppose we can remove the associated emotions behind these factors. In that case, we could even reach the state of mind where we can see every human for what they are and not what they are supposed to be," he said, concluding his speech.

Even I found his speech interesting. Maaya had taken notes worthy of recreating Homer's Odyssey.

Many people in the audience were asking questions of him and Yadin Sharat was also patiently answering them.

"We have already tested all this with rats. Now we need volunteers and even better Artificial Intelligence. If we get both correctly, we can start treating mental health issues like cough and fever," he said.

I also had a question from my side.

"Our memories are the product of our experiences. Either positive or negative, they are our experiences. If we take a spiritual angle on this, one of our actions and reactions could be the result of our karma. Can we not correct this with just therapy? Should we have to go through the editing route?"

"I do not know about karma. But what you said about our life experience is true. As I said, most of these high-end treatments are not required for 90% of people. But for those people with severe cases of PTSD, who have suffered horrific incidents, we will consider their cases like we would, say, cancer and treat them accordingly. If we can remove the memories like we would do cancer cells, I think there's nothing wrong in using that," Yadin replied.

"But if this technology reaches the wrong hands, the repercussions could be disastrous. How are you going to safeguard it?" I asked.

"That's not my job. We have experts here who will take care of that. We can follow the government's rules, take their suggestions, and do as per their ideas, too," he said.

While all this was happening, Maaya suddenly fainted. We did not know what had happened. The doctors there checked her up, said her blood pressure was high and took her aside to rest.

The workshop ended that evening. The entire afternoon, we were debating about what Yadin had said.

Maaya slept in her room when the evening session happened. At around 6 PM, she came to the place where we were working. Dhivya was the first person to check her out.

"How are you? You don't have to attend today's session. You can take a rest," she said.

"No! It has been an hour since I woke up. I feel quite different. I think most of you would have heard about what happened to me in my earlier project, a portion of my memories was deleted. But now, after I had slept and woken up, I could recollect all the incidents that had happened in Chennai," she said.

While uttering the words, her eyes searched for me. I was beside her, though, and she smiled at me. Her laugh seemed to say, "You're going to get it nicely from me!"

I had never told her everything that happened there. I had just given her only a primer, intentionally letting a few details slide. How could I even imagine that she would be getting those memories back like this?

Many people there were shocked on hearing what Maaya said.

Yadin alone smiled. "This is why we have to do all this carefully. If we superficially delete the memories of everyday events, then there is a possibility that memories could rekindle when similar incidents happen again in the future.

"Maaya had attended a similar project workshop in Chennai. And those memories had been deleted from her. And now when we discuss something similar in this workshop, her old memories got triggered and rekindled again.

"We cannot delete all the memories at a stretch. What happened to Maaya is just an example. Our brain has immense power. If we are conscious of whatever is happening around us and pay proper attention to our surroundings, we can even predict our future with reasonable accuracy." Yadin said.

Then he turned to Maaya and said, "Maaya, please come and meet me this evening. We could take a few tests and see what is really happening."

Vidhya and Karen documented the discussion points and emailed the documents to us. Once everyone left, I went near Maaya and asked, "What happened? How are you now?"

"What have we done da... We've experienced so much together! I re-lived those days again... That was one hell of a week for us," she said.

Before I could ask further, Vidhya arrived.

"What is this?! You are talking weirdly!"

"This is such a terrible feeling. It is one kind of horror to forget what happened to us, but it is an entirely different kind of horror to recollect those memories. Everything looks so different and a piece of small additional information is changing our perspective completely." Maaya said.

"Now, what has changed?" I asked.

"I'll tell you, but not here! We'll talk during dinner tonight," she said.

"Maaya, Yadin asked for you. He said he'd take you to dinner after the medical tests are over," Karen said.

"What? Dinner? With me?" Maaya looked surprised, and so did the rest of us.

"I don't know! Maybe he's asking you out on a date," Karen smiled.

Vidhya turned to me and said, "Then you've escaped!"

"I'm okay with that… What do you say, Ila?" Maaya asked me teasingly.

"If you're okay with that, then I am fine with it, too. Karen… Shall we go out to dinner tonight?" I asked.

Karen laughed. "Dhivya wants to meet you for dinner."

"I think even the people here know that you are an aunty-Indian," Maaya said.

Everyone laughed.

"This is just information for you. She is not asking if you will come. So be sure you are on time," Karen said.

"This looks like such a romantic invitation," I muttered.

"While we were chit-chatting here, Ilango was talking to someone from Medat Solutions.

He came back and said, "Guys! The head of Medat Solutions, Marco, has asked me to dinner."

With a laugh, Karen looked at Vidhya and said, "Then I'm inviting you for dinner!"

"Why? What happened?" Ilango asked.

I told him about all our plans.

"This doesn't look like a coincidence. Let's catch up post-dinner to see what's all this about." Ilango said.

I looked at Maaya, who looked back at me. We were both having second thoughts about going to dinner that night.

"Why are the love birds looking at each other without answering us?" Vidhya asked.

"I have to tell you guys a few things. Some things that happened in the earlier project that we need to discuss," Maaya said.

Maaya looked at me again, but I did not know how to answer. So I just nodded reassuringly at her. 'It's okay.' I communicated with my eyes.

* * *

Chapter 35

We all went to our rooms and got ready for dinner. I thought I should talk to Dhivya about our project if I got a chance.

While I was leaving for dinner, Kavya called me unexpectedly.

"Kavya! How come you've called this early in the morning?" I asked.

"Ilamara! Today is Raj's hearing. But it is a sealed hearing. I am a bit nervous as it is not clear why they are doing this," she said.

"What do you mean by sealed hearing?" I asked.

"We won't know any details about the hearing... For example, the details about who were the witnesses, what they said in court, and on what basis the judgment was given… they will not tell us anything at all," Kavya said.

"Then how can we know what happened inside?" I asked.

"We would only know the judgment. Even Raj will not be inside during the hearing. They will get a statement from him separately," she explained.

"Is this something that usually happens, Kavya?" I asked.

"Usually, they do such things for cases related to national security issues. So I don't know why they are doing the same for this…" she said.

On hearing that, I remembered Charles saying that Subha or her family could be terrorists or Naxalites. I told the same to Kavya.

"Did he say that, exactly?" Kavya asked.

"He said it could be one of the reasons. I did not take it seriously at that time. If that was the case, there's no way Raj did not know about it. Or at least have a hint. A person could not have acted so much," I said.

"How many more things have you hidden from me now?" Kavya asked.

"Ayyo! Not like that, Kavya. I did not even deem it important, so I did not remember it or think it was relevant." I explained.

"If, for some reason, what he said was true, the court could charge Raj for conspiracy and ask him details of where the family is. I can understand why they took away even that old woman," Kavya said, sounding puzzled and worried.

"Why?" I asked.

"It's like this… if Subha was associated with any kind of terrorist organization, they would inquire everyone related to her, including the old grandmother. Or at least have them under government supervision," she explained.

"Oh! Why would Charles get involved in this if that's the case?" I asked.

"He served in the army. So when he learned the details, he could not ignore them, or it could even have been handled by a special commission formed by the government. I think even Raj's sealed hearing would be because of this."

"Ayyo! I did not know it would have such ramifications. I took it so lightly," I said.

"If such a word comes from an army man, you should never have taken it lightly. They will never indulge in loose talk," Kavya said.

I did not reply and relapsed into silence.

"What is this, Ilamara? You have collected so much valuable information but kept it all a secret within you! Do you think you are James Bond? Don't you have the sense to know if these individual events are connected?" She demanded.

"I swear this is way beyond my understanding. I found it hard even to decide if I should get involved in all this. I could not differentiate between right and wrong and truth and lies here. In between all that, I had to do the work for the project, too," I said.

"If the government had classified all the details about Subha, then that could be the reason why we could gather any details about her, and all our leads have turned into dead ends. But if you had told me the things you had known beforehand, I could have worked out some other way to find the details. We could have contacted different sources to find the truth." Kavya said.

"It just didn't strike me, Kavya," I confessed.

"The issue is you still see me as Raj's wife. You forget that I am his lawyer, too. But to you, I am just a woman. Your boss's wife. That's it, right?" She asked again, sounding disappointed with me.

"Ayyo! It's not at all like that, Kavya," I reiterated.

"No matter how many decades pass, women will never get identified based on their profession instead their gender and family relationships become relevant. If it had been a man in my place, you would have told him everything you knew and asked for his advice. But you find it somehow unpalatable to ask me!"

"Ayyo, no! You're decking up so many accusations about me! When have I thought of you that way? Have I ever given you any indication that I think of you like this? I didn't take it too seriously and let it slip to the back of my mind. Why are you talking like this now?" I asked.

"Whether or not you thought that way… your actions look that way to me. In such a sensitive case, every bit of information will be useful to me. And your withholding this crucial information could be disastrous for this hearing. It could even go against him now," she said.

I did not know what to say, so I remained silent.

"Let us first get the judgement after this hearing. Then I will see what can be done. Thanks, though, for telling me all this, at least now. You send me Joseph's phone number. I think Charles has changed his number. The one you gave earlier is not active anymore. If Joseph's number is also inactive now, we could decide that they're both partners in crime.

"Did you inquire about the judge in Madurai?" I asked.

"I spoke to him directly. He had come to the police station that day regarding some other case. He claimed that he just knew Charles as an acquaintance, nothing else."

"Does this sound believable?"

"We have to believe it. Do we have a choice?"

"Okay, Kavya… no matter how late it is here, please call me after Raj's hearing." I requested.

"I'll surely do," she promised.

* * *

Once I ended the call, I went straight to dinner. Dhivya had already arrived.

"Hello, Dhivya," I said and sat at the table.

"Welcome to America. This is just a casual meet to catch up… a chance to get to know each other." Dhivya said.

"Nice, Dhivya! It's my pleasure to have dinner with you."

"But it did not sound so… based on how you spoke that day," she laughed.

"Ayyo! Not at all! I always have a lot of respect for you. But I am new to these things. We are working our way up after a bitter experience. So we were more cautious in everything we do. And to some extent, there is a lack of trust in anyone. We were not sure who to trust and when to believe others." I explained.

"I understand. You can trust me. I will help you guys. I looked at your work. You've done a great job. Maaya and Ilango are technically quite strong," she said.

'Aha! What's this… She's called me for dinner but is singing their praises?' I wondered.

"You're a keen observer. Even your empathy is a good thing. You can become a good leader. But you are a bit naïve," she said.

Here she was, casually talking so much about us. She obviously knew her stuff and has done her research. But Maaya was lamenting that Dhivya did not even see her or talk to her!

"Naive? Why do you say that?" I asked, curious.

"No… When I insisted that you should not come to America, you were okay with sending others and didn't fight for your place, recognition, and involvement," she pointed out.

"I could have come when I got the chance and if it were so ordained. But Maaya and Ilango did not want to give up this project. So I had to see their desire, too. The purpose of this project is more important than the individuals. So looking at the big picture, my ego is way too small. But my intuition told me even back then that I would be coming soon to the US," I shrugged.

"I thought so! You look like the kind of person who faces life with the 'come what may' approach. That's good, too, in a way… your decision-making becomes easier. But once you grow, doing this way will become increasingly difficult. So you may need to consider many other factors, and you cannot breeze through life like this…" Dhivya laughed softly and ordered a starter and wine.

"How's your start-up idea coming along? Tell me off the record," she prompted.

"We have a design ready. We're yet to decide on the commercial aspects," I said.

"Tell me about your idea now. We will look at the rest of the aspects later. This is off the record."

Once she asked, I shared all the details about our project.

"It sounds good. You can improve it, of course. But many companies out there are already doing what you are saying now. So they would have taken the patents for the idea already."

"Is that so? Are you talking about the big companies like Facebook/Meta?"

"Usually, only small companies like ours will initiate it. But big companies like Facebook will buy them out when they see the potential. Then they will expand on the idea and market it to the wider public as theirs," Dhivya said.

"So, are we late to the game?" I asked.

"No… I believe we can merge this idea with that of the third project that Yadin spoke about earlier. But if we get the details of the patents around it, we can work out a better idea. What we usually call Digital Assets, you called it a Digital World. This is the future. Now is a good time to invest in such concepts… Please share the details with us. We have people here who can prepare the presentation. We can use them for this. Once we go to San Francisco, we can meet the investors there," she suggested.

"Wow! If you're okay with this, it's a win for us, too," I said.

"Ilamaran! You're a young team. It will help if you need a mentor. You don't have big investors, either. So you lack clarity in your ideas and are trying to shift between ideas with no goal. I even found it difficult when I came to this company from a big workplace like Google. Now, I am going to present you with a proposal," she said.

I did not reply but was listening to her intently.

"We have an idea to expand our company in India. Yadin has agreed to manage a branch of our company in Israel. And we will merge with Medat Solutions in San Diego. Medat Solutions' head, Marco, is a Mexican. So he is going to start a branch there. I will take care of the San Diego and San Francisco offices from here. We have a few other ideas as you just told me. We've got money here in America. Israel has innovation and ideas. India has the resources. And many things that are difficult to do in these countries can be done in Mexico. This is a good combination for everyone involved. I think it would be better if you were our Indian partners," she said.

"Sorry, I do not know how to beat around the bush. Is this a partnership or a takeover?" I asked, holding her gaze.

"Why are you asking like that?" She asked sharply.

"No... It seems somehow pre-planned that Maaya and Ilango are also having dinner now with Yadin and Marco. And I am here. This does not look like any coincidence," I said.

"Oh! This is definitely not a coincidence," she said, laughing. "If our four companies have to work together, we must get to know each other at least a little bit – and align our visions, core principles, and ideas. The other two companies have been working together with us for the last couple of years. So we have some understanding. You are the new company for us. I knew a bit about you. But they do not, right? So...!" Dhivya explained.

"Hmmm... So why am I the one here?" I asked.

"That was just decided randomly. Yadin wanted to check Maaya up after she fainted today, so she has gone there, but that's about it."

"Sorry! I do not know how to beat around the bush, and I am a straight shooter. So don't mistake me if my questions sounded abrupt," I said.

"It's your age and inexperience," she said lightly. "No problem!"

"Okay. I will speak with Maaya and Ilango about this and let you know. I cannot decide anything by myself... Besides, Raj's hearing is happening in India now. If he comes out, he will also be working with us. So I will see how all this goes first and then let you know," I said.

"Surely you must discuss first, and then let me know," she said and muttered, "One minute!" before walking out.

She wore her earbud even as she walked out. Half an hour had gone by before she returned. And in the meanwhile, her dress had changed, and her face looked dull, even with her makeup obviously having been retouched.

"What happened, Dhivya? Is everything okay?" I asked.

"Everything's fine, of course! Unfortunately, my dress became wet while washing my hands, so I had to change it!" She said.

"I had wondered if you changed dresses often like a movie star," I said.

She laughed at that. She asked questions about our families and listened carefully. I asked about her. She said she was a huge fan of AR Rahman. And she said that she had been an atheist initially but not anymore.

"How did that change?" I asked, feeling curious.

"When we meet certain people in life, the happiness or sadness we get from them will transform us almost alchemically. In our twenties, we will question everything that happens to us or around us. But when we near forty, our beliefs will get a firmer base and root deeper in us. This is like that, too," she said.

I processed what she said and realized something.

"I have a cousin… She's now in Mumbai. She'd also speak a lot like you. When I saw your interviews online, I thought you'll be talking in American slang completely and was sure you won't speak Tamil properly. But you are nothing like that," I said.

She laughed softly for that, too, saying, "Come, let's go!"

After leaving the place, Maaya called me and asked me to come to her room even as I was walking to my room. So I went there directly.

* * *

Chapter 36

The five of us were in Maaya's room. Yes, nowadays, Karen had also taken to spending most of her time with us. When I entered, Karen was crying. I could not make head or tail of it.

Ilango gestured at me to keep quiet. I nodded and remained silent, trying to get a feel of the situation.

"Let me step out and get some air," Karen said, walking out. Vidhya and Maaya went along with her.

"What happened, da?" I asked Ilango once they left.

He then told me everything Steve Barmer had told him that day when he had been to Karen's house.

"When she heard about the shooting in New York today, Karen started crying and going into convulsive fits. Vidhya was the one who noticed her and calmed her down. She then brought Karen to her room to help her recover. The entire family has been affected by PTSD, da. Yadin was referring to patients like them in his speech at the workshop. I used to think this was a rarity. But it turns out millions of people are living amidst us with such ailments. We already know four people, after all, in our limited circle!" Ilango said.

"This is horrible! As Yadin said, we do underestimate the value of our memories!"

"There's more... Apparently, it's been eighteen years since Karen's mother, Kundavai, slept properly. She cannot even be in the dark... as in, not even at night for sleep. She could be normal only when some hymns or devotional songs are running in the background. She has even stopped coming out anywhere because of this reason. She shared this story with Vidhya and cried one day. When she was younger, some people kidnapped and gang-raped her, forcibly holding her for twenty days. She still has those nightmarish flashbacks and stress-induced responses to them,... hence the inability to be in the dark," Ilango said.

"Was all this in India or here?" I asked.

"Here, I think. I did not ask for these details... I mean, how could we pry into such a sensitive issue? Also, it does not end there. You know Karen's brother Aayan, right? His family had escaped Syria and come to Canada as refugees. Once their situation had become normal, his parents moved to the US to find better jobs. But a psycho here had shot both his parents, raging at them and demanding to know what foreigners were doing in America. Karen's and Aayan's parents had died on the same day in the same psycho-shooting incident... they're Chinese and Syrian immigrants, right?" he said.

"Ayyo! What horror is this? I cannot even think about it. My head is reeling. Our lives are surely a great blessing," I said.

"Correct! And now all of them are living as a family. Imagine what stories they have in their past. We should learn about survival and positivity just by seeing them," Ilango said.

The three girls came back in.

"Sorry, guys! This is why I never develop a friendship with anyone. I would just shuttle between home and work and keep to myself," Karen said.

"Karen... now you are also one of us. We are not just friends. We are your family," Ilango said.

Vidhya and Maaya fixed drinks for everyone and brought them out.

"How did your dinner go? Yadin mentioned something about tests... What happened?" I asked Maaya.

"Many of his questions were about the Russian company's setup. I told him what I knew. And he said, 'Very interesting! They have erased memories based on a particular time and date. They have done it quite carefully and using a very advanced technique. But if we were to get the government's approval for this, we must first complete what we are doing now. They went directly to university levels without attending kindergarten classes. But if all that is possible, what I am saying is possible, too'."

"It would be good if all this happens," Karen said.

Ilango, who had been listening intently, shrugged with a smile and added, "We did not speak about work in our meeting. We were discussing soccer and cars. Apparently, he is a huge fan of Elon Musk. He was speaking a lot about the tycoon."

"Now, you say… how did your meeting with Dhivya go?" Maaya asked.

I laughed. "In that regard, I guess I have to say a lot!"

And then, I explained Dhivya's proposal, her reaction to our project idea, and everything else that happened.

"Then… None of your dinner plans was a coincidence. The others had called you only to get to know you," I said, adding, "Dhivya spoke very sweetly."

"Did she speak all this after saying it was 'off the record'?" Karen asked.

"Yeah!"

"Then, tomorrow, you will know how she is. I have heard that she is very sweet when speaking off the record. But until now, she has never spoken to me like that. You're a bit lucky, I guess!" she said.

"Is that so? Let us see how this goes!" I said.

Then I told them about the call from Kavya. "Raj's hearing should have gotten over by now. I don't know why Kavya has not called me yet," I said.

I noticed Maaya's face changing when I spoke about Kavya. But she did not express her thoughts and instead asked, "What kind of a tale is this? Kavya was speaking positively, right?"

"She scolded me. She told me that accidentally omitting such important information would not help Raj. But she was mostly calm. I don't know how she manages to be so level-headed even amidst so many problems," I said.

We were talking about this and drinking well into the night. Then the five of us slept over at Maaya's place itself. I woke up quite early, at 6 AM, but Maaya had woken up before me. She was writing something in her diary.

"What are you writing?" I asked.

"Shall we go out for a coffee?" She asked in return, sidestepping my question.

We headed out to get some coffee. She walked while holding my hand very tightly.

"What's with the new habit?" I asked.

"I just felt like it… Why did you not tell me everything that happened in the resort? It had been such a beautiful experience. We have lived like a married couple. But you have omitted all that, da…" Maaya said, sighing.

"No… I was shocked beyond belief when you said you had forgotten all that. Then I lost my last breath when you told me that you had been acting to me throughout. While we were together in the resort, it did not look like acting. So I believed you completely. I thought that if my love were true, we would get back together again. I also believed that telling you everything that happened may seem like forcing you to love me. If what I felt in those days were true, then merely having your memories erased won't stop you from loving me. So I trusted my love and believed it would happen again. And so it did, too," I said, shrugging.

"I would have enjoyed it better if I had heard it all from you," she said.

"If I had told you all this myself, you could probably have understood. But you would not have been able to feel it. How could I have even predicted that you would get your memories back one day?" I asked.

She laughed and complained, "Had you known this, you would not have enacted the types of kisses scene again! You are a one-trick pony. To be honest, that day, I somehow felt like I had heard all that before. But you never did give me time to think."

"Cha! I missed the raw kiss this morning," I said.

"You'll never get it, lifelong," she swore, blushing.

While we were strolling along, Dhivya came walking toward us. Maaya tried to move away and take her hand out of mine. But I held her hand firmly in mine.

Dhivya wished us a good morning and walked away.

"Why are you doing this, da? Even if she had wanted to talk to us, she would not interrupt us when we were like this," she said.

"Exactly. I did that because she should not interrupt us. I am never getting any time to speak to you alone."

"You're planning all this correctly now! But when we are alone at home, you will call Ilango," she said.

"Oh, man! Again! Will you never let me forget that?!"

"I was in a great mood that day. But when you called him and spoke about the project. I wanted to break up with you. And that shameless fellow came to your house at midnight to discuss work! IDIOT!" She scolded him, too.

"Why are you scolding the poor guy?" I asked.

"Okay, leave that. What answer are you going to give Dhivya?" She asked.

"Why are you asking me that?" I asked.

"She likes only you. That's why she has called you personally and given you this responsibility," Maaya pointed out.

"It is more like handing the master keys of the house's treasury to the thief, asking him to take care of the wealth behind the doors. She has brought the business proposal directly to the guy who will create issues. Her logic is that if she puts it in my hands, I will not create any problems," I said.

"Oh, yes! You're the one who usually messes things up. So she has called and spoken to you sweetly, making sure you will accept," she agreed.

Even as we were talking, Ilango, Vidhya, and Karen came.

"Hey, love birds… You left us behind!" Vidhya commented.

"Come, join us! We were talking about Dhivya's proposal," Maaya said.

"What do you think?" Ilango asked.

"I am wondering how it would work out once Raj comes out. Otherwise, I feel there's no problem with this," I said.

"There shouldn't be any problems with that, too. Medat Solutions knows Raj quite well. Raj was telling Keshav even back then that we could ask them for help with the testing for that project. I feel Dhivya has called us only on Marco's recommendation," Maaya said.

"How do you know that?" Ilango asked.

"I remembered only yesterday. This was something that Raj was suggesting in a meeting in Chennai," Maaya said.

"Are you saying Raj already knows Marco?" I asked.

"I have heard the name before, and I am 90% sure it came from Raj. I think it is Marco who is overseeing the operations here, So yeah, there are chances that they know each other," Maaya said.

"I don't have a problem with this. Right now, it is good for us to work with them. We are anyway going to manage our company separately. But we would have the guidance of people like Dhivya, Yadin, Raj, and Kavya..." Ilango said.

Right then, Kavya called me.

"The hearing went on for six hours today. They are holding the judgment for tomorrow," she informed me.

"What really happened there?" I asked.

"We'll never know it until the end. The supreme powers and the God that Raj believes will have to save him," she sighed.

"You are his strength, Kavya. Everything will turn out well. Once you get the judgment, please call me even if it is midnight for me here. We are all waiting for the good news," I said fervently.

* * *

Chapter 37

Before the workshop began that day, Dhivya called and asked me about our decision.

"We're in-principle fine with this, but we have one condition. When Raj is released from prison, he will lead our company. I hope you don't have any problems with that. Please let me know now if you have any."

"That shouldn't be a problem," she said automatically. But I could sense that she was saying this without much conviction. Her face immediately changed, but I could not gauge her thoughts. I felt that she didn't have any great opinion of Raj. She might have thought that the court cases against him and his jail term might affect the company's reputation. I wondered if she did not want to discuss the matter further at this time and believed that they could make their own decision when the time came.

Now, there are a lot of start-ups in India. So Raj, with his experience, may not require help from the likes of Dhivya. But that's not the case with us. So I felt I should inform Kavya to take care of this. After speaking to me, Dhivya walked up to Yadin and Marco and said something. After that, she was missing for a while later. When she came back, her outfit was changed again. This weird habit of a person changing her outfits at least 4–5 times a day is something I had not even seen in the movies.

Dhivya inaugurated the day's workshop proceedings, as usual.

"I have an announcement for you all. This is going to be a milestone for the mental health industry and will help us achieve our dreams. We are all representing different companies and trying to work together to achieve something big here. If we all come under a common banner then we can make this an even bigger company and be a noticeable force with a wider global presence.

"In the US, our company will operate in San Diego and San Francisco. We plan to start our branches in Chennai, Mexico, and Israel. The head office will be in San Francisco. The facilities in San Diego and Israel will be our research centres and the ones in Mexico, and San Diego will be for our clinical testing. Chennai and San Francisco would be the software development centres.

"Dhiraj Systems, Medat Solutions, and Mibha Systems would come together, and our conglomerate would be named 'Cut Copy Paste,'" she said.

'Oh hell! They were referring to editing and deleting people's memories, and simply naming it as 'Cut-Copy-Paste.' What an innocuous, almost playful name for something so serious! Hey, wisecracks… This is about the human brain! But you guys are treating it with such a light-hearted approach!' I was thinking. It was probably good that no one could hear my mind voice – or I would have been in trouble.

"Now we're going to run this project from San Diego. We can do the clinical testing at the offices of Medat Solutions. We have a place there where we could also develop the software. Tonight, we should all go to San Diego from here. I have already spoken individually to the people here. A few people have expressed their wish to return to San Francisco and join us in San Diego.

"For the next three-four months, forget your families and other social obligations and commitments. This is a very important project. If we finish this properly, our company could reach much greater heights. Our Mibha Systems have proposed a new project idea, and we have a few more similar projects already in the pipeline. If we deliver this project to our investors, they would be interested in investing in our future projects too.

"As long as we have good people with us, we can achieve great success. I have poured my blood and sweat into putting this team together. And now I want all of you to help us take this project forward," she said.

Yadin stood up and said, "Dhivya took four months to convince me to join her on this journey. But when she spoke to me for the first time, she knew we would reach here. Dhivya, you are a great visionary!"

Then Marco spoke. "I know Dhivya from her Google days. Her clarity has always amazed us many times. She may change her outfits often, but I have never seen her change her decision once she makes it. She has worked and planned a lot to bring us together here."

Karen was talking to us quietly. "When we brought you here, I was speaking to Dhivya daily. But she never even mentioned all this. Did you see her foresightedness? She never forced you to come here, but instead brought you here to her company of your own volition."

"Even when she spoke to me yesterday, she did not talk about rebranding at all," I said.

Dhivya thanked Yadin and Marco. Then said, "Let us see what we should do next. We are going to split into three teams for this project. We have named the teams based on the limbic structure of the brain.

Thalamus – Marco will lead this team, and Ilango and Karen are going to help him.

Next is the Amygdala – Yadin would lead this.

Then we have the Hippocampus – I will lead this, and Maaya will help me.

And in addition, we will start a new project called 'Project Digital Fantasy.' Rick will lead this, and Ilamaran and Vidhya will work on this. Vidhya is an amazing artist. She will be quite an asset to this project," she said.

'Oh hell! Where did this Rick come from now? I hated the mere sight of him. Why had Dhivya put me with him in a team?' I wondered.

Maaya looked at my face and laughed softly. Ilango sent a message to our WhatsApp group, saying, 'You're done for.'

"Did you see that?! Dhivya never thinks emotionally. She fought with Rick that day about bringing you to the US. I was in the room when they argued. But knowing that Rick would be the right person for this project, she brought him on board. This is Dhivya's nature," Karen said.

'But why me? Can't she find someone else to appease him?' I thought to myself.

Karen was saying, "This is American culture."

"What bloody culture was this! I don't get it." I muttered, walking out to get coffee. Dhivya was there, too.

"What, Ilamaran?! You don't look happy at all?!" She asked.

"It's nothing! Rick does not like us much. I don't know how I am going to work with him," I said.

"Now you are working with us. If you can convince Rick, then this will work with investors too. You are not in college to only team up with the people you know and like… you have to work with everyone, especially those who might disagree with you. If this project is your dream, you have to convince Rick and take it to the next level," she said.

And without even waiting for my reply, she turned and walked away.

Karen, who had noticed this, came to me and said, "Ilamaran! Don't you understand even now? Dhivya is mentoring you. I have never seen her talking like this to anyone. It is always a mentor who chooses us and not the other way around."

I didn't understand. "What did I do for her to consider mentoring me?" I asked, confused.

"Only then you won't fight with her. That could be a reason!" Ilango chimed in, coming to see what we were discussing.

"Oh no, nothing like that! Dhivya has seen something in you. That's why she is taking extra efforts to mentor you… you should use it well," Karen insisted.

Even as I was hearing positive things, I was still wondering whether to enjoy this moment.

After lunch, we returned to the workshop. They had the San Diego plan ready. There was a huge bungalow in the city. We were all going to work together there. About four other people would also stay with me. Vidhya and I would be in one office. Maaya will be in a separate office with Dhivya, while Ilango and Karen will be in another office. They had a bus ready for us to go from here, and we boarded it.

San Diego is a city on the American-Mexico border. It was usually sunny, with many beaches, and housed America's navy base.

Maaya was sitting beside me on the bus. "Shall we get married?" she asked suddenly.

"Hey! Can't you wait till we get off the bus?" I joked.

"Haha… what a wonderful joke! I would first have to enquire if there's some option to delete such stupid jokes from your brain," she said.

I laughed too. "Then what will you do for timepass?" I demanded.

"Dei! Just stop goofing around and tell me!"

"What's the hurry now? Let's be like this for a few more days. Then, when we get bored of this life, we can get married," I said.

"Why? What's wrong with doing it now?" she asked.

"Let us finish this project first and then see. If we get married now, we will get stuck with work almost immediately. We won't even get time together as a newly married couple. So let us take some time and do it properly. I want to go on a honeymoon for a year with you," I said.

"Look at that! You have so many plans!" she said.

"You know how I am, right? So let us wait," I said.

I had successfully diverted the conversation. I did not like these new changes in Maaya at all. I hoped that she would return to her former self and find fulfillment in her career again without getting over-reliant on me. Even if we were to get married, I believed that it was crucial for us to maintain our individuality and lead separate wholesome, fulfilling lives. However, I was unsure how to express my thoughts to Maaya without offending her, so I resolved to choose my words carefully and not speak impulsively.

We eventually reached San Diego. The house was huge – an 8-bedroom bungalow.

Dhivya and Yadin were also on the same street, in their respective individual bungalows.

Marco had gone to Mexico, and he would be working from there. We had about 3–4 people who were yet to arrive and who will be staying with us.

* * *

Chapter 38

Kavya had texted me at one in the night. I called her immediately.

"Raj's hearing is over. They called me today to take my statement as well. The government also gave its side of the story in a sealed letter during the hearing. Raj got sentenced to four years in jail for causing threats to data security and national integrity and illegally collecting people's private data without their consent. They refused to accept his story about Subha. We can appeal after two years of prison term based on his behavior and health reasons. There is a possibility that he could be released earlier than the full four years..." She informed me.

"Sorry, Kavya. None of us could be with you at this time," I said.

"No, Ilamara! You've all been a huge support for me. This is something I expected, anyway. But I still nursed a small wish, hoping against hope, that I could somehow get him out of jail. I knew we would end up here when Keshav Patel was transferred," she said heavily.

"What happened to Sathyan and Suja?" I asked.

"Their sentence is also the same four years. Sathyan alone is forbidden from traveling overseas hereafter as he didn't plead guilty and defended his action. He must serve the full sentence while Suja and Raj can appeal for an early release." Kavya said.

"Is he mad? Why is he behaving like this?" I demanded.

"Let him do whatever he wants to! You go and sleep. We can speak tomorrow morning if you have the time. I am going to Chennai tomorrow. Inform Maaya too, and tell her that I will speak to her later. Revathi Periyasamy has said she will meet you guys in America."

I told Kavya everything that happened in America.

"Why did you agree immediately? It would have been useful if you had stayed as a partner for some more time before merging," she said.

"We could not talk to you when it was happening. And we did not want to trouble you with this, seeing as you had a lot of other things on your plate, too," I explained.

"That's okay! If we decide to come out of it, we can find a way out later. Get the terms from them and send the documents to me. I will go over them and let you know," she requested.

Maaya felt quite bad about Raj's prison term.

"Four years seems quite less! They should have been sentenced to life," Ilango said heatedly. He was still angry about Suja.

"They did not allow these people to go to Russia. If Sathyan had gone, he would have known the girls' true nature there," Vidhya commented.

Each of us there felt and expressed different emotions.

* * *

Our office was about two kilometers away from where we were staying. There were 4–5 bars right under the office floors. And there were also many other eateries. There were a lot of Mexican food outlets. So when we first went there, we looked at all the options and got excited.

But Dhivya was a real beast in the office. The targets that she set for us were really tough. 'Tough is an understatement here'. Maaya and Ilango had the most challenging tasks, with 13- to 15-hour work days. They were working on the weekends too. The work we would do in Chennai with ten people for six months was done by four people in one month here. While Maaya was my team leader in Chennai, I would call her a stern taskmaster. But here, even Maaya could not stop lamenting about Dhivya.

I told Rick about my project. First, he gave me the details of all the other companies doing similar projects. Then he said, "These people are doing something similar, so please check out the competition and similarities and fine-tune your idea."

I changed the ideas 4–5 times and took them to Rick repeatedly. But he did not even bother discussing those with me in detail. Instead, he kept coming up with many reasons to reject them every single time.

Dhivya did not even come anywhere near us. She would probably get involved only when we convince Rick. Dhivya had told me that she could connect their project to my idea. But Rick would blow a fuse if I brought that other project up and would reject my ideas with more force.

Only Ilango's project was going well. They had finished development and had started clinical testing. Their algorithm worked well, too. Soon they were ready to collect live data from real people and perform their testing. He told me that with the current speed, they could launch it in four months – which was remarkably soon.

In such a busy work life, six months passed like six days. We forgot what it is to have a life outside work. The people of San Diego were quite chill and happy. In a place full of parties and beaches, we were slaving at work instead. For our office version of summer barbecues, Dhivya seemed to be roasting us on her grill.

In between all this, Yadin alone went back and forth between Israel and the US about three times. Karen traveled to San Francisco often. Marco was still in Mexico. They were talking about starting the Mexican operations by next month.

If ever we asked for vacations, Dhivya apparently hit back with, "It has been seven years since I last went on a vacation. So why do you need a holiday so soon?"

I was constantly getting such updates from Maaya and Ilango, for I still had not spoken to Dhivya after the announcement.

Vidhya and I did a lot of designs for our Project Digital Fantasy – including the sets that resembled Disney movies and Indian movies like Bahubali. But nothing worked out.

"We could do designs like heaven and hell," Vidhya suggested one day.

"No! That Rick is thinking something else, but he is not telling us what it is and is trying to frustrate us into quitting… Or worse, presenting a substandard idea," I said.

"So we should first develop a technology to know what is in his brain. Then, likewise, we should also learn how these sadistic people think and devise an idea to make it work," Vidhya snapped in anger.

"Hey! This concept sounds good! Dhivya had already told something about combining this with Yadin's third project. How about this idea?" I asked, excited already."

"What idea?"

"Imagine if we could analyze the brain patterns of the world's greatest geniuses and store them as NFTs in humanoid robots that people could invest in. And whenever a major event happens in the world, we could create a digital version of it and feed it to the robots to see how their brain patterns analyze and respond to the situation. It's like we're using their genius brains to simulate how they would have tackled today's challenges if they were still alive! We'd use the brain patterns of experts in their respective fields and feed them real-time data to see how they would respond in the current situation. We could offer royalties to the descendants of the person whose brain patterns we use for this purpose," I suggested.

"Give me an example. I seem to get this, but I'm not sure," Vidhya said, suddenly giggly.

"See! We are doing this memory edit/delete thing already, right? So in this project, we are doing a reverse of it, kind of. Imagine if we could get our hands on the brain thought patterns of great leaders like Gandhi or Steve Jobs and store them digitally in humanoid robots. This would enable us to bring them back to life, in a sense, and seek their insights on current issues that we face today. Then, if we feed the information to the robots, they could analyze and respond to it, giving us an opinion based on the thought process of who they embody. It would be like having the person themselves in the room with us." I explained.

"This is too much," Vidhya said.

"This is just an idea. We may need to do a lot more research on this. It will take years. But for now, we should patent this. And then we could ask for investments to conduct more research. At least we will know how these people process things and think," I said.

"But if we see whatever they are saying… I feel as if anything is possible. Tell me one thing, though… Since the Gandhian times, for instance, a lot has changed. And the world is not the same. In fact, it has been evolving at a faster rate nowadays. What was relevant even ten years ago is obsolete now. All these changes have come through over the years because of a lot of events that happened since his days. Lots of technological changes have happened in the last couple of decades, and this information will be missing in Gandhi's NFT of his time. So how will it be relevant to obtain his opinion when his brain is not equipped to handle recent developments? Imagine teaching the Gandhian brain to handle mobile phones and the internet?" Vidhya asked.

"Good point. But we have to do it this way. We can only start with people in the current generation and not the past generation, anyway. Because we have to collect the brain patterns of those people and it is only possible if they are alive. I took Gandhi and Jobs as examples to show that if we had been able to do that, they could now be useful for us in this way. Once the brain patterns are recorded and stored, when they die, we will transfer that to a robot. Then we have to continuously feed it information about the world's current affairs and keep it up to date. Then we can determine how they would react to the current situations based on our past data."

"Sometimes, we may not fully understand why we act the way we do. Our personalities are shaped by the experiences we've been through, and most of the time, these are subconsciously formed. However, suppose we keep track of these changes and use behavioral analysis to study the data, we can figure out exactly how and why we respond in a certain way. This could even help us gain a better understanding of ourselves. We could also use this to see how our parents and elders make important family decisions and ensure we follow our family ethos and values." I said.

"Dei! This is a wonderful idea. We should prepare the proposal for this and send it across. If Rick rejects this, we will go straight to Dhivya, inform her about the same, and tell her that we have had enough with Rick," Vidhya said.

Immediately, we started to prepare the project proposal idea and sent it to Rick. Minutes after receiving the mail, Rick called us directly. We knew right then that this would work out.

He commented on our good presentation and said, "Only now have we got something exciting. I will talk to Dhivya and let you know."

Wondering why he had to talk to her about my plan, I sent an email directly to Dhivya.

Throughout the mail chain, Dhivya could see how many variations to the idea we had proposed that were rejected by Rick without proper reasons. Dhivya did not reply to me directly. She had once responded to Vidhya appreciating her artwork, though. I was flummoxed, wondering how aloof a person could be.

Rick did not answer me either, for a long while. So I mailed Dhivya again but did not get an answer.

Like the silt that had settled undisturbed at the bottom of a silent pond, there was no response of any kind for a long while. So I again started getting a lot of doubts. Dhivya may have brought me to the US only to bring Yadin here. And that was why she had cornered me by pushing me into a team under Rick, someone I was not comfortable working with. Maybe Vidhya was getting praised because she was unnecessarily dragged into this, and Dhivya felt sorry for her.

My thoughts kept spiraling in all directions.

Maaya was working with Dhivya daily, but she said that Dhivya would bite her head off if she even mumbled one extra word than what was strictly necessary.

"She will not let us think on our own. She just wants us to follow her orders without any deviation. So there is no room to improvise and do stuff on our own," Maaya was lamenting.

"This is just a mid-life crisis," Ilango said.

"What's that?" Maaya demanded.

"She's not married yet, so maybe she feels lonely… She is always at the office. That's why she is not allowing anyone else to have a life!" Ilango said.

"That Rick is like this, too. Maybe we should get them both married," I muttered.

"We made a great mistake. Big or small, we were working at our convenience. But now we are merely slaves for them… Marco, Yadin, and Dhivya are making all the decisions. And Rick has only ever rejected your projects so far," Maaya said.

"Ayyo! Why are all of you lamenting like this? You still have time. Once you finish this project, take this experience back to India, and you will get many more wonderful opportunities," Karen said bracingly.

She brought us a bottle of wine. We were drinking and talking until three in the night.

Finally, after two weeks, Rick mailed us.

'Are there any improvements?' He had asked.

I did not know what he was asking about.

'We're expecting an answer from you. You had last said you would speak to Dhivya and let us know,' I said, adding it to the mail he had sent and sending it back to him.

I also forwarded that mail to Dhivya.

Dhivya then asked Rick what the status was. In response, he had said, 'The theme will be ready in a week.'

But because Dhivya already had the mail I had sent earlier, she understood that Rick was unnecessarily holding something back. She then wrote a mail to us, asking us to work with her directly.

For the next month or so, we worked together with Dhivya and Yadin, whom she had appointed as the research head for this project. She decided that building such a concept be more feasible in Israel.

While working closely with her, I finally understood what the others were saying about Dhivya. She was pretty detail-oriented. Everything had to be perfect and to her exacting standards. She will never approve of anything easily. On one side, she will speak to Vidhya about her drawings – that's when I realized Dhivya herself was an excellent artist – and give her detailed comments on every fine aspect.

On another side, she will be speaking with Yadin about neuroscience. And then, she would talk to me about machine learning and robotics. I noticed that overall, Dhivya was knowledgeable enough to carry on conversations with industry experts in all aspects. She was also adept at presenting the concepts to investors in a way that could impress them. She was an all-rounder and was nothing short of a superwoman in the office. She slept only for five hours daily and worked for the rest of the day.

She would be with us all day but never speak anything personally. She was always focused on work. She really was the beast at work.

If there were one person to whom she spoke a bit docilely, mindful of his time and availability, it would be Yadin. Sometimes she would barrel through conversations even with the investors.

I could only laugh now when I realized that I had argued with such a person. It seemed almost childish now, seeing the other people she worked with on a regular basis and the conversations she had about really impactful, expensive projects with people in high positions of power.

I had spoken to her like she was a local team manager at a small organisation. But she had never kept that in mind or pushed me away… she had always had me around for the project. She had seen, even back then, what all of us had been blind to – that this project could work only with all of us on board, for we each added a different kind of value to this. This is also one of her strengths.

I understood that Dhivya never took anything personally and just managed the team wonderfully, retaining the people who were needed to work on the project and make her vision succeed. Only the end goal existed – and she just carved her path to it.

* * *

Chapter 39

"It has been nearly a year since we came to America. We haven't taken even a day off from work, and we've never had a chance to explore the vibrant city. None of us dared to approach Dhivya and talk about this. Back in India, my mom started asking when we'd return home. However, here they kept changing our visa status to ensure that we were continuously working in America. We would all be working here until the clinical testing was done and they obtained government approval.

First, we had to obtain approval from the investors and then submit it for FDA approval. Everything else could only be done after that. So we approached them multiple times and provided all the requested details, but they kept rejecting our proposals.

After much struggle, Dhivya and Yadin gained approval from the investors. Initially, they approved 100 million dollars, promising more after seeing our progress.

The Food and Drug Administration department rejected our proposals, stating that the testing we had done so far was insufficient. However, Dhivya felt that they didn't believe there was a need for this and were therefore rejecting it. We worked on this for about three months.

"To secure approval here, we need something emotionally overpowering to help them understand the importance of this. Just science and technology are not enough," Yadin said one evening.

We talked to the Buddhist Medical Centre, and they recorded the stories of a few volunteers and gave them to us. Karen and Steve shared their stories. They had even volunteered to come and speak in person if needed.

"For now, that won't be necessary," Yadin said.

"If you don't mind, may I suggest something?" Ilango asked.

We all turned to look at him.

"There are many important details in the videos we recorded... However, this isn't as emotionally overpowering as Yadin suggested earlier," he said."

"We're not making a movie here, developing this as a script," Dhivya countered.

"No! I've watched many TED Talks videos, and the ones that impacted me the most were those of rape survivors and individuals who've suffered sexual abuse. So if we could obtain even a couple of such videos, the impact would be much greater," he explained.

"This is utterly senseless. We can't ask a woman to relive such horrible experiences just to gain approval from a group of individuals. If that's the case, I don't need the damn approval at all," Dhivya said, getting up and attempting to leave the room in a sudden burst of emotion.

"Dhivya! Please wait a moment. What he's saying is correct," Yadin said.

Dhivya didn't respond, but she stood at the door, staring warily at us.

Immediately, Maaya chimed in. "Should we reach out to the people who shared their experiences with us earlier? They've already spoken about it, so if they were to share more personal details..."

"No! If the media finds out about all of this before we receive approval, it'll attract unnecessary attention," Dhivya argued.

"So should we approach the Buddhist Medical Centre then?" Vidhya suggested.

"When did you all become so heartless? Don't you feel uneasy about asking rape victims to discuss this? Put yourselves in their shoes and imagine the trauma they'll face. Don't be so self-centered, and don't get too absorbed in this. We'll find another way to solve this issue," Dhivya yelled and stormed out in anger.

Yadin asked us to stay where we were and followed her out.

I looked at Karen and asked, "Can you step out for a minute? I'd like to talk to you."

Maaya stared at me and shook her head warningly, signaling me not to proceed. Ilango and Vidhya facepalmed, already aware of what I was thinking. But Karen did follow me outside. Once I was out of earshot from the others, I wondered how to approach the topic with her. Yadin returned to our room, but Dhivya hadn't come back yet.

Karen looked at me and said, "I know what you're going to ask. But that won't happen! My mom can't do all of this! Please don't expect more from us."

"This is a great opportunity to help your mom overcome PTSD. If she talks about it once, she might not have to relive it again. We could facilitate that. Please consider it," I said.

"No! This isn't about that. There's an agreement that she shouldn't talk about any of this. She could face problems if she opens up," Karen said.

"Who would require an agreement for this?" I asked, confused.

"I don't want to discuss this further... my mother won't discuss it either. So please understand," she said and went back inside.

Yadin asked us to step outside and requested that only Karen remain inside. As we were exiting, Dhivya entered the room again.

Maaya looked at me and exclaimed, "Don't you have any sense? Have you sacrificed your empathy for the sake of success now? Until now, you've been the one adamantly against all of this, advocating against erasing memories and altering human experiences... where has all of that gone now?"

"What did I do wrong now? In any case, we're planning to do this during the treatment, right?" I asked.

"You're asking a daughter to approach her mother and say, 'Tell everyone how you were raped. We're going to erase your memories and test our project on you. So you need to assist us?'" Maaya seethed with anger."

"This is what we were planning to ask the other volunteers, right? How are those people any different from Karen's mom?" I demanded.

"Idiot! Karen is already a volunteer for this! She's contributed so much already. And wouldn't she have agreed to this if she were comfortable? So, if she's not doing it on her own, can't you understand that she doesn't like this?" Maaya yelled at me.

"It's not easy for anyone to talk about these things. But someone has to do it regardless," I said.

Karen came out, glanced at me, and said, "I don't even want to see your face anymore!" Then she angrily left the office.

Dhivya also emerged from the room and exited the building. Only Yadin remained inside, sitting and taking notes as if nothing had happened.

I entered and asked him, "What's going on?"

"Karen's mother's story will likely have an impact. It will elicit sympathy. But Karen mentioned that her mother wouldn't talk about all of that. Dhivya wants to have a direct conversation with Karen's mother and persuade her. So they're going to San Francisco. When they return, we'll assess what needs to be done next. Until then, the rest of you can continue your work," he said.

Maaya looked at me and said, "You're such a mess! Don't you realize that when Dhivya sets her mind on something, she'll achieve it no matter the cost? How could you put this idea in her head?"

"She was the one who said we shouldn't seek help from rape survivors or talk to them at all... if she's doing it now, she must know how to handle it. So what I suggested might turn out to be right, and it might even be the best course of action for the sake of this project. Hopefully, it could even benefit Karen's mother," I retorted, steadfastly defending myself.

"You still don't get it... If something goes wrong here, we won't be able to face Karen again," Maaya shouted and walked back to her desk.

Around ten minutes later, Karen texted me.

"Is there a way to stop Dhivya? I don't think this will end well. She can be forceful when she's determined. My mother is already reserved, and my father has a short temper. I'm very anxious now."

I called Karen and said, "Should I come with you? We can figure something out along the way to prevent this."

"What are you going to say?" she asked.

"I'm not sure, but we'll figure it out," I replied and left.

"Where are you going?" Maaya inquired.

"I'm going to San Francisco as well. Karen is quite scared," I explained.

"Dhivya won't agree to any of this! Don't create more problems," Maaya warned me.

"Who is she to decide? I'll handle everything. Don't worry," I assured her and left.

As I reached the apartment complex, Karen and Dhivya were getting into a car. I rushed to them and said, "I'll come with you too."

"Why, Ilamaran? There's so much work at the office. Why do you want to come?" Dhivya asked.

"No, it was me who initiated all of this. It was because of me that Karen had to open up about a lot of things here. So, I feel that I should be there for her now," I explained.

"So, you're coming along for some damage control, is that it?" Dhivya asked slyly. Her tone carried a hint of mockery.

"Not at all. I'll feel less guilty if I'm with Karen during this time," I replied.

Dhivya turned to Karen and asked, "Did you ask Ilamaran to come along?"

Before Karen could respond, I jumped in. "No, it was my decision to come. I want to see how you handle all of this and learn from you," I said.

"You've learned to speak well. There's a noticeable improvement! But, Karen, if you're seeking moral support, you should have invited someone else. Ilamaran will be more useful to me than to you," Dhivya remarked.

Karen let out a nervous laugh.

"It'll be beneficial for everyone if I'm around," I insisted. Even as I spoke, Dhivya took out her phone. While still looking at me, she made a call and said, "Another person is joining us."

We couldn't converse much in the car. Dhivya was constantly making calls, saying things like, "I need to talk to them urgently. Please arrange a suitable time."

It seemed like she was speaking to several influential individuals.

Karen was attentively listening to Dhivya. I thought I might have a chance to talk with Dhivya during the flight. However, I didn't realize it was a private jet. Once on board, she retreated to a private room, engrossed in work. Karen and I were left alone in another section of the aircraft.

I hadn't anticipated Dhivya traveling in a private plane. It seemed she held more influence than I had assumed. Had I known this back in Chennai, I'm not sure how I would have reacted.

I once again hoped for a chance to talk after landing, but Dhivya was already on a call when we touched down. We couldn't interrupt her conversation, nor could we engage in our own.

Karen appeared slightly nervous. We couldn't help overhearing Dhivya's phone conversation. She was speaking to the secretary of the women's wing of the United Nations.

"Have you seen my email? We need to ensure that this doesn't become public knowledge. I want to use this information solely to secure approval," Dhivya said.

"Can we handle this discreetly, without anyone else finding out? If this project succeeds, I'll offer a 50% discount to women seeking this treatment for the next ten years. If the UN covers 50% of the expenses, we could even offer it for free. Please discuss this and let me know. I'll also reach out to Ms. Revathy Periyasamy. If we collaborate, we can achieve a better outcome for all parties involved," Dhivya continued.

Karen and I exchanged glances, puzzled about who this might be. She raised an eyebrow, silently asking me if I knew. I shrugged, indicating my lack of knowledge. We both wondered who Dhivya was conversing with, and I felt a sense of unease.

As we entered Karen's house, Dhivya's phone rang again.

"Alright, I'll inquire about that and get back to you," was Dhivya's brief response.

We couldn't even speculate about the response from the person on the other end or their identity.

Once we entered Karen's house, Karen introduced her mother to Dhivya. I didn't know why, but Dhivya appeared oddly nervous too. She was visibly sweating, perhaps realizing the weight of her demands. Now that she was here, she probably didn't know how to initiate the conversation. Growing increasingly anxious, she tightly held my hand.

Karen also seemed quite apprehensive. Kundavai, on the other hand, gazed at Dhivya unwaveringly, her eyes fixed as if in discomfort. Devotional hymns played in the background as usual. Surprisingly, Dhivya didn't just look nervous, but utterly devastated. Had she finally come to terms with how incredibly challenging this was going to be? Without immediately addressing the task at hand, Dhivya asked to use the restroom and went inside, seemingly trying to compose herself for what lay ahead.

Kundavai observed her leave, pressing her fingers against her temples as her eyes remained closed, seemingly in distress. I felt sorry for putting this gentle, kind woman in such a position, albeit indirectly. My heart went out to all the women present; I was certain none of them liked the idea in the slightest. But I understood that this had to be done for the sake of the project and even for Kundavai herself.

Suddenly, Kundavai fainted. Karen immediately rushed to her side, helping her sit up on the couch. Dhivya returned about twenty minutes later, by which time Kundavai had managed to recover.

Dhivya looked at Steve and asked, "Were you in the army?"

"Yeah, but I'm retired now," he replied.

Dhivya mentioned that she wanted to speak to Kundavai privately and led her into a separate room. Half an hour later, she called Steve inside. Karen and I exchanged glances, curious about the nature of their conversation.

"Did you come just to stare at me like this?" Karen demanded, a mix of fear and anger in her voice.

"What could I do? She didn't give us a single moment to speak to her... she was constantly occupied," I said helplessly.

After an hour, Dhivya emerged from the room.

"Karen, please come with me," she said, then left the house.

"Steve, Ilamaran will come with you. Give him the documents, and I'll collect them from him at the airport," she instructed before leaving.

Kundavai said nothing and quietly followed Dhivya, with Karen trailing behind.

"Come, Ilamaran," Steve said, motioning for me to join him in the car.

"Where are we going now? And where are they going? What happened inside?" I inquired.

"She's heading to the Indian Embassy. You and I are going to my former house. We need to retrieve some documents from there, which you'll then hand over to Dhivya," he explained.

"Okay, but what happened inside? And why are they going to the embassy?" I asked.

"Dhivya specifically asked me not to tell you about what transpired inside. And honestly, I'm not aware of why they're going to the embassy either," he admitted.

"Sir, you're a military man. Didn't you inquire about the details?" I questioned.

"I might have a military background, but if my hunch is correct, Dhivya probably doesn't want you to know the reason. So I can't divulge this information either," he replied.

"Well, once again, everyone seems to know what's happening except me. This isn't new for me... it's how all of this began," I muttered.

Steve chuckled briefly. "I'm sorry, Ilamaran. Dhivya was quite particular about this."

Despite Dhivya bringing me along and doing everything in front of me, I still couldn't make sense of it all. I wondered how everyone unquestioningly followed her instructions.

I collected the documents from Steve and reached the airport. I messaged Karen to inquire about her whereabouts.

"We're still at the embassy. I don't know how much longer this will take," Karen replied.

I called Maaya and shared the events that had unfolded. She burst into laughter.

"I predicted this would happen. I told the folks here that I'd receive your call any moment now, and it's amusing to hear you grumble and complain," she said.

"Hey, Dhivya operates on an entirely different level. She's interacting with significant individuals. She even knows your Revathy Periyasamy," I said.

"Now I understand why Revathy never came to meet us like Kavya said she would," Maaya said, finally comprehending.

"I remember now. Kavya called me while I was on the flight. Let me call her and I'll call you back," I said.

"Why is she calling you at this hour? Alright, call her back, but don't forget to tell me what she says," Maaya urged.

I dialed Kavya's number, but she didn't pick up. It was now time for Raj's appeal. He had been in jail for almost two years now, with six months of imprisonment even before the hearing. I wondered if this was somehow related.

Dhivya arrived at the airport two hours later, accompanied by Kundavai. Karen informed me that she was unaware of what had transpired since they hadn't taken her into the embassy. She had waited outside. Karen added that Dhivya hadn't left Kundavai's side for even a moment.

Steve and Aayan also arrived at the airport. The entire group flew back to San Diego. Only Dhivya and Kundavai were privy to what had truly transpired.

From the airport, Dhivya took Kundavai directly to her house. Steve grew irritated, and Karen appeared concerned, but there wasn't much we could do. We returned to the office to meet the others. Maaya, Vidhya, and Ilango were eagerly waiting to learn what had transpired, but we couldn't provide them with many details.

"What's up with this woman? She's not sharing anything with us! Kundavai is going to reveal everything tomorrow anyway. Why all this secrecy now? We've all been with Kundavai for years, but I can't fathom why she's not even speaking to us and following Dhivya like a meek lamb... I've never seen her like this," Steve exclaimed.

"Mom hasn't heard a single devotional hymn in a long time... how is that even possible? What's going on here?" Karen questioned.

"Could this be another Dhivya magic trick? Many times, we've been left speechless by some of the things she's done. There's something extraordinary about her," I remarked.

I couldn't help but admire Dhivya. I've always been drawn to courageous women. When I recounted the incidents and expressed my admiration for Dhivya, Maaya laughed. Only she would understand the thoughts running through my mind.

"Aunty-Indian," she mouthed silently, teasing me.

I slapped my forehead and rolled my eyes at her playful remark.

"Exactly! Even in the military, we'd have similar thoughts when certain individuals spoke," Steve begrudgingly agreed, recalling my earlier comment about Dhivya.

Around thirty minutes later, we noticed Yadin heading toward Dhivya's home. All our eyebrows raised in suspicion. We pondered the topics of discussion among these influential individuals. Would we ever get to know the details of what was transpiring?

* * *

Chapter 40

The next morning, we were getting ready to go to the office. Steve was listlessly going around, wondering what had happened to Kundavai and why they had even come to San Diego. He said he would ask Dhivya directly about this when she came out.

Ilango came in and said, "Dhivya has started to the office. Kundavai is going along with her."

"Now Yadin would go right behind her," I was saying, just as Yadin got into his car and left. We all laughed.

Karen had not even had breakfast, but she said, "I'm going to the office too. I don't know what they are doing to my mother."

"Nothing untoward will happen! She would have arranged for a meeting regarding the approvals. And she is keeping your mother with her until then, so none of us confuses her," I guessed.

"I'm ready too, Karen. Come, let's go first." Vidhya said. Karen bit into a toast as she left.

"I'll come to your office, too. Kundavai is my partner. I must know what's happening to her," Steve said.

I felt sorry for him, wondering how Dhivya had made an army man lament like this. Ilango and Steve left in a few minutes.

I got a sudden call from Kavya.

"Ilamaran! What's happening there?" She asked, sounding flustered.

"What happened?" I asked.

"Raj was shifted to Delhi from Chennai yesterday. His two years of prison term ended, and I went for an appeal only last week. Revathy Periyasamy called me yesterday and asked about your project. Someone from the Indian Embassy there told her something about your project. She told me that they had inquired about Yadin too. So now I do not know if Raj was shifted to Delhi because of my appeal or if there was some other reason. I am not sure what links both of these, but there's surely something at the government level," she said.

I told her everything that had happened over here. "But only Dhivya knows what she is doing," I eventually said.

"You please follow Kundavai's story and keep me posted! I'm leaving for Delhi now," she informed me.

"Will do, Kavya!"

"One more thing... That Charles and Joseph are brothers. Also, the judge and Charles were schoolmates. The judge was lying when he said he did not know Charles. I think there is some connection between all this," she said.

"Brothers? Schoolmates? What! What's all this new confusion? Why would that judge hide this? Where is Charles now?" I asked.

"I don't know! Though Subha is dead, her story is not leaving us alone. They hurried through Raj's hearing too. In this country, such cases take years before the verdict is out, but we are expecting Raj's release in the next couple of weeks or months. This looks like they are trying to hush up the events and wrap up quickly. Apparently, the judge knew everything. There's something else beyond this here. And now I don't know what Joseph is doing or even who exactly he is," she said.

"When I hear all this, I feel like I'm reading a mystery thriller, Kavya. When Raj said Subha went missing, the confusion that rose in me has just taken another form now. The mystery seemingly never ends," I said.

"This is how I've been feeling for the last eighteen years!" Kavya sighed.

When I hung up the call, Maaya asked, "What happened?"

"My head is reeling when I see whatever is happening there," I said.

"How many more times are you going to say the same thing? We could tell this story to our grandkids... or maybe we could write a book out of this story and earn money," Maaya said.

"I'm going to write and publish a book on this," I said.

While I was talking thus, Karen called me.

"Where are you both? Why am I not able to reach Maaya's mobile? You come to the office immediately. The people from the FDA and the Indian Embassy are here. Some others – I don't know who they are – have also come. Yadin is not here. He left suddenly, but Marco is here," she said.

Maaya and I immediately left for the office. And everyone there was in a closed-room meeting.

"Dhivya! You're hurrying everyone into this. Is such high-pressure or high-command action required for this? The usual protocols we follow would have been enough," FDA officer Edward said.

"I'm not hurrying this. We're already 19 years behind schedule. If you hear Kundavai's story, you'll know the betrayal that this government has done to her. I am not doing this as a business or for any profit. We as a society have not given due importance to mental health and the relevant technology to cure mental ailments. We were able to engineer a vaccine for Covid-19 within 12 months of first knowing about such a disease, produce enough to compensate for the growing demand, distribute the vaccine worldwide, monitor its effects, and manufacture a booster dose when required.

"However, even though mental health issues have existed for a long time, they are not treated seriously – and are, to the contrary, completely stigmatized, too. The diagnosis and treatment methods are laughable, and the solutions are usually, 'do yoga and meditate' or 'go for counseling.'

"We're still in a state where we have to create awareness and reassure people the world over that it is not wrong to get oneself treated for mental health issues. Why? If we do yoga, we will not suffer from half the physical ailments affecting us now. But why are we spending on doctors and medicines for those diseases alone?" She demanded.

"Come to the point," said Stephen, one of the guys in the group.

"I am only answering your question. Kundavai's medical reports are in front of you. She's been suffering from this for the last nineteen years. Such problems are not even covered by insurance. She's lived so far only based on the therapy and treatments given at the Buddhist Medical Centre. It has taken her so many years to get a bit better… But she's still not completely healed. Steve is paying for her therapy from his military pension," Dhivya responded.

"Tell us what you expect us to do," Edward asked again.

"We've spoken a lot about this to you. We've built a technology that can edit and delete people's memories. And based on the comments we have received from you, the consensus is that this is not a big issue and does not need such high-technology treatment. You'd asked us to do some more basic testing and then get back to you," Dhivya said.

"What, now? You need your technology to cure Kundavai. So you want us to listen to her story, cry over it, and give you the approval you seek?" Edward demanded.

'Who was this fellow? He's interrupting Dhivya intentionally. It looks like he'd already decided to refuse.' I thought. We were all in the room, too, sitting in a corner.

"If you really had the heart to cry over this, the entire thing would have been over long back. We all have short-term memory loss. We hear about the news of a rape… a two-year-old child was sexually abused recently! But when a psycho conducted a mass shooting in a school… a terrorist attack like that put that other one out of the news. Then a bomb blast would have occurred… We will just ask, 'What is wrong with these people? Why are they doing this? What are they going to achieve with all this?' And maybe we will let slip a few swear words while sipping a coffee in our living room. Then we'd go back to our daily jobs.

"Such forgetfulness is also a disease. Because we remember only those things that affect us personally, so those who are actually affected by such incidents are suffering for life. They are unable to forget it and move on. In that case, even these memories are viruses. Where is the medicine for these viruses? Do you have a vaccine for this? How are we planning to cure it?" Dhivya demanded.

"We're not saying that this should not be cured. Nor are we saying this is not what we want. But how can we accept that what you say is the only solution? We're asking people like you to explore more solutions too. We're just asking you to take some more time and do it properly. That's all," a woman in the group named Katherine chipped in.

"Do we have a solution now? Could this be cured today? You will need answers via clinical testing to see the possible side effects, right? That's why we're asking for your approval," Dhivya said.

Throughout the day, Dhivya took everything head-on and spoke boldly.

"What do we do if this affects the general public? If this technology you're talking about reaches the wrong hands, it could have disastrous repercussions. It could create catastrophes the likes of which we could never even imagine in our worst nightmares. We have to see the other potential issues, too. There could be a lot of legal and political issues with this. You'd also have ethical problems. We cannot short-sightedly look at only one dimension like you," Edward pointed out.

"Look at it, yes! Look at all of those issues, and analyze our concept from all possible angles. We understand that it's your job. Please look at our processes carefully. But we'll finish clinical trials while you handle other issues. Maybe it'll take another six months or even a year. But we have to bring this to an end. Tell us what else we have to do according to the regulations. We'll do that, too. But, for now, we're just asking your approval to test this on the volunteers," Dhivya said.

"You're accessing deeply personal data. It will take time to approve all this. We cannot do it as per your urgent schedule. If we do this now, who'll answer the American Congress?" Stephen demanded.

"Then you are answerable to Kundavai, too," Dhivya gave a rhetorical response.

"What answer?" Stephen asked.

"How did she come to America? What happened to her parents? Is Kundavai her real name? Where was she born and brought up? Answer these questions, for instance!"

"What are you saying? How would we know all this?" One officer asked, confused.

"If you can't give us the answers, then we will tell the media everything. Then your government, the Indian Government, and the UN Human Rights Commission can give us the answers," Dhivya responded coolly.

None of us understood what was happening. The entire place was in a frenzy. It looked like only Dhivya knew the complete details about everything. Kundavai, who had been silent so far, started crying. Dhivya was consoling her, whispering encouraging words in her ear.

"You're saying a lot of irrelevant things. We're unable to follow your intentions or logic," Katherine said.

"I am suggesting that we should try this first. So you could see the effects better, in person. I'll now ask Kundavai to tell her story. Then we'll test her by erasing her memories during the trials. Then you could check her. All her medical reports are in front of you. If you are okay with this, give us the permission and approval to go further," Dhivya said.

"This looks like you're coercing us to give you the approval," Edward commented.

"I'm not threatening or coercing! I'm just trying to make you understand the importance of this. I'll tell you more. I'll also participate in these trials. I'll share my medical reports with you, too. If something happens to Kundavai because of this – nothing will – but if it does, let the same thing happen to me as well. Don't we all have things in our life that we wish to forget?"

Dhivya's eyes teared up when she said this. And for the first time since I had known her, I heard her voice falter. She composed herself quickly, though.

"If you need more details, Kundavai's adoptive family is here. They're all affected by PTSD, and they met in the place where they got the treatment for it. And now they have created a small world for themselves and are fighting their demons together, hand in hand. They're also ready to volunteer in these tests," Dhivya said.

Karen and Steve went up front and said, "We're ready for this."

"Give us an hour. We'll discuss it and get back to you," said Stephen.

The room was abuzz, with everyone talking back and forth. Then the officer from the Indian Embassy, Alok Varma, said something in Dhivya's ears. Dhivya listened to that, nodded, and went out immediately.

The other officers who had come there roamed around, all actively doing something. Some were calling others, probably people from the institutions they represented. Some were talking with the people beside them.

Kundavai alone stood immobile. Karen neared her and gestured, 'Are you okay?'

Kundavai just nodded and smiled at her. The rest of us were still in the corner of the room. Marco was standing with us. Maaya beckoned me to come out.

"What's happening here? What's Dhivya saying? What's the connection between Kundavai and the Indian government? Why are the people from the Indian Embassy here? I'm afraid we will be embroiled in another controversy here!" Maaya said, sounding quite tense.

"If you look at the guy from the embassy, it is he who seems to be caught in something," I observed.

"Dei! They're government employees. Your crush Dhivya aunty is not a cinema heroine. Everything here will not happen according to her will. This is not a scripted movie climax for everything to get over quickly," Maaya said, laughing.

"Crush?" I laughed. "Idiot," I said, knocking her on the head.

"I'm really scared, da. What's Dhivya trying to forget? What problems does she have?" she asked, absently biting her lip.

"Even I was quite surprised by that. Do people like Dhivya even have problems? And is she working so hard even amidst the problems?" I mused.

Maaya stared at me. "What am I saying, and what are you talking about?" She demanded.

Everyone there went for their lunch break. Then Dhivya came back inside and took Kundavai to her house. I went near Karen and asked, "What, were you able to talk about something with her?"

"Mom did not even open her mouth. She just said she'll tell me everything later, at home," she said.

"Do you know about Kundavai's parents, like Dhivya was saying? What is she trying to prove?" I asked.

"Mom gets convulsive fits if we even speak about her father… This is the first time I see her remain calm when discussing him. That is quite a surprise to me," Karen said.

"Could Dhivya and Kundavai be related? How is she able to control your mother like this?" I asked.

"I don't know! But Dhivya plays psychological games quite adeptly… She knows exactly what to say to people to control them," Karen said.

Maaya immediately looked at me and laughed. Her gaze and laugh implied that Dhivya had done the same to me.

"Nah… I was wondering if they could be childhood friends who studied at school together or something… if not related," I said.

"So do you want to hear tales about how they had fun together, eating out of the same plate, going for rides in the same bicycle… all those childhood memories?" Vidhya asked, smirking.

"You're such a movie addict, da. You associate movie-like scenarios with everything in real life. Everyone listens to Dhivya and what she says. That's her charisma," Ilango said.

Vidhya turned to Ilango with a dubious expression and asked, "When did you become an aunty-Indian, too?"

"Every guy here became an aunty-Indian since they came to America," Maaya said, laughing.

* * *

Chapter 41

Everyone finished lunch and returned to work. Edward started talking.

"We'll give you the conditional approval for the preliminary clinical trials. The affected ones will have to talk about the memories that you will be editing/deleting first. And we will be there when they talk about it. We will also be there when the memories are being edited/deleted. The testing should not be done with just your people. We'll also bring volunteers from our end. And the tests should have 100% the same effect on these people as they do on your volunteers.

"Whatever you do, say, or learn here should stay within these four walls. First, we all need to sign and abide by the non-disclosure agreement. And until we give the nod, this news should be embargoed – no media house or institution should know about this. These conditions apply to everyone, including your investors and your current and previous employees who were a part of this project," he said.

"We cannot expect anything beyond this from you. Thank you very much," Dhivya said.

"We're ready to come with our volunteers when you are ready," he said.

"If you give your agreements, we will sign them today… And we can start tomorrow," Dhivya said.

Once the delegates left, Yadin hugged Dhivya and patted her on the shoulders. Dhivya went and hugged Kundavai, crying copiously.

Then she turned to Marco and said, "All this would have been impossible without you. Thank you very much."

She also addressed Steve and Karen. "Thank you very much! For coming forward and agreeing to do this."

"If we come out of all this, we'd be indebted to you forever," Steve said.

Dhivya just smiled softly, gently caressed Aayan's hair, and went out.

"She's achieved what she wanted," I said to Ilango.

"What, da? We'd get the approval only if the tests go well tomorrow! Why is she happy already? Is she that sure about the project succeeding?" he asked.

"No! We have performed these testing many times, and our algorithm is a hundred percent ready," Maaya said.

"I understand that, but how can we be so confident without testing on humans so far?" Ilango demanded.

"I don't know that," Maaya said and tried to leave.

Ilango nodded and left before her. I called Maaya back into the room.

"Tell me the truth," I said.

"What truth?" she asked.

"No… it's not in your nature to not respond like this when Ilango is expressing such an important concern. I think you know something more than that, but you are not telling us. What is that?"

"There's nothing like that!"

"Look… There should be no secrets between us both. So don't hide what you know, that too on such important issues!"

"She's already done a lot of testing on humans. The data for all that came from Mexico. When Yadin says he is going to Israel, he'll instead go to work in the research center in Mexico… Even when he directly says he's going to Mexico to set up the research lab, he actually went to do such testing. A big black market for this exists even in the US. They're ready to facilitate anything if we give them good money. So these people have already done a lot of testing. We are a hundred percent ready. That's why Dhivya is so confident today," Maaya told me quietly.

"What are you saying, Maaya? How did you keep such a big thing from us all these days?" I demanded, a bit disoriented.

"It was Dhivya who asked me not to talk about this to anyone. Particularly you. If you reveal this to anyone else in a moment of anger, everything could be derailed," Maaya said.

"She will say a lot of things... but how could you keep this from me? What if you had gotten into some trouble again? Do you need all this nonsense?" I asked.

"Dhivya told me, 'There'll be no problems. And anyway, even if there are, all my emails to you are generic. That's the reason why I did not allow you people to make any decisions. Everything starts and ends with the three of us. If all this ends well, you can take on bigger responsibilities. There's so much risk in what we're doing now. And everything I am telling you now is off-the-record.'"

"Do you believe she'll do everything as she says? What if she had been saying and doing all this to pacify you?" I pointed out.

"There was truth in what she said. And I could see that she actually cared about the people... the volunteers, I mean. And even us. She spoke just like all good leaders will do. Like Karen said, she's quite engaging and honest when she speaks off the record," Maaya said.

"What is this off-the-record nonsense? I don't understand. Either you know, or you don't. Either you'll say or you won't. That's it! She can always be in this off-the-record mode, instead," I said and laughed.

"What? You've started admiring your crush again?"

"Hey! It's not a crush. But I can't stop admiring her."

"Dei! I know you well, da. You were staring at her open-mouthed while she was talking, so much so that you didn't even notice the two flies and four mosquitoes entering your mouth. You were so engrossed in her words!" She laughed.

"Cha! Nothing like that. She spoke quite inspiringly."

"Yeah! Dhivya is magic, and you are tragic," Maaya laughed.

"Are you jealous?" I raised an eyebrow at her.

"Not jealous! I like her, and I am allowed to like her but you aren't supposed to. I feel odd when you are praising her," she said.

"Idiot! She's like an elder sister to me! She's nearly forty now," I said.

"But you're an aunty-Indian! You wanted me to be bold and confident like I was before. But I cannot be like that with you.

When you are with me… I soften and melt… your hair, your smile… your eyes," she said, her eyes roving over my face as she stopped abruptly, blushing.

"Smile… eyes… and then?" I asked, grinning.

"I won't. I already blabbered a lot. I won't say more," she said and strode out hurriedly.

"Hey, wait! Where are you going? Say it and then go… you should not stop in between like this," I said, running after her.

"Stay in suspense. That's your punishment!"

"What did I do for you to punish me like this?"

She kept walking on even as I was asking this and following her. Eventually, I went close and pulled her back by her hand. She turned to me. Her eyes were a bit teary.

"Hey, what happened?" I asked.

"Nothing… then you'll call me weak. And I don't want that," she said and started walking again.

"Hey, wait…" I said and pulled her along with me to the bench on the street. We had walked into a park. There were a few restaurants nearby. Many kids were skating there. People were also walking back and forth.

It was drizzling mildly, and the chill air felt pleasant against her skin. Everyone was enjoying the drizzle and the smell of rain drenching the earth. Many couples were also there, only barely aware of their surroundings.

"I won't sit here," Maaya said. But I held her hand and pulled her down to sit beside me.

"What's your problem?" I asked.

"Nothing,"

"Nothing… as in you are not angry or upset with me… Right?"

"I won't say that… But, nothing…"

"Okay, I'll tell you what I think is your problem. You just say yes/no," I said.

She stayed silent.

I went and got ice cream from the shop nearby. We both like having ice creams in the rain and when the cold breeze blows around us. She started eating the ice cream, her gaze fixed on me.

"What are you looking at?" I asked.

"Nah… you said you were going to say something? I'm waiting for that," she said.

I looked intently at her and she laughed.

The ice cream started dripping down her hand. She looked around to see if anyone had noticed us and then wiped her hands with tissues.

"What? Did you think you could lick it away if no one was watching?" I asked.

"You'll talk about all this but not what you said you would be talking about," she snorted.

"Look at you! You should be the one talking. You're asking me about yourself," I pointed out.

"No da… It'll be good to hear about myself from you… If you say it correctly, it is a different heady feeling. If you get it wrong, that feeling is equivalent to getting a million dollars," she laughed.

I laughed too and got up to kneel before her. I looked deep into her eyes as I began talking.

"I think when I said, 'Be like the old Maaya. That's who I like,' it affected you deeply. Yes, I would love it if you were like that. But it is not the only thing I like about you. This caring side of yours is something I have not seen, and it is something I am enjoying immensely. I like this a lot, too. I like this version of Maaya, who manages all my craziness and understands me.

"I like the Maaya who wants to learn something from my mother, Kavya, and Dhivya and wants to change herself for the better. But, we'll get bored soon if we are of the same character. But if a woman like you is with me, I will always have something new to love you every single day. And if we keep loving each other with all these changes, our life will always be exciting. I don't know whether I am your perfect fit, but you are my life's biggest blessing," I said kissing her cheek.

Maaya, whose unwavering eyes had been fixed on me and whose face was devoid of reactions, blushed and laughed when I kissed her. Tears spilled from her eyes when she was laughing.

"Get lost! You've taken this conversation on a completely different track," she said and stood up from the bench.

"Hey! Am I right?" I demanded.

"No, you're wrong," she said and kissed my cheeks.

That evening, we had dinner alone – just the two of us – and went back home.

* * *

Chapter 42

Yadin and Maaya left for the office at 6 AM the following day. Ilango and Marco had spent the previous night working at the office. And a few more people were with them, too. Dhivya left with Kundavai at around 8 AM. Steve and I went together. We were all at the office by 08:30 AM. And the officers arrived at exactly 9 AM.

"Dhivya! We can begin immediately if you are all ready," they said.

"Have you checked the documents?" Stephen asked.

"Yeah, we have. Everything looks good!" Edward answered and then turned to Dhivya. "You can begin," he said. He then checked his watch and noted the time.

Dhivya took Kundavai to the lab there. Karen, Steve, and the rest of us followed them. A neuroscientist and psychiatrist were representing the government's side.

Yadin was speaking with the government's psychiatrist. They were preparing cameras there.

There was a big MRI scanning machine. And a few monitors and two VR glasses were beside it. Yadin pinned a lot of wires in Kundavai's body. There was a polygraph machine hooked up to her, too.

"We're unable to hear you," Edward said from outside.

Yadin pressed the speaker button from inside and asked, "Can you hear now?"

The officers showed a thumbs-up to indicate that they could hear now. Then Yadin pressed another button. The lighting in the room changed – the lights became a bit dull, and the room darkened too.

"Is the camera setting right?" Yadin asked.

They showed a thumbs-up again.

Yadin gave Kundavai an injection. Then he asked the basic details about her, including her name, where she came from, and why she had come here. Basically, he was confirming that she was conscious and aware of her surroundings by asking her the relevant questions to establish the facts and form a baseline.

"Did someone coerce or threaten you to come here, or did you come here of your own accord?" Yadin asked.

"I came here out of my wish," Kundavai said.

Yadin showed a thumbs-up to the people outside and asked, "Are you okay with this?"

They responded that they were.

"Kundavai… Tell us about the incident in your life that you wish to forget…" Yadin said.

Kundavai began her tale.

Nineteen years ago, one day, we – my mother, aunt, sisters, and I – had dinner outside and returned to our home. Someone was waiting for us in front of our house. Once he saw us, he informed us that my uncle had died in a car accident. When we heard that shocking news, we were all stunned.

My aunt fell to the floor right there and started crying. My sister fainted right there. We pulled ourselves together and they took my aunt to identify my uncle's body. My sister accompanied her to the hospital.

We all went inside the house. Soon after that, we got a phone call. I did not know who had called, but immediately on keeping the phone down, my mom switched on the TV. And then she started crying in great heart-rending gasps. My sister and I could not understand anything. The news scrolling on the TV said that Naxalites had killed a spy for the Indian government. And on the screen flashed a photo of our father.

I was shocked and did not know what to make of this. The stories I had heard about my father were different.

My mother had told us before that our father had left our home. She also told us that my father had lost interest in her after she had birthed children and didn't get her body back in shape.

After hearing this, I grew up hating my father. So I did not even feel like crying for him. But I was a bit shocked to know that he had been working as a spy for the government and started wondering whether everything my mother had said about him was true or not.

The stories did not add up. And if they were established as false, that would explain a lot here. So I slowly went near my mother and asked her about it. My mother said, 'He did fight with us and leave. But before going, he transferred all his properties to my name and said that this was my alimony. It is hard for people in such a line of work to have families. So now I feel he probably did it so his family will not get into trouble. But now the Indian government is claiming that they did not even know who he was. And that this news was just to blame them.'

I could not fully understand all this or even grasp the implications at that age. But my father was not as bad a man as I thought. That was when I understood that he might have left us for some other reason. It was traumatic to see my entire life from another perspective.

After some time, a car pulled up with a cop in it. "We need to make sure you people are safe. If your husband spilt the beans about this family, your lives would be in danger, too," he told us.

We all got into the car. My mother informed them about my uncle's accident and requested to pick up my aunt and cousin.

'Okay! We can pick them up from the hospital on our way,' he said.

The driver gave us some water to drink. Once we drank it, we all fainted. When we regained consciousness after a long time, we were all in a forest. Someone was tied up in front of us. It took little time to regain full vision. But once we did, I realised, with shock, that it was my father. Once he saw us, he started crying hard. My mother asked him if this was the reason he had left us all those years ago. But he could not answer her and continued to cry.

Then they tied up my mother and us girls, too. In about half an hour, they were dragging my other sister in as well… We did not know what had happened to my aunt.

They looked at my father and said, 'We made you a leader with the belief that you'll come to war with us. But instead, you worked against us getting the weapons. Because of you, our people lost their lives. You're a betrayer. For people like you, our lives are cheap, and you don't think twice about sacrifice for the sake of this inefficient government. So now you are going to suffer a consequence that is much worse than your death.'

'Did you not live away from your family so you could betray us? I assume you're seeing your daughter after a long time… She has grown up into a beautiful girl. Take a good look at her now, for as long as possible… After some time, you will not be able to recognize her at all!' he said.

My father did not answer at all and remained silent. They hit him quite hard and even kicked his genitals. They spewed so many bad words at my mother.

They removed our dresses right in front of our parents. My father shouted, screamed and closed his eyes, unable to see the horror. 'Look! Your daughter has grown up! She looks great, doesn't she? Look at her and enjoy her beauty!'

They then laughed loudly. And that laughter is still ringing in my ears. They never allowed my father to close his eyes. One guy forcefully held his eyelids open so he could not close his eyes; they ensured that he would not miss even one moment of what was happening to us.

They made us lie naked on the floor, lighted candles, and let the hot wax drop on our skin. There were five of them… they repeatedly raped us in front of our parents. And they put the forest critters, centipedes, millipedes, worms, and other insects on us. Then, they let those insects bite our private parts. I am still able to hear my mother's screams of agony.

They raped our mother in front of our eyes.

They kept us for about twenty days like this and tortured us. They gave us food only rarely. And if we asked for water, they pissed on us. They did not kill us. But they tortured us so much that death would have been a better alternative. As a result of their repeated gang-raping, many wounds in our bodies started leaking blood and pus. Then they would ask us, 'What kind of body is this?' and spit on us.

Suddenly, one day, they took all of us except our father in a car.

'Go and tell your government what happened. You should go naked on the streets. They'll be quite happy to see you like this. The police there are worse than us. Just don't get caught in their clutches,' they said.

They first pushed my mother out of the car when we had gone some distance. And then they threw me out on the road. My head hit a rock on the roadside, and I fainted.

And when I had regained consciousness, I was in America. I did not know what happened in between. I don't know what happened to my mother, father, or sisters. I was alone when I woke up.

Even my face had been changed by cosmetic surgery. I could not even recognise myself in the mirror when I saw my face here.

They told me, 'You must tell everyone you were born and brought up in America.'

'What name do you like?' They asked.

I like the name Kundavai – from a character who appeared in the famous Tamil novel series Ponniyin Selvan. So I assumed that name. I got the relevant identification papers with that name. For three years, I was in a hospital here. Then they discharged me from there and got me a job at a restaurant. But I couldn't find a permanent job because I was prone to convulsions.

One person took care of me for a while. But he never revealed his identity to me. Nor did he answer my questions. He always expressed his concern about my health and enquired about it. It was he who admitted me to this Buddhist Centre. And I spent many days there until I met Steve and the rest of my family, with whom I am living now.

Kundavai finished her story.

While listening to this, almost everyone was in tears. Even some of the officers who had come there shed tears. Alok Varma went out to call someone.

"We should report this to Homeland Security," Stephen said.

Dhivya alone was conspicuous by her absence. She had stepped out the moment Kundavai started talking.

"I need some time," Yadin said, looking shaken as he walked out of the room.

Maaya, Vidhya, and Karen had also stepped out and were crying profusely. Ilango was sitting with his head in his hands. Steve was trying to console Karen.

When Dhivya returned, it was evident that she had washed her face and changed her clothes. But her eyes were puffy and red. It looked like she had cried in the restroom. She went back into the room and helped Kundavai up.

"Is this enough?" Kundavai asked in a frail voice.

Dhivya hugged Kundavai and started crying again.

"You're a lioness. Who will get such courage? Now it's my responsibility to solve your problems," Dhivya said.

"Based on the calls you made yesterday, I think you know a lot of people. So please, somehow find out if my mother and sisters are alive." Kundavai requested Dhivya.

"I'll definitely do what I can," Dhivya said, wiping the tears from Kundavai's eyes. Kundavai also did the same for Dhivya and was gazing at her intently. Dhivya hugged her again and said, "Everything will turn out well hereafter."

Yadin came back in.

"Let everything hereafter happen behind closed doors," Edward said, sending us all out, too.

Once Steve, Karen, and Aayan had spoken about their lives, Dhivya went in too. She took the longest. It was 10 PM by the time she was done with her stories. The officers left immediately.

When we went inside, Dhivya was unconscious.

Alok Varma came out and told Karen, "This approval is not in our hands… We'll do what we can to give you the best treatment. You can call me directly."

It was a bit heartening to see them talking that way. They seemed to have gotten a grasp of the problem and were treating it with some seriousness now.

The impact of what I learned today will stay with me for a long while. Raj's problem was just a love story. Even that story had stuck with me since that day. But I didn't even have words to describe what had happened to these people. Just calling it torture or torment to normalize it will not convey even one per cent of the horror.

"If this project is approved, we should first delete our memories of today," Ilango said.

"What could be Dhivya's problem?" I asked, now really curious.

"I think it is not as serious as Kundavai. She did not get such reactions as Kundavai had," Vidhya said.

"No. We were not inside, so we cannot assume this," Ilango said.

"True! Whatever it is, Dhivya is such a bold person. She could even have done this to prove that this technology is safe," Maaya said.

"Even then, she'll have needed a lot of courage to open up about whatever bad thing she has in her past," I said.

"Okay, aunty-Indian," Maaya said.

"You're going to get it one day! Maaya is going to fly and give you a kick like Jackie Chan and knock you around," Ilango said.

"For all his antics, it's going to be a divorce even before we're married," Maaya said.

"Hey! She's like a sister to me. She's my mentor." I protested.

"Hello, aunty-Indian… won't you always call Raj your mentor? So now you've shifted to Dhivya?" Maaya hit back.

"Buggers! Have you already decided it is like that? You guys are perverted idiots," I said, shaking my head.

Karen looked at us and said, "I'll come to Chennai with you guys. No matter what problems surround you, you're always with each other and motivating one another… I don't know how I'll have been today were it not for you four…"

"Come, come! Looking at all this, Ilamaran will probably get settled here. You can come with us," Ilango said, pointing to me.

Talking and laughing like this, we reached home. While we were near the apartment, we noticed Yadin going to Dhivya's house.

"Why's he going to Dhivya's house often?" Vidhya asked.

"Ila! I think he's your biggest competition," Ilango commented.

"Maaya! Why don't you go and get settled in Israel?" Vidhya asked.

"I'll even marry a beggar from India but never do this," Maaya laughed.

"Now, who were you calling a beggar?" Karen demanded.

Though she asked it casually, everyone turned and laughed at me.

* * *

Chapter 43

We tried to keep things light-hearted that evening to ease our minds and unwind. However, none of us could get a good night's sleep.

Maaya went to work with Dhivya and Yadin. "It's an important day tomorrow. We need to prepare before that," they said before taking her away.

Ilango and I sat outside our house for a long while, just talking. Steve came and sat with us too. He also brought us beer. Karen and Vidhya were going here and there on some work or the other. Kundavai was sleeping inside.

Maaya was working in Dhivya's house. At about 2 AM, Marco came, and the four of them went straight to the office. We went to sleep only by 4 AM. Maaya came home at 6 AM, bathed, got ready, and went straight back to the office. Dhivya and Yadin stayed in the office.

The government officials from the different departments came to our office at 9 AM sharp. Now the recordings of their volunteers were being done. Maaya was sitting in a separate room and was working on something. She did not even reply to our texts. Once the recording of those volunteers was done, the officers went out, too.

Maaya and Dhivya were preparing a PowerPoint slide based on the data collated from yesterday's recording.

Dhivya called us to the meeting room after a while. "Now we'll see what to do next," she said. "Maaya is our project's lead," she added, introducing Maaya.

Maaya showed us a few images on the projector.

"When we speak and think now, the scanner captures the forms we see in our mind and projects them as images here. And based on the technology available today, there's a chance of an 80% match.

"The image you see now is the photograph of Kundavai's father. We also have the images of the beasts who tormented her. We have also captured recordings of her voice. By examining a graph resembling an electrocardiogram (ECG), we can observe Kundavai's emotional state and track when she experienced different emotions. As you can see, this shows happiness in green, sadness in orange, and shock and fear in red.

"Now, when we edit the memories, these people will repeat the same stories. Then you'll see the same type of images and graphs. We will match both of these and give you a report.

"For example, say we had captured a hundred images while they were talking yesterday. Today, at least ninety of those images will match. And if we compare those ninety images deeply, they will match at a minimum of 98%. If this happens, we can ensure that they were consistent with what they said on both days," Maaya said.

"Why? Can we not have a hundred per cent match?" Edward asked.

"That is humanly impossible. There are two important factors in this. Firstly, the images created from brain activity are only 80% accurate. Secondly, the human mind doesn't operate the same way every time, so that will result in some variations," Dhivya said.

"Besides, we don't even remember the same thing the same way every time. The memory will be edited 100%. But this is just evidence to demonstrate the similarity and the changes. We already share their medical report about their trauma, and you can test them based on their medical report," Yadin said.

They nodded to say they understood.

"I'll take over the explanations now," Yadin began.

"We're going to follow two practices and approaches here. First, we have one kind of mild treatment for people with mild trauma who feel that they can retain the memories of the incident but remove only the emotions associated with it. Second is an entirely different approach for people who want to completely forget the incident and all its associated memories, emotions, thoughts, and feelings.

"For the first kind – those who say they don't want to remember any emotions associated with the event. Your memory is in edit mode when they talk and relive it. We will ask them to do certain activities while talking about it, like playing video games or showing them different images on the TV, effectively confusing their brain by asking them to multitask on irrelevant channels. We will also give them medication to control blood pressure, and sleeping doses. They will sleep after speaking and wake only after 24 hours. You can begin your testing after that," he said.

"The next kind are people whose trauma is worse and who want to forget about the incident completely. We will give them similar medication and laser treatment. And when they recollect the memories, we will ask them to wear VR glasses and show them some pleasant scenes that will make them happy temporarily. And we will also change the room's temperature and mood to suit the scenes in the VR. They will also be undergoing shock treatments at this time, which disturbs the neural network and messaging to the brain for a few milliseconds. Once we finish this procedure, we will give them acupuncture treatments to increase the blood flow in certain places and activate their brain slowly and partially. Then they will also sleep for about 24 hours. While sleeping, if we let the Gayatri mantra or a religious chant in that frequency play in the room, their response will suit the frequency, and they will feel better. If all this goes well, we will know the results tomorrow night or the day after tomorrow," Yadin said.

"Will you do anything else while they are asleep?" Katherine asked.

"As usual, we'll check their blood pressure. And their ECG monitor will be running. There will always be nurses around to monitor them," Yadin replied.

"If something happens due to this, you'd be held responsible… You'll be under trial in the US and then face dire consequences. So think one last time!" Katherine warned.

"I'll undergo the procedure first. If anything happens, let it happen to me first," Dhivya volunteered.

"We'll do it as you say," Yadin said.

Once everyone went out, one of the officers said, "Looks like we'll fall into depression if we have to hear these stories again."

Maaya went and sat in a separate room. She was checking out the progress of the process as it happened. They sent the rest of us outside. Maaya's room was soundproof – she would hear no sound, just the images and output. The process will take about 24 hours in all.

They all had separate rooms. Doctors and nurses had arrived – both from the government and private institutions. Marco was with us.

Yadin called some of us occasionally and gave us odd jobs. But otherwise, we were all sitting and talking. Maaya alone was quite busy. Yadin would be going and checking out occasionally. The images and the voices were compared and processed.

Almost all the test volunteers' data came within the threshold limit. Only two people's data were outside the limits. And both of them were brought in by the officers. Yadin and Maaya shared whatever they had compared.

"We have two people's data that are not matching. Both of them are volunteers from your end. We will do further checks on this." Yadin said.

"It was we who asked them to change certain things intentionally. We wanted to see if your results were correct," the officers said.

Yadin did not react and merely muttered, "I expected this."

Maaya came out, looking exhausted. I dropped her home and came back. She had worked for fifty hours straight without rest.

They were strict about not allowing any of us to help her with the work. Yadin was still looking quite sprightly. He managed by taking just ten-minute power naps in between.

The officers there worked on a shift basis. When the process ended, they said, "So let's see tomorrow," and left.

Yadin asked us to remain there and take care of things in general. He asked us to call him if some problems arose, and left for home.

Ilango and I said we'd take care and asked Vidhya to get some sleep. Then while we were sleeping, Vidhya monitored things. We took shifts and kept an eye on the proceedings throughout the night.

The next morning, Yadin was back at 6 AM sharp, as if he were an alarm clock. The two officers arrived at 7 AM. The doctors and psychiatrists followed. Dhivya should be getting up first, as she had undergone the treatment first.

But it was Steve who got up first. The officers and government doctors started their testing then. It took about three hours to finish the testing. Karen, Aayan, and some other volunteers had woken up. Except for Dhivya, Kundavai, and one another person from their end, everyone else was awake by noon.

The volunteers were checked and medically tested, and then they came out. But they all claimed to be tired and went to their respective houses to sleep.

We were all waiting.

"I don't understand why Dhivya, Kundavai, and that other guy are taking so much time," I muttered.

That was when Maaya said, "We had completely deleted the memories only for these three people... The entire procedure. Everyone else's memories were just edited."

"How do you know this?" I asked.

"For these three people alone, we'd have to compare the image differently as we will have to omit the images from the VR and then compare. So I am saying this based on that process." Maaya explained.

These three people were hooked to drips, too and had many monitors running around them, checking their vitals. Finally, after nearly 70 hours since the procedure, Dhivya woke up. And her testing went on for about 5 hours after that.

The officers' side volunteer had also woken. Kundavai came last, and her test took 8 hours.

The officers, doctors, and psychiatrists discussed the results and said, "We'll let you know tomorrow."

We all felt like we had written major exams and were waiting for the results. Only Yadin remained expressionless and calm under duress.

Marco looked at Yadin and asked, "How can you be cool like this? We're all so tensed here."

"If I'd gotten tensed, I'll not have been able to do all this. We've done a lot of work towards this with trust and passion. Hereafter, whatever happens, will happen. If they do not approve, we will have to start again. That's all. But if my prediction goes right, I think the results will be in our favour. I know Dhivya well. Her tests have succeeded 100%. I checked her results. Everything else is left to God," Yadin said.

Everyone got back to normal but we'd been instructed not to go and test them with questions. We'd been warned that this had the potential to bring back their memories.

The people who had had their memories edited/deleted looked so happy. I was not sure whether we were assuming that or if they were really happy because a whole load of weight was off their shoulders.

Karen looked quite relaxed and chirpy. She was cracking a lot of jokes and teasing all of us. We had gone to see Dhivya.

"She's still quite exhausted. And my mother is still asleep," Karen said.

I looked at Dhivya and asked, "How are you?"

"Just so, Ilamaran. It looks like I have lost a few pages of my life and the book is so light right now," Dhivya said.

"That's good to know… the important pages are still intact," Maaya commented.

"Ilamaran keeps singing your praises. And talking about how you managed the entire thing wonderfully," Ilango added.

Dhivya looked at me, but I just smiled at her and saluted her.

"Oh, my! What's this? I just did my job, and all of you did yours, that's all!" She said.

"We cannot write it off that easily, Dhivya. Ilamaran was talking to me, too. This comes by your very nature, in your blood," Marco added.

"What is this, Ilamaran? When did you become my Public Relations Officer?" Dhivya asked me, smiling softly.

"This is more than that," Marco said, and everyone laughed. "I mean… mentor," Marco amended.

"What's happening here?" Dhivya asked, looking confused.

Thankfully, Kundavai came out just then, so the topics were changed quickly. We were all speaking to her for some time. Karen told us she had never seen Kundavai laugh or talk so much.

Now our responsibilities had increased. We knew the things they had forgotten. We should not bring them up. That was a huge challenge for us.

* * *

The next morning, the officers came. We were all there.

"We must first tell you one thing. I've been on many committees that would approve new technology for the health industry. But I have never had the same impact as this with any of the projects. To be honest, when I came here, I just wanted to hear what you had to say and reject it outright. But the way Dhivya spoke that day was quite passionate. Your stories made us realize the importance of such technology," Edward said.

"Then the way you all worked together, and how you anticipated what we'd ask, and had your answers ready… and the way you spoke about your project and your vision… we found all this quite satisfactory. We are fine with approving this for further clinical trials but under certain conditions.

"There is one legal issue here. In Kundavai's story, we should find out how she came to America. We have informed the Department of Homeland Security about it. They have banned testing on such people. They have already started an inquiry on us for the test on Kundavai and have been asking us many questions. Anyway, that is our problem… so we'll take care of it. Until they lift the ban, you cannot do any more testing. You may have to appeal to them about this.

"Like I already said, for the next twelve months, you have to come and undergo medical tests with us. We have to do this continuously. You can continue your work, and I hope everything goes well!" Edward said.

All of us gathered there did not even know how to react. On one side, we got their approval. But on the other hand, we had to cross another hurdle now.

Dhivya and Yadin smiled at each other but gave no other reaction. Once the officers went out, Dhivya looked at us. She probably understood our confusion.

Then she looked at Yadin with a laugh and said, "Guys! This is a win for us. Now we need to cross the next milestone. We will continue running this race. Leave this new approval business with me. We'll take care of what must be done next."

What I thought of as a hurdle was what Dhivya referred to as a milestone. This clearly showed the differences in our mindsets and clearly proved how she was different from all of us.

"Steve! I already spoke to you about this yesterday. You should join our team as a consultant. Your army experience will be helpful to navigate Homeland Security approval," she said.

Dhivya and Yadin were, as always, one step ahead. They had already anticipated what would happen and were prepared accordingly. So far, I had never seen them falter in any place or stumble about what to do.

Then Dhivya looked at me. "Ilamaran, it is time to pitch your idea to the investors. Let's speak more on that after lunch."

Then she turned to Steve and said, "Steve, I need to talk to you. Please come with me!" Steve nodded and followed her.

Marco and Yadin went with them, no doubt off to do the next step in the project.

* * *

Chapter 44

We had just finished one project and gotten the approval, but Dhivya had already started her work for the next project. Back in Chennai, it would be a big deal for us to complete the project in the first place. After that, we would take a break to celebrate before discussing the next one. But here, Dhivya had just done an amazing job on one major project this morning and already wanted to start the work on the next one by the afternoon.

I muttered to myself that her sense of duty was limitless.

Dhivya called me and said, "Our partners will join the call this afternoon. We can pitch it to investors only if our partners approve it. You have to get your presentation ready in the next four hours."

I felt light-headed. Marco assigned some work to Karen, Ilango, and Maaya. Vidhya and I started working on this and skipped lunch to complete it on time. I did not need to worry about preparing slides. If I shared the details with Vidhya, she would prepare them exceptionally well.

Dhivya called me around 3 PM.

"I urgently need to go to Washington DC. I'll join the presentation via video call," she informed me.

"Ayyo, Dhivya! How can I do this without you around?" I asked.

"This is your idea, so you should be the one presenting this. The secretary of Homeland Security has called me for an urgent meeting. Steve and I are going there now… you can do this. You speak to them in your usual style. Don't change anything just for this. Just use our real-life examples of why we would need such a project," she said encouragingly.

I could not speak anything against it when she was encouraging me like this. So I was just nodding my head and saying, "Yes, Dhivya! Okay, Dhivya!"

Vidhya started laughing at me. Once the call ended, she said, "Thankfully, Maaya is not here. In the last ten minutes, you said 'Dhivya' about a hundred times… What is this? A form of Dhivya-worship?"

"Oh, shut it! Dhivya is going to Washington, apparently. So she'll join the meeting only via video call. She's asking me to present it by myself. There are going to be about six partners, including Rick. Already Rick is quite miffed with me that I bypassed him and spoke directly to Dhivya. I am so nervous," I said.

"Why are you afraid now? Would you not have spoken boldly if this were you calling Dhivya from Chennai? Just speak like that. After seeing Dhivya and co here, you started doubting and underestimating yourself. But Dhivya sees you as the bold Ilamaran who spoke to her. So you speak in your usual style for this meeting too, and you'll have this in the bag," Vidhya encouraged me.

"Thanks, Vidhya. This gives me some positive affirmation." I said.

At exactly 4 PM, everyone joined the meeting. Maaya brought me a blazer. Dhivya joined via video call. She opened the meeting.

"Sorry I could not come to present this today. I am away on some other important work. Ilamaran is the lead from our Chennai team. He is also going to lead this project. So I'll be asking him to take over," she said.

And I started talking.

"Thanks, Dhivya," I said, feeling boldness return to me on her bolstering words. I addressed the others.

"Hello, all. I'm delighted to meet you all today. The idea I am going to present here started in some other form and has gone through many iterations to reach its current form. So I would first thank our Chennai team. Then Rick… He's helped us a lot with this. His critical supervision helped us think big. And it was Yadin and Dhivya who brought this to a grander scale. So thank you, everyone.

"Now, I'll go into the details of this project. In Indian Hindu beliefs, we have three gods who take care of the three main functions of this world – creation, preservation, and destruction. Likewise, our project before this was about deleting/editing memories. To put it simply, changing/destroying our memories.

"Now, can we preserve someone's memories instead? Today, we do it in the form of books and movies. But no matter how much we read books or see movies about them, it will only reflect our understanding and interpretation of the text and will not replace the feeling of them sharing their opinions and suggestions.

"In India, we call the people who won't die – the immortal ones –Markandeyan. Unfortunately, by the laws of nature, the concept of immortality does not exist for humans. But if we had the wish and the will, we could use today's technology to avail the functioning of people's brains even after their death.

"We can digitize people's brain patterns while they are alive and use machine learning to do behavioural analysis. And if we do that, we can have their brains preserved like today's NFTs post their death, and they could become digital brains."

"A significant distinction would be that the NFTs preserved as robots would require consistent ongoing feeding of current data, news, and other relevant events. With each update, the robots' accumulated experiences and brain pattern data would enable us to predict how they would have reacted to present-day circumstances. In effect, we could seek advice or opinions from these robots as if they were still alive."

"For instance, for this very idea, we might be curious to know how Steve Jobs would have reacted to it. Although he is no longer with us, we could have predicted his thought process if we had preserved his brain data and patterns. Then, instead of merely speculating, we could leverage that data to determine what advice or opinion he would have offered. This is the fundamental idea behind the project: to enable the brilliant minds living among us to remain with us indefinitely. We have presented this concept to you and welcome your feedback. Please don't hesitate to ask any questions you may have."

I did not mean it when I told them to ask any questions. But for the next half an hour, they asked me so many questions and squeezed every iota of my brain energy. I somehow managed.

Then once the call ended, Marco came to me and said, "Nicely done."

Yadin, as usual, did not say anything.

Maaya looked quite happy when she came to me. "You spoke well! I didn't expect you to speak like this," she said.

"Don't you remember whose mentorship this is?!" Ilango said and laughed.

"Oh, yeah," Maaya smirked.

Vidhya documented the meeting minutes and sent them. When she came out, I went straight to her and hugged her.

"What happened?" Maaya asked.

"Vidhya was the first one to have proposed this idea. While we were lamenting about torture from Rick, it was Vidhya who gave me this idea. And when Dhivya called me today to ask me to present this alone, I was nervous. It was

Vidhya who motivated me and prepped me for this meeting," I explained.

Vidhya laughed. "At first… Even Maaya's idea looked so huge to me. And then, your fantasy world concept looked bigger. But in the end, we have done something else completely different. But this looks like the next phase of the earlier project. So where did we start, and where have we come?!"

"I think Dhivya and Rick are the reasons for this. Though Rick looks like a bit of a psycho, he had also agreed that this idea is good. But Dhivya was constantly motivating us at every juncture. And as she promised, she has already taken this to the next step," Maaya said.

"And you guys would tease me if I said the same thing," I muttered.

"You're still an aunty-Indian even if you don't say it out loud, da," Maaya said dismissively, laughing at the expression on my face.

While we were talking, Dhivya called me. I laughed, showing the screen to Maaya before I answered. "Hello."

"The partners have approved. Nice job. Hereafter, don't use sensitive things like gods, religions, or castes in official meetings. Some people may not like these things and will start nit-picking about them instead of focusing on what you are trying to imply. Rick did not bring this up because you thanked him first. That was a good move," Dhivya said.

After returning from Washington, Dhivya called us for a meeting the next day.

"I spoke with the head of Homeland Security yesterday. He says the approval would take time. They said they'd have to talk with the Indian government, and the process is apparently lengthy. The Indian High Commissioner was also present at the meeting. We have to cooperate with them whenever they ask for details. And we cannot do much hereafter. So we'd just have to wait for this to come through," Dhivya said.

"How many more days will this take? Do you have any idea?" I asked.

"I think it will take months," Dhivya said. "But now, there's some happy news for you all. We're all going to India next week."

"This is unfair!" I said. "It has been nearly two years since we came here. But we have not even visited any places. We have just been shuttling between the house and the office. Back home, we'd have worked on a project like this for five years. But you finished it in 18 months and already started discussing the next project. Give us two weeks, please. Having come this far, we'd like to go around sightseeing here."

"He actually wished to have a beach wedding here," Ilango said.

"Wait, guys… Let me finish what I was saying. We're going to start an office in Chennai. Marco has already found a place there. A big company in India has come forward to invest in this project. I cannot tell you the name until Marco finalises the deal. Our partners have also agreed. So we should go and start that work. Then you can come here, have your wedding, and go on your honeymoon and do whatever you want," Dhivya said.

"Dhivya, with your permission," Maaya said and went and hugged her, expressing her thanks.

This was her longstanding dream! Long back, when we first spoke with Dhiraj Systems, she'd always wished to take care of their Chennai operations. And we did many things in between and eventually ended up doing exactly that.

That night, we all had a team dinner. Kundavai came along, too. Hearing that we were going to India, she asked, "Shall I come to Chennai, too?"

"We won't be going without you! Steve and Karen are working with us now. And if it were not for you, this project would not have come to this level. I'm also a part of your family now," Dhivya said.

"Dhivya, you forgot to mention that this was 'off the record,'" I said. And everyone laughed.

She gently slapped my back and said, "You've become quite cheeky."

While we were talking, Kavya called me.

"The appeal hearing got over. Raj is getting released next week and so is Suja. Only Sathyan has not been released yet," she said.

"That's the best news, Kavya! I'm really happy," I said, and then told her about everything that had happened here. "We're all coming to India next Wednesday. And we're opening that new office next Friday," I said.

"Super. Congratulations, Ilamaran. Your rise has been meteoric. And it will only go upwards," she said happily.

"Thanks, Kavya," I said fervently.

"Is Kundavai coming to Chennai?" She asked.

"Yeah, she's coming too. Why are you asking?" I asked.

"Just to know," she replied curtly.

"Will Raj be out before that? I would feel happy if you and Raj were there for the opening ceremony," I said.

"I think he'll be out by then. I will bring him," Kavya promised.

The week flew by in preparation for the trip. We finished shopping. Steve, Karen, and Kundavai went to San Francisco to their house and came to Chennai from there. Dhivya and Yadin went to Washington DC, then to San Francisco, and then flew to Chennai. Marco and the rest of us left San Diego.

I got a ring for Maaya from there. I planned to surprise her and propose to her once the company's opening ceremony was over. Her mother was coming to Chennai for the ceremony anyway, so I thought I could talk to Vidhya and her and arrange everything.

A lot of things we had never imagined had happened in America. But the only thing I thought would happen did not happen. Neither of my two dreams had come true. But I got the whole concept of this new project from my dreams, so technically, it did happen.

I still believed that our marriage would also happen as I had dreamed, some time in the near future.

∗ ∗ ∗

Chapter 45

We all reached Chennai. My mother had cooked a feast for me, celebrating my return. Maaya and Vidhya went to their house in Chennai. Their mother had come to that place for the first time. She had decided against her divorce after Maaya had spoken to her before leaving for the US. Consequently, the relationship between mother and daughter also improved. Maaya would often recollect how I had spoken to her about this that day and feel happy about it. And whenever she remembered this, I would get two extra kisses.

Ilango went to his house, where his parents gave him a grand welcome, too. The others who had come with us stayed in hotels. Kavya called us to inform us that Raj was getting released on Thursday. We went to see our new office. Dhivya was also there that day, organizing some last-minute things. The place was huge. About 80 people could work there, and we could build up to 5 floors.

"We can have one research center here," Ilango told Dhivya. "You draft a plan. We'll do this if we get the right people," Dhivya said. "We need to do more interior work here," she added. "I know a good company. We can contract them for this," Maaya said. "We should not seek anything outside when we have the talent right here with us," Dhivya said, looking at Vidhya. "I know only to draw," Vidhya said shyly. "It is not necessary to build grand interiors as of now. This place will take at least one year to become completely operational. You can learn the work before that and complete this. I will be coming here once every two months and will work here for two weeks. We can both do this design together," Dhivya said encouragingly.

We knew already that she was great at putting available talent to use. But we realized that she was also adept at enhancing existing talents. Vidhya had only been doing administrative jobs mostly, but the way Dhivya found out and nurtured her hidden talent had surprised us all.

* * *

On Friday morning, we all reached the office at 8 AM. My mother insisted that we should visit a temple first, so she woke me up at 5 AM and took me to a temple on the outskirts of Chennai. That day, the office looked like it was hosting a big family reunion. After having her memories deleted, Dhivya was almost always in her 'off-the-record' mode. I liked this version of her even more.

My mother and Maaya's mother met and spoke at length. My mother invited her to stay with us. "We'll all be together," she insisted. Maaya was in a green saree with a sleek chain and earrings, and she looked gorgeous. Wherever I was, I could not take my eyes off her. Only Maaya could pull off any outfit with such elegance. But when I saw her in this one, I wanted to get married to her right that moment.

I was just absently going around, my eyes and mind on Maaya, when Dhivya and Marco came near me. "Love is in the air, I guess," Marco commented. I laughed. "I'll see how good your romantic side is. Tell us a poem now," Dhivya challenged me, her eyes twinkling.

"Ayyo! I don't even read poems. Honestly, I don't even know how to be romantic." I said. "Just recite some poem of your own making… I will see how you'd fare in this," Dhivya prompted insistently. "Look at Maaya now! And just speak out what you are feeling. That should be easy," Marco suggested.

When I turned to look at Maaya, she was speaking something with Vidhya. I gazed at her intently. Without thinking much, I blurted, "Maaya… Even when I want to forget you, Your smile hits me like lightning, And I forget My forgetfulness."

As I was saying this, Maaya turned to me suddenly and blushed. I stared back, confused at her timing. Then realized that Dhivya had called Maaya before asking me to do this, so Maaya heard my poem and reacted. I laughed, feeling embarrassed. "Has our project affected you this much?" Marco asked, waggling his eyebrows at me.

"We should get this guy tested at your lab too. If we ask him to speak romantically, he's talking about trying to forget her," Dhivya said, shaking her head in mock sadness.

Once all the preparations were over, Dhivya looked around the place. She then called Aayan and asked him to light the lamp. When he did that, she said, "You should also start such a big company and come up in life." Dhivya had used this opportunity to motivate the poor boy from Syria who had undergone so much pain at such a young age and now simply wanted to come up in life.

Everyone went inside Dhivya's office room for the puja. Dhivya took up her laptop and said, "I am going to make an announcement today. Once this puja is over, that will be the first thing I will be doing. Karen, Vidhya, please come with me." She took them inside along with her.

Kavya called me then and said, "We've arrived." Maaya and I immediately went down to escort her and Raj inside. "How are you, guys?" Raj asked, hugging us both. "I'm incredibly happy to see your meteoric rise. Imagine where you started your career and where you are now! Your hard work over the last couple of years has yielded good results for you... My wishes for you to go onwards and upwards."

"This is just the beginning. You have a lot more to do," Kavya smiled. "When are you two going to get married?" Raj asked. "That's the next project, Raj," I laughed.

Ilango, Marco, and Steve were talking inside the office, standing to a side. My mother, Maaya's mother, and Kundavai were talking in another corner. Dhivya was working on something on her laptop in an inner room. Karen and Vidhya were also with her. I introduced Raj to Steve, Marco, and Ilango. Raj congratulated them, too. "It has taken me so long to meet you in person!" Marco said.

Kundavai had stopped talking and was looking at Raj unblinkingly. On seeing the tears in her eyes, Kavya looked at Raj. But Raj was occupied elsewhere. "Is this Dhivya?" He asked, trying to peek inside the room. "I have to thank her personally. I almost destroyed your career, but she put it back on the right path!"

"Why are you talking about all that now, Raj? Come, I will introduce you to the others," I said and took him inside. Seeing us going inside, Maaya called Kavya along. "Come, I will introduce you to Dhivya," she said.

Kundavai, meanwhile, was rushing towards Raj, looking nervous and confused. Kavya was watching Kundavai intently as she walked in. Even I did not understand what had happened to Kundavai suddenly.

Inside the room, Dhivya was drafting an email. I knocked on the door and entered, announcing, "Dhivya! This is Raj, our boss."

Still focused on the laptop, Dhivya asked, "So, am I not your boss then?" She then stood up and walked around her desk saying 'So Raj is always your boss ah'... and she came closer to Raj with her arm extended to shake his hand.

While their hands met, Raj began, "I should express my sincere thanks—" But he could not speak further and stood shocked. Dhivya's eyes widened too. Her lips started trembling, and she turned to clutch at Vidhya, who was standing beside her. Kundavai came in the right at that time and stood staring at Raj.

The rest of us looked at one another, unable to understand anything. Dhivya staggered back, her face showing many emotions. Then suddenly, she fell on the floor. Raj looked at Dhivya, his face going pale as he asked, "You... you... You're Subha, aren't you?" Dhivya started sobbing in great gasps.

None of us understood what was happening now. Kavya alone was looking at Raj unblinkingly. As the truth hit him with force, Raj held his chest and fell to the floor, too. That was when we realized that the woman he had been searching for since she disappeared eighteen years ago, the very woman he had recently assumed to be dead, had appeared right in front of his eyes.

Kundavai, who had been in shock for so long, recovered and went near Dhivya. "Are you Subha?" Kundavai demanded, looking at Dhivya. None of us understood what the relationship between Kundavai and Dhivya was. Dhivya did not look like the Subha we had seen in the photo, so we were puzzled and shocked at how Raj had identified that she was Subha, and why she had acknowledged it with such a potent reaction.

Dhivya was still crying, and she now looked at Kundavai through her tears. Kundavai then started hitting her repeatedly, demanding, "Did you know? Have you known about this the whole time? How could you pretend not to know me?" Kundavai then hugged her and kissed Dhivya's cheeks with tears streaming down her face. "No, Keerthi... I am not sure how safe it was to open up about us. I wanted to protect you and make sure you are alright and have a better life ahead. That's why I did not reveal anything and started to put an end to all this." Dhivya gasped.

The women hugged again, crying. "Then did you find out about our parents and Preethi too?" Kundavai asked. "No, I knew about you only when I heard your story. Only I know how much I suffered, unable to tell you the truth or claim my relationship with my sister, and hug and kiss you… Do you know how much I wanted to tell you that I was there for you and it would all be okay? But I held the truth back in the interest of our lives now. But more than anything, I wanted you to be cured and to create new memories with you."

It was only when she called Kundavai as Keerthi I understood that Kundavai was actually Subha's cousin from Delhi. Kundavai had talked about two sisters of hers. Could that be Preethi and Dhivya? Was that why Charles showed so much interest in this case? Would Charles have known that she was in America? I wondered.

How did these two women come to America? How could Dhivya be in such a good position in life? Why had Kundavai alone suffered? If Kundavai was Keerthi, what had happened to her other sister? I did not know if these were answers or if they were only more questions. My head reeled.

Kundavai, who had been speaking something amidst tears, suddenly fainted. The place buzzed with emotions. Karen gently took Kundavai on her lap. Then she turned to Dhivya and asked, "Did you also try to delete the memories of the same horror she had undergone?" "No… I just deleted the memories of my relationship with Raj. I had unfairly tormented him for 19 years. He had just recovered after thinking that I was dead. That's why I wanted to kill my memories. I have a lot of work left to do. I want to attain an influential position to eliminate human spy culture and destroy it at the grassroots level. I wanted to hold this anger and sorrow within me so that the fire would keep burning deep. I am preparing myself for this," Dhivya said, her chin held high.

That's when I understood her goal regarding the UN and American politics. Kavya was gently feeding water to Raj, who was still on the floor. He had been completely unconscious all this while. Kavya looked terribly worried. Raj had not uttered a single word yet. Kundavai had not yet regained consciousness, either. Dhivya still crying Some of us were with Raj and some others were with Dhivya and Kundavai. A few were standing in between, unable to understand what was happening.

The office which had been full of laughter and positivity just minutes ago was now in the complete opposite state. No matter how we developed the technology, no matter how much we deleted memories, we had just seen live proof that nothing could work when it came to memories. Two years of our work were wasted by the mere two seconds of their hands touching each other.

When Raj told his story, he often spoke about how he had walked holding Subha's hand and how his and Subha's hands spoke and expressed more emotions between them than their words. He would often say that he could not explain those emotions with words. I remembered how Raj had tears in his eyes when he said that Subha had written 'Love you. You are special' on his hands in their last few days of togetherness.

How did we even begin to think that such things could be deleted? Their 19-year penance had won. I realized that human memories are not just limited only to the brain. Our memories are connected to our very souls. There is no way that the genetic attributes of our ancestors – who we had not even seen – would be passed on to us and our children otherwise.

I felt that the memories we decided to 'cut' had been 'copy-pasted' by God. How did Subha become Dhivya, and eventually land up with the identity as a daughter of an American politician? How did Keerthi suffer so much and become Kundavai? How had both women come to America? Who had been the mysterious person who had resurrected Kundavai's life and done the cosmetic surgery on her?

Who would have the answers to these questions? Would that Charles know? Where would all this lead? How could we bridge the past and the present? Who were the people who could provide the proper information to us about these individual lives that were so intricately woven together? I had so many such questions in my mind.

Inside every answer we got, a hundred new questions were buried deep. If we were to answer all these unanswered questions, that would be a separate story by itself! There is still a lot more to know about these people. Life does not always give us the answers we seek like we were in a movie climax. Sometimes, these answers come with time and patience.

* * *

Let us meet again with the Journey of Subha and maybe explore a few more answers that would lead to few more questions! The cycle continues.

Thanks for reading along, and hope you would love the next story, too.

Yours, TE Aravind.

Beta Readers Review

I love reading books, and I read "The Memory Paradox" after a long break in my reading.

THE MEMORY PARADOX – A NOVEL - WITH A PLOT WE ARE NOT FAR AWAY FROM.

All the characters are introduced perfectly, making the reader remember every character until the end. The author keeps the reader engaged by executing plots and knots at perfect places so the reader doesn't get any lag. The book's worth is measured by what you carry away from it. It's an exciting book with all human emotions bundled up. I hope and wish everyone who read the book will feel the same.

All the best, Aravind. Miles to go expecting more and more awesome writing from you.

Rekha Bargavi

Great and innovative story, Aravind! I really enjoyed the suspense and imaginative ideas. The speculative medical concepts were fascinating - they may become reality one day! Thanks for an enjoyable and suspenseful story! As mentioned in the story - it may be a trend in the medical field in later years. This was truly an innovative story with great suspense. I appreciate you sharing your imaginative ideas. Keep up the great storytelling! Waiting for your next part of this story.

Manivel Poomalai

The Memory Paradox: Arvind predicts a new reality we all will soon enjoy.

This is the Author's first book; you won't feel it in any scenario.

The book takes you on a roller coaster ride from fun and romance to the vile cruelties of life.

I highly admire the female characters in this book.

The author takes various elements from real life and adds a bit of technology to create this magical book.

Nandhini

This book unravels the world of unimaginable technology that opens up a whole new world to indulge in. From characters with such complex backstories that make them feel like they are right next to you to a plot that transcends you into a whole other world, this book has it all. While mainly focusing on technology and psychology, the memory paradox also brings in elements of lightheartedness, misery, romance and mystery. This read would be a fantastic read for every person, regardless of your tastes. Opening up a portal into a whole new world allows us to take a sneak peek into a reality that may exist at a time when our current trends would be considered historical. I encourage each and every one to delve into these magical pages and be whisked away into a land so much more interesting than our own!

Sahaana Aravind

Note from my Family

This story is the creation of an aspiring author with a tremendous amount of creativity, which has been sprouting out on many occasions and has now finally grown into a talent tree holding loads of interesting fruits to be unleashed. Being his spouse, I had witnessed daily life situations where small things have been articulated into believable, fascinating and wonderful stories (examples as why the item is not available in the supermarket or why the task has not been completed) - the start had been small. Still, the result leads to a beautiful world of imagination, which the readers witness and enjoy. 'The memory paradox' is the author's first brainchild, portraying a different storyline with many plot twists and drama. It has a gripping energy that compels us to know the climax, an unanticipated one—wishing the author great success in following his passion and expecting more intriguing tales.

Shanmuga Priya

My first memory of stories from my dad (the author) was when I was five years old and was begging for bedtime stories to push me to a sweet slumber. Since then, I've been riveted by the creative and magical tales he originated in a moment's notice. Now, seeing such a tale present itself as a physical book brims my heart with happiness. As my mom and I would walk around the house, we would hear the sweet tunes of A.R Rahman floating through the house, and it would be known that the next chapter of the book was being created just a few feet away from us. Now, after hours of tireless work through the night and relentless modification, the book is finally perfected. The news of the book finally being ready to release created a ripple of happiness through our family due to the fact that the world would now be able to experience the fantastical world in my father's head that we have all grown to love and are sure you will too!

Sahaana Aravind

You Write. We Publish.

To publish your own book, contact us.

We publish poetry collections, short story collections, novellas and novels.

contact@thewriteorder.com

Instagram- thewriteorder

www.facebook.com/thewriteorder

Made in the USA
Monee, IL
07 July 2026